· · ·

MARK TWAIN

SHORT STORIES AND TALL TALES

MARK TWAIN

SHORT STORIES AND TALL TALES

COURAGE
BOOKS
an imprint of
RUNNING PRESS
Philadelphia, Pennsylvania

Canadian representatives: General Publishing Co., Ltd.,
30 Lesmill Road, Don Mills, Ontario M3B 2T6.

International representatives: Worldwide Media Services, Inc.,
30 Montgomery Street, Jersey City, New Jersey 07302.

9 8 7 6 5 4 3 2 1
Digit on the right indicates the number of this printing.

Library of Congress Catalog Card Number 93–70552
ISBN 1–56138–323–6

Edited by Virginia Mattingly
Cover illustration by Richard Loehle
Cover design by Toby Schmidt
Typography: ITC Berkeley Oldstyle by Deborah Lugar

Published by Courage Books, an imprint of
Running Press Book Publishers
125 South Twenty-second Street
Philadelphia, Pennsylvania 19103–4399

. . .

CONTENTS

Introduction

Born to a Virginian family in Florida, Missouri, Samuel Langhorne Clemens left school at the age of twelve to become a printer's apprentice. Over the next twenty years, Clemens set type for newspapers from New York to Iowa, piloted a steamboat on the Mississippi River, served briefly in the Confederate militia, worked as a newspaper correspondent in Nevada, and finally launched himself into the literary spotlight with the publication of his classic tale, "Jim Smiley and His Jumping Frog" (1865).

Writing under the pseudonym "Mark Twain," a riverboat pilot's call, Clemens captivated readers with his dry, humorous sketches, which were often inspired by his travels throughout the country. Audiences enjoyed his engaging style, his innate pessimism, and his shrewd but entertaining social commentary.

William Dean Howells said that "Twain was the first writer to use in writing the fashion we all use in thinking." This originality and immediacy are reflected in the thematic and narrative breadth of Clemens's works. From the hilarious satire of "The Stolen White Elephant" (1882) to the tainted, cynical perspective of "The $30,000 Bequest" (1904), he firmly established himself as a powerful critic and master storyteller.

In 1870, Clemens married Olivia Langdon and settled down as a best-selling author. The couple moved to Hartford, Connecticut, where Clemens wrote *The Adventures of Tom Sawyer* (1876) and *The Adventures of Huckleberry Finn* (1884). Short stories, including "Jim Baker's Bluejay Yarn" (1880), "How to Tell a Story" (1895), and "The Man that Corrupted Hadleyburg" (1900), followed in rapid succession.

But like many of his tales and characters, Clemens lived a somewhat wandering and erratic life, and bad investments bankrupted him in the 1890s. "The £1,000,000 Bank-Note" (1893), the story of a pauper who falls from honest poverty into wealthy corruption and hypocrisy, reflects Clemens's intensified pessimism and financial frustrations during this time.

Clemens died in 1910, after the untimely death of his wife and favorite daughter, leaving a legacy of works to entertain the generations to follow. Collected here are the best of his short stories and tall tales.

THE CELEBRATED JUMPING FROG OF CALAVERAS COUNTY

First published as "Jim Smiley and His Jumping Frog" in
New York's *Saturday Press*, November 18, 1865, this story won
instant acclaim. It later became the title of Twain's first book, *The
Celebrated Jumping Frog of Calaveras County and Other Sketches*,
published by C. H. Webb, New York, in 1867.

In compliance with the request of a friend of mine, who wrote me from the East, I called on good-natured, garrulous old Simon Wheeler, and inquired after my friend's friend, Leonidas W. Smiley, as requested to do, and I hereunto append the result. I have a lurking suspicion that *Leonidas W.* Smiley is a myth; that my friend never knew such a personage; and that he only conjectured that if I asked old Wheeler about him, it would remind him of his infamous *Jim* Smiley, and he would go to work and bore me to death with some exasperating reminiscence of him as long and as tedious as it should be useless to me. If that was the design, it succeeded.

I found Simon Wheeler dozing comfortably by the barroom stove of the dilapidated tavern in the decayed mining camp of Angel's, and I noticed that he was fat and bald-headed, and had no expression of winning gentleness and simplicity upon his tranquil countenance. He roused up, and gave me good-day. I told him a friend of mine had commissioned me to make some inquiries about a cherished companion of his boyhood named *Leonidas W.* Smiley—*Rev. Leonidas W.* Smiley, a young minister of the Gospel, who he had heard was at one time a resident of Angel's Camp. I added that if Mr. Wheeler could tell me anything about this Rev. Leonidas W. Smiley, I would feel under many obligations to him.

Simon Wheeler backed me into a corner and blockaded me there with his chair, and then sat down and reeled off the monotonous narrative which follows this paragraph. He never smiled, he never frowned, he never changed his voice from the gentle-flowing key to which he turned his initial sentence, he never betrayed the slightest suspicion of enthusiasm; but all through the interminable narrative there ran a vein of impressive earnestness and sincerity, which showed me plainly that, so far from his imagining that there was anything ridiculous or funny about his story, he regarded it as a really important matter, and admired its two heroes as men of transcendent genius in *finesse*. I let him go on in his own way, and never interrupted him once.

"Rev. Leonidas W. H'm, Reverend Le—well, there was a feller here once by the name of *Jim* Smiley, in the winter of '49—or may be it was the spring of '50—I don't recollect exactly, somehow, though what makes me think it was one or the other is because I remember the big flume warn't finished when he first come to the camp; but any way, he was the curiosest man about always betting on anything that turned up you ever see, if he could get anybody to bet on the other side; and if he couldn't he'd change sides. Any way that suited the other man would suit *him*—any way just so's he got a bet, *he* was satisfied. But still he was lucky, uncommonly lucky; he most always come out winner. He was always ready and laying for a chance; there couldn't be no soli-t'ry thing mentioned but that feller'd offer to bet on it, and take any side you please, as I was just telling you. If there was a horse-race, you'd find him flush or you'd find him busted at the end of it; if there was a dog-fight, he'd bet on it; if there was a cat-fight, he'd bet on it; if there was a chicken-fight, he'd bet on it; why, if there was two birds setting on a fence, he would bet you which one would fly first; or if there was a camp-meeting, he would be there reg'lar to bet on Parson Walker, which he judged to be the best exhorter about here, and so he was too, and a good man. If he even see a straddle-bug start to go anywheres, he would bet you how long it would take him to get to – to wherever he was going to, and if you took him up, he would foller that straddle-bug to Mexico but what he would find out where he was bound for and how long he was on the road. Lots of boys here has seen that Smiley, and can tell you about him. Why, it never made no difference to *him* – he'd bet on *any* thing – the dangdest feller. Parson Walker's wife laid very sick once, for a good while, and it seemed as if they warn't going to save her; but one morning he come, in, and Smiley up and asked him how she was, and he said she was considable better – thank the Lord for his inf'nite mercy – and coming on so smart that with the blessing of Prov'dence she'd get well yet; and Smiley before he thought, says, "Well, I'll resk two-and-a-half she don't anyway."

Thish-yer Smiley had a mare – the boys called her the fifteen-minute nag, but that was only in fun, you know, because of course she was faster than that – and he used to win money on that horse for all she was so slow and always had the asthma, or the distemper, or the consumption, or something of that kind. They used to give her two or three hundred yards start, and then pass her under way; but always at the fag end of the race she'd get excited and desperate like, and come cavorting and straddling up, and scattering her legs around limber, sometimes in the air, and sometimes out to one side among the fences, and kicking up m-o-r-e dust and raising m-o-r-e racket with her coughing and sneezing and blowing her nose – and *always* fetch up at the stand just about a neck ahead, as near as you could cipher it down.

And he had a little small bull-pup, that to look at him you'd think he warn't worth a cent but to set around and look ornery and lay for a chance to steal something. But as soon as money was up on him he was a different dog; his under-jaw'd begin to stick out like the fo'castle of a steamboat, and his teeth would uncover and shine like the furnaces. And a dog might tackle him and bully-rag him, and bite him, and throw him over his shoulder two or three times, and Andrew Jackson – which was the name

of the pup—Andrew Jackson would never let on but what *he* was
satisfied, and hadn't expected nothing else—and the bets being
doubled and doubled on the other side all the time, till the money
was all up; and then all of a sudden he would grab that other
dog jest by the j'int of his hind leg and freeze to it—not chaw,
you understand, but only just grip and hang on till they throwed
up the sponge, if it was a year. Smiley always come out winner
on that pup, till he harnessed a dog once that didn't have no hind
legs, because they'd been sawed off in a circular saw, and when
the thing had gone along far enough, and the money was all up,
and he come to make a snatch for his pet holt, he see in a minute
how he'd been imposed on, and how the other dog had him in
the door, so to speak, and he 'peared surprised, and then he looked
sorter discouraged-like, and didn't try no more to win the fight,
and so he got shucked out bad. He give Smiley a look, as much
as to say his heart was broke, and it was *his* fault, for putting up
a dog that hadn't no hind legs for him to take holt of, which was
his main dependence in a fight, and then he limped off a piece
and laid down and died. It was a good pup, was that Andrew Jackson, and would have made a name for hisself if he'd lived, for
the stuff was in him and he had genius—I know it, because he
hadn't no opportunities to speak of, and it don't stand to reason
that a dog could make such a fight as he could under them circumstances if he hadn't no talent. It always makes me feel sorry
when I think of that last fight of his'n, and the way it turned out.

Well, thish-yer Smiley had rat-tarriers, and chicken cocks, and
tomcats and all them kind of things, till you couldn't rest, and
you couldn't fetch nothing for him to bet on but he'd match you.
He ketched a frog one day, and took him home, and said he
cal'lated to educate him; and so he never done nothing for three
months but set in his back yard and learn that frog to jump. And
you bet you he *did* learn him, too. He'd give him a little punch
behind, and the next minute you'd see that frog whirling in the
air like a doughnut—see him turn one summerset, or may be a

couple, if he got a good start, and come down flat-footed and all
right, like a cat. He got him up so in the matter of ketching flies,
and kep' him in practice so constant, that he'd nail a fly every
time as fur as he could see him. Smiley said all a frog wanted
was education, and he could do 'most anything—and I believe
him. Why, I've seen him set Dan'l Webster down here on this
floor—Dan'l Webster was the name of the frog—and sing out, "Flies,
Dan'l, flies!" and quicker'n you could wink he'd spring straight
up and snake a fly off'n the counter there, and flop down on the
floor ag'in as solid as a gob of mud, and fall to scratching the
side of his head with his hind foot as indifferent as if he hadn't
no idea he'd been doin' any more'n any frog might do. You never
see a frog so modest and straightfor'ard as he was, for all he was
so gifted. And when it come to fair and square jumping on a dead
level, he could get over more ground at one straddle than any
animal of his breed you ever see. Jumping on a dead level was
his strong suit, you understand; and when it come to that, Smiley
would ante up money on him as long as he had a red. Smiley
was monstrous proud of his frog, and well he might be, for fellers
that had traveled and been everywheres all said he laid over any
frog that ever *they* see.

Well, Smiley kep' the beast in a little lattice box, and he used
to fetch him down town sometimes and lay for a bet. One day
a feller—a stranger in the camp, he was—come acrost him with
his box, and says:

"What might it be that you've got in the box?"

And Smiley says, sorter indifferent-like, "It might be a parrot,
or it might be a canary, maybe, but it ain't—its only just a frog."

And the feller took it, and looked at it careful, and turned it
round this way and that, and says, "H'm—so 'tis. Well, what's *he*
good for?"

"Well," Smiley says, easy and careless, "he's good enough
for *one* thing, I should judge—he can outjump any frog in
Calaveras county."

The feller took the box again, and took another long, particular look, and give it back to Smiley, and says, very deliberate, "Well," he says, "I don't see no p'ints about that frog that's any better'n any other frog."

"Maybe you don't," Smiley says. "Maybe you understand frogs and maybe you don't understand 'em; maybe you've had experience, and maybe you ain't only a amature, as it were. Anyways, I've got *my* opinion, and I'll resk forty dollars that he can out-jump any frog in Calaveras county."

And the feller studied a minute, and then says, kinder sad like, "Well, I'm only a stranger here, and I ain't got no frog; but if I had a frog, I'd bet you."

And then Smiley says, "That's all right – that's all right – if you'll hold my box a minute, I'll go and get you a frog." And so the feller took the box, and put up his forty dollars along with Smiley's, and set down to wait.

So he set there a good while thinking and thinking to hisself, and then he got the frog out and prized his mouth open and took a teaspoon and filled him full of quail shot – filled him pretty near up to his chin – and set him on the floor. Smiley he went to the swamp and slopped around in the mud for a long time, and finally he ketched a frog, and fetched him in, and give him to this feller, and says:

"Now, if you're ready, set him alongside of Dan'l, with his forepaws just even with Dan'l's, and I'll give the word." Then he says, "One – two – three – *git!*" and him and the feller touched up the frogs from behind, and the new frog hopped off lively, but Dan'l give a heave, and hysted up his shoulders – so – like a Frenchman, but it warn't no use – he couldn't budge: he was planted as solid as a church, and he couldn't no more stir than if he was anchored out. Smiley was a good deal surprised, and he was disgusted too, but he didn't have no idea what the matter was, of course.

The feller took the money and started away; and when he was going out the door, he sorter jerked his thumb over his shoulder –

so–at Dan'l, and says again, very deliberate, "Well," he says, "*I don't see no p'ints about that frog that's any better'n any other frog.*"

Smiley he stood scratching his head and looking down at Dan'l a long time, and at last he says, "I do wonder what in the nation that frog throw'd off for–I wonder if there ain't something the matter with him–he 'pears to look mighty baggy, somehow." And he ketched Dan'l by the nap of the neck, and hefted him, and turned him upside down and he belched out a double handful of shot. And then he see how it was, and he was the maddest man–he set the frog down and took out after that feller, but he never ketched him. And—"

[Here Simon Wheeler heard his name called from the front yard, and got up to see what was wanted.] And turning to me as he moved away, he said: "Just set where you are, stranger, and rest easy–I ain't going to be gone a second."

But, by your leave, I did not think that a continuation of the history of the enterprising vagabond *Jim* Smiley would be likely to afford me much information concerning the Rev. *Leonidas W.* Smiley, and so I started away.

At the door I met the sociable Wheeler returning, and he button-holed me and re-commenced:

"Well, thish-yer Smiley had a yaller one-eyed cow that didn't have no tail, only just a short stump like a bannanner, and—"

However, lacking both time and inclination, I did not wait to hear about the afflicted cow, but took my leave.

A Visit to Niagara

Appearing in Twain's *Buffalo Express* column on
August 21, 1869, this travelogue was originally entitled
"A Day at Niagara." John Camden Hotten pirated the work for his
collection, *Practical Jokes,* in 1872. The following year the story
was published in a Philadelphia collection called *One Hundred
Choice Selections,* then retitled "A Visit to Niagara" for the
American Publishing Company's *Mark Twain's
Sketches New and Old* in 1875.

Niagara Falls is a most enjoyable place of resort. The hotels
are excellent, and the prices not at all exorbitant. The opportunities for fishing are not even equalled elsewhere. Because, in other
localities, certain places in the streams are much better than others;
but at Niagara one place is just as good as another, for the reason
that the fish do not bite anywhere, and so there is no use in your
walking five miles to fish, when you can depend on being just
as unsuccessful nearer home. The advantages of this state of things
have never heretofore been properly placed before the public.

The weather is cool in summer, and the walks and drives are
all pleasant and none of them fatiguing. When you start out to
"do" the Falls you first drive down about a mile, and pay a small
sum for the privilege of looking down from a precipice into the
narrowest part of the Niagara river. A railway "cut" through a hill
would be as comely if it had the angry river tumbling and foam-
ing through its bottom. You can descend a staircase here a hundred
and fifty feet down, and stand at the edge of the water. After you
have done it, you will wonder why you did it; but you will then
be too late.

The guide will explain to you, in his blood-curdling way, how
he saw the little steamer, *Maid of the Mist,* descend the fearful
rapids—how first one paddle-box was out of sight behind the rag-
ing billows, and then the other, and at what point it was that her

smokestack toppled overboard, and where her planking began to break and part asunder – and how she did finally live through the trip, after accomplishing the incredible feat of travelling seventeen miles in six minutes, or six miles in seventeen minutes, I have really forgotten which. But it was very extraordinary, anyhow. It is worth the price of admission to hear the guide tell the story nine times in succession to different parties, and never miss a word or alter a sentence or a gesture.

Then you drive over the Suspension Bridge, and divide your misery between the chances of smashing down two hundred feet into the river below, and the chances of having the railway train overhead smashing down on to you. Either possibility is discomforting taken by itself, but mixed together, they amount in the aggregate to positive unhappiness.

On the Canada side you drive along the chasm between long ranks of photographers standing guard behind their cameras, ready to make an ostentatious frontispiece of you and your decaying ambulance, and your solemn crate with a hide on it, which you are expected to regard in the light of a horse, and a diminished and unimportant background of sublime Niagara; and a great many people have the incredible effrontery or the native depravity to aid and abet this sort of crime.

Any day, in the hands of these photographers, you may see stately pictures of papa and mamma, Johnny and Bub and Sis, or a couple of country cousins, all smiling vacantly, and all disposed in studied and uncomfortable attitudes in their carriage, and all looming up in their awe-inspiring imbecility before the snubbed and diminished presentment of that majestic presence whose ministering spirits are the rainbows, whose voice is the thunder, whose awful front is veiled in clouds, who was monarch here dead and forgotten ages before this hackful of small reptiles was deemed temporarily necessary to fill a crack in the world's unnoted myriads, and will still be monarch here ages and decades of ages after they shall have gathered themselves to their blood

relations, the other worms, and been mingled with the unremem-
bering dust.

There is no actual harm in making Niagara a background
whereon to display one's marvelous insignificance in a good strong
light, but it requires a sort of superhuman self-complacency to
enable one to do it.

When you have examined the stupendous Horseshoe Fall till
you are satisfied you cannot improve on it, you return to America
by the new Suspension Bridge, and follow up the bank to where
they exhibit the Cave of the Winds.

Here I followed instructions, and divested myself of all my
clothing, and put on a waterproof jacket and overalls. This costume
is picturesque, but not beautiful. A guide, similarly dressed, led
the way down a flight of winding stairs, which wound and wound,
and still kept on winding long after the thing had ceased to be
a novelty, and then terminated long before it had begun to be
a pleasure. We were then well down under the precipice, but still
considerably above the level of the river.

We now began to creep along flimsy bridges of a single plank,
our persons shielded from destruction by a crazy wooden rail-
ing, to which I clung with both hands – not because I was afraid,
but because I wanted to. Presently the descent became steeper,
and the bridge flimsier, and sprays from the American Fall began
to rain down on us in fast-increasing sheets that soon became
blinding, and after that our progress was mostly in the nature
of groping. Now a furious wind began to rush out from behind
the waterfall, which seemed determined to sweep us from the
bridge, and scatter us on the rocks and among the torrents below.
I remarked that I wanted to go home; but it was too late. We were
almost under the monstrous wall of water thundering down from
above, and speech was in vain in the midst of such a pitiless crash
of sound.

In another moment the guide disappeared behind the deluge,
and bewildered by the thunder, driven helplessly by the wind,

and smitten by the arrowy tempest of rain, I followed. All was darkness. Such a mad storming, roaring, and bellowing of warring wind and water never crazed my ears before. I bent my head, and seemed to receive the Atlantic on my back. The world seemed going to destruction, I could not see anything, the flood poured down so savagely. I raised my head, with open mouth, and the most of the American cataract went down my throat. If I had sprung a leak now, I had been lost. And at this moment I discovered that the bridge had ceased, and we must trust for a foothold to the slippery and precipitous rocks. I never was so scared before and survived it. But we got through at last, and emerged into the open day, where we could stand in front of the laced and frothy and seething world of descending water, and look at it. When I saw how much of it there was, and how fearfully in earnest it was, I was sorry I had gone behind it.

The noble Red Man has always been a friend and darling of mine. I love to read about him in tales and legends and romances. I love to read of his inspired sagacity, and his love of the wild free life of mountain and forest, and his general nobility of character, and his stately metaphorical manner of speech, and his chivalrous love for the dusky maiden, and the picturesque pomp of his dress and accoutrements. Especially the picturesque pomp of his dress and accoutrements. When I found the shops at Niagara Falls full of dainty Indian bead-work, and stunning moccasins, and equally stunning toy figures representing human beings who carried their weapons in holes bored through their arms and bodies, and had feet shaped like a pie, I was filled with emotion. I knew that now, at last, I was going to come face to face with the noble Red Man.

A lady clerk in a shop told me, indeed, that all her grand array of curiosities were made by the Indians, and that they were plenty about the Falls, and that they were friendly, and it would not be dangerous to speak to them. And sure enough, as I approached the bridge leading over to Luna Island, I came upon a noble Son of the Forest sitting under a tree, diligently at work on a bead reticule. He wore a slouch hat and brogans, and had a short black pipe in his mouth. Thus does the baneful contact with our effeminate civilization dilute the picturesque pomp which is so natural to the Indian when far removed from us in his native haunts. I addressed the relic as follows: –

"Is the Wawhoo-Wang-Wang of the Whack-a-Whack happy? Does the great Speckled Thunder sigh for the warpath, or is his heart contented with dreaming of the dusky maiden, the Pride of the Forest? Does the mighty Sachem yearn to drink the blood of his enemies, or is he satisfied to make bead reticules for the papooses of the paleface? Speak, sublime relic of bygone grandeur – venerable ruin, speak!"

The relic said –

"An' is it mesilf, Dennis Hooligan, that ye'd be takin' for a dirty Injin, ye drawlin', lantern-jawed, spider-legged divil! By the piper that played before Moses, I'll ate ye!"

I went away from there.

By and by, in the neighborhood of the Terrapin Tower, I came upon a gentle daughter of the aborigines in fringed and beaded buckskin moccasins and leggins, seated on a bench, with her pretty wares about her. She had just carved out a wooden chief that had a strong family resemblance to a clothes-pin, and was now boring a hole through his abdomen to put his bow through, I hesitated a moment, and then addressed her:

"Is the heart of the forest maiden heavy? Is the Laughing Tadpole lonely? Does she mourn over the extinguished council-fires of her race, and the vanished glory of her ancestors? Or does her sad spirit wander afar toward the hunting grounds whither her brave Gobbler-of-the-Lightning is gone? Why is my daughter silent? Has she aught against the paleface stranger?"

The maiden said –

"Faix, an' is it Biddy Malone ye dare to be callin' names? Lave this, or I'll shy your lean carcass over the cataract, ye sniveling blaggard!"

I adjourned from there also.

"Confound these Indians!" I said. "They told me they were tame; but, if appearances go for anything, I should say they were all on the warpath."

I made one more attempt to fraternize with them, and only one. I came upon a camp of them gathered in the shade of a great tree, making wampum and moccasins, and addressed them in the language of friendship:

"Noble Red Men, Braves, Grand Sachems, War Chiefs, Squaws, and High Muck-a-Mucks, the paleface from the land of the setting sun greets you! You, Beneficent Polecat—you, Devourer of Mountains—you, Roaring Thundergust—you, Bully Boy with a Glass eye—the paleface from beyond the great waters greets you all! War and pestilence have thinned your ranks, and destroyed your once proud nation. Poker and seven-up, and a vain modern expense for soap, unknown to your glorious ancestors, have depleted your purses. Appropriating, in your simplicity, the property of others, has gotten you into trouble. Misrepresenting facts, in your simple innocence, has damaged your reputation with the soulless usurper. Trading for forty-rod whisky, to enable you to get drunk and happy and tomahawk your families, has played the everlasting mischief with the picturesque pomp of your dress, and here you are, in the broad light of the nineteenth century, gotten up like the ragtag and bobtail of the purlieus of New York. For shame! Remember your ancestors! Recall their mighty deeds! Remember Uncus!—and Red Jacket!—and Hole in the Day!—and Whoopdedoodledo! Emulate their achievements! Unfurl yourselves under my banner, noble savages, illustrious guttersnipes"—

"Down wid him!" "Scoop the blaggard!" "Burn him!" "Hang him!" "Dhround him!"

It was the quickest operation that ever was. I simply saw a sudden flash in the air of clubs, brickbats, fists, bead-baskets, and moccasins—a single flash, and they all appeared to hit me at once, and no two of them in the same place. In the next instant the entire tribe was upon me. They tore half the clothes off me; they broke my arms and legs; they gave me a thump that dented the top of my head till it would hold coffee like a saucer; and, to crown their disgraceful proceedings and add insult to injury, they threw me over the Niagara Falls, and I got wet.

About ninety or a hundred feet from the top, the remains of my vest caught on a projecting rock, and I was almost drowned before I could get loose. I finally fell, and brought up in a world of white foam at the foot of the Fall, whose celled and bubbly masses towered up several inches above my head. Of course I got into the eddy. I sailed round and round in it forty-four times— chasing a chip and gaining on it—each round trip a half mile— reaching for the same bush on the bank forty-four times, and just exactly missing it by a hair's-breadth every time.

At last a man walked down and sat down close to that bush, and put a pipe in his mouth, and lit a match, and followed me with one eye and kept the other on the match, while he sheltered it in his hands from the wind. Presently a puff of wind blew it out. The next time I swept around he said—

"Got a match?"

"Yes, in my other vest. Help me out, please."

"Not for Joe."

When I come round again, I said—

"Excuse the seemingly impertinent curiosity of a drowning man, but will you explain this singular conduct of yours?"

"With pleasure. I am the coroner. Don't hurry on my account. I can wait for you. But I wish I had a match."

I said—"Take my place, and I'll go and get you one."

He declined. This lack of confidence on his part created a coldness between us, and from that time forward I avoided him. It was my idea, in case anything happened, to so time the occurrence as to throw my custom into the hands of the opposition coroner over on the American side.

At last a policeman came along, and arrested me for disturbing the peace by yelling at people on shore for help. The judge fined me, but I had the advantage of him. My money was with my pantaloons, and my pantaloons were with the Indians.

Thus I escaped. I am now lying in a very critical condition. At least I am lying anyway – critical or not critical. I am hurt all over, but I cannot tell the full extent yet, because the doctor is not done taking inventory. He will make out my manifest this evening. However, thus far he thinks only sixteen of my wounds are fatal. I don't mind the others.

Upon regaining my right mind, I said –

"It is an awful savage tribe of Indians that do the bead work and moccasins for Niagara Falls, doctor. Where are they from?"

"Limerick, my son."

JOURNALISM IN TENNESSEE

Written for Twain's column in the *Buffalo Express*, this short story later appeared in *Mark Twain's Sketches New and Old*, as well as in a pamphlet issued in Girard, Kansas, around 1923.

– Editor

The editor of the Memphis Avalanche *swoops thus mildly down upon a correspondent who posted him as a Radical:* –"*While he was writing the first word, the middle, dotting his i's, crossing his t's, and punching his period, he knew he was concocting a sentence that was saturated with infamy and reeking with falsehood."* –Exchange

I was told by the physician that a Southern climate would improve my health, so I went down to Tennessee, and got a berth on the *Morning Glory and Johnson County War-Whoop* as associate editor. When I went on duty I found the chief editor sitting tilted back in a three-legged chair with his feet on a pine table. There was another pine table in the room and another afflicted chair, and both were half buried under newspapers and scraps and sheets of manuscript. There was a wooden box of sand, sprinkled with cigar stubs and "old soldiers," and a stove with a door hanging by its upper hinge. The chief editor had a long-tailed black cloth frock coat on, and white linen pants. His boots were small and neatly blacked. He wore a ruffled shirt, a large seal ring, a standing collar of obsolete pattern, and a checkered neckerchief with the ends hanging down. Date of costume about 1848. He was smoking a cigar, and trying to think of a word, and in pawing his hair he had rumpled his locks a good deal. He was scowling fearfully, and I judged that he was concocting a particularly knotty editorial. He told me to take the exchanges and skim through them and write up the "Spirit of the Tennessee Press," condensing into the article all of their contents that seemed of interest.

I wrote as follows: –

"SPIRIT OF THE TENNESSEE PRESS

"The editors of the *Semi-Weekly Earthquake* evidently labor under a misapprehension with regard to the Ballyhack railroad. It is not the object of the company to leave Buzzardville off to one side. On the contrary, they consider it one of the most important points along the line, and consequently can have no desire to slight it. The gentlemen of the *Earthquake* will, of course, take pleasure in making the correction.

"John W. Blossom, Esq., the able editor of the Higginsville *Thunderbolt and Battle Cry of Freedom,* arrived in the city yesterday. He is stopping at the Van Buren House.

"We observe that our contemporary of the Mud Springs *Morning Howl* has fallen into the error of supposing that the election of Van Werter is not an established fact, but he will have discovered his mistake before this reminder reaches him, no doubt. He was doubtless misled by incomplete election returns.

"It is pleasant to note that the city of Blathersville is endeavoring to contact with some New York gentlemen to pave its well-nigh impassable streets with the Nicholson pavement. The *Daily Hurrah* urges the measure with ability, and seems confident of ultimate success."

I passed my manuscript over to the chief editor for acceptance, alteration, or destruction. He glanced at it and his face clouded. He ran his eye down the pages, and his countenance grew portentous. It was easy to see that something was wrong. Presently he sprang up and said –

"Thunder and lightning! Do you suppose I am going to speak of those cattle that way? Do you suppose my subscribers are going to stand such gruel as that? Give me the pen!"

I never saw a pen scrape and scratch its way so viciously, or plough through another man's verbs and adjectives so relentlessly. While he was in the midst of his work, somebody shot at him through the open window, and marred the symmetry of my ear.

"Ah," said he, "that is that scoundrel Smith, of the *Moral Volcano* – he was due yesterday." And he snatched a navy revolver from his belt and fired. Smith dropped, shot in the thigh. The shot spoiled Smith's aim, who was just taking a second chance, and he crippled a stranger. It was me. Merely a finger shot off.

Then the chief editor went on with his erasures and interlineations. Just as he finished them a hand-grenade came down the stove pipe, and the explosion shivered the stove into a thousand fragments. However, if did no further damage, except that a vagrant piece knocked a couple of my teeth out.

"That stove is utterly ruined," said the chief editor.

I said I believed it was.

"Well, no matter—don't want it this kind of weather. I know the man that did it. I'll get him. Now, here is the way this stuff ought to be written."

I took the manuscript. It was scarred with erasures and interlineations till its mother wouldn't have known it if it had had one. It now read as follows:—

"SPIRIT OF THE TENNESSEE PRESS

"The inveterate liars of the Semi-Weekly Earthquake are evidently endeavoring to palm off upon a noble and chivalrous people another of their vile and brutal falsehoods with regard to that most glorious conception of the nineteenth century, the Ballyhack railroad. The idea that Buzzardville was to be left off at one side originated in their own fulsome brains—or rather in the settlings which they regard as brains. They had better swallow this lie if they want to save their abandoned reptile carcasses the cowhiding they so richly deserve.

"That ass, Blossom, of the Higginsville Thunderbolt and Battle Cry of Freedom, is down here again sponging at the Van Buren.

"We observe that the besotted blackguard of the Mud Springs Morning Howl is giving out, with his usual propensity for lying, that Van Werter is not elected. The heaven-born mission of journalism is to disseminate truth; to eradicate error; to educate, refine, and elevate the tone of public morals and manners, and make all men more gentle, more virtuous, more charitable, and in all ways better, and holier, and happier; and yet this black-hearted scoundrel degrades his great office persistently to the dissemination of falsehood, calumny, vituperation, and vulgarity.

"Blathersville wants a Nicholson pavement – it wants a jail and a poorhouse more. The idea of a pavement in a one horse town composed of two gin mills, a blacksmith's shop, and that mustard-plaster of a newspaper, the *Daily Hurrah!* The crawling insect, Buckner, who edits the *Hurrah,* is braying about this business with his customary imbecility, and imagining that he is talking sense."

"Now *that* is the way to write – peppery and to the point. Mush-and-milk journalism gives me the fan-tods."

About this time a brick came through the window with a splintering crash, and gave me a considerable of a jolt in the back. I moved out of range – I began to feel in the way.

The chief said, "That was Colonel, likely. I've been expecting him for two days. He will be up, now, right away."

He was correct. The Colonel appeared in the door a moment afterward with a dragoon revolver in his hand.

He said, "Sir, have I the honor of addressing the poltroon who edits this mangy sheet?"

"You have. Be seated, sir. Be careful of the chair, one of its legs is gone. I believe I have the honor of addressing the putrid liar, Col. Blatherskite Tecumseh?"

"Right, sir. I have a little account to settle with you. If you are at leisure we will begin."

"I have an article on the 'Encouraging Progress of Moral and Intellectual Development in America' to finish, but there is no hurry. Begin."

Both pistols rang out their fierce clamor at the same instant. The chief lost a lock of his hair, and the Colonel's bullet ended its career in the fleshy part of my thigh. The Colonel's left shoulder was clipped a little. They fired again. Both missed their men this time, but I got my share, a shot in the arm. At the third fire both gentlemen were wounded slightly, and I had a knuckle chipped. I then said, I believed I would go out and take a walk, at this was a private matter, and I had a delicacy about participating in it further. Both gentlemen begged me to keep my seat, and assured me that I was not in the way.

They then talked about the elections and the crops while they reloaded, and I fell to tying up my wounds. But presently they opened fire again with animation, and every shot took effect – but it is proper to remark that five out of the six fell to my share. The sixth one mortally wounded the colonel, who remarked, with fine humor, that he would have to say good morning now, as he had business up town. He then inquired the way to the undertaker's and left.

The chief turned to me and said, "I am expecting company to dinner, and shall have to get ready. It will be a favor to me if you will read proof and attend to the customers."

I winced a little at the idea of attending to the customers, but I was too bewildered by the fusilade that was still ringing in my ears to think of anything to say.

He continued, "Jones will be here at 3 – cowhide him. Gillespie will call earlier, perhaps – throw him out of the window. Ferguson will be along about 4 – kill him. That is all for today, I believe. If you have any odd time, you may write a blistering article on the police – give the Chief Inspector rats. The cowhides are under the table; weapons in the drawer – ammunition there in the corner – lint and bandages up there in the pigeon-holes. In case of accident, go to Lancet, the surgeon, downstairs. He advertises – we take it out in trade."

He was gone. I shuddered. At the end of the next three hours I had been through perils so awful that all peace of mind and all cheerfulness were gone from me. Gillespie had called and thrown *me* out the window. Jones arrived promptly, and when I got ready to do the cowhiding he took the job off my hands. In an encounter with a stranger, not in the bill of fare, I had lost my scalp. Another stranger, by the name of Thompson, left me a mere wreck and ruin of chaotic rags. And at last, at bay in the corner, and beset by an infuriated mob of editors, blacklegs,

politicians, and desperadoes, who raved and swore and flourished
their weapons about my head till the air shimmered with glanc-
ing flashes of steel, I was in the act of resigning my berth on the
paper when the chief arrived, and with him a rabble of charmed
and enthusiastic friends. Then ensued a scene of riot and car-
nage such as no human pen, or steel one either, could describe.
People were shot, probed, dismembered, blown up, thrown out
of the window. There was a brief tornado of murky blasphemy,
with a confused and frantic war-dance glimmering through it, and
then all was over. In five minutes there was silence, and the gory
chief and I sat alone and surveyed the sanguinary ruin that strewed
the floor around us.

He said, "You'll like this place when you get used to it."

I said, "I'll have to get you to excuse me; I think maybe I might
write to suit you after a while; as soon as I had had some practice and learned the language I am confident I could. But, to speak
the plain truth, that sort of energy of expression has its incon-
veniences, and a man is liable to interruption. You see that yourself.
Vigorous writing is calculated to elevate the public, no doubt, but,
then I do not like to attract so much attention as it calls forth.
I can't write with comfort when I am interrupted so much as I
have been today. I like this berth well enough, but I don't like
to be left here to wait on the customers. The experiences are novel,
I grant you, and entertaining too, after a fashion, but they are not
judiciously distributed. A gentleman shoots at you through the
window and cripples *me;* a bomb-shell comes down the stove-
pipe for your gratification and sends the stove-door down *my*
throat; a friend drops in to swap compliments with you, and
freckles *me* with bullet-holes till my skin won't hold my principles; you go to dinner, and Jones comes with his cowhide, Gillespie
throws me out of the window, Thompson tears all my clothes off,
and an entire stranger takes my scalp with the easy freedom of
an old acquaintance; and in less than five minutes all the black-
guards in the country arrive in their war-paint, and proceed to

scare the rest of me to death with their tomahawks. Take it altogether, I never had such a spirited time in all my life as I have had today. No; I like you, and I like your calm unruffled way of explaining things to the customers, but you see I am not used to it. The Southern heart is too impulsive; Southern hospitality is too lavish with the stranger. The paragraphs which I have written today, and into whose cold sentences your masterly hand has infused the fervent spirit of Tennessean journalism, will wake up another nest of hornets. All that mob of editors will come — and they will come hungry, too, and want somebody for breakfast. I shall have to bid you adieu. I decline to be present at these festivities. I came South for my health, I will go back on the same errand, and suddenly. Tennesseean journalism is too stirring for me."

After which we parted with mutual regret, and I took apartments at the hospital.

A MYSTERIOUS VISIT

Collected in *Mark Twain's Sketches New and Old* in 1875,
this tale was first published in Twain's *Buffalo Express*
column on March 19, 1870.

The first notice that was taken of me when I "settled down" recently, was by a gentleman who said he was an assessor, and connected with the U.S. Internal Revenue Department. I said I had never heard of his branch of business before, but I was very glad to see him all the same—would he sit down? He sat down. I did not know anything particular to say, and yet I felt that people who have arrived at the dignity of keeping house must be conversational, must be easy and sociable in company. So, in default of anything else to say, I asked him if he was opening his shop in our neighborhood?

He said he was. [I did not wish to appear ignorant, but I *had* hoped he would mention what he had for sale.]

I ventured to ask him "How was trade?" and he said "So-so."

I then said we would drop in, and if we liked his house as well as any other, we would give him our custom.

He said he thought we would like his establishment well enough to confine ourselves to it—said he never saw anybody who would go off and hunt up another man in his line after trading with him once.

That sounded pretty complacent, but barring that natural expression of villainy which we all have, the man looked honest enough.

I do not know how it came about exactly, but gradually we appeared to melt down and run together, conversationally speaking, and then everything went along as comfortably as clockwork.

We talked, and talked, and talked—at least I did; and we laughed, and laughed, and laughed—at least he did. But all the time I had my presence of mind about me – I had my native shrewdness turned on "full head," as the engineers say. I was determined to find out all about his business in spite of his obscure answers – and I was determined I would have it out of him without his suspecting what I was at. I meant to trap him with a deep, deep ruse. I would tell him all about my own business, and he would naturally so warm to me during this seductive burst of confidence that he would forget himself, and tell me all about *his* affairs before he suspected what I was about. I thought to myself, My son, you little know what an old fox you are dealing with. I said –

"Now you never would guess what I made lecturing this winter and last spring?"

"No – don't believe I could, to save me. Let me see – let me see. About two thousand dollars, maybe? But no; no sir, I know you couldn't have made that much. Say seventeen hundred, maybe?"

"Ha! ha! I knew you couldn't. My lecturing receipts for last spring and this winter were fourteen thousand seven hundred and fifty dollars. What do you think of that?"

"Why, it is amazing – perfectly amazing. I will make a note of it. And you say even this wasn't all?"

"All! Why bless you, there was my income from the *Daily Warwhoop* for four months – about – about – well, what should you say to about eight thousand dollars, for instance?"

"Say! Why, I should say I should like to see myself rolling in just such another ocean of affluence. Eight thousand! I'll make a note of it. Why man! – and on top of all this I am to understand that you had still more income?"

"Ha! ha! ha! Why, you're only in the suburbs of it, so to speak. There's my book, 'The Innocents Abroad'– price $3.50 to $5.00, according to the binding. Listen to me. Look me in the eye. During the last four months and a half, saying nothing of sales before that, but just simply during the four months and a half, we've sold ninety-five thousand copies of that book. Ninety-five thousand! Think of it. Average four dollars a copy, say. It's nearly four hundred thousand dollars, my son. I get half."

"The suffering Moses! I'll set *that* down. Fourteen-seven-fifty—eight—two hundred. Total, say—well, upon my word, the grand total is about two hundred and thirteen or fourteen thousand dollars! *Is* that possible?"

"Possible! If there's any mistake it's the other way. Two hundred and fourteen thousand, cash, is my income for this year if *I* know how to cipher."

Then the gentleman got up to go. It came over me most uncomfortably that maybe I had made revelations for nothing, besides being flattered into stretching them considerably by the stranger's astonished exclamations. But no; at the last moment the gentleman handed me a large envelope, and said it contained his advertisement; and that I would find out all about his business in it; and that he would be happy to have my custom—would in fact, be *proud* to have the custom of a man of such prodigious income; and that he used to think there were several wealthy men in the city, but when they came to trade with him, he discovered that they barely had enough to live on; and that, in truth it had been such a weary, weary age since he had seen a rich man face to face, and talked to him, and touched him with his hands, that he could hardly refrain from embracing me—in fact, would esteem it a great favor if I would *let* him embrace me.

This so pleased me that I did not try to resist, but allowed this simple-hearted stranger to throw his arms about me and weep a few tranquilizing tears down the back of my neck. Then he went his way.

As soon as he was gone I opened his advertisement. I studied it attentively for four minutes. I then called up the cook, and said—

"Hold me while I faint! Let Marie turn the griddle-cakes."

By and by, when I came to, I sent down to the rum mill on the corner and hired an artist by the week to sit up nights and curse that stranger, and give me a lift occasionally in the daytime when I came to a hard place.

Ah, what a miscreant he was! His "advertisement" was nothing in the world but a wicked tax-return – a string of impertinent questions about my private affairs, occupying the best part of four foolscap pages of fine print – questions, I may remark, gotten up with such marvelous ingenuity, that the oldest man in the world couldn't understand what the most of them were driving at – questions, too, that were calculated to make a man report about four times his actual income to keep from swearing to a falsehood. I looked for a loophole, but there did not appear to be any. Inquiry No. 1 covered my case as generously and as amply as an umbrella could cover an ant hill –

> "What were your profits, during the past year, from any trade, business, or vocation, wherever carried on?"

And that inquiry was backed up by thirteen others of an equally searching nature, the most modest of which required information as to whether I had committed any burglary or highway robbery, or by any arson or other secret source of emolument, had acquired property which was not enumerated in my statement of income as set opposite to inquiry No. 1.

It was plain that that stranger had enabled me to make a goose of myself. It was very, very plain; and so I went out and hired another artist. By working on my vanity, the stranger had seduced me into declaring an income of $214,000. By law, $1000 of this was exempt from income-tax – the only relief I could see, and it was only a drop in the ocean. At the legal five per cent, I must pay to the Government the sum of ten thousand six hundred and fifty dollars, income-tax!

[I may remark, in this place, that I did not do it.]

I am acquainted with a very opulent man, whose house is a palace, whose table is regal, whose outlays are enormous, yet a man who has no income, as I have often noticed by the revenue returns; and to him I went for advice, in my distress. He took my dreadful exhibition of receipts, he put on his glasses, he took his pen, and presto! – I was a pauper! It was the neatest thing that ever was. He did it simply by deftly manipulating the bill of "DEDUCTIONS." He set down my "State, national, and municipal taxes" at so much; my "losses by shipwreck, fire, etc.," at so much; my "losses on sales of real estate"– on "live stock sold"– on "payments for rent of homestead"– on "repairs, improvements, interest"– on "previously taxed salary as an officer of the United States' army, navy, revenue service," and other things. He got astonishing "deductions" out of each and every one of these matters – each and every one of them. And when he was done he handed me the paper, and I saw at a glance that during the year my income, in the way of profits, had been *one thousand two hundred and fifty dollars and forty cents.*

"Now," said he, "the thousand dollars is exempt by law. What you want to do is to go and swear this document in and pay tax on the two hundred and fifty dollars."

[While he was making this speech his little boy Willie lifted a two dollar greenback out of his vest pocket and vanished with it, and I would wager anything that if my stranger were to call on that little boy tomorrow he would make a false return of his income.]

"Do you," said I, "do you always work up the 'deductions' after this fashion in your own case, sir?"

"Well, I should say so! If it weren't for those eleven saving clauses under the head of 'Deduction' I should be beggared every year to support this hateful and wicked, this extortionate and tyrannical government."

This gentleman stands away up among the very best of the solid men of the city–the men of moral weight, of commercial integrity, of unimpeachable social spotlessness–and so I bowed to his example. I went down to the revenue office, and under the accusing eyes of my old visitor I stood up and swore to lie after

lie, fraud after fraud, villainy after villainy, till my soul was coated
inches and inches thick with perjury, and my self-respect gone
for ever and ever.

But what of it? It is nothing more than thousands of the richest
and proudest, and most respected, honored, and courted men in
America do every year. And so I don't care. I am not ashamed.
I shall simply, for the present, talk little, and eschew fire-proof
gloves, lest I fall into certain dreadful habits irrevocably.

THE UNDERTAKER'S CHAT

First appearing in *Galaxy* magazine as "Reminiscences of a Back Settlement," "The Undertaker's Chat" was published in the volume *Sketches, New and Old,* by The American Publishing Company, Hartford, Connecticut, in 1875.

"Now that corpse," said the undertaker, patting the folded hands of deceased approvingly, "was a brick—every way you took him he was a brick. He was so real accommodating, and so modest-like and simple in his last moments. Friends wanted metallic burial-case—nothing else would do. I couldn't get it. There warn't going to be time—anybody could see that.

"Corpse said never mind, shake him up some kind of a box he could stretch out in comfortable, *he* warn't particular 'bout the general style of it. Said he went more on room than style, anyway in the last final container.

"Friends wanted a silver doorplate on the coffin, signifying who he was and wher' he was from. Now *you* know a fellow couldn't roust out such a gaily thing as that in a little country town like this. What did the corpse say?

"Corpse said, whitewash his old canoe and dob his address and general destination onto it with a blacking brush and a stencil plate, 'long with a verse from some likely hymn or other, and p'int him for the tomb, and mark him C.O.D., and just let him flicker. *He* warn't distressed any more than you be—on the contrary just as ca'm and collected as a hearse-horse; said he judged that wher' he was going to a body would find it considerable better to attract attention by a picturesque moral character than a natty burial case with a swell doorplate on it.

"Splendid man, he was. I'd druther do for a corpse like that 'n any I've tackled in seven year. There's some satisfaction in buryin' a man like that. You feel that what you're doing is appreciated.

Lord bless you, so's he got planted before he sp'iled, he was perfectly satisfied; said his relations meant well, *perfectly* well, but
all them preparations was bound to delay the thing more or less,
and he didn't wish to be kept layin' around. You never see such
a clear head as what he had – and so ca'm, and so cool. Just a
hunk of brains – that is what *he* was. Perfectly awful. It was a ripping
distance from one end of that man's head to t'other. Often and
over again he's had brain fever a-raging in one place, and the rest
of the pile didn't know anything about it – didn't affect it any more
than an Injun insurrection in Arizona affects the Atlantic States.

"Well, the relations they wanted a big funeral, but corpse said
he was down on flummery – didn't want any procession – fill the
hearse full of mourners, and get out a stern line and tow *him*
behind. He *was* the most down on style of any remains I ever
struck. A beautiful simple-minded creature – it was what he was,
you can depend on that. He was just set on having things the way
he wanted them, and he took a solid comfort in laying his little
plans. He had me measure him and take a whole raft of directions; then he had the minister stand up behind a long box with
a tablecloth over it, to represent the coffin, and read his funeral
sermon saying, 'Angcore, angcore!' at the good places, and making him scratch out every bit of brag about him, and all the
hifalutin; and then he made them trot out the choir so's he could
help them pick out the tunes for the occasion, and he got them
to sing 'Pop Goes the Weasel,' because he'd always liked that tune
when he was down-hearted, and solemn music made him sad;
and when they sung that with tears in their eyes (because they
all loved him), and his relations grieving around, he just laid there
as happy as a bug, and trying to beat time and showing all over
how much he enjoyed it; and presently he got worked up and
excited, and tried to join in, for, mind you, he was pretty proud
of his abilities in the singing line; but the first time he opened
his mouth and was just going to spread himself his breath took
a walk.

"I never saw a man snuffed out so sudden. Ah, it was a great loss – a powerful loss to this poor little one-horse town. Well, well, well, I hain't got time to be palavering along here – got to nail on the lid and mosey along with him; and if you'll just give me a lift we'll skeet him into the hearse and meander along. Relations bound to have it so – don't pay no attention to dying injunctions, minute a corpse's gone; but, if I had *my* way, if I didn't respect his last wishes and tow him behind the hearse *I'll* be cuss'd. I consider that whatever a corpse wants done for his comfort is little enough matter, and a man hain't got no right to deceive him or take advantage of him; and whatever a corpse trusts me to do I'm a-going to *do*, you know, even if it's to stuff him and paint him yaller and keep him for a keepsake – you hear *me!*"

He cracked his whip and went lumbering away with his ancient ruin of a hearse, and I continued my walk with a valuable lesson learned – that a healthy and wholesome cheerfulness is not necessarily impossible to *any* occupation. The lesson is likely to be lasting, for it will take many months to obliterate the memory of the remarks and circumstances that impressed it.

THE DANGER OF LYING IN BED

This short story was first published in Twain's *Galaxy* column in
1871. It was later collected in *The $30,000 Bequest and Other
Stories,* published in 1906 by Harper and Brothers,
New York and London.

The man in the ticket office said:

"Have an accident insurance ticket, also?"

"No," I said, after studying the matter over a little. "No, I believe
not; I am going to be travelling by rail all day today. However,
tomorrow I don't travel. Give me one for tomorrow."

The man looked puzzled. He said:

"But it is for accident insurance, and if you are going to travel
by rail—"

"If I am going to travel by rail, I shan't need it. Lying at home
in bed is the thing I am afraid of."

I had been looking into this matter. Last year I travelled twenty
thousand miles, almost entirely by rail; the year before, I travelled
over twenty-five thousand miles, half by sea and half by rail; and
the year before that I travelled in the neighborhood of ten thousand miles, exclusively by rail. I suppose if I put in all the little
odd journeys here and there, I may say I have travelled sixty thousand miles during the three years I have mentioned. *And never
an accident.*

For a good while I said to myself every morning: "Now I have
escaped thus far, and so the chances are just that much increased
that I shall catch it this time. I will be shrewd, and buy an accident ticket." And to a dead moral certainty I drew a blank, and
went to bed that night without a joint started or a bone splin-
tered. I got tired of that sort of daily bother, and fell to buying
accident tickets that were good for a month. I said to myself, "A
man *can't* buy thirty blanks in one bundle."

But I was mistaken. There was never a prize in the lot. I could read of railway accidents every day–the newspaper atmosphere was foggy with them; but somehow they never came my way. I found I had spent a good deal of money in the accident business, and had nothing to show for it. My suspicions were aroused, and I began to hunt around for somebody that had won in this lottery. I found plenty of people who had invested, but not an individual that had ever had an accident or made a cent. I stopped buying accident tickets and went to ciphering. The result was astounding. THE PERIL LAY NOT IN TRAVELLING, BUT IN STAYING AT HOME.

I hunted up statistics, and was amazed to find that after all the glaring newspaper headings concerning railroad disasters, less than *three hundred* people had really lost their lives by those disasters in the preceding twelve months. The Erie road was set down as the most murderous in the list. It had killed forty-six–or twenty-six, I do not exactly remember which, but I know the number was double that of any other road. But the fact straightway suggested itself that the Erie was an immensely long road, and did more business than any other line in the country; so the double number of killed ceased to be matter for surprise.

By further figuring, it appeared that between New York and Rochester the Erie ran eight passenger trains each way every day–sixteen altogether; and carried a daily average of 6,000 persons. That is about a million in six months–the population of New York city. Well, the Erie kills from thirteen to twenty-three persons out of *its* million in six months; and in the same time 13,000 of New York's million die in their beds! My flesh crept, my hair stood on end. "This is appalling!" I said. "The danger isn't in travelling by rail, but in trusting to those deadly beds. I will never sleep in a bed again."

I had figured on considerably less than one-half the length of the Erie road. It was plain that the entire road must transport at least eleven or twelve thousand people every day. There are many short roads running out of Boston that do fully half as much;

a great many such roads. They are many roads scattered about the Union that do a prodigious passenger business. Therefore it was fair to presume that an average of 2,500 passengers a day for each road in the country would be about correct. There are 846 railway lines in our country, and 846 times 2,500 are 2,115,000. So the railways of America move more than two millions of people every day; six hundred and fifty millions of people a year, without counting the Sundays. They do that, too – there is no question about it; though where they get the raw material is clear beyond the jurisdiction of arithmetic; for I have hunted the census through and through, and I find that there are not that many people in the United States, by a matter of six hundred and ten millions at the very least. They must use some of the same people over again, likely.

San Francisco is one-eighth as populous as New York; there are 60 deaths a week in the former and 500 a week in the latter – if they have luck. That is 3,120 deaths a year in San Francisco, and eight times as many in New York – say about 25,000 or 26,000. The health of the two places is the same. So we will let it stand as a fair presumption that this will hold good all over the country, and that consequently 25,000 out of every million of people we have must die every year. That amounts to one-fortieth of our total population. Out of this million ten or twelve thousand are stabbed, shot, drowned, hanged, poisoned, or meet a similarly violent death in some other popular way, such as perishing by kerosene lamp and hoop-skirt conflagrations, getting buried in coal mines, falling off housetops, breaking through church or lecture-room floors, taking patent medicines, or committing suicide in other forms. The Erie railroad kills from 23 to 46; the other 845 railroads kill an average of one-third of a man each; and the rest of that million, amounting in the aggregate to the appalling figure of nine hundred and eighty-seven thousand six hundred and thirty-one corpses, die naturally in their beds!

You will excuse me from taking any more chances on those beds. The railroads are good enough for me.

And my advice to all people is, Don't stay at home any more than you can help; but when you have *got* to stay at home a while, buy a package of those insurance tickets and sit up nights. You cannot be too cautious.

[One can see now why I answered that ticket agent in the manner recorded at the top of this sketch.]

The moral of this composition is, that thoughtless people grumble more than is fair about railroad management in the United States. When we consider that every day and night of the year full fourteen thousand railway trains of various kinds, freighted with life and armed with death, go thundering over the land, the marvel is *not* that they kill three hundred human beings in a twelvemonth, but that they do not kill three hundred times three hundred!

A True Story Repeated Word For Word As I Heard It

Written in 1874 during a stay at Quarry Farm, one of Twain's
common retreats, this tale was the first of Twain's many
contributions to the *Atlantic Monthly*. It is an account
as told to Twain by Auntie Cord, the cook at
Quarry Farm, of her experiences as a slave.

It was summer time, and twilight. We were sitting on the porch
of the farmhouse, on the summit of the hill, and "Aunt Rachel"
was sitting respectfully below our level, on the steps – for she was
our servant, and colored. She was of mighty frame and stature;
she was sixty years old, but her eye was undimmed and her
strength unabated. She was a cheerful, hearty soul, and it was no
more trouble for her to laugh than it is for a bird to sing. She
was under fire now, as usual when the day was done. That is to
say, she was being chaffed without mercy, and was enjoying it.
She would let off peal after peal of laughter, and then sit with
her face in her hands and shake with throes of enjoyment which
she could no longer get breath enough to express. At such a
moment as this a thought occurred to me, and I said:

"Aunt Rachel, how is it that you've lived sixty years and never
had any trouble?"

She stopped quaking. She paused, and there was a moment
of silence. She turned her face over her shoulder toward me, and
said, without even a smile in her voice:

"Misto C—, is you in 'arnest?"

It surprised me a good deal; and it sobered my manner and
my speech, too, I said:

"Why, I thought–that is, I meant–why, you *can't* have had any trouble. I've never seen your eye when there wasn't a laugh in it."

She faced fairly around now, and was full of earnestness.

"Has I had any trouble? Misto C——, I's gwyne to tell you, den I leave it to you. I was bawn down 'mongst de slaves; I knows all 'bout slavery, 'case I ben one of 'em my own se'f. Well, sah, my ole man–dat's my husban'–he was lovin' and kind to me, jist as kind as you is to yo' own wife. An' we had chil'en–seven chil'en–an' we loved dem chil'en jist de same as you loves yo' chil'en. Dey was black, but de Lord can't make no chil'en so black but what dey mother loves 'em an' wouldn't give 'em up, no, not for anything dat's in dis whole world.

"Well, sah, I was raised in ole Fo'ginny, but my mother she was raised in Maryland; an' my *souls!* she was turrible when she'd git started! My *lan'!* but she'd make de fur fly! When she'd git into dem tantrums, she always had one word dat she said. She'd straighten herse'f up an put her fists in her hips an' say, 'I want you to understan' dat I wa'nt bawn in the mash to be fool' by trash! I's one o' de ole Blue Hen's Chickens, *I* is!' 'Ca'se, you see, dat's what folks dat's bawn in Maryland calls deyselves, an' dey's proud of it. Well, dat was her word. I don't ever forgit it, beca'se she said it so much, an' beca'se she said it one day when my little Henry tore his wris' awful, and most busted his head, right up at de top of his forehead, an' de niggers didn't fly aroun' fas' enough to 'tend to him. An' when dey talk' back at her, she up an' she says, 'Look-a-heah!' she says, 'I want you niggers to understan' dat I wa'nt bawn in de mash to be fool' by trash! I's one o' de old Blue Hen's Chickens, *I* is!' an' den she clar' dat kitchen an' bandage up de chile herse'f. So I says dat word, too, when I's riled.

"Well, bymeby my ole mistis say she's broke, an' she got to sell all de niggers on de place. An' when I heah dat dey gwyne to sell us all off at oction in Richmon', oh, de good gracious! I know what dat mean!"

Aunt Rachel had gradually risen, while she warmed to her subject, and how she towered above us, black against the stars.

"Dey put chains on us an' put us on a stan' as high as dis po'ch – twenty foot high – an' all de people stood aroun', crowds an' crowds. An' dey'd come up dah an' look at us all roun', an' squeeze our arm, an' make us git up an' walk, an' den say, 'Dis one too ole,' or 'Dis one lame,' or 'Dis one don't 'mount to much.' An' dey sole my ole man, an' took him away, an' dey begin to sell my chil'en an' take *dem* away, an' I begin to cry; an' de man say, 'Shet up yo' dem blubberin',' an' hit me on de mouf wid his han'. An' when de las' one was gone but my little Henry, I grab' *him* clost up to my breas' so, an' I ris up an' says, 'You shan't take him away,' I says; 'I'll kill de man dat tetches him!' I says. But my little Henry whisper an' say, 'I gwyne to run away, an' den I work an' buy yo' freedom.' Oh, bless de chile, he always so good! But dey got him – dey got him, de men did; but I took and tear de clo'es mos' off of 'em an' beat 'em over de head wid my chain; an' *dey* give it to *me,* too, but I didn't mine dat.

"Well, dah was my old man gone, an' all my chil'en, all my seven chil'en – an' six of 'em I hain't set eyes on ag'in to dis day, an' dat's twenty-two year ago las' Easter. De man dat bought me b'long' in Newbern, an' he took me dah. Well, bymeby de years roll on an' de waw come. My marster he was a Confedrit colonel, an' I was his family's cook. So when de Unions took dat town, day all run away an' lef' me all by myse'f wid de other niggers in dat mons'us big house. So de big Union officers move in dah, an' dey ask me would I cook for *dem.* 'Lord bless you,' says I, 'dat's what I's *for.*'

"Dey wa'nt no small-fry officers, mine you, dey was de biggest dey *is;* an' de way dey made dem sojers mosey roun'! De Gen'l he tole me to boss dat kitchen; an' he say, 'If anybody come meddlin' wid you, you jist make 'em walk chalk; don't you be afeared,' he say; 'you's 'mong frens now.'

"Well, I thinks to myse'f, if my little Henry ever got a chance to run away, he'd make to de Norf, o' course. So one day I comes in dah whar de big officers was, in de parlor, an' I drops a kurtchy, so, an' I up an' tole 'em 'bout my Henry, dey a-listenin' to my trouble jist de same as if I was white folks; an' I says, 'What I come for is beca'se if he got away and got up Norf whar you gemmen comes from, you might' a' seen him, maybe, an' could tell me so as I could fine him ag'in; he was very little, an' he had a sk-yar on his lef' wris' an' at de top of his forehead.' Den dey look mournful, an' de Gen'l says, 'How long sence you los' him?' an' I say, 'Thirteen year.' Den de Gen'l say, 'He wouldn't be little no mo' now—he's a man!'

"I never thought o' dat befo'! He was only dat little feller to *me* yit. I never thought 'bout him growin' up an' bein' big. But I see it den. None o' de gemmen had run acrost him, so dey couldn't do nothin' for me. But all dat time, do' I didn't know it, my Henry *was* run off to de Norf, years an' years, an' he was a barber, too, an' worked for hisse'f. An' bymeby, when de waw come he ups an' he says: 'I's done barberin',' he says, 'I's gwyne to fine my ole mammy, less'n she's dead.' So he sole out an' went to whar dey was recruitin', an' hired hisse'f out to de colonel for his servant; an' den he went all froo de battles everywhah, huntin' for his ole mammy; yes, indeedy, he's hire to fust one officer an' den another, tell he'd ransacked do whole Souf; but you see I didn't know nuffin 'bout *dis*. How was *I* gwyne to know it?

"Well, one night we had a big sojer ball; de sojers dah at Newbern was always havin' balls an' carryin' on. Dey had 'em in my kitchen, heaps o' times, 'ca'se it was so big. Mine you. I was *down* on sich doin's; beca'se my place was wid de officers, an' it rasp me to have dem common sojers cavortin' roun' my kitchen like dat. But I alway' stood aroun' an' kep' things straight, I did; an' sometimes dey'd get my dander up, an' den I'd make 'em clar dat kitchen, mine I *tell* you!

"Well, one night—it was a Friday night—dey comes a whole plattoon f'm a *nigger* ridgment dat was on guard at de house—de house was headquarters, you know—an' den I was jist a-*bilin'!* Mad? I was jist a-*boomin'!* I swelled aroun' an' swelled aroun'; I jist was a-itchin' for 'em to do somefin for to start me. *An'* dey was a-waltzin' an' a-dancin'! *my!* but dey was havin' a time! an' I jist a-swellin' an' a-swellin' up! Pooty soon, 'long come *sich* a spruce young nigger a-sailin' down de room wid a yaller wench roun' de wais'; an' roun' an' roun' an roun' dey went, enough to make a body drunk to look at 'em; an' when dey got abreas' o' me, dey went to kin' o' balacin' aroun' fust on one leg an' den on t'other, an' smilin' at my big red turban, an' makin' fun, an' I ups an' says '*Git* along wid you! rubbage!' De young man's face kin' o' changed, all of a sudden, for 'bout a second, but den he went to smilin' ag'in, same as he was befo'. Well, 'bout dis time, in comes some niggers dat played music an b'long' to de ban', an' dey *never* could git along widout puttin' on airs. An' de very fust air dey put on dat night, I lit into 'em! Dey laughed, an' dat made me wuss. De res' o' de niggers got to laughin', an' den my soul *alive* but I was hot! My eye was jist a-blazin'! I jist straightened myself up so—jist as I is now, plum to de ceilin', mos'—an' I digs my fists into my hips, an' I says, 'Look-a-heah!' I says, 'I want you niggers to understan' dat I wa'nt bawn in de mash to be fool' by trash! I's one o' de ole Blue Hen's Chickens, *I* is!' an' den I see dat young man stan' a-starin' an' stiff, lookin' kin' o' up at de ceilin' like he fo'got somefin, an' couldn't 'member it no mo'. Well, I jist march' on dem niggers— so, lookin' like a gen'l—an' dey jist cave' away befo' me an' out at de do'. An' as dis young man was a-goin' out, I heah him say to another nigger, 'Jim,' he says, 'you go 'long an' tell de cap'n I be on han' 'bout eight o'clock in de mawnin'; dey's somefin on my mine,' he says; 'I don't sleep no mo' dis night. You go 'long,' he says, 'an' leave me by my own se'f.'

"Dis was 'bout one o'clock in de mawnin'. Well, 'bout seven, I was up an' on han', gettin' de officers' breakfast. I was a-stoopin' down by de stove—jist so, same as if yo' foot was de stove—an' I'd opened de stove do' wid my right han'—so, pushin' it back, jist

as I pushes yo' foot – an' I'd jist got de pan o' hot biscuits in my
han' an' was 'bout to raise up, when I see a black face come aroun'
under mine, an' de eyes a-lookin' up into mine, jist as I's a-lookin'
up clost under yo' face now; an I jist stopped *right dah,* an' never
budged! jist gazed an' gazed so; an' de pan begin to tremble, an'
all of a sudden I *knowed!* De pan drop' on de flo' an' I grab his
lef' han' an shove back his sleeve – jist so, as I's doin' to you – an'
I says, 'if you an't my Henry, what is you doin' wid dis welt on
yo' wris' an' dat sk-yar on yo' forehead? De Lord God ob heaven
be praise', I got my own ag'in!'

"Oh, no Misto C—, *I* hain't had no trouble. An' no *joy!*"

AN ENCOUNTER
WITH AN INTERVIEWER

Three years after appearing as a contribution to *Lotus Leaves* in
1875, this tale was included in *Punch, Brothers, Punch! and Other
Sketches*, published by Slote, Woodman and Company of New
York. It surfaces again in *The Stolen White Elephant, Etc.*, in 1882
in Boston, by James R. Osgood and Company and finally in
*Tom Sawyer Abroad, Tom Sawyer, Detective, and Other Stories, Etc.,
Etc.*, published by Harper and Brothers, New York, in 1896.

The nervous, dapper, "peart" young man took the chair I offered
him, and said he was connected with the *Daily Thunderstorm*, and
added –

"Hoping it's no harm, I've come to interview you."

"Come to what?"

"*Interview* you."

"Ah! I see. Yes–yes. Um! Yes–yes."

I was not feeling bright that morning. Indeed, my powers
seemed a bit under a cloud. However, I went to the bookcase, and
when I had been looking six or seven minutes, I found I was
obliged to refer to the young man. I said–

"How do you spell it?"

"Spell what?"

"Interview."

"Oh my goodness! what do you want to spell it for?"

"I don't want to spell it; I want to see what it means."

"Well, this is astonishing, I must say. *I* can tell you what it
means, if you–if you–"

"Oh, all right! That will answer, and much obliged to you, too."

"In, *in,* ter, *ter, inter*–"

"Then you spell it with an *I*?"

"Why, certainly!"

"Oh, that is what took me so long."

"Why, my *dear* sir, what did *you* propose to spell it with?"

"Well, I–I–hardly know. I had the Unabridged, and I was ciphering around in the back end, hoping I might tree her among the pictures. But it's a very old edition."

"Why, my friend, they wouldn't have a *picture* of it even the latest e– My dear sir, I beg your pardon, I mean no harm in the world, but you do not look as–as–intelligent as I had expected you would. No harm–I mean no harm at all."

"Oh, don't mention it! It has often been said, and by people who would not flatter and who could have no inducement to flatter, that I am quite remarkable in that way. Yes–yes; they always speak of it with rapture."

"I can easily imagine it. But about this interview. You know it is the custom, now, to interview any man who has become notorious."

"Indeed, I had not heard of it before. It must be very interesting. What do you do it with?"

"Ah, well–well–well–this is disheartening. It *ought* to be done with a club in some cases; but customarily it consists in the interviewer asking questions and the interviewed answering them. It is all the rage now. Will you let me ask you certain questions calculated to bring out the salient points of your public and private history?"

"Oh, with pleasure–with pleasure. I have a very bad memory, but I hope you will not mind that. That is to say, it is an irregular memory–singularly irregular. Sometimes it goes in a gallop, and then again it well be as much as a fortnight passing a given point. This is a great grief to me."

"Oh, it is no matter, so you will try to do the best you can."

"I will. I will put my whole mind on it."

"Thanks. Are you ready to begin?"

"Ready."

Q. How old are you?

A. Nineteen, in June.

Q. Indeed! I would have taken you to be thirty-five or six. Where were you born?

A. In Missouri.

Q. When did you begin to write?

A. In 1836.

Q. Why, how could that be, if you are only nineteen now?

A. I don't know. It does seem curious, somehow.

Q. It does, indeed. Whom do you consider the most remarkable man you ever met?

A. Aaron Burr.

Q. But you have never met Aaron Burr, if you are only nineteen years –

A. Now, if you know more about me than I do, what do you ask me for?

Q. Well, it was only a suggestion; nothing more. How did you happen to meet Burr?

A. Well, I happened to be at his funeral one day, and he asked me to make less noise, and –

Q. But, good heavens! if you were at his funeral, he must have been dead; and if he was dead, how could he care whether you made a noise or not?

A. I don't know. He was always a particular kind of a man that way.

Q. Still, I don't understand it at all. You say he spoke to you, and that he was dead.

A. I didn't say he was dead.

Q. But wasn't he dead?

A. Well, some said he was, some said he wasn't.

Q. What did you think?

A. Oh, it was none of my business! It wasn't any of my funeral.

Q. Did you – However, we can never get this matter straight. Let me ask about something else. What was the date of your birth?

A. Monday, October 31st, 1693.

Q. What! Impossible! That would make you a hundred and eighty years old. How do you account for that?

A. I don't account for it at all.

Q. But you said at first you were only nineteen, and now you make yourself out to be one hundred and eighty. It is an awful discrepancy.

A. Why, have you noticed that? (Shaking hands.) Many a time it has seemed to me like a discrepancy, but somehow I couldn't make up my mind: How quick you notice a thing!

Q. Thank you for the compliment, as far as it goes. Had you, or have you, any brothers or sisters?

A. Eh! I—I—I think so—yes—but I don't remember.

Q. Well, that is the most extraordinary statement I ever heard!

A. Why, what makes you think that?

Q. How could I think otherwise? Why, look here! Who is this a picture of on the wall? Isn't that a brother of yours?

A. Oh! Yes, yes, yes! Now you remind me of it; that *was* a brother of mine. that's William—*Bill* we called him. Poor old Bill!

Q. Why? Is he dead, then?

A. Ah! well, I suppose so. We never could tell. There was a great mystery about it.

Q. That is sad, very sad. He disappeared, then?

A. Well, yes, in a sort of general way. We buried him.

Q. Buried him! *Buried* him, without knowing whether he was dead or not?

A. Oh, no! Not that. He was dead enough.

Q. Well, I confess that I can't understand this. If you buried him, and you knew he was dead—

A. No! no! We only thought he was.

Q. Oh, I see! He came to life again?

A. I bet he didn't.

Q. Well, I never heard anything like this. *Somebody* was dead. *Somebody* was buried. Now, where was the mystery?

A. Ah! that's just it! That's it exactly. You see, we were twins—

defunct and I—and we got mixed in the bath-tub when we were only two weeks old, and one of us was drowned. But we didn't know which. Some think it was Bill. Some think it was me.

Q. Well, that *is* remarkable. What do *you* think!

A. Goodness knows! I would give whole worlds to know. This solemn, this awful mystery has cast a gloom over my whole life. But I will tell you a secret now, which I never have revealed to any creature before. One of us had a peculiar mark—a large mole on the back of his left hand; that was *me*. *That child was the one that was drowned!*

Q. Very well, then, I don't see that there is any mystery about it, after all.

A. You don't? Well, *I* do. Anyway, I don't see how they could ever have been such a blundering lot as to go and bury the wrong child. But, 'sh!—don't mention it where the family can hear of it. Heaven knows they have heartbreaking troubles enough without adding this.

Q. Well, I believe I have got material enough for the present, and I am very much obliged to you for the pains you have taken. But I was a good deal interested in that account of Aaron Burr's funeral. Would you mind telling me what particular circumstance it was that made you think Burr was such a remarkable man?

A. Oh! it was a mere trifle! Not one man in fifty would have noticed it at all. When the sermon was over, and the procession all ready to start for the cemetery, and the body all arranged nice in the hearse, he said he wanted to take a last look at the scenery, and so he *got up and rode with the driver.*

Then the young man reverently withdrew. He was a very pleasant company, and I was sorry to see him go.

ABOUT BARBERS

As he did with many of his other works, Twain first introduced this story in his *Galaxy* column. four years later, in 1875, it was published in *Sketches, New and Old,* by The American Publishing Company of Hartford, Connecticut.

All things change except barbers, the ways of barbers, and the surroundings of barbers. These never change. What one experiences in a barber's shop the first time he enters one is what he always experiences in barbers' shops afterward till the end of his days. I got shaved this morning as usual. A man approached the door from Jones street as I approached it from Main—a thing that always happens. I hurried up, but it was of no use; he entered the door one little step ahead of me, and I followed in on his heels and saw him take the only vacant chair, the one presided over by the best barber. It always happens so. I sat down, hoping that I might fall heir to the chair belonging to the better of the remaining two barbers, for he had already begun combing his man's hair, while his comrade was not quite done rubbing up and oiling his customer's locks. I watched the probabilities with strong interest. When I saw that No. 2 was gaining on No. 1 my interest grew to solicitude. When No. 1 stopped a moment to make change on a bath ticket for a new comer, and lost ground in the race, my solicitude rose to anxiety. When No. 1 caught up again, both he and his comrade were pulling the towels away and brushing the powder from their customer's cheeks, and it was about an even thing which would say "Next!" first, my very breath stood still with the suspense. But when at the culminating moment No. 1 stopped to pass a comb a couple of times through his customer's eyebrows, I saw that he had lost the race by a single instant, and I rose indignant and quitted the shop, to keep from falling into the hands of No. 2; for I have none of that enviable firmness that enables a man to look calmly into the eyes of a waiting barber and tell him he will wait for his fellow-barber's chair.

I stayed out fifteen minutes, and then went back, hoping for better luck. Of course all the chairs were occupied now, and four men sat waiting, silent, unsociable, distraught, and looking bored, as men always do who are waiting their turn in a barber's shop. I sat down in one of the iron-armed compartments of an old sofa, and put in the time for a while reading the framed advertisements of all sorts of quack nostrums for dyeing and coloring the hair. Then I read the greasy names on the private bay-rum bottles; read the names and noted the numbers on the private shaving cups in the pigeon-holes; studied the stained and damaged cheap prints on the walls, of battles, early Presidents, and voluptuous recumbent sultanas, and the tiresome and everlasting young girl putting her grandfather's spectacles on; execrated in my heart the cheerful canary and the distracting parrot that few barbers' shops are without. Finally, I searched out the least dilapidated of last year's illustrated papers that littered the foul center-table, and conned their unjustifiable misrepresentations of old forgotten events.

At last my turn came. A voice said "Next!" and I surrendered to – No. 2, of course. It always happens so. I said meekly that I was in a hurry, and it affected him as strongly as if he had never heard it. He shoved up my head, and put a napkin under it. He plowed his fingers into my collar and fixed a towel there. He explored my hair with his claws and suggested that it needed trimming. I said I did not want it trimmed. He explored again and said it was pretty long for the present style – better have a little taken off; it needed it behind especially. I said I had had it cut only a week before. He yearned over it reflectively a moment, and then asked with a disparaging manner, who cut it? I came back at him promptly with a "You did!" I had him there. Then he fell to stirring up his lather and regarding himself in the glass, stopping now and then to get close and examine his chin critically or inspect a pimple. then he lathered one side of my face thoroughly, and was about to lather the other, when a dog fight attracted his attention, and he ran to the window and stayed and saw it out, losing two shillings on the result in bets with the other barbers, a thing which gave me great satisfaction. He finished lathering, and then began to rub in the suds with his hand.

He now began to sharpen his razor on an old suspender, and was delayed a good deal on account of a controversy about a cheap masquerade ball he had figured at the night before, in red cambric and bogus ermine, as some kind of a king. He was so gratified with being chaffed about some damsel whom he had smitten with his charms that he used every means to continue the controversy by pretending to be annoyed at the chaffings of his fellows. This matter begot more surveyings of himself in the glass, and he put down his razor and brushed his hair with elaborate care, plastering an inverted arch of it down on his forehead, accomplishing an accurate "part" behind, and brushing the two wings forward over his ears with nice exactness. In the meantime the lather was drying on my face, and apparently eating into my vitals.

Now he began to shave, digging his fingers into my countenance to stretch the skin and bundling and tumbling my head this way and that as convenience in shaving demanded. As long as he was on the tough sides of my face I did not suffer; but when he began to rake, and rip, and tug at my chin, the tears came. He now made a handle of my nose, to assist him in shaving the corners of my upper lip, and it was by this bit of circumstantial evidence that I discovered that a part of his duties in the shop was to clean the kerosene lamps. I had often wondered in an indolent way whether the barbers did that, or whether it was the boss.

About this time I was amusing myself trying to guess where he would be most likely to cut me this time, but he got ahead of me, and sliced me on the end of the chin before I had got my mind made up. He immediately sharpened his razor—he might have done it before. I do not like a close shave, and would not let him go over me a second time. I tried to get him to put up his razor, dreading that he would make for the side of my chin, my pet tender spot, a place which a razor cannot touch twice without making trouble; but he said he only wanted to just smooth off one little roughness, and in the same moment he slipped his razor along the forbidden ground, and the dreaded pimple-signs of a close shave rose up smarting and answered to the call. Now he soaked his towel in bay rum, and slapped it all over my face nastily; lapped it over as if a human being ever yet washed his face in that way. Then he dried it by slapping with the dry part of the towel, as if a human being ever dried his face in such a fashion; but a barber seldom rubs you like a Christian. Next he poked bay rum into the cut place with his towel, then choked the wound with powdered starch, then soaked it forevermore, no doubt, if I had not rebelled and begged off. He powdered my whole face now, straightened me up, and began to plow my hair thoughtfully with his hands. Then he suggested a shampoo, and said my hair needed it badly, very badly. I observed that I shampooed it myself very thoroughly in the bath yesterday. I "had him" again. He next recommended some of "Smith's Hair Glorifier," and offered to sell me a bottle. I declined. He praised the new perfume, "Jones's Delight of the Toilet," and proposed to sell me some of that. I declined again. He tendered me a toothwash atrocity of his own invention, and when I declined offered to trade knives with me.

He returned to business after the miscarriage of this last enterprise, sprinkled me all over, legs and all, greased my hair in defiance of my protest against it, rubbed and scrubbed a good deal of it out by the roots, and combed and brushed the rest, parting it behind, and plastering the eternal inverted arch of hair down on my forehead, and then, while combing my scant eyebrows and defiling them with pomade, strung out an account of the achievements of a six-ounce black and tan terrier of his till I heard the whistles blow for noon, and knew I was five minutes too late for the train. Then he snatched away the towel, brushed it lightly about my face, passed his comb through my eyebrows once more, and gaily sang out "Next!"

This barber fell down and died of apoplexy two hours later. I am waiting over a day for my revenge—I am going to attend his funeral.

THE FACTS CONCERNING THE RECENT CARNIVAL OF CRIME IN CONNECTICUT

Written during the peak of Twain's career, "The Facts Concerning
the Recent Carnival of Crime in Connecticut" was first published
in the *Atlantic Monthly* in June of 1876, the same year *The
Adventures of Tom Sawyer* was published. Twain was inspired by
his own experiences, as well as one of his favorite books, William
E.H. Lecky's *History of European Morals*. Six years later, the story
was collected in *The Stolen Elephant, Etc.*

I was feeling blithe, almost jocund. I put a match to my cigar, and just then the morning's mail was handed in. The first superscription I glanced at was in a handwriting that sent a thrill of pleasure through and through me. It was Aunt Mary's; and she was the person I loved and honored most in all the world, outside of my own household. She had been my boyhood's idol; maturity, which is fatal to so many enchantments, had not been able to dislodge her from her pedestal; no, it had only justified her right to be there, and placed her dethronement permanently among the impossibilities. To show how strong her influence over me was, I will observe that long after everybody else's "*do*-stop-smoking" had ceased to affect me in the slightest degree, Aunt Mary could still stir my torpid conscience into faint signs of life when she touched upon the matter. but all things have their limit, in this world. A happy day came at last, when even Aunt Mary's words could no longer move me. I was not merely glad to see that day arrive; I was more than glad—I was grateful; for when its sun had set, the one alloy that was able to mar my enjoyment of my aunt's society was gone. The remainder of her stay with us that winter was in every way a delight. Of course she pleaded with me just as earnestly as ever, after that blessed day, to quit my pernicious habit, but to no purpose whatever; the moment she opened the subject I at once became calmly, peacefully, contentedly indifferent – absolutely, adamantinely indifferent. Consequently the closing weeks of that memorable visit melted away as pleasantly as a dream, they were so freighted, for me, with tranquil satisfaction. I could not have enjoyed my pet vice more if my gentle tormentor had been a smoker herself, and an advocate of the practice. Well, the sight of her handwriting reminded me that I was getting very hungry to see her again. I easily guessed what I should find in her letter. I opened it. Good! just as I expected; she was coming! Coming this very day, too, and by the morning train; I might expect her any moment.

I said to myself, "I am thoroughly happy and content, now. If my most pitiless enemy could appear before me at this moment, I would freely right any wrong I may have done him."

Straightway the door opened, and a shrivelled, shabby dwarf entered. He was not more than two feet high. He seemed to be about forty years old. Every feature and every inch of him was a trifle out of shape; and so, while one could not put his finger upon any particular part and say, "This is a conspicuous deformity," the spectator perceived that this little person was a deformity as a whole – a vague, general, evenly blended, nicely adjusted deformity. There was a fox-like cunning in the face and the sharp little eyes, and also alertness and malice. And yet, this vile bit of human rubbish seemed to bear a sort of remote and ill-defined resemblance to me! It was dully perceptible in the mean form, the countenance, and even the clothes, gestures, manner, and attitudes of the creature. He was a far-fetched, dim suggestion of a burlesque upon me, a caricature of me in little. One thing about him struck me forcibly, and most unpleasantly: he was covered all over with a fuzzy, greenish mould, such as one sometimes sees upon mildewed bread. The sight of it was nauseating.

He stepped along with a chipper air, and flung himself into a doll's chair in a very free-and-easy way, without waiting to be asked. He tossed his hat into the waste-basket. He picked up my old chalk pipe from the floor, gave the stem a wipe or two on his knee, filled the bowl from the tobacco-box at his side, and said to me in a tone of pert command—

"Gimme a match!"

I blushed to the roots of my hair; partly with indignation, but mainly because it somehow seemed to me that this whole performance was very like an exaggeration of conduct which I myself had sometimes been guilty of in my intercourse with familiar friends—but never, never with strangers, I observed to myself. I wanted to kick the pygmy into the fire, but some incomprehensible sense of being legally and legitimately under his authority forced me to obey his order. He applied the match to the pipe, took a contemplative whiff or two, and remarked, in an irritatingly familiar way—

"Seems to me it's devilish odd weather for this time of year."

I flushed again, and in anger and humiliation as before; for the language was hardly an exaggeration of some that I have uttered in my day, and moreover was delivered in a tone of voice and with an exasperating drawl that had the seeming of a deliberate travesty of my style. Now there is nothing I am quite so sensitive about as a mocking imitation of my drawling infirmity of speech. I spoke up sharply and said—

"Look here, you miserable ash-cat! you will have to give a little more attention to your manners, or I will throw you out of the window!"

The manikin smiled a smile of malicious content and security, puffed a whiff of smoke contemptuously toward me, and said, with a still more elaborate drawl—

"Come—go gently, now; don't put on *too* many airs with your betters."

This cool snub rasped me all over, but it seemed to subjugate me, too, for a moment. The pygmy contemplated me awhile with his weasel eyes, and then said, in a peculiarly sneering way—

"You turned a tramp away from your door this morning."

I said crustily—

"Perhaps I did, perhaps I didn't. How do *you* know?"

"Well, I know. It isn't any matter *how* I know."

"Very well. Suppose I *did* turn a tramp away from the door— what of it?"

"Oh, nothing; nothing in particular. Only you lied to him."

"I *didn't!* That is, I—"

"Yes, but you did; you lied to him."

I felt a guilty pang—in truth I had felt it forty times before that tramp had travelled a block from my door—but still I resolved to make a show of feeling slandered; so I said—

"That is a baseless impertinence. I said to the tramp—"

"There—wait. You were about to lie again. *I* know what you said to him. You said the cook was gone down town and there was nothing left behind the door, and plenty of provisions behind *her.*"

This astonishing accuracy silenced me; and it filled me with wondering speculations, too, as to how this cub could have got his information. Of course he could have culled the conversation from the tramp, but by what sort of magic had he contrived to find out about the concealed cook? Now the dwarf spoke again:—

"It was rather pitiful, rather small, in you to refuse to read that poor young woman's manuscript the other day, and give her an opinion as to its literary value; and she had come so far, too, and *so* hopefully. Now *wasn't* it?"

I felt like a cur! And I had felt so every time the thing had recurred to my mind, I may as well confess. I flushed hotly and said—

"Look here, have you nothing better to do than prowl around prying into other people's business? Did that girl tell you that?"

"Never mind whether she did or not. The main thing is, you

did that contemptible thing. And you felt ashamed of it afterwards. Aha! you feel ashamed of it *now!*"

This with a sort of devilish glee. With fiery earnestness I responded –

"I told that girl, in the kindest, gentlest way, that I could not consent to deliver judgment upon *any* one's manuscript, because an individual's verdict was worthless. It might underrate a work of high merit and lose it to the world, or it might overrate a trashy production and so open the way for its infliction upon the world. I said that the great public was the only tribunal competent to sit in judgment upon a literary effort, and therefore it must be best to lay it before that tribunal in the outset, since in the end it must stand or fall by that mighty court's decision anyway."

"Yes, you said all that. So you did, you juggling, small-souled shuffler! And yet when the happy hopefulness faded out of that poor girl's face, when you saw her furtively slip beneath her shawl the scroll she had so patiently and honestly scribbled at – so ashamed of her darling now, so proud of it before – when you saw the gladness go out of her eyes and the tears come there, when she crept away so humbly who had come so –"

"Oh, peace! peace! peace! Blister your merciless tongue, haven't all these thoughts tortured me enough without *your* coming here to fetch them back again!"

Remorse! remorse! It seemed to me that it would eat the very heart out of me! And yet that small fiend only sat there leering at me with joy and contempt, and placidly chuckling. Presently he began to speak again. Every sentence was an accusation, and every accusation a truth. Every clause was freighted with sarcasm and derision, every slow-dropping word burned like vitriol. The dwarf reminded me of times when I had flown at my children in anger and punished them for faults which a little inquiry would have taught me that others, and not they, had committed. He reminded me of how I had disloyally allowed old friends to be traduced in my hearing, and been too craven to utter a word in their defence. He reminded me of many dishonest things which I had done; of many which I had procured to be done by children and other irresponsible persons; of some which I had planned, thought upon, and longed to do, and been kept from the performance by fear of consequences only. With exquisite cruelty he recalled to my mind, item by item, wrongs and unkindnesses I had inflicted and humiliations I had put upon friends since dead, "who died thinking of those injuries, maybe, and grieving over them," he added, by way of poison to the stab.

"For instance," said he, "take the case of your younger brother, when you two were boys together, many a long year ago. He always lovingly trusted in you with a fidelity that your manifold treacheries were not able to shake. He followed you about like a dog, content to suffer wrong and abuse if he might only be with you; patient under these injuries so long as it was your hand that inflicted them. The latest picture you have of him in health and strength must be such a comfort to you! You pledged your honor that if he would let you blindfold him no harm should come to him; and then, giggling and choking over the rare fun of the joke, you led him to a brook thinly glazed with ice, and pushed him in; and how you did laugh! Man you will never forget the gentle, reproachful look he gave you as he struggled shivering out, if you live a thousand years! Oho! you see it now, you see it *now!*"

"Beast, I have seen it a million times, and shall see it a million more! and may you rot away piecemeal, and suffer till doomsday what I suffer now, for bringing it back to me again!"

The dwarf chuckled contentedly, and went on with his accusing history of my career. I dropped into a moody, vengeful state, and suffered in silence under the merciless lash. At last this remark of his gave me a sudden rouse:—

"Two months ago, on a Tuesday, you woke up, away in the night, and fell to thinking, with shame, about a peculiarly mean and pitiful act of yours toward a poor ignorant Indian in the wilds of the Rocky Mountains in the winter of eighteen hundred and—"

"Stop a moment, devil! Stop! Do you mean to tell me that even my very *thoughts* are not hidden from you?"

"It seems to look like that. Didn't you think the thoughts I have just mentioned?"

"If I didn't, I wish I may never breathe again! Look here, friend – look me in the eye. Who *are* you?"

"Well, who do you think?"

"I think you are Satan himself. I think you are the devil."

"No."

"No? Then who *can* you be?"

"Would you really like to know?"

"*Indeed* I would."

"Well, I am your *Conscience!*"

In an instant I was in a blaze of joy and exultation. I sprang at the creature, roaring –

"Curse you, I have wished a hundred million times that you were tangible, and that I could get my hands on your throat once! Oh, but I will wreak a deadly vengeance on –"

Folly! Lightning does not move more quickly than my Conscience did! He darted aloft so suddenly that in the moment my fingers clutched the empty air he was already perched on the top of the high bookcase, with his thumb at his nose in token of derision. I flung the poker at him, and missed. I fired the boot-jack. In a blind rage I flew from place to place, and snatched and hurled any missile that came handy; the storm of books, inkstands, and chunks of coal gloomed the air and beat about the manikin's perch relentlessly, but all to no purpose; the nimble figure dodged every shot; and not only that, but burst into a cackle of sarcastic and triumphant laughter as I sat down exhausted. While I puffed and gasped with fatigue and excitement, my Conscience talked to this effect: –

"My good slave, you are curiously witless – no, I mean characteristically so. In truth, you are always consistent, always yourself, always an ass. Otherwise it must have occurred to you that if you attempted this murder with a sad heart and a heavy conscience, I would droop under the burdening influence instantly. Fool, I should have weighed a ton, and could not have budged from the floor; but instead, you are so cheerfully anxious to kill me that your conscience is as light as a feather; hence I am away up here out of your reach. I can almost respect a mere ordinary sort of fool; but *you* – pah!"

I would have given anything, then, to be heavy-hearted, so that I could get this person down from there and take his life, but I could no more be heavy-hearted over such a desire than I could have sorrowed over its accomplishment. So I could only look long-ingly up at my master, and rave at the ill-luck that denied me a heavy conscience the one only time that I had ever wanted such a thing in my life. By-and-by I got to musing over the hour's strange adventure, and of course my human curiosity began to work. I set myself to framing in my mind some questions for this fiend to answer. Just then one of my boys entered, leaving the door open behind him, and exclaimed, –

"My, what *has* been going on, here? The bookcase is all one riddle of –"

I sprang up in consternation, and shouted –

"Out of this! Hurry! Jump! Fly! Shut the door! Quick, or my Conscience will get away!"

The door slammed to, and I locked it. I glanced up and was grateful, to the bottom of my heart, to see that my owner was still my prisoner. I said –

"Hang you, I might have lost you! Children are the heedless-est creatures. But look here, friend, the boy did not seem to notice you at all; how is that?"

"For a good reason. I am invisible to all but you."

I made mental note of that piece of information with a good deal of satisfaction. I could kill this miscreant now, if I got a chance, and no one would know it. But this very reflection made me so light-hearted that my Conscience could hardly keep his seat, but was like to float aloft toward the ceiling like a toy balloon. I said, presently—

"Come, my Conscience, let us be friendly. Let us fly a flag of truce for a while. I am suffering to ask you some questions."

"Very well. Begin."

"Well, then, in the first place, why were you never visible to me before?"

"Because you never asked to see me before; that is, you never asked in the right spirit and the proper form before. You were just in the right spirit this time, and when you called for your most pitiless enemy I was that person by a very large majority, though you did not suspect it."

"Well, did that remark of mine turn you into flesh and blood?"

"No. It only made me visible to you. I am unsubstantial, just as other spirits are."

This remark prodded me with a sharp misgiving. If he was unsubstantial, how was I going to kill him? But I dissembled, and said persuasively—

"Conscience, it isn't sociable of you to keep at such a distance. Come down and take another smoke."

This was answered with a look that was full of derision, and with this observation added—

"Come where you can get at me and kill me? The invitation is declined with thanks."

"All right," said I to myself; "so it seems a spirit *can* be killed, after all; there will be one spirit lacking in this world, presently, or I lose my guess." Then I said aloud—

"Friend—"

"There; wait a bit. I am not your friend, I am your enemy; I am not your equal, I am your master. Call me 'my lord,' if you please. You are too familiar."

"I don't like such titles. I am willing to call you *sir.* That is as far as—"

"We will have no argument about this. Just obey; that is all. Go on with your chatter."

"Very well, my lord – since nothing but my lord will suit you – I was going to ask you how long you will be visible to me?"

"Always!"

I broke out with strong indignation: "This is simply an outrage. That is what I think of it. You have dogged, and dogged, and *dogged* me, all the days of my life, invisible. That was misery enough; now to have such a looking thing as you tagging after me like another shadow all the rest of my days is an intolerable prospect. You have my opinion, my lord; make the most of it."

"My lad, there was never so pleased a conscience in this world as I was when you made me visible. It gives me an inconceivable advantage. *Now,* I can look you straight in the eye, and call you names, and leer at your, jeer at you, sneer at you; and *you* know what eloquence there is in visible gesture and expression, more especially when the effect is heightened by audible speech. I shall always address you henceforth in your o-w-n s-n-i-v-e-l-l-in-g d-r-a-w-l – baby!"

I let fly with the coal-hod. No result. My lord said –

"Come, come! Remember the flag of truce!"

"Ah, I forgot that. I will try to be civil; and *you* try it, too, for a novelty. The idea of a *civil* conscience! It is a good joke; an excellent joke. All the consciences I have every heard of were nagging, badgering, fault-finding, execrable savages! Yes; and always in a sweat about some poor little insignificant trifle or other – destruction catch the lot of them, I say! I would trade mine for the small-pox and seven kinds of consumption, and be glad of the chance. Now tell me, why *is* it that a conscience can't haul a man over the coals once, for an offence, and then let him alone? Why is it that it wants to keep in pegging at him, day and night and night and day, week in and week out, forever and ever, about the same old thing? There is no sense in that, and no reason in it.

I think a conscience that will act like that is meaner than the very dirt itself."

"Well, *we* like it; that suffices."

"Do you do it with the honest intent to improve a man?"

That question produced a sarcastic smile, and this reply:—

"No, sir. Excuse me. We do it simply because it is 'business.' It is our trade. The *purpose* of it *is* to improve the man, but *we* are merely disinterested agents. We are appointed by authority, and haven't anything to say in the matter. We obey orders and leave the consequences where they belong. But I am willing to admit this much: we *do* crowd the orders a trifle when we get a chance, which is most of the time. We enjoy it. We are instructed to remind a man a few times of any error; and I don't mind acknowledging that we try to give pretty good measure. And when we get hold of a man of a peculiarly sensitive nature, oh, but we do haze him! I have known consciences to come all the way from China and Russia to see a person of that kind put through his paces, on a special occasion. Why, I knew a man of that sort who had accidentally crippled a mulatto baby; the news went abroad, and I wish you may never commit another sin if the consciences didn't flock from all over the earth to enjoy the fun and help his master exercise him. That man walked the floor in torture for forty-eight hours, without eating or sleeping, and then blew his brains out. The child was perfectly well again in three weeks."

"Well, you are a precious crew, not to put it too strong. I think I begin to see, now, why you have always been a trifle inconsistent with me. In your anxiety to get all the juice you can out of a sin, you make a man repent of it in three or four different ways. For instance, you found fault with me for lying to that tramp, and I suffered over that. But it was only yesterday that I told a tramp the square truth, to whit, that, it being regarded as bad citizenship to encourage vagrancy, I would give him nothing. What did you do *then?* Why, you made me say to myself, 'Ah, it would have been so much kinder and more blameless to ease him off with

a little white lie, and send him away feeling that if he could not
have bread, the gentle treatment was at least something to be grateful for!' Well, I suffered all day about *that.* Three days before I
had fed a tramp, and fed him freely, supposing it a virtuous act.
Straight off you said, 'O false citizen, to have fed a tramp!' and
I suffered as usual. I gave a tramp work; you objected to it–*after*
the contract was made, of course; you never speak up beforehand.
Next, I *refused* a tramp work; you objected to *that.* Next I proposed to kill a tramp; you kept me awake all night, oozing remorse
at every pore. Sure I was going to be right *this* time, I sent the
next tramp away with my benediction; and I wish you may live
as long as I do, if you didn't make me smart all night again because
I didn't kill him. Is there *any* way of satisfying that malignant invention which is called a conscience?"

"Ha, ha! this is luxury! Go on!"

"But come, now, answer me that question. *Is* there any way?"

"Well, none that I propose to tell *you,* my son. Ass! I don't
care *what* act you may turn your hand to, I can straightway
whisper a word in your ear and make you think you have committed a dreadful meanness. It is my *business*–and my joy–to
make you repent of *every*thing you do. If I have fooled away any
opportunities it was not intentional; I beg to assure you it was
not intentional!"

"Don't worry; you haven't missed a trick that *I* know of. I never
did a thing in all my life, virtuous or otherwise, that I didn't repent
of in twenty-four hours. In church last Sunday I listened to a charity sermon. My first impulse was to give three hundred and fifty
dollars; I repented of that and reduced it another hundred;
repented of that and reduced it another hundred; repented of that
and reduced the remaining fifty to twenty-five; repented of that
and came down to fifteen; repented of that and dropped to two
dollars and a half; when the plate came around at last, I repented
once more and contributed ten cents. Well, when I got home,
I did wish goodness I had that ten cents back again! You never

did let me get through a charity sermon without having something to sweat about."

"Oh, and I never shall, I never shall. You can always depend on me."

"I think so. Many and many's the restless night I've wanted to take you by the neck. If I could only get hold of you now!"

"Yes, no doubt. But I am not an ass; I am only the saddle of an ass. But go on, go on. You entertain me more than I like to confess."

"I am glad of that. (You will not mind my lying a little, to keep in practice.) Look here; not to be too personal, I think you are about the shabbiest and most contemptible little shrivelled-up reptile that can be imagined. I am grateful enough that you are invisible to other people, for I should die with shame to be seen with such a mildewed monkey of a conscience as *you* are. Now if you were five or six feet high and –"

"Oh, come! who is to blame?"

"*I* don't know."

"Why, you are; nobody else."

"Confound you, I wasn't consulted about your personal appearance."

"I don't care, you had a good deal to do with it, nevertheless. When you were eight or nine years old, I was seven feet high, and as pretty as a picture."

"I wish you had died young! So you have grown the wrong way, have you?"

"Some of us grow one way and some the other. You had a large conscience once; if you've a small conscience now, I reckon there are reasons for it. However, both of us are to blame, you and I. You see, you used to be conscientious about a great many things; morbidly so, I may say. It was a great many years ago. You probably do not remember it, now. Well, I took a great interest in my work, and I so enjoyed the anguish which certain pet sins of yours afflicted you with, that I kept pelting at you until I rather overdid the matter. You began to rebel. Of course I began to lose ground, then, and shrivel a little,–diminish in stature, get mouldy, and grow deformed. The more I weakened, the more stubbornly you fastened on to those particular sins; till at last the places on my person that represent those vices became as callous as shark skin. Take smoking, for instance. I played that card a little too long, and I lost. When people plead with you at this late day to quit that vice, that old callous place seems to enlarge and cover me all over, like a shirt of mail. It exerts a mysterious, smother-ing effect; and presently I, your faithful hater, your devoted Conscience, go sound asleep! Sound? It is no name for it. I couldn't hear it thunder at such a time. You have some few other vices– perhaps eighty, or maybe ninety–that affect me in much the same way."

"This is flattering; you must be asleep a good part of your time."

"Yes, of late years. I should be asleep *all* the time, but for the help I get."

"Who helps you?"

"Other consciences. Whenever a person whose conscience I am acquainted with tries to plead with you about the vices you are callous to, I get my friend to give his client a pang concerning some villany of his own, and that shuts off his meddling and starts him off to hunt personal consolation. My field of usefulness is about trimmed down to tramps, budding authoresses, and that line of goods, now; but don't you worry–I'll harry you on *them* while they last! Just you put your trust in me."

"I think I can. But if you had only been good enough to men-tion these facts some thirty years ago, I should have turned my particular attention to sin, and I think that by this time I should not only have had you pretty permanently asleep on the entire list of human vices, but reduced to the size of a homeopathic pill, at that. That is about the style of conscience *I* am pining for. If I only had you shrunk down to a homeopathic pill, and could get my hands on you, would I put you in a glass case for a keepsake? No, sir. I would give you to a yellow dog! That is where *you* ought to be—you and all your tribe. You are not fit to be in society, in my opinion. Now another question. Do you know a good many consciences in this section?"

"Plenty of them."

"I would give anything to see some of them! Could you bring them here? And would they be visible to me?"

"Certainly not."

"I suppose I ought to have known that, without asking. But no matter, you can describe them. Tell me about my neighbor Thompson's conscience, please."

"Very well. I know him intimately; have known him many years. I knew him when he was eleven feet high and of a faultless figure. But he is very rusty and tough and misshapen now, and hardly ever interests himself about anything. As to his present size—well, he sleeps in a cigar box."

"Likely enough. There are few smaller, meaner men in this region that Hugh Thompson. Do you know Robinson's conscience?"

"Yes. He is a shade under four and a half feet high; used to be a blonde; is a brunette, now, but still shapely and comely."

"Well, Robinson is a good fellow. Do you know Tom Smith's conscience?"

"I have known him from childhood. He was thirteen inches high, and rather sluggish, when he was two years old—as nearly all of us are, at that age. He is thirty-seven feet high, now, and the stateliest figure in America. His legs are still racked with growing-pains, but he has a good time, nevertheless. Never sleeps. He is the most active and energetic member of the New England Conscience Club; is president of it. Night and day you can find him pegging away at Smith, panting with his labor, sleeves rolled up, countenance all alive with enjoyment. He has got his victim splendidly dragooned, now. He can make poor Smith imagine that the most innocent little thing he does is an odious sin; and then he sets to work and almost tortures the soul out of him about it."

"Smith is the noblest man in all this section, and the purest; and yet is always breaking his heart because he cannot be good! Only a conscience *could* find pleasure in heaping agony upon a spirit like that. Do you know my aunt Mary's conscience?"

"I have seen her at a distance, but am not acquainted with her. She lives in the open air altogether, because no door is large enough to admit her."

"I can believe that. Let me see. Do you know the conscience of that publisher who once stole some sketches of mine for a 'series' of his, and then left me to pay the law expenses I had to incur in order to choke him off?"

"Yes. He has a wide fame. He was exhibited, a month ago, with some other antiquities, for the benefit of a recent Member of the Cabinet's conscience, that was starving in exile. Tickets and fares were high, but I travelled for nothing by pretending to be the conscience of an editor, and got in for half-price by representing myself to be the conscience of a clergyman. However, the publisher's conscience, which was to have been the main feature of the entertainment, was a failure – as an exhibition. He was there, but what of that? The management had provided a microscope with a magnifying power of only thirty thousand diameters, and so nobody got to see him, after all. There was great and general dissatisfaction, of course, but–"

Just here there was an eager footstep on the stair; I opened the door, and my aunt Mary burst into the room. It was a joyful meeting, and a cheery bombardment of questions and answers concerning family matters ensued. by-and-by my aunt said–

"But I am going to abuse you a little now. You promised me, the day I saw you last, that you would look after the needs of the poor family around the corner as faithfully as I had done it myself. Well, I found out by accident that you failed of your promise. *Was* that right?"

In simple truth, I never had thought of that family a second time! And now such a splintering pang of guilt shot through me!

I glanced up at my Conscience. Plainly, my heavy heart was affecting him. His body was drooping forward; he seemed about to fall from the bookcase. My aunt continued: –

"And think how you have neglected my poor *protégée* at the almshouse, you dear, hard-hearted promise-breaker!"

I blushed scarlet, and my tongue was tied. As the sense of my guilty negligence waxed sharper and stronger, my Conscience began to sway heavily back and forth; and when my aunt, after a little pause, said in a grieved tone, "Since you never once went to see her, maybe it will distress you now to know that that poor child died, months ago, utterly friendless and forsaken!" my Conscience could no longer bear up under the weight of my sufferings, but tumbled headlong from his high perch and struck the floor with a dull, leaden thump. He lay there writhing with pain and quaking with apprehension, but straining every muscle in frantic efforts to get up. In a fever of expectancy I sprang to the door, locked it, placed my back against it, and bent a watchful gaze upon my struggling master. Already my fingers were itching to begin their murderous work.

"Oh, what *can* be the matter!" exclaimed my aunt, shrinking from me, and following with her frightened eyes the direction of mine. My breath was coming in short, quick gasps now, and my excitement was almost uncontrollable. My aunt cried out,–

"Oh, do not look so! You appall me! Oh, what can the matter be? What is it you see? Why do you stare so? Why do you work your fingers like that?"

"Peace, woman!" I said, in a hoarse whisper. "Look elsewhere; pay no attention to me; it is nothing–nothing. I am often this way. It will pass in a moment. It comes from smoking too much."

My injured lord was up, wild-eyed with terror, and trying to hobble toward the door. I could hardly breathe, I was so wrought up. My aunt wrung her hands, and said–

"Oh, I knew how it would be; I knew it would come to this at last! Oh, I implore you to crush out that fatal habit while it may yet be time! You must not, you shall not be deaf to my supplications longer!" My struggling Conscience showed sudden signs of weariness! "Oh, promise me you will throw off this hateful slavery of tobacco!" My Conscience began to reel drowsily, and grope with his hands – enchanting spectacle! "I beg you, I beseech you, I implore you! Your reason is deserting you! There is madness in your eye! It flames with frenzy! Oh, hear me, hear me, and be saved! See, I plead with you on my very knees!" As she sank before me my Conscience reeled again, and then drooped languidly to the floor, blinking toward me a last supplication for mercy, with heavy eyes. "Oh, promise, or you are lost! Promise, and be redeemed! Promise! Promise and live!" With a long-drawn sigh my conquered Conscience closed his eyes and fell fast asleep!

With an exultant shout I sprang past my aunt, and in an instant I had my life-long foe by the throat. After so many years of waiting and longing, he was mine at last. I tore him to shreds and fragments. I rent the garments to bits. I cast the bleeding rubbish into the fire, and drew into my nostrils the grateful incense of my burnt-offering. At last, and forever, my Conscience was dead!

I was a free man! I turned upon my poor aunt, who was almost petrified with terror, and shouted –

"Out of this with your paupers, your charities, your reforms, your pestilent morals! You behold before you a man whose life-conflict is done, whose soul is at peace; a man whose heart is dead to sorrow, dead to suffering, dead to remorse; a man WITHOUT A CONSCIENCE! In my joy I spare you, though I could throttle you and never feel a pang! Fly!"

She fled. Since that day my life is all bliss. Bliss, unalloyed bliss. Nothing in all the world could persuade me to have a conscience again. I settled all my old outstanding scores, and began the world anew. I killed thirty-eight persons during the first two weeks – all of them on account of ancient grudges. I burned a dwelling that interrupted my view. I swindled a widow and some orphans out of their last cow, which is a very good one, though not thoroughbred, I believe. I have also committed scores of crimes, of various kinds, and have enjoyed my work exceedingly, whereas it would formerly have broken my heart and turned my hair gray, I have no doubt.

In conclusion I wish to state, by way of advertisement, that medical colleges desiring assorted tramps for scientific purposes, either by the gross, by cord measurement, or per ton, will do well to examine the lot in my cellar before purchasing elsewhere, as these were all selected and prepared by myself, and can be had at a low rate, because I wish to clear out my stock and get ready for the spring trade.

THE JOURNALS OF GERMANY

This short story originated as an appendix in Twain's
Tramp Abroad, published by The American Publishing
Company of Hartford, Connecticut in 1880.

The daily journals of Hamburg, Frankfort, Baden, Munich, and
Augsburg are all constructed on the same general plan. I speak
of these because I am more familiar with them than with any other
German papers. They contain no "editorials" whatever; no "per-
sonals,"–and this is rather a merit than a demerit, perhaps; no
funny-paragraph column; no police court reports; no reports of
proceedings of higher courts; no information about prize fights
or other dog fights, horse races, walking matches, yachting con-
tests, rifle matches, or other sporting matters of any sort; no reports
of banquet speeches; no department of curious odds and ends
of floating fact and gossip; no "rumors" about anything or anybody; no lists of patents granted or sought, or any reference to
such things; no abuse of public officials, big or little, or complaints against them, or praises of them; no religious columns
Saturdays, no rehash of cold sermons Mondays; no "weather indications"; no "local item" unveilings of what is happening in
town–nothing of a local nature, indeed, is mentioned, beyond
the movements of some prince, or the proposed meeting of some
deliberative body.

After so formidable a list of what one can't find in a German
daily, the question may well be asked, What *can* be found in it?
It is easily answered: A child's handful of telegrams, mainly about
European national and international political movements; letter-
correspondence about the same things; market reports. There you
have it. That is what a German daily is made of. A German daily
is the slowest and saddest and dreariest of the inventions of man.
Our own dailies infuriate the reader, pretty often; the German

daily only stupefies him. Once a week the German daily of the
highest class lightens up its heavy columns,–that is, it thinks it
lightens them up,–with a profound, an abysmal, book criticism;
a criticism which carries you down, down, down into the scientific bowels of the subject,–for the German critic is nothing if
not scientific,–and when you come up at last and scent the fresh
air and see the bonny daylight once more, you resolve without
a dissenting voice that a book criticism is a mistaken way to lighten
up a German daily. Sometimes, in place of the criticism, the first-
class daily gives you what it thinks is a gay and chipper essay,–
about ancient Grecian funeral customs, or the ancient Egyptian
method of tarring a mummy, or the reasons for believing that some
of the peoples who existed before the flood did not approve of
cats. These are not unpleasant subjects; they are not uninterest-
ing subjects; they are even exciting subjects,–until one of these
massive scientists gets hold of them. He soon convinces you that
even these matters can be handled in such a way as to make a
person low-spirited.

As I have said, the average German daily is made up solely
of correspondence,–a trifle of it by telegraph, the rest of it by
mail. Every paragraph has the side-head, "London," "Vienna," or
some other town, and a date. And always, before the name of the
town, is placed a letter or a sign, to indicate who the correspondent is, so that the authorities can find him when they want to
hang him. Stars, crosses, triangles, squares, half-moons, suns,–
such are some of the signs used by correspondents.

Some of the dailies move too fast, others too slowly. For
instance, my Heidelberg daily was always twenty-four hours old
when it arrived at the hotel; but one of my Munich evening papers used to come a full twenty-four hours before it
was due.

Some of the less important dailies give one a tablespoonful
of a continued story every day; it is strung across the bottom of
the page, in the French fashion. By subscribing for the paper for

five years I judge that a man might succeed in getting pretty much all of the story.

If you ask a citizen of Munich which is the best Munich daily journal, he will always tell you that there is only one good Munich daily, and that it is published in Augsburg, forty or fifty miles sway. It is like saying that the best daily paper in New York is published out in New Jersey somewhere. Yes, the Augsburg *Allgemeine Zeitung* is "the best Munich paper," and it is the one I had in my mind when I was describing a "first-class German daily" above. The entire paper, opened out, is not quite as large as a single page of the New York *Herald*. It is printed on both sides, of course; but in such large type that its entire contents could be put, in *Herald* type, upon a single page of the *Herald*,—and there would still be room enough on the page for the *Zeitung's* "supplement" and some portion of the *Zeitung's* next day's contents.

Such is the first-class daily. The dailies actually printed in Munich are all called second-class by the public. If you ask which is the best of these second-class papers they say there is no difference; one is as good as another. I have preserved a copy of one of them; it is called the *Munchener Tages-Anzeiger,* and bears date January 25, 1879. Comparisons are odious, but they need not be malicious; and without any malice I wish to compare this journal, published in a German city of 170,000 inhabitants, with journals of other countries. I know of no other way to enable the reader to "size" the thing.

A column of an average daily paper in America contains from 1,800 to 2,500 words; the reading matter in a single issue consists of from 25,000 to 50,000 words. The reading matter in my copy of the Munich journal consists of a total of 1,654 words,— for I counted them. That would be nearly a column of one of our dailies. A single issue of the bulkiest daily newspaper in the world—the London *Times*—often contains 100,000 words of reading matter. Considering that the *Daily Anzeiger* issues the usual twenty-six numbers per month, the reading matter in a single number of the London *Times* would keep it in "copy" two months and a half!

The *Anzeiger* is an eight-page paper; its page is one inch wider and one inch longer than a foolscap page; that is to say, the dimensions of its page are somewhere between those of a schoolboy's slate and a lady's pocket handkerchief. One-fourth of the first page is taken up with the heading of the journal; this gives it a rather top-heavy appearance; the rest of the first page is reading matter; all of the second page is reading matter; the other six pages are devoted to advertisements.

The reading matter is compressed into two hundred and five small pica lines, and is lighted up with eight pica head-lines. The bill of fare is as follows: First, under a pica head-line, to enforce attention and respect, is a four-line sermon urging mankind to remember that, although they are pilgrims here below, they are yet heirs of heaven; and that "When they depart from earth they soar to heaven." Perhaps a four-line sermon in a Saturday paper is the sufficient German equivalent of the eight or ten columns of sermons which the New Yorkers get in their Monday morning papers. The latest news (two days old) follows the four-line sermon, under the pica head-line "Telegrams,"– these are "telegraphed" with a pair of scissors out of the *Augsburger Zeitung* of the day before. These telegrams consist of fourteen and two-thirds lines from Berlin, fifteen lines from Vienna, and two and five-eighths lines from Calcutta. Thirty-three small pica lines of telegraphic news in a daily journal in a King's Capital of 170,000 inhabitants is surely not an overdose. Next we have the pica heading, "News of the Day," under which the following facts are set forth: Prince Leopold is going on a visit to Vienna, six lines; Prince Arnulph is coming back from Russia, two lines; the Landtag will meet at ten o'clock in the morning and consider an election law, three lines and one word over; a city government item, five and one-half lines; prices of tickets to the proposed grand Charity Ball, twenty-three lines,– for this one item occupies almost one-fourth

of the entire first page; there is to be a wonderful Wagner con-
cert in Frankfurt-on-the-Main, with an orchestra of one hundred
and eight instruments, seven and one-half lines. That concludes
the first page. Eighty-five lines, altogether, on that page, including three headlines. About fifty of those lines, as one perceives,
deal with local matters; so the reporters are not overworked.

Exactly one-half of the second page is occupied with an opera
criticism, fifty-three lines (three of them being headlines), and
"Death Notices," ten lines.

The other half of the second page is made up of two paragraphs under the head of "Miscellaneous News." One of these
paragraphs tells about a quarrel between the Czar of Russia and
his eldest son, twenty-one and a half lines; and the other tells
about the atrocious destruction of a peasant child by its parents,
forty lines, or one-fifth of the total of the reading matter contained
in the paper.

Consider what a fifth part of the reading matter of an American daily paper issued in a city of 170,000 inhabitants amounts
to! Think what a mass it is. Would any one suppose I could so
snugly tuck away such a mass in a chapter of this book that it
would be difficult to find it again if the reader slot his place? Surely
not. I will translate that child murder word for word, to give the
reader a realizing sense of what a fifth part of the reading matter
of a Munich daily actually is when it comes under measurement
of the eye:

"From Oberkreuzberg, January 21, the *Donau Zeitung* receives
a long account of a crime, which we shorten as follows: In Rametu-
ach, a village near Eppenschlag, lived a young married couple with
two children, one of which, a boy aged five, was born three years
before the marriage. For this reason, and also because a relative
at Iggensbach had bequeathed M400 ($100) to the boy, the heart-
less father considered him in the way; so the unnatural parents
determined to sacrifice him in the cruelest possible manner. They
proceeded to starve him slowly to death, meantime frightfully

maltreating him,—as the village people now make known, when
it is too late. The boy was shut up in a hole, and when people
passed by he cried, and implored them to give him bread. His
long-continued tortures and deprivations destroyed him at last,
on the third of January. The sudden (sic) death of the child created
suspicion, the more so as the body was immediately clothed and
laid upon the bier. Therefore the coroner gave notice, and an
inquest was held on the 6th. What a pitiful spectacle was dis-
closed then! The body was a complete skeleton. The stomach and
intestines were utterly empty; they contained nothing whatever.
The flesh on the corpse was not as thick as the back of a knife,
and incisions in it brought not a drop of blood. There was not
a piece of sound skin the size of a dollar on the whole body;
wounds, scars, bruises, discolored extravasated blood, everywhere,—even on the soles of the feet there were wounds. The cruel
parents asserted that the boy had been so bad that they had been
obliged to use severe punishments, and that he finally fell over
a bench and broke his neck. However, they were arrested two seeks
after the inquest and put in the prison at Deggendorf."

Yes, they were arrested "two weeks after the inquest." What
a home sound that has. That kind of police briskness rather more
reminds me of my native land than German journalism does.

I think a German daily journal doesn't do any good to speak
of, but at the same time it doesn't do any harm. That is a very
large merit, and should not be lightly weighed nor lightly
thought of.

The German humorous papers are beautifully printed upon
fine paper, and the illustrations are finely drawn, finely engraved,
and are not vapidly funny, but deliciously so. So, also, generally
speaking, are the two or three terse sentences which accompany
the pictures. I remember one of these pictures: A most dilapidated tramp is ruefully contemplating some coins which lie in
his open palm. He says: "Well, begging is getting played out. Only
about five marks ($1.25) for the whole day; many an official makes

more!" And I call to mind a picture of a commercial traveler who is about to unroll his samples:

Merchant (pettishly).– No, don't. I don't want to buy anything!

Drummer.– If you please, I was only going to show you–

Merchant.– But I don't wish to see them!

Drummer (after a pause, pleadingly).– But do you mind letting *me* look at them! I haven't seen them for three weeks!

PLAYING COURIER

Originating in the English periodical *The Illustrated London News*
in December, 1881, this tale reappeared in *The New York Sun*
one month later. It was collected in *The £1,000,000
Bank-Note and Other Stories,* published by
C. L. Webster, New York, in 1893.

A time would come when we must go from Aixles-Bains to Geneva, and from thence, by a series of day-long and tangled journeys, to Bayreuth in Bavaria. I should have to have a courier, of course, to take care of so considerable a party as mine.

But I procrastinated. The time slipped along, and at last I woke up one day to the fact that we were ready to move and had no courier. I then resolved upon what I felt was a foolhardy thing, but I was in the humor of it. I said I would make the first stage without help – I did it.

I brought the party from Aix to Geneva by myself – four people. The distance was two hours and more, and there was one change of cars. There was not an accident of any kind, except leaving a valise and some other matters on the platform – a thing which can hardly be called an accident, it is so common. So I offered to conduct the party all the way to Bayreuth.

This was a blunder, though it did not seem so at the time. There was more detail than I thought there would be: 1, two persons whom we had left in a Genevan pension some weeks before must be collected and brought to the hotel; 2, I must notify the people on the Grand Quay who store trunks to bring seven of our stored trunks to the hotel and carry back seven which they would find piled in the lobby; 3, I must find out what part of Europe Bayreuth was in and buy seven railway tickets for that point; 4, I must send a telegram to a friend in the Netherlands; 5, it was now two in the afternoon, and we must look sharp and be ready for the first night train and make sure of sleeping-car tickets; 6, I must draw money at the bank.

It seemed to me that the sleeping-car tickets must be the most important thing, so I went to the station myself to make sure; hotel messengers are not always brisk people. It was a hot day and I ought to have driven, but it seemed better economy to walk. It did not turn out so, because I lost my way and trebled the distance. I applied for the tickets, and they asked me which route I wanted to go by, and that embarrassed me and made me lose my head, there were so many people standing around, and I not knowing anything about the routes and not supposing there were going to be two; so I judged it best to go back and map out the road and come again.

I took a cab this time, but on my way upstairs at the hotel I remembered that I was out of cigars, so I thought it would be well to get some while the matter was in my mind. It was only round the corner and I didn't need the cab. I asked the cabman to wait where he was. Thinking of the telegram and trying to word it in my head, I forgot the cigars and the cab, and walked on indefinitely. I was going to have the hotel people send the telegram, but as I could not be far from the post-office by this time, I thought I would do it myself. But it was further than I had supposed. I found the place at last and wrote the telegram and handed it in. The clerk was a severe-looking, fidgety man, and he began to fire French questions at me in such a liquid form that I could not detect the joints between his words, and this made me lose my head again. But an Englishman stepped up and said the clerk wanted to know where he was to send the telegram. I could not tell him, because it was not my telegram, and I explained that I was merely sending it for a member of my party. But nothing would pacify the clerk but the address; so I said that if he was so particular I would go back and get it.

However, I thought I would go and collect those lacking two persons first, for it would be best to do everything systematically and in order, and one detail at a time. Then I remembered the cab was eating up my substances down at the hotel yonder; so I called another cab and told the man to go down and fetch it to the post office and wait till I came.

I had a long hot walk to collect those people, and when I got there they couldn't come with me because they had heavy satchels and must have a cab. I went away to find one, but before I ran across any I noticed that I had reached the neighborhood of the Grand Quay–at least I thought I had–so I judged I could save time by stepping around and arranging about the trunks. I stepped around about a mile, and although I did not find the Grand Quay, I found a cigar shop, and remembered about the cigars. I said I was going to Bayreuth, and wanted enough for the journey. The man asked me which route I was going to take. I said I did not know. He said he would recommend me to go by Zurich and various other places which he named, and offered to sell me seven second-class through tickets for $22 apiece, which would be throwing off the discount which the railroads allowed him. I was already tired of riding second-class on first-class tickets, so I took him up.

By and by I found Natural & Co.'s storage office, and told them to send seven of our trunks to the hotel and pile them up in the lobby. It seemed to me that I was not delivering the whole of the message, still it was all I could find in my head.

Next I found the bank and asked for some money, but I had left my letter of credit somewhere and was not able to draw. I remembered now that I must have left it lying on the table where I wrote my telegram; so I got a cab and drove to the post-office and went upstairs, and they said that a letter of credit had indeed been left on the table, but that it was now in the hands of the police authorities, and it would be necessary for me to go there

and prove property. They sent a boy with me, and we went out
the back way and walked a couple of miles and found the place;
and then I remembered about my cabs, and asked the boy to send
them to me when he got back to the post-office. It was nightfall
now, and the Mayor had gone to dinner. I thought I would go to
dinner myself, but the officer on duty thought differently, and
I stayed. The Mayor dropped in at half-past ten, but said it was
too late to do anything tonight – come at 9:30 in the morning.
The officer wanted to keep me all night, and said I was a suspicious looking person, and probably did not own the letter of credit,
and didn't know what a letter of credit was, but merely saw the
real owner leave it lying on the table, and wanted to get it because
I was probably a person that would want anything he could get,
whether it was valuable or not. But the Mayor said he saw nothing suspicious about me, and that I seemed a harmless person
and nothing the matter with me but a wandering mind, and not
much of that. So I thanked him and he set me free, and I went
home in my three cabs.

As I was dog-tired and in no condition to answer questions
with discretion, I thought I would not disturb the Expedition at
that time of night, as there was a vacant room I knew of at the
other end of the hall; but I did not quite arrive there, as a watch
had been set, the Expedition being anxious about me. I was placed
in a galling situation. The Expedition sat stiff and forbidding on
four chairs in a row, with shawls and things all on, satchels and
guide-books in lap. They had been sitting like that for four hours,
and the glass going down all the time. Yes, and they were waiting –
waiting for me. It seemed to me that nothing but a sudden, happily contrived, and brilliant *tour de force* could break this iron
front and make a diversion in my favor; so I shied my hat into
the arena and followed it with a skip and a jump, shouting blithely:

"Ha, ha, here we all are, Mr. Merryman!"

Nothing could be deeper or stiller than the absence of applause which followed. But I kept on; there seemed no other way, though my confidence, poor enough before, had got a deadly check and was in effect gone.

I tried to be jocund out of a heavy heart. I tried to touch the other hearts there and soften the bitter resentment in those faces by throwing off bright and airy fun and making of the whole ghastly thing a joyously humorous incident, but this idea was not well conceived. It was not the right atmosphere for it. I got not one smile; not one line in those offended faces relaxed; I thawed nothing of the winter that looked out of those frosty eyes. I started one more breezy, poor effort, but the head of the Expedition cut into the center of it and said:

"Where have you been?"

I saw by the manner of this that the idea was to get down to cold business now. So I began my travels, but was cut short again.

"Where are the two others? We have been in frightful anxiety about them."

"Oh, they're all right. I was to fetch a cab. I will go straight off, and—"

"Sit down! Don't you know it is eleven o'clock? Where did you leave them?"

"At the pension."

"Why didn't you bring them?"

"Because we couldn't carry the satchels. And so I thought—"

"Thought! You should not try to think. One cannot think without the proper machinery. It is two miles to that pension. Did you go there without a cab?"

"I—well I didn't intend to; it only happened so."

"How did it happen so?"

"Because I was at the post-office and I remembered that I had left a cab waiting here, and so, to stop the expense, I sent another cab to—to—"

"To what?"

"Well, I don't remember now, but I think the new cab was to have the hotel pay the old cab, and send it away."

"What good would that do?"

"What good would it do? It would stop the expense, wouldn't it?"

"By putting the new cab in its place to continue the expense?"

I didn't say anything.

"Why didn't you have the new cab come back for you?"

"Oh, that is what I did. I remember now. Yes, that is what I did. Because I recollect that when I—"

"Well, then why didn't it come back for you?"

"To the post-office? Why, it did."

"Very well, then, how did you come to walk to the pension?"

"I—I don't quite remember how that happened. Oh, yes, I do remember now. I wrote the dispatch to send to the Netherlands, and—"

"Oh, thank goodness, you did accomplish something! I wouldn't have had you fail to send—what makes you look like that! You are trying to avoid my eye. That dispatch is the most important thing that—You haven't sent that dispatch!"

"I haven't said I didn't send it."

"You don't need to. Oh, dear, I wouldn't have had that telegram fail for anything. Why didn't you send it?"

"Well, you see, with so many things to do and think of, I—they're very particular there, and after I had written the telegram—"

"Oh, never mind, let it go, explanations can't help the matter now—what will he think of us?"

"Oh, that's all right, that's all right, he'll think we gave the telegram to the hotel people, and that they—"

"Why, certainly! Why didn't you do that? There was no other rational way."

"Yes, I know, but then I had it on my mind that I must be sure and get to the bank and draw some money—"

"Well, you are entitled to some credit, after all, for thinking of that, and I don't wish to be too hard on you, though you
must acknowledge yourself that you have cost us all a good
deal of trouble, and some of it not necessary. How much did
you draw?"

"Well, I–I had an idea that–that–"

"What are you mooning about? Do turn your face this way
and let me–why, you haven't drawn any money!"

"Well, the banker said–"

"Never mind what the banker said. You must have had a reason of your own. Not a reason, exactly, but something which–"

"Well, then, the simple fact was that I hadn't my letter of credit."

"Hadn't your letter of credit?"

"Hadn't my letter of credit."

"Don't repeat me like that. Where was it?"

"At the post-office."

"What was it doing there?"

"Well, I forgot it and left it there."

"Upon my word, I've seen a good many couriers, but of all the
couriers that ever I–"

"I've done the best I could."

"Well, so you have, poor thing, and I'm wrong to abuse you
so when you've been working yourself to death while we've been
sitting here only thinking of our vexations instead of feeling grateful for what you were trying to do for us. It will all come out right.
We can take the 7:30 train in the morning just as well. You've
bought the tickets?"

"I have–and it's a bargain, too. Second class."

"I'm glad of it. Everybody else travels second class, and we might
just as well save that ruinous extra charge. What did you pay?"

"Twenty-two dollars apiece–through to Bayreuth."

"Why, I didn't know you could buy through tickets anywhere
but in London and Paris."

"Some people can't, maybe; but some people can – of whom I am one of which, it appears."

"It seems a rather high price."

"On the contrary, the dealer knocked off his commission."

"Dealer?"

"Yes – I bought them at a cigar shop."

"That reminds me. We shall have to get up pretty early, and so there should be no packing to do. Your umbrella, your rubbers, your cigars – what is the matter?"

"Hang it, I've left the cigars at the bank."

"Just think of it! Well, your umbrella?"

"I'll have that all right. There's no hurry."

"What do you mean by that?"

"Oh, that's all right; I'll take care of –"

"Where is that umbrella?"

"It's just the merest step – it won't take me –"

"Where is it?"

"Well, I think I left it at the cigar shop; but anyway –"

"Take your feet out from under that thing. It's just as I expected! Where are your rubbers?"

"It's got so dry now – well, everybody says there's not going to be another drop of –"

"Where – are – your – rubbers?"

"Well, you see – well, it was this way. First, the officer said –"

"What officer?"

"Police officer; but the Mayor, he –"

"What Mayor?"

"Mayor of Geneva; but I said –"

"Wait. What is the matter with you?"

"Who, me? Nothing. They both tried to persuade me to stay, and –"

"Stay where?"

"Well – the fact is –"

"Where have you been? What's kept you out till half-past ten at night?"

"Oh, you see, after I lost my letter of credit, I—"

"You are beating around the bush a good deal. Now, answer the question in just one straightforward word. Where are those rubbers?"

"They—well; they're in the county jail."

I started a placating smile, but it petrified. The climate was unsuitable. Spending three or four hours in jail did not seem to the Expedition humorous. Neither did it to me, at bottom.

I had to explain the whole thing, and, of course, it came out then that we couldn't take the early train, because that would leave my letter of credit in hock still. It did look as if we had all got to go to bed estranged and unhappy, but by good luck that was prevented. There happened to be mention of the trunks, and I was able to say I had attended to that feature.

"There, you are just as good and thoughtful and painstaking and intelligent as you can be, and it's a shame to find so much fault with you, and there sha'n't be another word of it. You've done beautifully, admirably, and I'm sorry I ever said one ungrateful word to you."

This hit deeper than some of the other things and made me uncomfortable, because I wasn't feeling as solid about that trunk errand as I wanted to. There seemed somehow to be a defect about it somewhere, though I couldn't put my finger on it, and didn't like to stir the matter just now, it being late and maybe well enough to let well enough alone.

Of course there was music in the morning, when it was found that we couldn't leave by the early train. But I had no time to wait; I got only the opening bars of the overture, and then started out to get my letter of credit.

It seemed a good time to look into the trunk business and

rectify it if it needed it, and I had a suspicion that it did. I was too late. The concierge said he had shipped the trunks to Zurich the evening before. I asked him how he could do that without exhibiting passage tickets.

"Not necessary in Switzerland. You pay for your trunks and send them where you please. Nothing goes free but your hand baggage."

"How much did you pay on them?"

"A hundred and forty francs."

"Twenty-eight dollars. There's something wrong about that trunk business, sure."

Next I met the porter. He said:

"You have not slept well, is it not. You have the worn look. If you would like a courier, a good one has arrived last night, and is not engaged for five days already, by the name of Ludi. We recommend him; das heisst, the Grand Hotel Beau Rivage recommends him."

I declined with coldness. My spirit was not broken yet. And I did not like having my condition taken notice of in this way. I was at the country jail by nine o'clock hoping that the Mayor might chance to come before his regular hour; but he didn't. It was dull there. Every time I offered to touch anything, or look at anything, or do anything, or refrain from doing anything, the policeman said it was "defendu." I thought I would practice my French on him, but he wouldn't have that either. It seemed to make him particularly bitter to hear his own tongue.

The Mayor came at last, and then there was no trouble; for the minute he had convened the Supreme Court—they always do whenever there is valuable property in dispute—and got everything shipshape and sentries posted, and had prayer by the chaplain; my unsealed letter was brought and opened, and there wasn't anything in it but some photographs; because, as I remembered now, I had taken out the letter of credit so as to make room for the photographs, and had put the letter in my other pocket, which I proved to everybody's satisfaction by fetching it out and showing it with a good deal of exultation. So then the court looked at each other in a vacant kind of way, and then at me, and then at each other again, and finally let me go, but said it was imprudent for me to be at large, and asked me what my profession was. I said I was a courier. They lifted up their eyes in a kind of reverent way and said, "Du lieber Gott!" and I said a word of courteous thanks for their apparent admiration, and hurried off to the bank.

However, being a courier was already making me a great stickler for order and system and one thing at a time and each thing in its own proper turn; so I passed by the bank and branched off and started for the two lacking members of the Expedition. A cab lazied by, and I took it upon persuasion. I gained no speed by this, but it was a reposeful turnout and I liked reposefulness. The week-long jubilations over the six hundredth anniversary of the birth of Swiss liberty and the Signing of the Compact was at flood tide, and all the street were clothed in fluttering flags.

The horse and the driver had been drunk three days and nights, and had known no stall nor bed meantime. They looked as I felt— dreamy and seedy. But we arrived in course of time. I went in and rang, and asked a housemaid to rush out the lacking members. She said something which I did not understand, and I returned to the chariot. The girl had probably told me that those people did not belong on her floor, and that it would be judicious for me to go higher, and ring from floor to floor till I found them; for in those Swiss flats there does not seem to be any way to find the right family but to be patient and guess your way along up. I calculated that I must wait fifteen minutes, there being three details inseparable from an occasion of this sort: 1, put on hats and come down and climb in; 2, return of one to get "My other glove;" 3, presently return of the other one to fetch "my *French*

Verbs at a Glance." I would muse during the fifteen minutes and take it easy.

A very still and blank interval ensued, and then I felt a hand on my shoulder and started. The intruder was a policeman. I glanced up and perceived that there was new scenery. There was a good deal of a crowd, and they had that pleased and interested look which such a crowd wears when they see that somebody is out of luck. The horse was asleep, and so was the driver, and some boys had hung them and me full of gaudy decorations stolen from the innumerable banner poles. It was a scandalous spectacle. The officer said:

"I'm sorry, but we can't have you sleeping here all day."

I was wounded and said with dignity:

"I beg your pardon, I was not sleeping; I was thinking."

"Well, you can think if you want to, but you've got to think to yourself; you disturb the whole neighborhood."

It was a poor joke, and it made the crowd laugh. I snore at night sometimes, but it is not likely that I would do such a thing in the daytime and in such a place. The officer undecorated us, and seemed sorry for our friendlessness, and really tried to be humane, but he said we mustn't stop there any longer or he would have to charge us rent—it was the law, he said, and he went on to say in a sociable way that I was looking pretty mouldy, and he wished he knew—

I shut him off pretty austerely, and said I hoped one might celebrate a little these days, especially when one was personally concerned.

"Personally?" he asked. "How?"

"Because 600 years ago an ancestor of mine signed the compact."

He reflected a moment, then looked me over and said:

"Ancestor! It's my opinion you signed it yourself. For of all the old ancient relics that ever I—but never mind about that. What is it you are waiting here for so long?"

I said:

"I'm not waiting here so long at all. I'm waiting fifteen minutes till they forget a glove and a book and go back and get them." Then I told him who they were that I had come for.

He was very obliging, and began to shout inquiries to the tiers of heads and shoulders projecting from the windows above us. Then a woman away up there sang out:

"Oh, they? Why I got them a cab and they left here long ago – half-past eight, I should say."

It was annoying. I glanced at my watch, but didn't say anything. The officer said:

"It is a quarter of twelve, you see. You should have inquired better. You have been asleep three-quarters of an hour, and in such a sun as this. You are baked – baked black. It is wonderful. And you will miss your train, perhaps. You interest me greatly. What is your occupation?"

I said I was a courier. It seemed to stun him, and before he could come to we were gone.

When I arrived in the third story of the hotel I found our quarters vacant. I was not surprised. The moment a courier takes his eye off his tribe they go shopping. The nearer it is to train time the surer they are to go. I sat down to try and think out what I had best do next, but presently the hall boy found me there, and said the Expedition had gone to the station half an hour before. It was the first time I had known them to do a rational thing, and it was very confusing. This is one of the things that make a courier's life so difficult and uncertain. Just as matters are going the smoothest, his people will strike a lucid interval, and down go all his arrangements to wreck and ruin.

The train was to leave at twelve noon sharp. It was now ten minutes after twelve. I could be at the station in ten minutes. I saw I had no great amount of leeway, for this was the lightning express and on the Continent the lightning expresses are pretty fastidious about getting away some time during the advertised day. My people were the only ones remaining in the waiting-room; everybody else had passed through and "mounted the train," as they say in those regions. They were exhausted with nervousness and fret, but I comforted them and heartened them up, and we made our rush.

But no; we were out of luck again. The doorkeeper was not satisfied with the tickets. He examined them cautiously, deliberately, suspiciously; then glared at me a while, and after that he called another official. The two examined the tickets and called another official. These called others, and the convention discussed and discussed, and gesticulated and carried on, until I begged that they would consider how time was flying, and just pass a few resolutions and let us go. Then they said very courteously that there was a defect in the tickets, and asked me where I got them.

I judged I saw what the trouble was not. You see, I had bought the tickets in a cigar shop, and, of course, the tobacco smell was on them; without doubt, the thing they were up to was to work the tickets through the Custom House and to collect duty on that smell. So I resolved to be perfectly frank; it is sometimes the best way. I said:

"Gentlemen, I will not deceive you. These railway tickets—"

"Ah, pardon, monsieur! These are not railway tickets."

"Oh," I said, "is that the defect?"

"Ah, truly yes, monsieur. These are lottery tickets, yes; and it is a lottery which has been drawn two years ago."

I affected to be greatly amused; it is all one can do in such circumstances; it is all one can do, and yet there is no value in it; it deceives nobody, and you can see that everybody around pities you and is ashamed of you. One of the hardest situations in life, I think, is to be full of grief and a sense of defeat and shabbiness that way, and yet have to put on an outside of archness and gayety, while all the time you know that your own expedition, the treasures of your heart, and whose love and reverence you are by the custom of our civilization entitled to, are being consumed with humiliation before strangers to see you earning and getting a compassion which is a stigma, a brand—a brand which certifies you to be—oh, anything and everything which is fatal to human respect.

I said, cheerily, it was all right, just one of those little accidents that was likely to happen to anybody—I would have the right tickets in two minutes, and we would catch the train yet, and, moreover, have something to laugh about all through the journey. I did get the tickets in time, all stamped and complete, but then it turned out that I couldn't take them, because in taking so much pains about the two missing members, I had skipped the bank and hadn't the money. So then the train left, and there didn't seem to be anything to do but go back to the hotel, which we did; but it was kind of melancholy and not much said. I tried to start a few subjects, like scenery and transubstantiation, and those sorts of things, but they didn't seem to hit the weather right.

We had lost our good rooms, but we got some others which were pretty scattering, but would answer. I judged things would brighten now, but the Head of the Expedition said, "Send up the trunks." It made me feel pretty cold. There was a doubtful something about the trunk business. I was almost sure of it. I was going to suggest—

But a wave of the hand sufficiently restrained me, and I was informed that we would now camp for three days and see if we could rest up.

I said all right, never mind ringing: I would go down and attend to the trunks myself. I got a cab and went straight to Mr. Charles Natural's place, and asked what order it was I had left there.

"To send seven trunks to the hotel."

"And were you to bring any back?"

"No."

"You are sure I didn't tell you to bring back seven that would be found piled in the lobby?"

"Absolutely sure you didn't."

"Then the whole fourteen are gone to Zurich or Jericho or somewhere, and there is going to be more debris around that hotel when the Expedition—"

I didn't finish, because my mind was getting to be in a good deal of a whirl, and when you are that way you think you have finished a sentence when you haven't, and you go mooning and dreaming away, and the first thing you know you get run over by a dray or a cow or something.

I left the cab there—I forgot it—and on my way back I thought it all out and concluded to resign, because otherwise I should be nearly sure to be discharged. But I didn't believe it would be a good idea to resign in person; I could do it by message. So I sent for Mr. Ludi and explained that there was a courier going to resign on account of incompatibility or fatigue or something, and as he had four or five vacant days, I would like to insert him into that vacancy if he thought he could fill it. When everything was arranged I got him to go up and say to the Expedition that, owing to an error made by Mr. Natural's people, we were out of trunks here, but would have plenty in Zurich, and we'd better take the first train, freight, gravel, or construction, and move right along.

He attended to that and came down with an invitation for me to go up—yes, certainly; and, while we walked along over to the bank to get money, and collect my cigars and tobacco, and to the cigar shop to trade back the lottery tickets and get my umbrella, and to Mr. Natural's to pay that cab and send it away, and to the county jail to get my rubbers and leave p.p.c. cards for the Mayor and Supreme Court, he described the weather to me that was prevailing on the upper levels there with the Expedition, and I saw that I was doing well where I was.

I stayed out in the woods till four P.M., to let the weather moderate, and then turned up at the station just in time to take the three o'clock express for Zurich along with the Expedition, now in the hands of Ludi, who conducted its complex affairs with little apparent effort or inconvenience.

Well, I had worked like a slave while I was in office, and done the very best I knew how; yet all that these people dwelt upon or seemed to care to remember was the defects of my adminis- tration, not its creditable features. They would skip over a thousand creditable features to remark upon and reiterate and fuss about just one fact, till it seemed to me they would wear it out; and not much of a fact, either, taken by itself—the fact that I elected myself courier in Geneva, and put in work enough to carry a circus to Jerusalem, and yet never even got my gang out of the town. I finally said I didn't wish to hear any more about the subject, it made me tired. And I told them to their faces that I would never be a courier again to save anybody's life. And if I live long enough I'll prove it. I think it's a difficult, brain-racking, overworked, and thoroughly ungrateful office, and the main bulk of its wages is a sore heart and a bruised spirit.

On the Decay of the Art of Lying

This short story made its debut in *The Stolen White Elephant, Etc.,* published by James R. Osgood and Company, Boston, in 1882.
— Editor

ESSAY, FOR DISCUSSION, READ AT A MEETING OF THE HISTORICAL AND ANTIQUARIAN CLUB OF HARTFORD, AND OFFERED FOR THE THIRTY-DOLLAR PRIZE. NOW FIRST PUBLISHED.*

Observe, I do not mean to suggest that the *custom* of lying has suffered any decay or interruption—no, for the Lie, as a Virtue, a Principle, is eternal; the Lie, as a recreation, a solace, a refuge in time of need, the fourth Grace, the tenth Muse, man's best and surest friend, is immortal, and cannot perish from the earth while this Club remains. My complaint simply concerns the decay of the *art* of lying. No high-minded man, no man of right feeling, can contemplate the lumbering and slovenly lying of the present day without grieving to see a noble art so prostituted. In this veteran presence I naturally enter upon this theme with diffidence; it is like an old maid trying to teach nursery matters to the mothers in Israel. It would not become me to criticise you, gentlemen, who are nearly all my elders—and my superiors, in this thing—and so, if I should here and there *seem* to do it, I trust it will in most cases be more in a spirit of admiration than of fault-finding; indeed if this finest of the fine arts had everywhere received the attention, encouragement, and conscientious practice and development which this Club has devoted to it, I should not need to utter this lament, or shed a single tear. I do not say this to flatter: I say it in a spirit of just and appreciative recognition. [It had been my

*Did not take the prize.

intention, at this point, to mention names and give illustrative specimens, but indications observable about me admonished me to beware of particulars and confine myself to generalities.]

No fact is more firmly established than that lying is a necessity of our circumstances – the deduction that it is then a Virtue goes without saying. No virtue can reach its highest usefulness without careful and diligent cultivation – therefore, it goes without saying, that this one ought to be taught in the public schools – at the fireside – even in the newspapers. What chance has the ignorant, uncultivated liar against the educated expert? What chance have I against Mr. Per – against a lawyer? *Judicious* lying is what the world needs. I sometimes think it were even better and safer not to lie at all than to lie injudiciously. An awkward, unscientific lie is often as ineffectual as the truth.

Now let us see what the philosophers say. Note that venerable proverb: Children and fools *always* speak the truth. The deduction is plain – adults and wise persons *never* speak it. Parkman, the historian, says, "The principle of truth may itself be carried into an absurdity." In another place in the same chapter he says, "The saying is old that truth should not be spoken at all times; and those whom a sick conscience worries into habitual violation of the maxim are imbeciles and nuisances." It is strong language, but true. None of us could *live* with an habitual truth-teller; but thank goodness none of us has to. An habitual truth-teller is simply an impossible creature; he does not exist; he never has existed. Of course there people who *think* they never lie, but it is not so – and this ignorance is one of the very things that shame our so-called civilization. Everybody lies – every day; every hour; awake; asleep; in his dreams; in his joy; in his mourning; if he keeps his tongue still, his hands, his feet, his eyes, his attitude will convey deception – and purposely. Even in sermons – but that is a platitude.

In a far country where I once lived the ladies used to go around paying calls, under the humane and kindly pretence of wanting to see each other; and when they returned home, they would cry out with a glad voice, saying, "We made sixteen calls and found fourteen of them out"–not meaning that they found out anything against the fourteen–no, that was only a colloquial phrase to signify that they were not at home–and their manner of saying it expressed their lively satisfaction in that fact. Now their pretence of wanting to see the fourteen–and the other two whom they had been less lucky with–was that commonest and mildest form of lying which is sufficiently described as a deflection from the truth. Is it justifiable? Most certainly. It is beautiful, it is noble; for its object is, *not* to reap profit, but to convey a pleasure to the sixteen. The iron-souled truth-monger would plainly manifest, or even utter the fact that he didn't want to see those people–and he would be an ass, and inflict a totally unnecessary pain. And next, those ladies in that far country–but never mind, they had a thousand pleasant ways of lying, that grew out of gentle impulses, and were a credit to their intelligence and an honor to their hearts. Let the particulars go.

The men in that far country were liars, every one. Their mere howdy-do was a lie, because *they* didn't care how you did, except they were undertakers. To the ordinary inquirer you lied in return; for you made no conscientious diagnosis of your case, but answered at random, and usually missed it considerably. You lied to the undertaker, and said your health was failing–a wholly commendable lie, since it cost you nothing and pleased the other man. If a stranger called and interrupted you, you said with your hearty tongue, "I'm glad to see you." and said with your heartier soul, "I wish you were with the cannibals and it was dinner-time." When he went, you said regretfully, "*Must* you go?" and followed it with a "Call again;" but you did no harm, for you did not deceive anybody nor inflict any hurt, whereas the truth would have made you both unhappy.

I think that all this courteous lying is a sweet and loving art, and should be cultivated. The highest perfection of politeness is only a beautiful edifice, built, from the base to the dome, of graceful and gilded forms of charitable and unselfish lying.

What I bemoan is the growing prevalence of the brutal truth. Let us do what we can to eradicate it. An injurious truth has no merit over an injurious lie. Neither should ever be uttered. The man who speaks an injurious truth lest his soul be not saved if he do otherwise, should reflect that that sort of a soul is not strictly worth saving. The man who tells a lie to help a poor devil out of trouble, is one of whom the angels doubtless say, "Lo, here is an heroic soul who casts his won welfare into jeopardy to succor his neighbor's; let us exalt this magnanimous liar."

An injurious lie is an uncommendable thing; and so, also, and in the same degree, is an injurious truth—a fact which is recognized by the law of libel.

Among other common lies, we have the *silent* lie—the deception which one conveys by simply keeping still and concealing the truth. Many obstinate truth-mongers indulge in this dissipation, imagining that if they *speak* no lie, they lie not at all. In that far country where I once lived, there was a lovely spirit, a lady whose impulses were always high and pure, and whose character answered to them. One day I was there at dinner, and remarked, in a general way, that we are all liars. She was amazed, and said, "Not *all?*" It was before "Pinafore's" time, so I did not make the response which would naturally follow in our day, but frankly said, "Yes, *all*—we are all liars; there are no exceptions." She looked almost offended, and said, "Why, do you include *me?*" "Certainly," I said. "I think you even rank as an expert." She said, "'Sh–'sh! the children!" So the subject was changed in deference to the children's presence, and we went on taking about other things. But as soon as the young people were out of the way, the lady came warmly back to the matter and said, "I have made it the rule of my life to never tell a lie; and I have never departed from it in a single instance." I said, "I don't mean the least harm or disrespect, but really you have been lying like smoke ever since I've been sitting here. It has caused me a good deal of pain, because I am not used to it." She required of me an instance – just a single instance. So I said –

"Well, here is the unfilled duplicate of the blank which the Oakland hospital people sent to you by the hand of the sick-nurse when she came here to nurse your little nephew through his dangerous illness. This blank asks all manner of questions as to the conduct of that sick-nurse: 'Did she ever sleep on her watch? Did she ever forget to give the medicine?' and so forth and so on. You are warned to be very careful and explicit in your answers, for the welfare of the service requires that the nurses be promptly fined or otherwise punished for derelictions. You told me you were perfectly delighted with that nurse – that she had a thousand perfections and only one fault; you found you never could depend on her wrapping Johnny up half sufficiently while he waited in a chilly chair for her to rearrange the warm bed. You filled up the duplicate of this paper, and sent it back to the hospital by the hand of the nurse. How did you answer this question – 'Was the nurse at any time guilty of a negligence which was likely to result in the patient's taking cold?' Come – everything is decided by a bet here in California: ten dollars to ten cents you lied when you answered that question." She said, "I didn't; *I left it blank!*" "Just so – you have told a *silent* lie; you have left it to be inferred that you had no fault to find in that matter." She said, "Oh, was that a lie? And how *could* I mention her one single fault, and she so good? – it would have been cruel." I said, "One ought always to lie, when one can do good by it; your impulse was right, but your judgment was crude; this comes of unintelligent practice. Now observe the result of this inexpert deflection of yours. You know Mr. Jones's Willie is lying very low with scarlet-fever; well, your recommendation was so enthusiastic that that girl is there nursing him, and the worn-out family have all been trusting sound asleep for the last fourteen hours, leaving their darling with full confidence in those fatal hands, because you, like young George Washington, have a reputa—However, if you are not going to have anything to do, I will come around tomorrow and we'll attend the funeral together, for of course, you'll naturally feel a peculiar interest in Willie's case—as personal a one, in fact, as the undertaker."

But that was all lost. Before I was halfway through she was in a carriage and making thirty miles an hour toward the Jones mansion to save what was left of Willie and tell all she knew about the deadly nurse. All of which was unnecessary, as Willie wasn't sick; I had been lying myself. But that same day, all the same, she sent a line to the hospital which filled up the neglected blank, and stated the *facts,* too, in the squarest possible manner.

Now, you see, this lady's fault was *not* in lying, but only in lying injudiciously. She should have told the truth, *there,* and made it up to the nurse with a fraudulent compliment further along in the paper. She could have said, "In one respect this sick-nurse is perfection—when she is on watch, she never snores." Almost any little pleasant lie would have taken the sting out of that troublesome but necessary expression of the truth.

Lying is universal—we *all* do it; we all *must* do it. Therefore, the wise thing is for us diligently to train ourselves to lie thoughtfully, judiciously; to lie with a good object, and not an evil one; to lie for others' advantage, and not our own; to lie healingly, charitably, humanely, not cruelly, hurtfully, maliciously; to lie gracefully and graciously, not awkwardly and clumsily; to lie firmly, frankly, squarely, with head erect, not haltingly, tortuously, with pusillanimous mien, as being ashamed of our high calling. Then shall we be rid of the rank and pestilent truth that is rotting the land; then shall we be great and good and beautiful, and worthy dwellers in a world where even benign Nature habitually lies, except when she promises execrable weather. Then—But I am but a new and feeble student in this gracious art; I cannot instruct *this* Club.

Joking aside, I think there is much need of wise examination into what sorts of lies are best and wholesomest to be indulged, seeing we *must* all lie and *do* all lie, and what sorts it may be best to avoid – and this is a thing which I feel I can confidently put into the hands of this experienced Club – a ripe body, who may be termed, in this regard, and without undue flattery, Old Masters.

The Stolen White Elephant *

Spoofing the roles of detectives, who were commonly
championed in the popular fiction of the period, "The Stolen
White Elephant" was first published in a volume of the same
name by James R. Osgood and Company in 1882.

I

The following curious history was related to me by a chance
railway acquaintance. He was a gentleman more than seventy years
of age, and his thoroughly good and gentle face and earnest and
sincere manner imprinted the unmistakable stamp of truth upon
every statement which fell from his lips. He said:—

You know in what reverence the royal white elephant of Siam
is held by the people of that country. You know it is sacred to
kings, only kings may possess it, and that it is indeed in a measure even superior to kings, since it receives not merely honor but
worship. Very well; five years ago, when the troubles concerning
the frontier line arose between Great Britain and Siam, it was
presently manifest that Siam had been in the wrong. Therefore
every reparation was quickly made, and the British representative stated that he was satisfied and the past should be forgotten.
This greatly relieved the King of Siam, and partly as a token of
gratitude, but partly also, perhaps, to wipe out any little remaining vestige of unpleasantness which England might feel toward
him, he wished to send the Queen a present,—the sole sure way
of propitiating an enemy, according to Oriental ideas. This present
ought not only to be a royal one, but transcendently royal. Where-
fore, what offering could be so meet as that of a white elephant?
My position in the Indian civil service was such that I was deemed
peculiarly worthy of the honor of conveying the present to her

*Left out of "A Tramp Abroad," because it was feared that some of the particulars had been
exaggerated, and that others were not true. Before these suspicions had been proven ground-
less, the book had gone to press.—M.T.

Majesty. A ship was fitted out for me and my servants and the officers and attendants of the elephant, and in due time I arrived in New York harbor and placed my royal charge in admirable quarters in Jersey City. It was necessary to remain awhile in order to recruit the animal's health before resuming the voyage.

All went well during a fortnight,—then my calamities began. The white elephant was stolen! I was called up at dead of night and informed of this fearful misfortune. For some moments I was beside myself with terror and anxiety; I was helpless. Then I grew calmer and collected my faculties. I soon saw my course,—for indeed there was but the one course for an intelligent man to pursue. Late as it was, I flew to New York and got a policeman to conduct me to the headquarters of the detective force. Fortunately I arrived in time, though the chief of the force, the celebrated Inspector Blunt, was just on the point of leaving for his home. He was a man of middle size and compact frame, and when he was thinking deeply he had a way of knitting his brows and tapping his forehead reflectively with his finger, which impressed you at once with the conviction that you stood in the presence of a person of no common order. The very sight of him gave me confidence and made me hopeful. I stated my errand. It did not flurry him in the least; it had no more visible effect upon his iron self-possession than if I had told him somebody had stolen my dog. He motioned me to a seat, and said calmly,—

"Allow me to think a moment, please."

So saying, he sat down at his office table and leaned his head upon his hand. Several clerks were at work at the other end of the room; the scratching of their pens was all the sound I heard during the next six or seven minutes. Meantime the inspector sat there, buried in thought. Finally he raised his head, and there was that in the firm lines of his face which showed me that his brain had done its work and his plan was made. Said he,—and his voice was low and impressive,—

"This is no ordinary case. Every step must be warily taken;

each step must be made sure before the next is ventured. And secrecy must be observed,—secrecy profound and absolute. Speak to no one about the matter, not even the reporters. I will take care of *them;* I will see that they get only what it may suit my ends to let them know." He touched a bell; a youth appeared. "Alaric, tell the reporters to remain for the present." The boy retired. "Now let us proceed to business,—and systematically. Nothing can be accomplished in this trade of mine without strict and minute method."

He took a pen and some paper. "Now—name of the elephant?"

"Hassan Ben Ali Ben Selim Abdallah Mohammed Moisé Alhammal Jamsetjejeebhoy Dhuleep Sultan Ebu Bhudpoor."

"Very well. Given name?"

"Jumbo."

"Very well. Place of birth?"

"The capital city of Siam."

"Parents living?"

"No—dead."

"Had they any other issue besides this one?"

"None. He was an only child."

"Very well. These matters are sufficient under that head. Now please describe the elephant, and leave out no particular, however insignificant,—that is, insignificant from *your* point of view. To men in my profession there *are* no insignificant particulars; they do not exist."

I described,—he wrote. When I was done, he said,—

"Now listen. If I have made any mistakes, correct me."

He read as follows:—

"Height, 19 feet; length from apex of forehead to insertion of tail, 26 feet; length of trunk, 16 feet; length of tail, 6 feet; total length, including trunk and tail, 48 feet; length of tusks, 9½ feet; ears in keeping with these dimensions; footprint resembles the mark left when one up-ends a barrel in the snow; color of the elephant, a dull white; has a hole the size of a plate in each ear

for the insertion of jewelry, and possesses the habit in a remarkable degree of squirting water upon spectators and of maltreating
with his trunk not only such persons as he is acquainted with,
but even entire strangers; limps slightly with his right hind leg,
and has a small scar in his left armpit caused by a former boil;
had on, when stolen, a castle containing seats for fifteen persons,
and a gold-cloth saddle-blanket the size of an ordinary carpet."

There were no mistakes. The inspector touched the bell,
handed the description to Alaric, and said,–

"Have fifty thousand copies of this printed at once and mailed
to every detective office and pawnbroker's shop in the continent."
Alaric retired. "There,–so far, so good. Next, I must have a photograph of the property."

I gave him one. He examined it critically, and said,–

"It must do, since we can do no better; but he has his trunk
curled up and tucked into his mouth. That is unfortunate, and
is calculated to mislead, for of course he does not usually have
it in that position." He touched his bell.

"Alaric, have fifty thousand copies of this photograph made,
the first thing in the morning, and mail them with the descriptive circulars."

Alaric retired to execute his orders. The inspector said,–

"It will be necessary to offer a reward, of course. Now as to
the amount?"

"What sum would you suggest?"

"To *begin* with, I should say,–well, twenty-five thousand dollars. It is an intricate and difficult business; there are a thousand
avenues of escape and opportunities of concealment. These thieves
have friends and pals everywhere–"

"Bless me, do you know who they are?"

The wary face, practised in concealing the thoughts and feelings within, gave me no token, nor yet the replying words, so
quietly uttered:–

"Never mind about that. I may, and I may not. We generally

gather a pretty shrewd inkling of who our man is by the manner of his work and the size of the game he goes after. We are not dealing with a pickpocket or a hall thief, now, make up your mind to that. This property was not 'lifted' by a novice. But, as I was saying, considering the amount of travel which will have to be done, and the diligence with which the thieves will cover up their traces as they move along, twenty-five thousand may be too small a sum to offer, yet I think it worth while to start with that."

So we determined upon that figure, as a beginning. Then this man, whom nothing escaped which could by any possibility be made to serve as a clew, said: –

"There are cases in detective history to show that criminals have been detected through peculiarities in their appetites. Now, what does this elephant eat, and how much?"

"Well, as to *what* he eats, – he will eat *anything*. He will eat a man, he will eat a Bible, – he will eat anything *between* a man and a Bible."

"Good, – very good indeed, but too general. Details are necessary, – details are the only valuable things in our trade. Very well, – as to men. At one meal, – or, if you prefer, during one day, – how many men will he eat, if fresh?"

"He would not care whether they were fresh or not; at a single meal he would eat five ordinary men."

"Very good; five men; we will put that down. What nationalities would he prefer?"

"He is indifferent about nationalities. He prefers acquaintances, but is not prejudiced against strangers."

"Very good. Now, as to Bibles. How many Bibles would he eat at a meal?"

"He would eat an entire edition."

"It is hardly succinct enough. Do you mean the ordinary octavo, or the family illustrated?"

"I think he would be indifferent to illustrations; that is, I think he would not value illustrations above simple letter-press."

"No, you do not get my idea. I refer to bulk. The ordinary octavo Bible weighs about two pounds and a half, while the great quarto with illustrations weighs ten or twelve. How many Doré Bibles would he eat at a meal?"

"If you knew this elephant, you could not ask. He would take what they had."

"Well, put it in dollars and cents, then. We must get at it somehow. The Doré costs a hundred dollars a copy, Russia leather, bevelled."

"He would require about fifty thousand dollars' worth,–say an edition of five hundred copies."

"Now that is more exact. I will put that down. Very well; he likes men and Bibles; so far, so good. What else will he eat? I want particulars."

"He will leave Bibles to eat bricks, he will leave bricks to eat bottles, he will leave bottles to eat clothing, he will leave clothing to eat cats, he will leave cats to eat oysters, he will leave oysters to eat ham, he will leave ham to eat sugar, he will leave sugar to eat pie, he will leave pie to eat potatoes, he will leave potatoes to eat bran, he will leave bran to eat hay, he will leave hay to eat oats, he will leave oats to eat rice, for he was mainly raised on it. There is nothing whatever that he will not eat but European butter, and he would eat that if he could taste it."

"Very good. General quantity at a meal,–say about–"

"Well, anywhere from a quarter to half a ton."

"And he drinks–"

"Everything that is fluid. Milk, water, whiskey, molasses, castor oil, camphene, carbolic acid,–it is no use to go into particulars; whatever fluid occurs to you set it down. He will drink anything that is fluid, except European coffee."

"Very good. As to quantity?"

"Put it down five to fifteen barrels,–his thirst varies; his other appetites do not."

"These things are unusual. They ought to furnish quite good clews toward tracing him."

He touched the bell.

"Alaric, summon Captain Burns."

Burns appeared. Inspector Blunt unfolded the whole matter to him, detail by detail. Then he said in the clear, decisive tones of a man whose plans are clearly defined in his head, and who is accustomed to command,—

"Captain Burns, detail Detectives Jones, Davis, Halsey, Bates, and Hackett to shadow the elephant."

"Yes, sir."

"Detail Detectives Moses, Dakin, Murphy, Rogers, Tupper, Higgins, and Bartholomew to shadow the thieves."

"Yes, sir."

"Place a strong guard—a guard of thirty picked men, with a relief of thirty—over the place from whence the elephant was stolen, to keep strict watch there night and day, and allow none to approach—except reporters—without written authority from me."

"Yes, sir."

"Place detectives in plain clothes in the railway, steamship, and ferry depots, and upon all roadways leading out of Jersey City, with orders to search all suspicious persons."

"Yes, sir."

"Furnish all these men with photograph and accompanying description of the elephant, and instruct them to search all trains and outgoing ferry-boats and other vessels."

"Yes, sir."

"If the elephant should be found, let him be seized, and the information forwarded to me by telegraph."

"Yes, sir."

"Let me be informed at once if any clews should be found,—footprints of the animal, or anything of that kind."

"Yes, sir."

"Get an order commanding the harbor police to patrol the frontages vigilantly."

"Yes, sir."

"Despatch detectives in plain clothes over all the railways, north as far as Canada, west as far as Ohio, south as far as Washington."

"Yes, sir."

"Place experts in all the telegraph offices to listen to all messages; and let them require that all cipher despatches be interpreted to them."

"Yes, sir."

"Let all these things be done with the utmost secrecy,—mind, the most impenetrable secrecy."

"Yes, sir."

"Report to me promptly at the usual hour."

"Yes, sir."

"Go!"

"Yes, sir."

He was gone.

Inspector Blunt was silent and thoughtful a moment, while the fire in his eye cooled down and faded out. Then he turned to me and said in a placid voice,—

"I am not given to boasting, it is not my habit; but—we shall find the elephant."

I shook him warmly by the hand and thanked him; and I *felt* my thanks, too. The more I had seen of the man the more I liked him, and the more I admired him and marvelled over the mysterious wonders of his profession. Then we parted for the night, and I went home with a far happier heart than I had carried with me to his office.

II

Next morning it was all in the newspapers, in the minutest detail. It even had additions,—consisting of Detective This, Detective That, and Detective The Other's "Theory" as to how the robbery was done, who the robbers were, and whither they had flown with their booty. There were eleven of these theories, and they covered all the possibilities; and this single fact shows what independent thinkers detectives are. No two theories were alike, or even much resembled each other, save in one striking particular, and in that one all the eleven theories were absolutely agreed. That was, that although the rear of my building was torn out and the only door remained locked, the elephant had not been removed through the rent, but by some other (undiscovered) outlet. All agreed that the robbers had made that rent only to mislead the detectives. That never would have occurred to me or to any other layman, perhaps, but it had not deceived the detectives for a moment. Thus, what I had supposed was the only thing that had no mystery about it was in fact the very thing I had gone furthest astray in. The eleven theories all named the supposed robbers, but no two named the same robbers; the total number of suspected persons was thirty-seven. The various newspaper accounts all closed with the most important opinion of all,—that of Chief Inspector Blunt. A portion of this statement read as follows:—

> "The chief knows who the principals are, namely, 'Brick' Duffy and 'Red' McFadden. Ten days before the robbery was achieved he was already aware that it was to be attempted, and had quietly proceeded to shadow these two noted villains; but unfortunately on the night in question their track was lost, and before it could be found again the bird was flown,—that is, the elephant.
>
> "Duffy and McFadden are the boldest scoundrels in the profession; the chief has reasons for believing that they are the men who stole the stove out of the detective headquarters on a bitter night last winter,—in consequence of which the chief and every detective present were in the hands of the physicians before morning, some with frozen feet, others with frozen fingers, ears, and other members."

When I read the first half of that I was more astonished than ever at the wonderful sagacity of this strange man. He not only saw everything in the present with a clear eye, but even the future could not be hidden from him. I was soon at his office, and said I could not help wishing he had had those men arrested, and so prevented the trouble and loss; but his reply was simple and unanswerable:—

"It is not our province to prevent crime, but to punish it. We cannot punish it until it is committed."

I remarked that the secrecy with which we had begun had been marred by the newspapers; not only all our facts but all our plans and purposes had been revealed; even all the suspected persons had been named; these would doubtless disguise themselves now, or go into hiding.

"Let them. They will find that when I am ready for them my hand will descend upon them, in their secret places, as unerringly as the hand of fate. As to the newspapers, we *must* keep in with them. Fame, reputation, constant public mention,– these are the detective's bread and butter. He must publish his facts, else he will be supposed to have none; he must publish his theory, for nothing is so strange or striking as a detective's theory, or brings him so much wondering respect; we must publish our plans, for these the journals insist upon having, and we could not deny them without offending. We must constantly show the public what we are doing, or they will believe we are doing nothing. It is much pleasanter to have a newspaper say, 'Inspector Blunt's ingenious and extraordinary theory is as follows,' than to have it say some harsh thing, or, worse still, some sarcastic one."

"I see the force of what you say. But I noticed that in one part of your remarks in the papers this morning you refused to reveal your opinion upon a certain minor point."

"Yes, we always do that; it has a good effect. Besides, I had not formed any opinion on that point, any way."

I deposited a considerable sum of money with the inspector, to meet current expenses, and sat down to wait for news. We were expecting the telegrams to begin to arrive at any moment now. Meantime I reread the newspapers and also our descriptive circular, and observed that our $25,000 reward seemed to be offered only to detectives. I said I thought it ought to be offered to anybody who would catch the elephant. The inspector said:–

"It is the detectives who will find the elephant, hence the reward will go to the right place. If other people found the animal, it would only be by watching the detectives and taking advantage of clews and indications stolen from them, and that would entitle the detectives to the reward, after all. The proper office of a reward is to stimulate the men who deliver up their time and their trained sagacities to this sort of work, and not to confer benefits upon chance citizens who stumble upon a capture without having earned the benefits by their own merits and labors."

This was reasonable enough, certainly. Now the telegraphic machine in the corner began to click, and the following despatch was the result: —

> FLOWER STATION, N.Y., 7.30 A M
> Have got a clew. Found a succession of deep tracks across a farm near here. Followed them two miles east without result; think elephant went west. Shall now shadow him in that direction.
> DARLEY, *Detective.*

"Darley's one of the best men on the force," said the inspector. "We shall hear from him again before long."

Telegram No. 2 came: —

> BARKER'S, N.J., 7.40 A.M.
> Just arrived. Glass factory broken open here during night, and eight hundred bottles taken. Only water in large quantity near here is five miles distant. Shall strike for there. Elephant will be thirsty. Bottles were empty.
> BAKER, *Detective.*

"That promises well, too," said the inspector. "I told you the creature's appetites would not be bad clews."

Telegram No. 3: —

> TAYLORVILLE, L.I., 8.15 A.M.
> A haystack near here disappeared during night. Probably eaten. Have got a clew and am off.
> HUBBARD, *Detective.*

"How he does move around!" said the inspector. "I knew we had a difficult job on hand, but we shall catch him yet."

> FLOWER STATION, N.Y., 9 A.M.
> Shadowed the tracks three miles westward. Large, deep and ragged. Have just met a farmer who says they are not elephant tracks. Says they are holes where he dug up saplings for shade-trees when ground was frozen last winter. Give me orders how to proceed.
> DARLEY, *Detective.*

"Aha! a confederate of the thieves! The thing grows warm," said the inspector.

He dictated the following telegram to Darley:—

> Arrest the man and force him to name his pals. Continue to follow the tracks,—to the Pacific, if necessary.
> *Chief* BLUNT.

Next telegram:—

> CONEY POINT, PA., 8.45 A.M.
> Gas office broken open here during night and three months' unpaid gas bills taken. Have got a clew and am away.
> MURPHY, *Detective.*

"Heavens!" said the inspector; "would he eat gas bills?"

"Through ignorance,—yes; but they cannot support life. At least, unassisted."

Now came this exciting telegram:—

> IRONVILLE, N.Y., 9.30 A.M.
> Just arrived. This village in consternation. Elephant passed through here at five this morning. Some say he went east, some say west, some north, some south,—but all say they did not wait to notice particularly. He killed a horse; have secured a piece of it for a clew. Killed it with his trunk; from style of blow, think he struck it left-handed. From position in which horse lies, think elephant travelled northward along line of Berkley railway. Has four and a half hours' start, but I move on his track at once.
> HAWES, *Detective.*

I uttered exclamations of joy. The inspector was as self-contained as a graven image. He calmly touched his bell.

"Alaric, send Captain Burns here."

Burns appeared.

"How many men are ready for instant orders?"

"Ninety-six, sir."

"Send them north at once. Let them concentrate along the line of the Berkley road north of Ironville."

"Yes, sir."

"Let them conduct their movements with the utmost secrecy. As fast as others are at liberty, hold them for orders."

"Yes, sir."

"Go!"

"Yes, sir."

Presently came another telegram: –

> SAGE CORNERS, N.Y., 10.30.
> Just arrived. Elephant passed through here at 8.15. All escaped from the town but a policeman. Apparently elephant did not strike at policeman, but at the lamp-post. Got both. I have secured a portion of the policeman as clew.
> STUMM, *Detective.*

"So the elephant has turned westward," said the inspector. "However, he will not escape, for my men are scattered all over that region."

The next telegram said: –

> GLOVER'S, 11.15.
> Just arrived. Village deserted, except sick and aged. Elephant passed through three quarters of an hour ago. The anti-temperance mass meeting was in session; he put his trunk in at a window and washed it out with water from cistern. Some swallowed it – since dead; several drowned. Detectives Cross and O'Shaughnessy were passing through town, but going south, – so missed elephant. Whole region for many miles around in terror, – people flying from their homes. Wherever they turn they meet elephant, and many are killed.
> BRANT, *Detective.*

I could have shed tears, this havoc so distressed me. But the inspector only said,—

"You see,—we are closing in on him. He feels our presence; he has turned eastward again."

Yes further troublous news was in store for us. The telegraph brought this:—

> HOGANPORT, 12.19.
> Just arrived. Elephant passed through half an hour ago, creating wildest fright and excitement. Elephant raged around streets; two plumbers going by, killed one—other escaped. Regret general.
> O'FLAHERTY, *Detective.*

"Now he is right in the midst of my men," said the inspector. "Nothing can save him."

A succession of telegrams came from detectives who were scattered through New Jersey and Pennsylvania, and who were following clews consisting of ravaged barns, factories, and Sunday school libraries, with high hopes,—hopes amounting to certainties, indeed. The inspector said,—

"I wish I could communicate with them and order them north, but that is impossible. A detective only visits a telegraph office to send his report; then he is off again, and you don't know where to put your hand on him."

Now came this despatch:—

> BRIDGEPORT, CT., 12.15.
> Barnum offers rate of $4,000 a year for exclusive privilege of using elephant as travelling advertising medium from now till detectives find him. Wants to paste circus-posters on him. Desires immediate answer.
> BOGGS, *Detective.*

"That is perfectly absurd!" I exclaimed.

"Of course it is," said the inspector. "Evidently Mr. Barnum, who thinks he is so sharp, does not know me,—but I know him."

Then he dictated this answer to the despatch:—

Mr. Barnum's offer declined. Make it $7,000 or nothing.

Chief BLUNT.

"There. We shall not have to wait long for an answer. Mr. Barnum is not at home; he is in the telegraph office,—it is his way when he has business on hand. Inside of three—"

DONE.—P.T. BARNUM.

So interrupted the clicking telegraphic instrument. Before I could make a comment upon this extraordinary episode, the following despatch carried my thoughts into another and very distressing channel:—

BOLIVIA, N.Y., 12.50.

Elephant arrived here from the south and passed through toward the forest at 11.50, dispersing a funeral on the way, and diminishing the mourners by two. Citizens fired some small cannon-balls into him, and then fled. Detective Burke and I arrived ten minutes later, from the north, but mistook some excavations for footprints, and so lost a good deal of time; but at last we struck the right trail and followed it to the woods. We then got down on our hands and knees and continued to keep a sharp eye on the track, and so shadowed it into the brush. Burke was in advance. Unfortunately the animal had stopped to rest; therefore, Burke having his head down, intent upon the track, butted up against the elephant's hind legs before he was aware of his vicinity. Burke instantly rose to his feet, seized the tail, exclaimed joyfully, "I claim the re—" but got no further, for a single blow of the huge trunk laid the brave fellow's fragments low in death. I fled rearward, and the elephant turned and shadowed me to the edge of the wood, making tremendous speed, and I should inevitably have been lost, but that the remains of the funeral providentially intervened again and diverted his attention. I have just learned that nothing of that funeral is now left; but this is no loss, for there is an abundance of material for another. Meantime, the elephant has disappeared again.

MULROONEY, *Detective.*

We heard no news except from the diligent and confident detectives scattered about New Jersey, Pennsylvania, Delaware, and

Virginia,–who were all following fresh and encouraging clews,–
until shortly after 2 P.M., when this telegram came:–

> BAXTER CENTRE, 2.15.
>
> Elephant been here, plastered over with circus-bills, and broke up
> a revival, striking down and damaging many who were on the point
> of entering upon a better life. Citizens penned him up, and established
> a guard. When Detective Brown and I arrived, some time after, we
> entered enclosure and proceeded to identify elephant by photograph
> and description. All marks tallied exactly except one, which we could
> not see,–the boil-scar under armpit. To make sure, Brown crept under
> to look, and was immediately brained,–that is, head crushed and des-
> troyed, though nothing issued from debris. All fled; so did elephant,
> striking right and left with much effect. Has escaped, but left bold
> blood-track from cannon-wounds. Rediscovery certain. He broke south-
> ward, through a dense forest.
>
> BRENT, *Detective.*

That was the last telegram. At nightfall a fog shut down which
was so dense that objects but three feet away could not be dis-
cerned. This lasted all night. The ferry-boats and even the
omnibuses had to stop running.

III

Next morning the papers were as full of detective theories as
before; they had all our tragic facts in detail also, and a great many
more which they had received from their telegraphic correspondents. Column after column was occupied, a third of its way down,
with glaring head-lines, which it made my heart sick to read. Their
general tone was like this:–

> THE WHITE ELEPHANT AT LARGE! HE MOVES UPON HIS FATAL MARCH! WHOLE
> VILLAGES DESERTED BY THEIR FRIGHT-STRICKEN OCCUPANTS! PALE TERROR GOES
> BEFORE HIM. DEATH AND DEVASTATION FOLLOW AFTER! AFTER THESE, THE DETEC-
> TIVES. BARNS DESTROYED, FACTORIES GUTTED, HARVESTS DEVOURED, PUBLIC
> ASSEMBLAGES DISPERSED, ACCOMPANIED BY SCENES OF CARNAGE IMPOSSIBLE TO
> DESCRIBE! THEORIES OF THIRTY-FOUR OF THE MOST DISTINGUISHED DETECTIVES ON
> THE FORCE! THEORY OF CHIEF BLUNT!

"There!" said Inspector Blunt, almost betrayed into excitement, "this is magnificent! This is the greatest windfall that any detective organization ever had. The fame of it will travel to the ends of the earth, and endure to the end of time, and my name with it."

But there was no joy for me. I felt as if I had committed all those red crimes, and that the elephant was only my irresponsible agent. And how the list had grown! In one place he had "interfered with an election and killed five repeaters." He had followed this act with the destruction of two poor fellows, named O'Donahue and McFlannigan, who had "found a refuge in the home of the oppressed of all lands only the day before, and were in the act of exercising for the first time the noble right of American citizens at the polls, when stricken down by the relentless hand of the Scourge of Siam." In another, he had "found a crazy sensation preacher preparing his next season's heroic attacks on the dance, the theatre, and other things which can't strike back, and had stepped on him." And in still another place he had "killed a lightning-rod agent." And so the list went on, growing redder and redder, and more and more heart-breaking. Sixty persons had been killed, and two hundred and forty wounded. All the accounts bore just testimony to the activity and devotion of the detectives, and all closed with the remark that "three hundred thousand citizens and four detectives saw the dread creature, and two of the latter he destroyed."

I dreaded to hear the telegraphic instrument begin to click again. By and by the messages began to pour in, but I was happily disappointed in their nature. It was soon apparent that all trace of the elephant was lost. The fog had enabled him to search out a good hiding-place unobserved. Telegrams from the most absurdly distant points reported that a dim vast mass had been glimpsed there through the fog at such and such an hour, and was "undoubtedly the elephant." This dim vast mass had been glimpsed in New Haven, in New Jersey, in Pennsylvania, interior New York, in Brooklyn, and even in the city of New York itself!

But in all cases the dim vast mass had vanished quickly and left no trace. Every detective of the large force scattered over this huge extent of country sent his hourly report, and each and every one of them had a clew, and was shadowing something, and was hot upon the heels of it.

But the day passed without other result.

The next day the same.

The next just the same.

The newspaper reports began to grow monotonous with facts that amounted to nothing, clews which led to nothing, and theories which had nearly exhausted the elements which surprise and delight and dazzle.

By advice of the inspector I doubled the reward.

Four more dull days followed. Then came a bitter blow to the poor, hard-working detectives,—the journalists declined to print their theories, and coldly said, "Give us a rest."

Two weeks after the elephant's disappearance I raised the reward to $75,000 by the inspector's advice. It was a great sum, but I felt that I would rather sacrifice my whole private fortune than lose my credit with my government. Now that the detectives were in adversity, the newspapers turned upon them, and began to fling the most stinging sarcasms at them. This gave the minstrels an idea, and they dressed themselves as detectives and hunted the elephant on the stage in the most extravagant way. The caricaturists made pictures of detectives scanning the country with spy-glasses, while the elephant, at their backs, stole apples out of their pockets. And they made all sorts of ridiculous pictures of the detective badge,—you have seen that badge printed in gold on the back of detective novels, no doubt,—it is a wide-staring eye, with the legend, "WE NEVER SLEEP." When detectives called for a drink, the would-be facetious bar-keeper resurrected an obsolete form of expression and said, "Will you have an eye-opener?" All the air was thick with sarcasms.

But there was one man who moved calm, untouched,

unaffected, through it all. It was that heart of oak, the Chief Inspector. His brave eye never drooped, his serene confidence never wavered. He always said,—

"Let them rail on; he laughs best who laughs last."

My admiration for the man grew into a species of worship. I was at his side always. His office had become an unpleasant place to me, and now became daily more and more so. Yet if he could endure it I meant to do so also; at least, as long as I could. So I came regularly, and stayed,—the only outsider who seemed to be capable of it. Everybody wondered how I could, and often it seemed to me that I must desert, but at such times I looked into that calm and apparently unconscious face, and held my ground.

About three weeks after the elephant's disappearance I was about to say, one morning, that I should have to strike my colors and retire, when the great detective arrested the thought by proposing one more superb and masterly move.

This was to compromise with the robbers. The fertility of this man's invention exceeded anything I have ever seen, and I have had a wide intercourse with the world's finest minds. He said he was confident he could compromise for $100,000 and recover the elephant. I said I believed I could scrape the amount together, but what would become of the poor detectives who had worked so faithfully? He said,—

"In compromises they always get half."

This removed my only objection. So the inspector wrote two motes, in this form:—

> Dear Madam,—Your husband can make a large sum of money (and be entirely protected from the law) by making an immediate appointment with me.
>
> *Chief* Blunt.

He sent one of these by his confidential messenger to the "reputed wife" of Brick Duffy, and the other to the reputed wife of Red McFadden.

Within the hour these offensive answers came: –

Yᴇ Oᴡʟᴅ Fᴏᴏʟ: brick McDuffys bin ded 2 yere.
Bʀɪᴅɢᴇᴛ Mᴀʜᴏɴᴇʏ.

Cʜɪᴇꜰ Bᴀᴛ, – Red McFadden is hung and in heving 18 month. Any
Ass but a detective knose that.
Mᴀʀʏ O'Hᴏᴏʟɪɢᴀɴ.

"I had long suspected these facts," said the inspector; "this testimony proves the unerring accuracy of my instinct."

The moment one resource failed him he was ready with
another. He immediately wrote an advertisement for the morning papers, and I kept a copy of it: –

A. – xwblv.242 N. Tjnd – fz328wmlg. Ozpo, – ; 2m!ogw. Mum.

He said that if the thief was alive this would bring him to the
usual rendezvous. He further explained that the usual rendezvous
was a place where all business affairs between detectives and criminals were conducted. This meeting would take place at twelve
the next night.

We could do nothing till then, and I lost no time in getting
out of the office, and was grateful indeed for the privilege.

At 11 the next night I brought $100,000 in bank-notes and put
them into the chief's hands, and shortly afterward he took his
leave, with the brave old undimmed confidence in his eye. An
almost intolerable hour dragged to a close; then I heard his welcome tread, and rose gasping and tottered to meet him. How his
fine eyes flamed with triumph! He said, –

"We've compromised! The jokers will sing a different tune
tomorrow! Follow me!"

He took a lighted candle and strode down into the vast vaulted
basement where sixty detectives always slept, and where s score
were now playing cards to while the time. I followed close after
him. He walked swiftly down to the dim remote end of the place,
and just as I succumbed to the pangs of suffocation and was

swooning away he stumbled and fell over the outlying members of a mighty object, and I heard him exclaim as he went down,—

"Our noble profession is vindicated. Here is your elephant!"

I was carried to the office above and restored with carbolic acid. The whole detective force swarmed in, and such another season of triumphant rejoicing ensued as I had never witnessed before. The reporters were called, baskets of champagne were opened, toasts were drunk, the handshakings and congratulations were continuous and enthusiastic. Naturally the chief was the hero of the hour, and his happiness was so complete and had been so patiently and worthily and bravely won that it made me happy to see it, though I stood there a homeless beggar, my priceless charge dead, and my position in my country's service lost to me through what would always seem my fatally careless execution of a great trust. Many an eloquent eye testified its deep admiration for the chief, and many a detective's voice murmured, "Look at him,—just the king of the profession,—only give him a clew, it's all he wants, and there ain't anything hid that he can't find." The dividing of the $50,000 made great pleasure; when it was finished the chief made a little speech while he put his share in his pocket, in which he said, "Enjoy it, boys, for you've earned it; and more than that you've earned for the detective profession undying fame."

A telegram arrived, which read:—

> MONROE, MICH., 10 P.M.
>
> First time I've struck a telegraph office in over three weeks. Have followed those footprints, horseback, through the woods, a thousand miles to here, and they get stronger and bigger and fresher every day. Don't worry—inside of another week I'll have the elephant. This is dead sure.
>
> DARLEY, *Detective.*

The chief ordered three cheers for "Darley, one of the finest minds on the force," and then commanded that he be telegraphed to come home and receive his share of the reward.

So ended that marvelous episode of the stolen elephant. The newspapers were pleasant with praises once more, the next day, with one contemptible exception. This sheet said, "Great is the detective! He may be a little slow in finding a little thing like a mislaid elephant,—he may hunt him all day and sleep with his rotting carcass all night for three weeks, but he will find him at last—if he can get the man who mislaid him to show him the place!"

Poor Hassan was lost to me forever. The cannon-shots had wounded him fatally, he had crept to that unfriendly place in the fog, and there, surrounded by his enemies and in constant danger of detection, he had wasted away with hunger and suffering till death gave him peace.

The compromise cost me $100,000; my detective expenses were $42,000 more; I never applied for a place again under my government; I am a ruined man and a wanderer in the earth,—but my admiration for that man, whom I believe to be the greatest detective the world has ever produced, remains undimmed to this day, and will so remain unto the end.

THE £1,000,000 BANK-NOTE

Twain created the plot of "The £1,000,000 Bank-Note" during
June of 1883, a happy time for Twain and his family. But the
story was not published until the following year, when Twain was
facing financial ruin and had to write to pay his debts. The story
was later published in The £1,000,000 Bank-Note and Other New
Stories, although it was the only story in the "collection."

When I was twenty-seven years old, I was a mining-broker's
clerk in San Francisco, and an expert in all the details of stock
traffic. I was alone in the world, and had nothing to depend upon
but my wits and a clean reputation; but these were setting
my feet in the road of eventual fortune, and I was content with
the prospect.

My time was my own after the afternoon board, Saturdays, and
I was accustomed to put it in on a little sail-boat on the bay. One
day I ventured too far, and was carried out to sea. Just at nightfall, when hope was about gone, I was picked up by a small brig
which was bound for London. It was a long and stormy voyage,
and they made me work my passage without pay, as a common
sailor. When I stepped ashore in London my clothes were ragged
and shabby, and I had only a dollar in my pocket. This money
fed and sheltered me twenty-four hours. During the next twenty-
four I went without food and shelter.

About ten o'clock on the following morning, seedy and hungry, I was dragging myself along Portland Place, when a child that
was passing, towed by a nurse-maid, tossed a luscious big pear—
minus one bite—into the gutter. I stopped, of course, and fastened
my desiring eye on that muddy treasure. My mouth watered for
it, my stomach craved it, my whole being begged for it. But every
time I made a move to get it some passing eye detected my purpose, and of course I straightened up then, and looked indifferent,
and pretended that I hadn't been thinking about the pear at all.

This same thing kept happening and happening, and I couldn't get the pear. I was just getting desperate enough to brave all the shame, and to seize it, when a window behind me was raised, and a gentleman spoke out of it, saying:

"Step in here, please."

I was admitted by a gorgeous flunkey, and shown into a sumptuous room where a couple of elderly gentlemen were sitting. They sent away the servant, and made me sit down. They had just finished their breakfast, and the sight of the remains of it almost overpowered me. I could hardly keep my wits together in the presence of that food, but as I was not asked to sample it, I had to bear my trouble as best I could.

Now, something had been happening there a little before, which I did not know anything about until a good many days afterwards, but I will tell you about it now. Those two old brothers had been having a pretty hot argument a couple of days before, and had ended by agreeing to decide it by a bet, which is the English way of settling everything.

You will remember that the Bank of England once issued two notes of a million pounds each, to be used for a special purpose connected with some public transaction with a foreign country. For some reason or other only one of these had been used and canceled; the other still lay in the vaults of the Bank. Well, the brothers, chatting along, happened to get to wondering what might be the fate of a perfectly honest and intelligent stranger who should be turned adrift in London without a friend, and with no money but that million-pound bank-note, and no way to account for his being in possession of it. Brother A said he would starve to death; Brother B said he wouldn't. Brother A said he couldn't offer it at a bank or anywhere else, because he would be arrested on the spot. So they went on disputing till Brother B said he would bet twenty thousand pounds that the man would live thirty days, *anyway,* on that million, and keep out of jail, too. Brother A took him up. Brother B went down to the Bank and bought that note. Just like an Englishman, you see; pluck to the backbone. Then he dictated a letter, which one of his clerks wrote out in a beautiful round hand, and then the two brothers sat at the window a whole day watching for the right man to give it to.

They saw many honest faces go by that were not intelligent enough; many that were intelligent, but not honest enough; many that were both, but the possessors were not poor enough, or, if poor enough, were not strangers. There was always a defect, until I came along; but they agreed that I filled the bill all around; so they elected me unanimously, and there I was now waiting to know why I was called in. They began to ask me questions about myself and pretty soon they had my story. Finally they told me I would answer their purpose. I said I was sincerely glad, and asked what it was. Then one of them handed me an envelope, and said I would find the explanation inside. I was going to open it, but he said no, take it to my lodgings, and look it over carefully, and not be hasty or rash. I was puzzled, and wanted to discuss the matter a little further, but they didn't; so I took my leave, feeling hurt and insulted to be made the butt of what was apparently some kind of a practical joke, and yet obliged to put up with it, not being in circumstances to resent affronts from rich and strong folk.

I would have picked up the pear now and eaten it before all the world, but it was gone; so I had lost that by this unlucky business, and the thought of it did not soften my feeling towards those men. As soon as I was out of sight of that house I opened my envelope, and saw that it contained money! My opinion of those people changed, I can tell you! I lost not a moment, but shoved note and money into my vest pocket, and broke for the nearest cheap eating house. Well, how I did eat! When at last I couldn't hold any more, I took out my money and unfolded it, took one glimpse and nearly fainted. Five millions of dollars! Why, it made my head swim.

I must have sat there stunned and blinking at the note as much as a minute before I came rightly to myself again. The first thing

I noticed, then, was the landlord. His eye was on the note, and he was petrified. He was worshipping, with all his body and soul, but he looked as if he couldn't stir hand or foot. I took my cue in a moment, and did the only rational thing there was to do. I reached the note towards him, and said, carelessly:

"Give me the change, please."

Then he was restored to his normal condition, and made a thousand apologies for not being able to break the bill, and I couldn't get him to touch it. He wanted to look at it, and keep on looking at it; he couldn't seem to get enough of it to quench the thirst of his eye, but he shrank from touching it as if it had been something too sacred for poor common clay to handle. I said:

"I am sorry if it is an inconvenience, but I must insist. Please change it; I haven't anything else."

But he said that wasn't any matter; he was quite willing to let the trifle stand over till another time. I said I might not be in his neighborhood again for a good while; but he said it was of no consequence, he could wait, and, moreover, I could have anything I wanted, any time I chose, and let the account run as long as I pleased. He said he hoped he wasn't afraid to trust as rich a gentleman as I was, merely because I was of a merry disposition, and chose to play larks on the public in the matter of dress. By this time another customer was entering, and the landlord hinted to me to put the monster out of sight; then he bowed me all the way to the door, and I started straight for the house and those brothers, to correct the mistake which had been made before the police should hunt me up and help me do it. I was pretty nervous; in fact, pretty badly frightened, though, of course, I was no way in fault; but I knew men well enough to know that when they find they've given a tramp a million-pound bill when they thought it was a one-pounder, they are in a frantic rage against *him* instead of quarreling with their own near-sightedness, as they ought. As I approached the house my excitement began to abate, for all was quiet there, which made me feel pretty sure the blunder

was not discovered yet. I rang. The same servant appeared. I asked
for those gentlemen.

"They are gone." This in the lofty, cold way of that fellow's tribe.

"Gone? Gone where?"

"On a journey."

"But whereabouts?"

"To the Continent, I think."

"The Continent?"

"Yes, sir."

"Which way–by what route?"

"I can't say, sir."

"When will they be back?"

"In a month, they said."

"A month! Oh, this is awful! Give me some sort of idea of how
to get a word to them. It's of the last importance."

"I can't, indeed. I've no idea where they've gone, sir."

"Then I must see some member of the family."

"Family's away, too; been abroad months–in Egypt and India,
I think."

"Man, there's been an immense mistake made. They'll be back
before night. Will you tell them I've been here, and that I will
keep coming till it's all made right, and they needn't be afraid?"

"I'll tell them, if they come back, but I am not expecting them.
They said you would be here in an hour to make inquiries, but
I must tell you it's all right, they'll be here on time and expect you."

So I had to give it up and go away. What a riddle it all was!
I was like to lose my mind. They would be here "on time."
What could that mean? Oh, the letter would explain, maybe.
I had forgotten the letter; I got it out and read it. This is what
it said:

"You are an intelligent and honest man, as one may see by your
face. We conceive you to be poor and a stranger. Enclosed you will
find a sum of money. It is lent to you for thirty days, without interest.

Report at this house at the end of that time. I have a bet on you. If
I win it you shall have any situation that is in my gift – any, that is,
that you shall be able to prove yourself familiar with and competent
to fill."

No signature, no address, no date.

Well, here was a coil to be in! You are posted on what had
preceded all this, but I was not. It was just a deep, dark puzzle
to me. I hadn't the least idea what the game was, nor whether
harm was meant me or a kindness. I went into a park, and
sat down to try to think it out, and to consider what I had
best do.

At the end of an hour my reasonings had crystallized into
this verdict.

Maybe those men mean me well, maybe they mean me ill; no
way to decide that – let it go. They've got a game, or a scheme,
or an experiment, of some kind on hand; no way to determine
what it is – let it go. There's a bet on me; no way to find out what
it is – let it go. That disposes of the indeterminable quantities;
the remainder of the matter is tangible, solid, and may be classed
and labeled with certainty. If I ask the Bank of England to place
this bill to the credit of the man it belongs to, they'll do it, for
they know him, although I don't; but they will ask me how I
came in possession of it, and if I tell the truth, they'll put me in
the asylum, naturally, and a lie will land me in jail. The same
result would follow if I tried to bank the bill anywhere or to borrow money on it. I have got to carry this immense burden around
until those men come back, whether I want to or not. It is useless to me, as useless as a handful of ashes, and yet I must take
care of it, and watch over it, while I beg my living. I couldn't *give*
it away, if I should try, for neither honest citizen nor highwayman
would accept it or meddle with it for anything. Those brothers
are safe, because they can stop payment, and the Bank will make
them whole; but meantime I've got to do a month's suffering
without wages or profit – unless I help win that bet, whatever it

may be, and get that situation that I am promised. I *should* like to get that; men of their sort have situations in their gift that are worth having.

I got to thinking a good deal about that situation. My hopes began to rise high. Without doubt the salary would be large. It would begin in a month; after that I should be all right. Pretty soon I was feeling first-rate. By this time I was tramping the streets again. The sight of a tailor-shop gave me a sharp longing to shed my rags, and to clothe myself decently once more. Could I afford it? No; I had nothing in the world but a million pounds. So I forced myself to go on by. But soon I was drifting back again. The temptation persecuted me cruelly. I must have passed that shop back and forth six times during that manful struggle. At last I gave in; I had to. I asked if they had a misfit suit that had been thrown on their hands. The fellow I spoke to nodded his head towards another fellow, and gave me no answer. I went to the indicated fellow, and he indicated another fellow with *his* head, and no words. I went to him, and he said:

"'Tend to you presently."

I waited till he was done with what he was at, then he took me into a back room, and overhauled a pile of rejected suits, and selected the rattiest one for me. I put it on. It didn't fit, and wasn't in any way attractive, but it was new, and I was anxious to have it; so I didn't find any fault, but said, with some diffidence:

"It would be an accommodation to me if you could wait some days for the money. I haven't any small change about me."

The fellow worked up a most sarcastic expression of countenance, and said:

"Oh, you haven't? Well, of course, I didn't expect it. I'd only expect gentlemen like you to carry large change."

I was nettled, and said:

"My friend, you shouldn't judge a stranger always by the clothes he wears. I am quite able to pay for this suit; I simply didn't wish to put you to the trouble of changing a large note."

He modified his style a little at that, and said, though still with
something of an air:

"I didn't mean any particular harm, but as long as rebukes are
going, I might say it wasn't quite your affair to jump to the conclusion that we couldn't change any note that you might happen
to be carrying around. On the contrary, we *can*."

I handed the note to him, and said:

"Oh, very well; I apologize."

He received it with a smile, one of those large smiles which
goes all around over, and has folds in it, and wrinkles, and spirals,
and looks like the place where you have thrown a brick in a pond;
and then in the act of his taking a glimpse of the bill, this smile
froze solid, and turned yellow, and looked like those wavy, wormy
spreads of larva which you find hardened on little levels on the
side of Vesuvius. I never before saw a smile like that, and per-
petuated. The man stood there holding the bill, and looking like
that, and the proprietor hustled up to see what was the matter,
and said briskly:

"Well, what's up? what's the trouble? what's wanting?"

I said; "There isn't any trouble. I'm waiting for my change."

"Come, come; get him his change, Tod; get him his change."

Tod retorted: "Get him his change! It's easy to say, sir; but look
at the bill yourself."

The proprietor took a look, gave a low, eloquent whistle, then
made a dive for the pile of rejected clothing, and began to snatch
it this way and that, talking all the time excitedly, and as if
to himself:

"Sell an eccentric millionaire such an unspeakable suit as that!
Tod's a fool—a born fool. Always doing something like this. Drives
every millionaire away from this place, because he can't tell a millionaire from a tramp, and never could. Ah, here's the thing I am
after. Please get those things off, sir, and throw them in the fire.
Do me the favor to put on this shirt and this suit; it's just the
thing, the very thing—plain, rich, modest, and just ducally nobby;

made to order for a foreign prince—you may know him, sir, his Serene Highness the Hospodar of Halifax; and to leave it with us and take a mourning-suit because his mother was going to die—which she didn't. But that's all right; we can't always have things the way we—that is, they way they—there! trousers all right, they fit you to a charm, sir; now the waistcoat; aha, right again! now the coat—lord! look at that, now! Perfect—the whole thing! I never saw such a triumph in all my experience."

I expressed my satisfaction.

"Quite right, sir, quite right; it'll do for a make-shift. I'm bound to say. But wait till you see what we'll get up for you on your own measure. Come, Tod, book and pen; get at it. Length of leg, 32"—and so on. Before I could get in a word he had measured me, and was giving orders for dress suits, morning suits, shirts, and all sorts of things. When I got a chance I said:

"But my dear sir, I *can't* give these orders, unless you can wait indefinitely, or change the bill."

"Indefinitely! It's a weak word, sir, a weak word. Eternally—*that's* the word, sir. Tod, rush these things through, and send them to the gentleman's address without any waste of time. Let the minor customers wait. Set down the gentleman's address and—"

"I'm changing my quarters. I will drop in and leave the new address."

"Quite right, sir, quite right. One moment—let me show you out, sir. There—good day, sir, good day."

Well, don't you see what was bound to happen? I drifted naturally into buying whatever I wanted, and asking for change. Within a week I was sumptuously equipped with all needful comforts and luxuries, and was housed in an expensive private hotel in Hanover Square. I took my dinners there, but for breakfast I stuck by Harris's humble feeding house, where I had got my first meal on my million-pound bill. I was the making of Harris. The fact had gone all abroad that the foreign crank who carried million-pound bills in his vest pocket was the patron saint of the place.

That was enough. From being a poor, struggling, little hand-to-mouth enterprise, it had become celebrated, and over crowded with customers. Harris was so grateful that he forced loans upon me, and would not be denied; and so, pauper as I was, I had money to spend, and was living like the rich and the great. I judged that there was going to be a crash by and by, but I was in now and must swim across or drown. You see there was just that element of impending disaster to give a serious side, a sober side, yes, a tragic side, to a state of things which would otherwise have been purely ridiculous. In the night, in the dark, the tragedy part was always to the front, and always warning, always threatening; and so I moaned and tossed, and sleep was hard to find. But in the cheerful day-light the tragedy element faded out and disappeared, and I walked on air, and was happy to giddiness, to intoxication, you may say.

And it was natural; for I had become one of the notorieties of the metropolis of the world, and it turned my head, not just a little but a good deal. You could not take up a newspaper, English, Scotch, or Irish, without finding in it one or more references to the "vest-pocket million-pounder" and his latest doings and sayings. At first, in these mentions, I was at the bottom of the personal-gossip column; next, I was listed above the knights, next above the baronets, next above the barons, and so on, and so on, climbing steadily, as my notoriety augmented, until I reached the highest altitude possible, and there I remained, taking precedence of all dukes not royal, and of all eccesiastics except the primate of all England. But mind, this was not fame; as yet I had achieved only notoriety. Then came the climaxing stroke – the accolade, so to speak – which in a single instant transmuted the perishable dross of notoriety into the enduring gold of fame; *Punch* caricatured me! Yes, I was a made man now; my place was established. I might be joked about still, but reverently, not hilariously, not rudely; I could be smiled at, but not laughed at. The time for that had gone by. *Punch* pictured me all a-flutter with rags, dickering with a beef-eater for the Tower of London. Well, you can imagine how it was with a young fellow who had never been taken notice of before, and now all of a sudden couldn't say a thing that wasn't taken up and repeated everywhere; couldn't stir abroad without constantly overhearing the remark flying from lip to lip. "There he goes; that's him!" couldn't take his breakfast without a crowd to look on; couldn't appear in an opera-box without concentrating there the fire of a thousand lorgnettes. Why, I just swam in glory all day long—that is the amount of it.

You know, I even kept my old suit of rags, and every now and then appeared in them, so as to have the old pleasure of buying trifles, and being insulted, and then shooting the scoffer dead with the million-pound bill. But I couldn't keep that up. The illustrated papers made the outfit so familiar that when I went out in it I was at once recognized and followed by a crowd, and if I attempted a purchase the man would offer me his whole shop on credit before I could pull my note on him.

About the tenth day of my fame I went to fulfil my duty to my flag by paying my respects to the American minister. He received me with the enthusiasm proper in my case, upbraided me for being so tardy in my duty, and said that there was only one way to get his forgiveness, and that was to take the seat at his dinner-party that night made vacant by the illness of one of his guests. I said I would, and we got to talking. It turned out that he and my father had been schoolmates in boyhood, Yale students together later, and always warm friends up to my father's death. So then he required me to put in at his house all the odd time I might have to spare, and I was very willing, of course.

In fact, I was more than willing; I was glad. When the crash should come, he might somehow be able to save me from total destruction; I didn't know how, but he might think of a way, maybe. I couldn't venture to unbosom myself to him at this late date, a thing which I would have been quick to do in the beginning of this awful career of mine in London. No, I couldn't venture it now;

I was in too deep; that is, too deep for me to be risking revelations to so new a friend, though not clear beyond my depth, as
I looked at it. Because, you see, with all my borrowing, I was carefully keeping within my means – I mean within my salary. Of
course, I couldn't *know* what my salary was going to be, but
I had a good enough basis for an estimate in the fact, that if
I won the bet I was to have *choice* of any situation in that rich
old gentleman's gift provided I was competent – and I should certainly prove competent; I hadn't any doubt about that. And as
to the bet, I wasn't worrying about that; I had always been lucky.
Now my estimate of the salary was six hundred to a thousand
a year; say, six hundred for the first year, and so on up year by
year, till I struck the upper figure by proved merit. At present I
was only in debt for my first year's salary. Everybody had been
trying to lend me money, but I had fought off the most of them
on one pretext or another; so this indebtedness represented
only £300 borrowed money, the other £300 represented my
keep and my purchases. I believed my second year's salary would
carry me through the rest of the month if I went on being cautious and economical, and I intended to look sharply out for that.
My month ended, my employer back from his journey, I should
be all right once more, for I should at once divide the two years'
salary among my creditors by assignment, and get right down to
my work.

It was a lovely dinner-party of fourteen. The Duke and Duchess
of Shoreditch, and their daughter the Lady Anne-Grace-Eleanor-
Celeste-and-so-forth-and-so-forth-de-Bohun, the Earl and Coun-
tess of Newgate, Viscount Cheapside, Lord and Lady Blatherskite,
some untitled people of both sexes, the minister and his wife
and daughter, and his daughter's visiting friend, an English girl
of twenty-two, named Portia Langham, whom I fell in love within two minutes, and she with me – I could see it without glasses.
There was still another guest, an American – but I am a little ahead
of my story. While the people were still in the drawing-room,

whetting up for dinner, and coldly inspecting the late comers, the servant announced:

"Mr. Lloyd Hastings."

The moment the usual civilities were over, Hastings caught sight of me, and came straight with cordially outstretched hand; then stopped short when about to shake, and said, with an embarrassed look:

"I beg your pardon, sir, I thought I knew you."

"Why, you do know me, old fellow."

"No. Are *you* the – the –"

"Vest-pocket monster? I am, indeed. Don't be afraid to call me by my nickname; I'm used to it."

"Well, well, well, this is a surprise. Once or twice I've seen your own name coupled with the nickname, but it never occurred to me that *you* could be the Henry Adams referred to. Why, it isn't six months since you were clerking away for Blake Hopkins in Frisco on a salary, and sitting up nights on an extra allowance, helping me arrange and verify the Gould and Curry Extension papers and statistics. The idea of your being in London, and a vast millionaire, and a colossal celebrity! Why, it's the Arabian Nights come again. Man, I can't take it in at all; can't realize it; give me time to settle the whirl in my head."

"The fact is, Lloyd, you are no worse off than I am. I can't realize it myself."

"Dear me, it *is* stunning, now isn't it? Why, it's just three months today since we went to the Miners' restaurant –"

"No; the What Cheer."

"Right, it *was* the What Cheer; went there at two in the morning, and had a chop and coffee after a hard six-hours grind over those Extension papers, and I tried to persuade you to come to London with me, and offered to get leave of absence for you and pay all your expenses, and give you something over if I succeeded in making the sale; and you would not listen to me, said I wouldn't succeed, and you couldn't afford to lose the run of business and be no end of time getting the hang of things again when you got back home. And yet here you are. How odd it all is! How did you happen to come, and whatever *did* give you this incredible start?"

"Oh, just an accident. It's a long story—a romance, a body may say. I'll tell you all about it, but not now."

"When?"

"The end of this month."

"That's more than a fortnight yet. It's too much of a strain on a person's curiosity. Make it a week."

"I can't. You'll know why, by and by. But how's the trade getting along?"

His cheerfulness vanished like a breath, and he said with a sigh:

"You were a true prophet, Hal, a true prophet. I wish I hadn't come. I don't want to talk about it."

"But you must. You must come and stop with me tonight, when we leave here, and tell me all about it."

"Oh, may I? Are you in earnest?" and the water showed in his eyes.

"Yes; I want to hear the whole story, every word."

"I'm so grateful! Just to find a human interest once more, in some voice and in some eye, in me and affairs of mine, after what I've been through here—lord! I could go down on my knees for it!"

He gripped my hand hard, and braced up, and was all right and lively after that for the dinner—which didn't come off. No; the usual thing happened, the thing that is always happening under that vicious and aggravating English system—the matter of precedence couldn't be settled, and so there was no dinner. Englishmen always eat dinner before they go out to dinner, because *they* know the risks they are running; but nobody ever warns the stranger, and so he walks placidly into the trap. Of course, nobody was hurt this time, because we had all been to dinner, none of us being novices excepting Hastings, and he having been informed by the minister at the time that he invited him that in deference to the

English custom he had not provided any dinner. Everybody took
a lady and processioned down to the dining-room, because it is
usual to go through the motions; but there the dispute began.
The Duke of Shoreditch wanted to take precedence, and sit at
the head of the table, holding that he outranked a minister who
represented merely a nation and not a monarch; but I stood for
my rights, and refused to yield. In the gossip column I ranked
all dukes not royal, and said so, and claimed precedence of this
one. It couldn't be settled, of course, struggle as we might and
did, he finally (and injudiciously) trying to play birth and antiquity, and I "seeing" his Conqueror and "raising" him with Adam,
whose direct posterity I was, as shown by my name, while *he* was
of a collateral branch, as shown by *his,* and by his recent Nor-
man origin; so we all processioned back to the drawing-room again
and had a perpendicular lunch – plate of sardines and a strawberry, and you group yourself and stand up and eat it. Here the
religion of precedence is not so strenuous; the two persons of
highest rank chuck up a shilling, the one that wins has first go
at his strawberry, and the loser gets the shilling. The next two
chuck up, then the next two, and so on. After refreshment, tables
were brought, and we all played cribbage, sixpence a game. The
English never play any game for amusement. If they can't
make something or lose something – they don't care which – they
won't play.

We had a lovely time; certainly two of us had. Miss Langham
and I. I was so bewitched with her that I couldn't count my hands
if they went above a double sequence; and when I struck home
I never discovered it, and started up the outside row again, and
would have lost the game every time, only the girl did the same,
she being in just my condition, you see; and consequently neither
one of us ever got out, or cared to wonder why we didn't; we only
just knew we were happy, and didn't wish to know anything else,
and didn't want to be interrupted. And I *told* her – I did, indeed –
told her I loved her; and she – well, she blushed till her hair turned

red, but she liked it; she *said* she did. Oh, there was never such an evening! Every time I pegged I put on a postscript; every time she pegged she acknowledged receipt of it, counting the hands the same. Why, I couldn't even say "Two for his heels" without adding, "*My,* how sweet you do look!" and she would say, "Fifteen two, fifteen four, fifteen six, and a pair are eight, and eight are sixteen – *do* you think so?"– peeping out aslant from under her lashes, you know, so sweet and cunning. Oh, it was just *too*-too!

Well, I was perfectly honest and square with her; told her I hadn't a cent in the world but just the million-pound note she'd heard so much talk about, and *it* didn't belong to me, and that started her curiosity; and then I talked low, and told her the whole history right from the start, and it nearly killed her laughing. What in the nation she could find to laugh about *I* couldn't see, but there it was; every half-minute some new detail would fetch her, and I would have to stop as much as a minute and a half to give her a chance to settle down again. Why, she laughed herself lame – she did, indeed; I never saw anything like it. I mean I never saw a painful story – a story of a person's troubles and worries and fears – produce just *that* kind of effect before. So I loved her all the more, seeing she could be so cheerful when there wasn't anything to be cheerful about; for I might soon need that kind of wife, you know, the way things looked. Of course, I told her we should have to wait a couple of years, till I could catch up on my salary; but she didn't mind that, only she hoped I would be as careful as possible in the matter of expenses, and not let them run the least risk of trenching on our third year's pay. Then she began to get a little worried, and wondered if we were making any mistake, and starting the salary on a higher figure for the first year than I would get. This was good sense, and it made me feel a little less confident than I had been feeling before; but it gave me a good business idea, and I brought it frankly out.

"Portia, dear, would you mind going with me that day, when I confront those old gentlemen?"

She shrank a little, but said:

"N-o; if my being with you would help hearten you. But—would it be quite proper, do you think?"

"No, I don't know that it would—in fact, I'm afraid it wouldn't; but, you see, there's so *much* dependent upon it that—"

"Then I'll go anyway, proper or improper," she said, with a beautiful and generous enthusiasm. "Oh, I shall be so happy to think I'm helping!"

"Helping, dear? Why, you'll be doing it all. You're so beautiful and so lovely and so winning, that with you there I can pile our salary up till I break those good old fellows, and they'll never have the heart to struggle."

Sho! you should have seen the rich blood mount, and her happy eyes shine!

"You wicked flatterer! There isn't a word of truth in what you say, but still I'll go with you. Maybe it will teach you not to expect other people to look with your eyes."

Were my doubts dissipated? Was my confidence restored? You may judge by this fact: privately I raised my salary to twelve hundred the first year on the spot. But I didn't tell her; I saved it for a surprise.

All the way home I was in the clouds, Hastings talking, I not hearing a word. When he and I entered my parlor, he brought me to myself with his fervent appreciations of my manifold comforts and luxuries.

"Let me just stand here a little and look my fill. Dear me! it's a palace—it's just a palace! And in it everything a body *could* desire, including cosey coal fire and supper standing ready. Henry, it doesn't merely make me realize how rich you are; it makes me realize, to the bone, to the marrow, how poor I am—how poor I am, and how miserable, how defeated, routed, annihilated!"

Plague take it! this language gave me the cold shudders. It scared me broad awake, and made me comprehend that I was standing on a half-inch crust, with a crater underneath. *I* didn't know I had been dreaming—that is, I hadn't been allowing myself to know it for a while back; but *now*—oh, dear! Deep in debt, not a cent in the world, a lovely girl's happiness or woe in my hands, and nothing in front of me but a salary which might never—oh, *would* never—materialize! Oh, oh, oh! I am ruined past hope! nothing can save me!

"Henry, the mere unconsidered drippings of your daily income would—"

"Oh, my daily income! Here, down with this hot Scotch, and cheer up your soul. Here's with you! Or, no—you're hungry; sit down and—"

"Not a bite for me; I'm past it. I can't eat, these days; but I'll drink with you till I drop. Come!"

"Barrel for barrel, I'm with you! Ready? Here we go! Now, then, Lloyd, unreel your story while I brew."

"Unreel it? What, again?"

"Again? What do you mean by that?"

"Why, I mean do you want to hear it *over* again?"

"Do I want to hear it *over* again? This *is* a puzzler. Wait; don't take any more of that liquid. You don't need it."

"Look here, Henry, you alarm me. Didn't I tell you the whole story on the way here?"

"You?"

"Yes, I."

"I'll be hanged if I heard a word of it."

"Henry, this is a serious thing. It troubles me. What did you take up yonder at the minister's?"

Then it all flashed on me, and I owned up like a man.

"I took the dearest girl in this world—prisoner!"

So then he came with a rush, and we shook, and shook, and shook till our hands ached; and he didn't blame me for not having heard a word of a story which had lasted while we walked three miles. He just sat down them, like the patient, good fellow he was, and told it all over again. Synopsized, it amounted to this: He had come to England with what he thought was a grand opportunity; he had on "option" to sell the Gould and Curry Extension for the "locators" of it, and keep all he could get over a million dollars. He had worked hard, had pulled every wire he knew of, had left no honest expedient untried, had spent nearly all the money he had in the world, had not been able to get a solitary capitalist to listen to him, and his option would run out at the end of the month. In a word, he was ruined. Then he jumped up and cried out:

"Henry, you can save me! You can save me, and you're the only man in the universe that can. Will you do it? *Won't* you do it?"

"Tell me how. Speak out, my boy."

"Give me a million and my passage home for my 'option'! Don't, *don't* refuse!"

I was in a kind of agony. I was right on the point of coming out with the words, "Lloyd, I'm a pauper myself – absolutely penniless, and in *debt*!" But a white-hot idea came flaming through my head, and I gripped my jaws together, and calmed myself down till I was as cold as a capitalist. Then I said, in a commercial and self-possessed way:

"I will save you, Lloyd –"

"Then I'm already saved! God be merciful to you forever! If ever I –"

"Let me finish, Lloyd. I will save you, but not in that way; for that would not be fair to you, after your hard word, and the risks you've run. I don't need to buy mines; I can keep my capital moving, in a commercial center like London, without that; it's what I'm at, all the time; but here is what I'll do. I know all about that mine, of course; I know its immense value, and can swear to it if anybody wishes it. You shall sell out inside of the fortnight for three millions cash, using my name freely, and we'll divide, share and share alike."

Do you know, he would have danced the furniture to kindling-wood in his insane joy, and broken everything on the place, if I hadn't tripped him up and tied him.

Then he lay there, perfectly happy, saying:

"I may use your name! Your name – think of it! Man, they'll flock in droves, these rich Londoners; they'll *fight* for that stock! I'm a made man, I'm a made man forever, and I'll never forget you as long as I live!"

In less than twenty-four hours London was abuzz! I hadn't anything to do, day after day, but sit at home, and say to all comers:

"Yes; I told him to refer to me. I know the man, and I know the mine. His character is above reproach, and the mine is worth far more than he asks for it."

Meantime I spent all my evenings at the minister's with Portia. I didn't say a word to her about the mine; I saved it for a surprise. We talked salary; never anything but salary and love; sometimes love, sometimes salary, sometimes love and salary together. And my! the interest the minister's wife and daughter took in our little affair, and the endless ingenuities they invented to save us from interruption, and to keep the minister in the dark and unsuspicious – well, it was just lovely of them!

When the month was up at last, I had a million dollars to my credit in the London and County Bank, and Hastings was fixed in the same way. Dressed at my level best, I drove by the house in Portland Place, judged by the look of things that my birds were home again, went on towards the minister's and got my precious, and we started back, talking salary with all our might. She was so excited and anxious that it made her just intolerably beautiful. I said:

"Dearie, the way you're looking it's a crime to strike for a salary a single penny under three thousand a year."

"Henry, Henry, you'll ruin us!"

"Don't you be afraid. Just keep up those looks, and trust to me. It'll all come out right."

So, as it turned out, I had to keep bolstering up *her* courage all the way. She kept pleading with me, and saying:

"Oh, please remember that if we ask for too much we may

get no salary at all; and then what will become of us, with no way in the world to earn our living?"

We were ushered in by that same servant, and there they were, the two old gentlemen. Of course, they were surprised to see that wonderful creature with me, but I said:

"It's all right, gentlemen; she is my future stay and helpmate."

And I introduced them to her, and called them by name. It didn't surprise them; they knew I would know enough to consult the directory. They seated us, and were very polite to me, and very solicitous to relieve her from embarrassment, and put her as much at her ease as they could. Then I said:

"Gentlemen, I am ready to report."

"We are glad to hear it," said my man, "for now we can decide the bet which my brother Abel and I made. If you have won for me, you shall have any situation in my gift. Have you the million-pound note?"

"Here it is, sir," and I handed it to him.

"I've won!" he shouted, and slapped Abel on the back. "*Now* what do you say, brother?"

"I say he *did* survive, and I've lost twenty thousand pounds. I—I never would have believed it."

"I've a further report to make," I said, "and a pretty long one. I want you to let me come soon, and detail my whole month's history; and I promise you it's worth hearing. Meantime, take a look at that."

"What, man! Certificate of deposit for £200,000. Is it yours?"

"Mine. I earned it by thirty days' judicious use of that little loan you let me have. And the only use I made of it was to buy trifles and offer the bill in change."

"Come, this is astonishing! It's incredible, man!"

"Never mind, I'll prove it. Don't take my word unsupported."

But now Portia's turn was come to be surprised. Her eyes were spread wide, and she said:

"Henry, is that really your money? Have you been fibbing to me?"

"I have, indeed, dearie. But you'll forgive me, I know."

She put up an arch pout, and said:

"Don't you be so sure. You are a naughty thing to deceive me so!"

"Oh, you'll get over it, sweetheart, you'll get over it; it was only fun, you know. Come, lets be going."

"But wait, wait! The situation, you know. I want to give you the situation," said my man.

"Well," I said, "I'm just as grateful as I can be, but really I don't want one."

"But you can have the very choicest one in my gift."

"Thanks again, with all my heart; but I don't even want *that* one."

"Henry, I'm ashamed of you. You don't half thank the good gentleman. May I do it for you?"

"Indeed, you shall, dear, if you can improve it. Let us see you try."

She walked to the man, got up in his lap, put her arm round his neck, and kissed him right on the mouth. Then the two old gentlemen shouted with laughter, but I was dumfounded, just petrified, as you may say. Portia said:

"Papa, he has said you haven't a situation in your gift that he'd take; and I feel just as hurt as –"

"My darling, is that your papa?"

"Yes; he's my step-papa, and the dearest one that ever was. You understand now, don't you, why I was able to laugh when you told me at the minister's, not knowing my relationships, what trouble and worry papa's and Uncle Abel's scheme was giving you?"

Of course, I spoke right up now, without any fooling, and went straight to the point.

"Oh, my dearest dear sir, I want to take back what I said. You *have* got a situation open that I want."

"Name it."

"Son-in-law."

"Well, well, well! But you know, if you haven't ever served in that capacity, you, of course, can't furnish recommendations of a sort to satisfy the conditions of the contract, and so –"

"Try me – oh, do, I beg of you! Only just try me thirty or forty years, and if –"

"Oh, well, all right; it's but a little thing to ask, take her along."

Happy, we two? There are not words enough in the unabridged to describe it. And when London got the whole history, a day or two later, of my month's adventures with that bank-note, and how they ended, did London talk, and have a good time? Yes.

My Portia's papa took that friendly and hospitable bill back to the Bank of England and cashed it; then the Bank canceled it and made him a present of it, and he gave it to us at our wedding, and it has always hung in its frame in the sacredest place in our home ever since. For it gave me my Portia. But for it I could not have remained in London, would not have appeared at the minister's, never should have met her. And so I always say, "Yes, it's a million-pounder, as you see; but it never made but one purchase in its life, and *then* got the article for only about a tenth part of its value."

EXTRACTS FROM ADAM'S DIARY

Translated from the original Ms.

The original version of this story, "Adam's Diary," was composed
sometime before the spring of 1893 when Twain desperately
needed money. Charles and Irving Underhill came to Twain
looking for a humorous piece involving Niagara Falls. Although
he originally resisted the offer, Twain realized that he could adapt
his unpublished "Adam's Diary" by relocating the Garden of Eden
to Niagara Falls. The finished version appeared in *The Niagara
Book*, published by Underhill and Nichols in Buffalo in 1893.
Twain cut all the references to Niagara Falls when the story
appeared in the London edition of *Tom Sawyer, Detective* in 1897.
The original version was later reprinted in 1931 along with
"Eve's Diary" as *The Private Lives of Adam and Eve*.

–Editor

*[NOTE.–I translated a portion of this diary some years ago, and a
friend of mine printed a few copies in an incomplete form, but the public
never got them. Since then I have deciphered some more of Adam's hiero-
glyphics, and think he has now become sufficiently important as a public
character to justify this publication.–M.T.]*

Monday

This new creature with the long hair is a good deal in the way.
It is always hanging around and following me about. I don't like
this; I am not used to company. I wish it would stay with the other
animals. . . . Cloudy today, wind in the east; think we shall have
rain. . . . *We?* Where did I get that word? . . . I remember now—
the new creature uses it.

Tuesday

Been examining the great waterfall. It is the finest thing on
the estate, I think. The new creature calls it Niagara Falls—why,

I am sure I do not know. Says it *looks* like Niagara Falls. That is
not a reason; it is mere waywardness and imbecility. I get no chance
to name anything myself. The new creature names everything that
comes along, before I can get in a protest. And always that same
pretext is offered – it *looks* like the thing. There is the dodo, for
instance. Says the moment one looks at it one sees at a glance
that it "looks like a dodo." It will have to keep that name, no doubt.
It wearies me to fret about it, and it does no good, anyway. Dodo!
It looks no more like a dodo than I do.

Wednesday

Built me a shelter against the rain, but could not have it to
myself in peace. The new creature intruded. When I tried to put
it out it shed water out of the holes it looks with, and wiped it
away with the back of its paws, and made a noise such as some
of the other animals make when they are in distress. I wish it
would not talk; it is always talking. That sounds like a cheap fling
at the poor creature, a slur; but I do not mean it so. I have heard
the human voice before, and any new and strange sound intruding itself here upon the solemn hush of these dreaming solitudes
offends my ear and seems a false note. And this new sound is
so close to me; it is right at my shoulder, right at my ear, first
on one side and then on the other, and I am used only to sounds
that are more or less distant from me.

Friday

The naming goes recklessly on, in spite of anything I can do.
I had a very good name for the estate, and it was musical and
pretty – Garden-of-Eden. Privately, I continue to call it that, but not
any longer publicly. The new creature says it is all woods and
rocks and scenery, and therefore has no resemblance to a
garden. Says it *looks* like a park, and does not look like anything
but a park. Consequently, without consulting me, it has been

new-named–Niagara Falls Park. This is sufficiently high-handed, it seems to me. And already there is a sign up:

```
┌─────────────┐
│  KEEP OFF   │
│  THE GRASS  │
└─────────────┘
```

My life is not as happy as it was.

Saturday

The new creature eats too much fruit. We are going to run short, most likely. "We" again – that is *its* word; mine too, now, from hearing it so much. Good deal of fog this morning. I do not go out in the fog myself. The new creature does. It goes out in all weathers, and stumps right in with its muddy feet. And talks. It used to be so pleasant and quiet here.

Sunday

Pulled through. This day is getting to be more and more trying. It was selected and set apart last November as a day of rest. I already had six of them per week, before. This morning found the new creature trying to clod apples out of that forbidden tree.

Monday

The new creature says its name is Eve. That is all right, I have no objections. Says it is to call it by when I want it to come. I said it was superfluous, then. The word evidently raised me in its respect; and indeed it is a large, good word, and will bear repetition. It says it is not an It, it is a She. This is probably doubtful; yet it is all one to me; what she is were nothing to me if she would but go by herself and not talk.

Tuesday

She has littered the whole estate with execrable names and offensive signs:

☞ THIS WAY TO THE WHIRLPOOL.

☞ THIS WAY TO GOAT ISLAND.

☞ CAVE OF THE WINDS THIS WAY.

She says this park would make a tidy summer resort, if there was any custom for it. Summer resort – another invention of hers – just words, without any meaning. What is a summer resort? But it is best not to ask her, she has such a rage for explaining.

Friday

She has taken to beseeching me to stop going over the Falls. What harm does it do? Says it makes her shudder. I wonder why. I have always done it – always liked the plunge, and the excitement, and the coolness. I supposed it was what the Falls were for. They have no other use that I can see, and they must have been made for something. She says they were only made for scenery – like the rhinoceros and the mastodon.

I went over the Falls in a barrel – not satisfactory to her. Went over in a tub – still not satisfactory. Swam the Whirlpool and the Rapids in a fig-leaf suit. It got much damaged. Hence, tedious complaints about my extravagance. I am too much hampered here. What I need is change of scene.

Saturday

I escaped last Tuesday night, and travelled two days, and built me another shelter, in a secluded place, and obliterated my tracks as well as I could, but she hunted me out by means of a beast which she has tamed and calls a wolf, and came making that pitiful noise again, and shedding that water out of the places she looks with. I was obliged to return with her, but will presently emigrate again, when occasion offers. She engages herself in many foolish things: among others, trying to study out why the animals called lions and tigers live on grass and flowers, when, as she says, the sort of teeth they wear would indicate that they were intended to eat each other. This is foolish, because to do that would be to kill each other, and that would introduce what, as I understand it, is called "death"; and death, as I have been told, has not yet entered the Park. Which is a pity, on some accounts.

Sunday
Pulled through.

Monday
I believe I see what the week is for: it is to give time to rest up from the weariness of Sunday. It seems a good idea.... She has been climbing that tree again. Clodded her out of it. She said nobody was looking. Seems to consider that a sufficient justification for chancing any dangerous thing. Told her that. The word justification moved her admiration – and envy too, I thought. It is a good word.

Tuesday
She told me she was made out of a rib taken from my body. This is at least doubtful, if not more than that. I have not missed any rib.... She is in much trouble about the buzzard; says grass does not agree with it; is afraid she can't raise it; thinks it was intended to live on decayed flesh. The buzzard must get along the best it can with what is provided. We cannot overturn the whole scheme to accommodate the buzzard.

Saturday
She fell in the pond yesterday, when she was looking at herself in it, which she is always doing. She nearly strangled, and

said it was most uncomfortable. This made her sorry for the creatures which live in there, which she calls fish, for she continues
to fasten names on to things that don't need them and don't come
when they are called by them, which is a matter of no consequence to her, as she is such a numskull anyway; so she got a
lot of them out and brought them in last night and put them in
my bed to keep warm, but I have noticed them now and then
all day, and I don't see that they are any happier there than they
were before, only quieter. When night comes I shall throw them
outdoors. I will not sleep with them again, for I find them clammy
and unpleasant to lie among when a person hasn't anything on.

Sunday
    Pulled through.

Tuesday
    She has taken up with a snake now. The other animals are
glad, for she was always experimenting with them and bothering
them; and I am glad, because the snake talks, and this enables
me to get a rest.

Friday
    She says the snake advises her to try the fruit of that tree, and
says the result will be a great and fine and noble education. I told
her there would be another result, too – it would introduce death
into the world. That was a mistake – it had been better to keep
the remark to myself; it only gave her an idea – she could save
the sick buzzard, and furnish fresh meat to the despondent lions
and tigers. I advised her to keep away from the tree. She said she
wouldn't. I foresee trouble. Will emigrate.

Wednesday
    I have had a variegated time. I escaped that night, and rode
a horse all night as fast as he could go, hoping to get clear out

of the Park and hide in some other country before the trouble should begin; but it was not to be. About an hour after sunup, as I was riding through a flowery plain where thousands of animals were grazing, slumbering, or playing with each other, according to their wont, all of a sudden they broke into a tempest of frightful noises, and in one moment the plain was in a frantic commotion and every beast was destroying its neighbor. I knew what it meant – Eve had eaten that fruit, and death was come into the world. . . . The tigers ate my horse, paying no attention when I ordered them to desist, and they would even have eaten me if I had stayed – which I didn't, but went away in much haste. . . . I found this place, outside the Park, and was fairly comfortable for a few days, but she has found me out. Found me out, and has named the place Tonawanda – says it *looks* like that. In fact, I was not sorry she came, for there are but meagre pickings here, and she brought some of those apples. I was obliged to eat them, I was so hungry. It was against my principles, but I find that principles have no real force except when one is well fed. . . . She came curtained in boughs and bunches of leaves, and when I asked her what she meant by such nonsense, and snatched them away and threw them down, she tittered and blushed. I had never seen a person titter and blush before, and to me it seemed unbecoming and idiotic. She said I would soon know how it was myself. This was correct. Hungry as I was, I laid down the apple half eaten – certainly the best one I ever saw, considering the lateness of the season – and arrayed myself in the discarded boughs and branches, and then spoke to her with some severity and ordered her to go and get some more and not make such a spectacle of herself. She did it, and after this we crept down to where the wildbeast battle had been, and collected some skins, and I made her patch together a couple of suits proper for public occasions. They are uncomfortable, it is true, but stylish, and that is the main point about clothes. . . . I find she is a good deal of a companion. I see I should be lonesome and depressed without her, now that

I have lost my property. Another thing, she says it is ordered that we work for our living hereafter. She will be useful. I will superintend.

Ten Days Later

She accuses *me* of being the cause of our disaster! She says, with apparent sincerity and truth, that the Serpent assured her that the forbidden fruit was not apples, it was chestnuts. I said I was innocent, then, for I had not eaten any chestnuts. She said the Serpent informed her that "chestnut" was a figurative term meaning an aged and mouldy joke. I turned pale at that, for I have made many jokes to pass the weary time, and some of them could have been of that sort, though I had honestly supposed that they were new when I made them. She asked me if I had made one just at the time of the catastrophe. I was obliged to admit that I had made one to myself, though not aloud. It was this. I was thinking about the Falls, and I said to myself, "How wonderful it is to see that vast body of water tumble down there!" Then in an instant a bright thought flashed into my head, and I let it fly, saying, "It would be a deal more wonderful to see it tumble *up* there!"—and I was just about to kill myself with laughing at it when all nature broke loose in war and death, and I had to flee for my life. "There," she said, with triumph, "that is just it; the Serpent mentioned that very jest, and called it the First Chestnut, and said it was coeval with the creation." Alas, I am indeed to blame. Would that I were not witty; oh, would that I had never had that radiant thought!

Next Year

We have named it Cain. She caught it while I was up country trapping on the North Shore of the Erie; caught it in the timber a couple of miles from our dug-out—or it might have been four, she isn't certain which. It resembles us in some ways, and may be a relation. That is what she thinks, but this is an error, in my judgement. The difference in size warrants the conclusion that it is a different and new kind of animal – a fish, perhaps, though when I put it in the water to see, it sank, and she plunged in and snatched it out before there was opportunity for the experiment to determine the matter. I still think it is a fish, but she is indifferent about what it is, and will not let me have it to try. I do not understand this. The coming of the creature seems to have changed her whole nature and made her unreasonable about experiments. She thinks more of it than she does of any of the other animals, but is not able to explain why. Her mind is disordered – everything shows it. Sometimes she carries the fish in her arms half the night when it complains and wants to get to the water. At such times the water comes out of the places in her face that she looks out of, and she pats the fish on the back and makes soft sounds with her mouth to soothe it, and betrays sorrow and solicitude in a hundred ways. I have never seen her do like this with any other fish, and it troubles me greatly. She used to carry the young tigers around so, and play with them, before we lost our property; but it was only play; she never took on about them like this when their dinner disagreed with them.

Sunday

She doesn't work Sundays, but lies around all tired out, and likes to have the fish wallow over her; and she makes fool noises to amuse it, and pretends to chew its paws, and that makes it laugh. I have not seen a fish before that could laugh. This makes me doubt. . . . I have come to like Sunday myself. Superintending all the week tires a body so. There ought to be more Sundays. In the old days they were tough, but now they come handy.

Wednesday

It isn't a fish. I cannot quite make out what it is. It makes curious, devilish noises when not satisfied, and says "goo-goo" when it is. It is not one of us, for it doesn't walk; it is not a bird, for it doesn't fly; it is not a frog, for it doesn't hop; it is not a snake, for it doesn't crawl; I feel sure it is not a fish, though I cannot get a chance to find out whether it can swim or not. It merely lies around, and mostly on its back, with its feet up. I have not seen any other animal do that before. I said I believed it was an enigma, but she only admired the word without understanding it. In my judgment it is either an enigma or some kind of a bug. If it dies, I will take it apart and see what its arrangements are. I never had a thing perplex me so.

Three Months Later

The perplexity augments instead of diminishing. I sleep but little. It has ceased from lying around, and goes about on its four legs now. Yet it differs from the other four-legged animals in that its front legs are unusually short, consequently this causes the main part of its person to stick up uncomfortably high in the air, and this is not attractive. It is built much as we are, but its method of travelling shows that it is not of our breed. The short front legs and long hind ones indicate that it is of the kangaroo family, but it is a marked variation of the species, since the true kangaroo hops, whereas this one never does. Still, it is a curious and interesting variety, and has not been catalogued before. As I discovered it, I have felt justified in securing the credit of the discovery by attaching my name to it, and hence have called it *Kangaroorum Adamiensis*.... It must have been a young one when it came, for it has grown exceedingly since. It must be five times as big, now, as it was then, and when discontented is able to make from twenty-two to thirty-eight times the noise it made at first. Coercion does not modify this, but has the contrary effect. For this reason I discontinued the system. She reconciles it by persuasion, and by giving it things which she had previously told it she wouldn't give it. As already observed, I was not at home when it first came, and she told me she found it in the woods. It seems odd that it should be the only one, yet it must be so, for I have worn myself out these many weeks trying to find another one to add to my collection, and for this one to play with; for surely then it would be quieter, and we could tame it more easily. But I find none, nor any vestige of any; and strangest of all, no tracks. It has to live on the ground, it cannot help itself; therefore, how does it get about without leaving a track? I have set a dozen traps, but they do no good. I catch all small animals except that one; animals that merely go into the trap out of curiosity, I think, to see what the milk is there for. They never drink it.

Three Months Later

The kangaroo still continues to grow, which is very strange and perplexing. I never knew one to be so long getting its growth. It has fur on its head now; not like kangaroo fur, but exactly like our hair, except that it is much finer and softer, and instead of being black is red. I am like to lose my mind over the capricious and harassing developments of this unclassifiable zoological freak. If I could catch another one—but that is hopeless; it is a new variety, and the only sample; this is plain. But I caught a true kangaroo and brought it in, thinking that this one, being lonesome, would rather have that for company than have no kin at all, or any animal it could feel a nearness to or get sympathy from in its forlorn condition here among strangers who do not know its ways or habits, or what to do to make it feel that it is among friends; but it was a mistake—it went into such fits at the sight of the kangaroo that I was convinced it had never seen one before. I pity the poor noisy little animal, but there is nothing I can do to make it happy. If I could tame it—but that is out of the question; the more I try, the worse I seem to make it. It grieves me to the heart to see it in its little storms of sorrow and passion. I wanted to let it go, but she wouldn't hear of it. That seemed cruel and not like her; and yet she may be right. It might be lonelier than ever; for since I cannot find another one, how could *it*?

Five Months Later

It is not a kangaroo. No, for it supports itself by holding to her finger, and thus goes a few steps on its hind legs, and then falls down. It is probably some kind of a bear; and yet it has no tail – as yet – and no fur, except on its head. It still keeps on growing – that is a curious circumstance, for bears get their growth earlier than this. Bears are dangerous – since our catastrophe – and I shall not be satisfied to have this one prowling about the place much longer without a muzzle on. I have offered to get her a kangaroo if she would let this one go, but it did no good – she is determined to run us into all sorts of foolish risks, I think. She was not like this before she lost her mind.

A Fortnight Later

I examined its mouth. There is no danger yet; it has only one tooth. It has no tail yet. It makes more noise now than it ever did before – and mainly at night. I have moved out. But I shall go over, mornings, to breakfast, and to see if it has more teeth. If it gets a mouthful of teeth, it will be time for it to go, tail or no tail, for a bear does not need a tail in order to be dangerous.

Four Months Later

I have been off hunting and fishing a month, up in the region that she calls Buffalo; I don't know why, unless it is because there are not any buffaloes there. Meantime the bear has learned to paddle around by itself on its hind legs, and says "poppa" and "momma." It is certainly a new species. This resemblance to words may be purely accidental, of course, and may have no purpose or meaning; but even in that case it is still extraordinary, and is a thing which no other bear can do. This imitation of speech, taken together with general absence of fur and entire absence of tail, sufficiently indicates that this is a new kind of bear. The further study of it will be exceedingly interesting. Meantime I will go off on a far expedition among the forests of the North and make an exhaustive search. There must certainly be another one somewhere, and this one will be less dangerous when it has company of its own species. I will go straightway; but I will muzzle this one first.

Three Months Later

It has been a weary, weary hunt, yet I have had no success. In the mean time, without stirring from the home estate, she has caught another one! I never saw such luck. I might have hunted these woods a hundred years, I never should have run across that thing.

Next Day

I have been comparing the new one with the old one, and it is perfectly plain that they are the same breed. I was going to stuff one of them for my collection, but she is prejudiced against it for some reason or other; so I have relinquished the idea, though I think it is a mistake. It would be an irreparable loss to science of they should get away. The old one is tamer than it was, and can laugh and talk like the parrot, having learned this, no doubt, from being with the parrot so much, and having the imitative faculty in a highly developed degree. I shall be astonished if it turns out to be a new kind of parrot; and yet I ought not to be astonished, for it has already been everything else it could think of, since those first days when it was a fish. The new one is as ugly now as the old one was at first; has the same sulphur-and-raw-meat complexion and the same singular head without any fur on it. She calls it Abel.

Ten Years Later

They are boys; we found it out long ago. It was their coming in that small, immature shape that puzzled us; we were not used to it. There are some girls now. Abel is a good boy, but if Cain had stayed a bear it would have improved him. After all these

years, I see that I was mistaken about Eve in the beginning; it
is better to live outside the Garden with her than inside it without
her. At first I thought she talked too much; but now I should be
sorry to have that voice fall silent and pass out of my life. Blessed
be the chestnut that brought us near together and taught me to
know the goodness of her heart and the sweetness of her spirit!

FENIMORE COOPER'S
LITERARY OFFENSES

Written during the winter of 1893–94, this satirical essay has
been proclaimed one of Twain's funniest works. "Fenimore
Cooper's Literary Offenses" was later collected in *How To
Tell a Story and Other Essays,* published in 1897
by Harper and Brothers, New York.

– Editor

The Pathfinder and The Deerslayer *stand at the head of Cooper's
novels as artistic creations. There are others of his works which contain
parts as perfect as are to be found in these, and scenes even more thrill-
ing. Not one can be compared with either of them as a finished whole.*

*The defects in both of these tales are comparatively slight. They were
pure works of art.* – Prof. Lounsbury.

The five tales reveal an extraordinary fulness of invention.

. . . One of the very greatest characters in fiction, "Natty Bumppo." . . .

*The craft of the woodsman, the tricks of the trapper, all the delicate
art of the forest, were familiar to Cooper from his youth up.* – Prof. Brander
Matthews.

*Cooper is the greatest artist in the domain of romantic fiction yet
produced by America.* – Wilkie Collins.

It seems to me that it was far from right for the Professor of
English Literature in Yale, the Professor of English Literature in
Columbia, and Wilkie Collins, to deliver opinions on Cooper's
literature without having read some of it. It would have been
much more decorous to keep silent and let persons talk who have
read Cooper.

Cooper's art has some defects. In one place in *Deerslayer,* and
in the restricted space of two-thirds of a page, Cooper has scored
114 offences against literary art out of a possible 115. It breaks
the record.

There are nineteen rules governing literary art in the domain of romantic fiction – some say twenty-two. In *Deerslayer* Cooper violated eighteen of them. These eighteen require:

1. That a tale shall accomplish something and arrive somewhere. But the *Deerslayer* tale accomplishes nothing and arrives in the air.

2. They require that the episodes of a tale shall be necessary parts of the tale, and shall help to develop it. But as the *Deerslayer* tale is not a tale, and accomplishes nothing and arrives nowhere, the episodes have no rightful place in the work, since there was nothing for them to develop.

3. They require that the personages in a tale shall be alive, except in the case of corpses, and that always the reader shall be able to tell the corpses from the others. But this detail has often been overlooked in the *Deerslayer* tale.

4. They require that the personages in a tale, both dead and alive, shall exhibit a sufficient excuse for being there. But this detail also has been overlooked in the *Deerslayer* tale.

5. They require that when the personages of a tale deal in conversation, the talk shall sound like human talk, and be talk such as human beings would be likely to talk in the given circumstances, and have a discoverable meaning, also a discoverable purpose, and a show of relevancy, and remain in the neighborhood of the subject in hand, and be interesting to the reader, and help out the tale, and stop when the people cannot think of anything more to say. But this requirement has been ignored from the beginning of the *Deerslayer* tale to the end of it.

6. They require that when the author describes the character of a personage in his tale, the conduct and conversation of that personage shall justify said description. But this law gets little or no attention in the *Deerslayer* tale, as "Natty Bumppo's" case will amply prove.

7. They require that when a personage talks like an illustrated, gilt-edged, tree-calf, hand-tooled, seven-dollar Friendship's Offering

in the beginning of a paragraph, he shall not talk like a negro minstrel in the end of it. But this rule is flung down and danced upon in the *Deerslayer* tale.

8. They require that crass stupidities shall not be played upon the reader as "the craft of the woodsman, the delicate art of the forest," either by the author or the people in the tale. But this rule is persistently violated in the *Deerslayer* tale.

9. They require that the personages of a tale shall confine themselves to possibilities and let miracles alone; or, if they venture a miracle, the author must so plausibly set it forth as to make it look possible and reasonable. But these rules are not respected in the *Deerslayer* tale.

10. They require that the author shall make the reader feel a deep interest in the personages of his tale and in their fate; and that he shall make the reader love the good people in the tale and hate the bad ones. But the reader of the *Deerslayer* tale dislikes the good people in it, is indifferent to the others, and wishes they would all get drowned together.

11. They require that the characters in a tale shall be so clearly defined that the reader can tell beforehand what each will do in a given emergency. But in the *Deerslayer* tale this rule is vacated.

In addition to these large rules there are some little ones. These require that the author shall

12. *Say* what he is proposing to say, not merely come near it.

13. Use the right word, not its second cousin.

14. Eschew surplusage.

15. Not omit necessary details.

16. Avoid slovenliness of form.

17. Use good grammar.

18. Employ a simple and straightforward style.

Even these seven are coldly and persistently violated in the *Deerslayer* tale.

Cooper's gift in the way of invention was not a rich endowment; but such as it was he liked to work it, he was pleased with the effects, and indeed he did some quite sweet things with it. In his little box of stage properties he kept six or eight cunning devices, tricks, artifices for his savages and woodsmen to deceive and circumvent each other with, and he was never so happy as when he was working these innocent things and seeing them go. A favorite one was to make a moccasined person tread in the tracks of the moccasined enemy, and thus hide his own trail. Cooper wore out barrels and barrels of moccasins in working that trick. Another stage-property that he pulled out of his box pretty frequently was his broken twig. He prized his broken twig above all the rest of his effects, and worked it the hardest. It is a restful chapter in any book of his when somebody doesn't step on a dry twig and alarm all the reds and whites for two hundred yards around. Every time a Cooper person is in peril, and absolute silence is worth four dollars a minute, he is sure to step on a dry twig. There may be a hundred handier things to step on, but that wouldn't satisfy Cooper. Cooper requires him to turn out and find a dry twig; and if he can't do it, go and borrow one. In fact the Leather Stocking Series ought to have been called the Broken Twig Series.

I am sorry there is not room to put in a few dozen instances of the delicate art of the forest, as practiced by Natty Bumppo and some of the other Cooperian experts. Perhaps we may venture two or three samples. Cooper was a sailor—a naval officer; yet he gravely tells us how a vessel, driving toward a lee shore in a gale, is steered for a particular spot by her skipper because he knows of an *undertow* there which will hold her back against the gale and save her. For just pure woodcraft, or sailorcraft, or whatever it is, isn't that neat? For several years Cooper was daily in the society of artillery, and he ought to have noticed that when a cannon-ball strikes the ground it either buries itself or skips a hundred feet or so; skips a gain a hundred feet or so—and so on, till it finally gets tired and rolls. Now in one place he loses some "females"—as he always calls women—in the edge of a wood near a plain at night in a fog, on purpose to give Bumppo a chance to show off the delicate art of the forest before the reader. These mislaid people are hunting for a fort. They hear a cannon-blast, and a cannon-ball presently comes rolling into the wood and stops at their feet. To the females this suggests nothing. The case is very different with the admirable Bumppo. I wish I may never know peace again if he doesn't strike out promptly and *follow the track* of that cannon-ball across the plain through the dense fog and find the fort. Isn't it a daisy? If Cooper had any real knowledge of Nature's ways of doing things, he had a most delicate art in concealing the fact. For instance: one of his acute Indian experts, Chingachgook (pronounced Chicago, I think), has lost the trail of a person he is tracking through the forest. Apparently that trail is hopelessly lost. Neither you nor I could ever have guessed out the way to find it. It was very different with Chicago. Chicago was not stumped for long. He turned a running stream out of its course, and there, in the slush in its old bed, were that person's moccasin-tracks. The current did not wash them away, as it would have done in all other like cases—no, even the eternal laws of Nature have to vacate when Cooper wants to put up a delicate job of wood-craft on the reader.

We must be a little wary when Brander Matthews tells us that Cooper's books "reveal an extraordinary fullness of invention." As a rule, I am quite willing to accept Brander Matthews's literary judgments and applaud his lucid and graceful phrasing of them; but that particular statement needs to be taken with a few tons of salt. Bless your heart, Cooper hadn't any more invention than a horse; and I don't mean a high-class horse, either; I mean a clothes-horse. It would be very difficult to find a really clever "situation" in Cooper's books; and still more difficult to find one of any kind which he has failed to render absurd by his handling of it. Look at the episodes of "the caves;" and at the celebrated scuffle between Maqua and those others on the table-land a few days later; and at Hurry Harry's queer water-transit from the castle to the ark; and at Deerslayer's half hour with his first corpse;

and at the quarrel between Hurry Harry and Deerslayer later; and at – but choose for yourself; you can't go amiss.

If Cooper had been an observer, his inventive faculty would have worked better, not more interestingly, but more rationally, more plausibly. Cooper's proudest creations in the way of "situations" suffer noticeably from the absence of the observer's protecting gift. Cooper's eye was splendidly inaccurate. Cooper seldom saw anything correctly. He saw nearly all things as through a glass eye, darkly. Of course a man who cannot see the commonest little everyday matters accurately is working at a disadvantage when he is constructing a "situation." In the *Deerslayer* tale Cooper has a stream which is fifty feet wide, where it flows out of a lake; it presently narrows to twenty as it meanders along for no given reason, and yet, when a stream acts like that it ought to be required to explain itself. Fourteen pages later the width of the brook's outlet from the lake has suddenly shrunk thirty feet, and become "the narrowest part of the stream." This shrinkage is not accounted for. The stream has bends in it, a sure indication that it has alluvial banks, and cuts them; yet these bends are only thirty and fifty feet long. If Cooper had been a nice and punctilious observer he would have noticed that the bends were oftener nine hundred feet long than short of it.

Cooper made the exit of that stream fifty feet wide in the first place, for no particular reason; in the second place, he narrowed it to less than twenty to accommodate some Indians. He bends a "sapling" to the form of an arch over this narrow passage, and conceals six Indians in its foliage. They are "laying" for a settler's scow or ark which is coming up the stream on its way to the lake; it is being hauled against the stiff current by a rope whose stationary end is anchored in the lake; its rate of progress cannot be more than a mile an hour. Cooper describes the ark, but pretty obscurely. In the matter of dimensions "it was little more than a modern canal boat." Let us guess, then, that it was about 140 feet long. It was of "greater breadth than common." Let us guess, then, that it was about sixteen feet wide. This leviathan had been prowling down bends which were but a third as long as itself, and scraping between banks where it had only two feet of space to spare on each side. We cannot too much admire this miracle. A low-roofed log dwelling occupies "two-third's of the ark's length"–a dwelling ninety feet long and sixteen feet wide, let us say–a kind of vestibule train. The dwelling has two rooms–each forty-five feet long and sixteen feet wide, let us guess. One of them is the bed-room of the Hutter girls, Judith and Hetty; the other is the parlor, in the day time, at night it is papa's bed chamber. The ark is arriving at the stream's exit, now, whose width has been reduced to less than twenty feet to accommodate the Indians– say to eighteen. There is a foot to spare on each side of the boat. Did the Indians notice that there was going to be a tight squeeze there? Did they notice that they could make money by climbing down out of that arched sapling and just stepping aboard when the ark scraped by? No; other Indians would have noticed these things, but Cooper's Indians never notice anything. Cooper thinks they are marvelous creatures for noticing, but he was almost always in error about his Indians. There was seldom a sane one among them.

The ark is 140 feet long; the dwelling is 90 feet long. The idea of the Indians is to drop softly and secretly from the arched sapling to the dwelling as the ark creeps along under it at the rate of a mile an hour, and butcher the family. It will take the ark a minute and a half to pass under. It will take the 90-foot dwelling a minute to pass under. Now, then, what did the six Indians do? It would take you thirty years to guess, and even then you would have to give it up, I believe. Therefore, I will tell you what the Indians did. Their chief, a person of quite extraordinary intellect for a Cooper Indian, warily watched the canal boat as it squeezed along under him, and when he had got his calculations fined down to exactly the right shade, as he judged, he let go and dropped. And *missed the house!* That is actually what he did. He missed the house, and landed in the stern of the scow. It was not much of a fall, yet it knocked him silly. He lay there unconscious. If the house had been 97 feet long, he would have made the trip. The fault was Cooper's, not his. The error lay in the construction of the house. Cooper was no architect.

There still remained in the roost five Indians. The boat has passed under and is now out of their reach. Let me explain what the five did—you would not be able to reason it out for yourself. No. 1 jumped for the boat, but fell in the water astern of it. Then No. 2 jumped for the boat, but fell in the water still further astern of it. Then No. 3 jumped for the boat, and fell a good way astern of it. Then No. 4 jumped for the boat, and fell in the water *away* astern. Then even No. 5 made a jump for the boat—for he was a Cooper Indian. In the matter of intellect, the difference between a Cooper Indian and the Indian that stands in front of the cigar shop is not spacious. The scow episode is really a sublime burst of invention; but it does not thrill, because the inaccuracy of the details throws a sort of air of fictitiousness and general improbability over it. This comes of Cooper's inadequacy as an observer.

The reader will find some examples of Cooper's high talent for inaccurate observation in the account of the shooting match in *The Pathfinder.* "A common wrought nail was driven lightly into the target, its head having been first touched with paint." The color of the paint is not stated—an important omission, but Cooper deals freely in important omissions. No, after all, it was not an important omission; for this nail head is a *hundred yards* from the marksman and could not be seen by them at that distance no matter what its color might be. How far can the best eyes see a common house fly? A hundred yards? It is quite impossible. Very well, eyes that cannot see a house fly that is a hundred yards away cannot see an ordinary nail head at that distance, for the size of the two objects is the same. It takes a keen eye to see a fly or a nail head at fifty yards—one hundred and fifty feet. Can the reader do it?

The nail was lightly driven, its head painted, and game called. Then the Cooper miracles began. The bullet of the first marksman chipped an edge of the nail head; the next man's bullet drove the nail a little way into the target—and removed all the paint. Haven't the miracles gone far enough now? Not to suit Cooper; for the purpose of this whole scheme is to show off his prodigy, Deerslayer-Hawkeye-Long-Rifle-Leather-Stocking-Pathfinder-Bumppo before the ladies.

> "Be all ready to clench it, boys!" cried out Pathfinder, stepping into his friend's tracks the instant they were vacant. "Never mind a new nail; I can see that, though the paint is gone, and what I can see, I can hit at a hundred yards, though it were only a mosquito's eye. Be ready to clench!"
>
> The rifle cracked, the bullet sped its way and the head of the nail was buried in the wood, covered by the piece of flattened lead.

There, you see, is a man who could hunt flies with a rifle, and command a ducal salary in a Wild West show today, if we had him back with us.

The recorded feat is certainly surprising, just as it stands; but it is not surprising enough for Cooper. Cooper adds a touch. He had made Pathfinder do this miracle with another man's rifle, and not only that, but Pathfinder did not have even the advantage of loading it himself. He had everything against him, and yet he made that impossible shot, and not only made it, but did it with absolute confidence, saying, "Be ready to clench." Now a person like that would have undertaken that same feat with a brickbat, and with Cooper to help he would have achieved it, too.

Pathfinder showed off handsomely that day before the ladies. His very first feat was a thing which no Wild West show can touch. He was standing with the group of marksmen, observing—a hundred yards from the target, mind; one Jasper raised his rifle and drove the centre of the bull's-eye. Then the quartermaster fired. The target exhibited no result this time. There was a laugh. "It's a dead miss," said Major Lundie. Pathfinder waited an impressive moment or two, than said in that calm, indifferent, know-it-all way of his, "No, Major—he has covered Jasper's bullet, as will be seen if any one will take the trouble to examine the target."

Wasn't it remarkable! How *could* he see that little pellet fly through the air and enter that distant bullet-hole? Yet that is what he did; for nothing is impossible to a Cooper person. Did any of those people have any deep-seated doubts about this thing? No; for that would imply sanity, and these were all Cooper people.

> The respect for Pathfinder's skill and for his *quickness and accuracy of sight* (the italics are mine) was so profound and general, that the instant he made this declaration the spectators began to distrust their own opinions, and a dozen rushed to the target in order to ascertain the fact. There, sure enough, it was found that the quartermaster's bullet had gone through the hold made by Jasper's, and that, too, so accurately as to require a minute examination to be certain of the circumstances, which, however, was soon established by discovering one bullet over the other in the stump against which the target was placed.

They made a "minute" examination; but never mind, how could they know that there were two bullets in that hole without digging the latest one out? for neither probe nor eyesight could prove the presence of any more than one bullet. Did they dig? No; as we shall see. It is the Pathfinder's turn now; he steps out before the ladies, takes aim, and fires.

But alas! here is a disappointment; an incredible, an unimaginable disappointment—for the target's aspect is unchanged; there is nothing there but the same old bullet hole!

> "If one dared to hint at such a thing," cried Major Duncan, "I should say that the Pathfinder has also missed the target."

As nobody had missed it yet, the "also" was not necessary; but never mind about that, for the Pathfinder is going to speak.

> "No, no, Major," said he, confidently, "that *would* be a risky declaration. I didn't load the piece, and can't say what was in it, but if it

was lead, you will find the bullet driving down those of the Quartermaster and Jasper, else is not my name Pathfinder."
A shout from the target announced the truth of this assertion.

Is the miracle sufficient as it stands? Not for Cooper. The
Pathfinder speaks again, as he "now slowly advances towards the
stage occupied by the females:"

> "That's not all, boys, that's not all: if you find the target touched
> at all, I'll own to a miss. The Quartermaster cut the wood, but you'll
> find no wood cut by that last messenger."

The miracle is at last complete. He knew–doubtless *saw*–at
the distance of a hundred yards–that his bullet had passed into
the hole *without fraying the edges*. There were now three bullets
imbedded processionally in the body of the stump back of the
target. Everybody knew this–somehow or other–and yet nobody
had dug any of them out to make sure. Cooper is not a close
observer, but he is interesting. He is certainly always that, no matter
what happens. And he is more interesting when he is not noticing what he is about than when he is. This is a considerable merit.

The conversations in the Cooper books have a curious sound
in our modern ears. To believe that such talk really ever came
out of people's mouths would be to believe that there was a time
when time was of no value to a person who thought he had something to say; when a man's mouth was a rolling-mill, and busied
itself all day long in turning four-foot pigs of thought into thirty-
foot bars of conversational railroad iron by attenuation; when subjects were seldom faithfully stuck to, but the talk wandered all
around and arrived nowhere; when conversations consisted mainly
of irrelevances, with here and there a relevancy, a relevancy with
an embarrassed look, as not being able to explain how it got there.

Cooper was certainly not a master in the construction of dialogue. Inaccurate observation defeated him here as it defeated him
in so many other enterprises of his. He even failed to notice that
the man who talks corrupt English six days in the week must and

will talk it on the seventh, and can't help himself. In the *Deer-slayer* story he lets Deerslayer talk the showiest kind of book talk sometimes, and at other times the basest of base dialects. For instance, when some one asks him if he has a sweetheart, and if so, where she abides, this is his majestic answer:

> "She's in the forest – hanging from the boughs of the trees, in a soft rain – in the dew on the open grass – the clouds that float about in the blue heavens – the birds that sing in the woods – the sweet springs where I slake my thirst – and in all the other glorious gifts that come from God's Providence!"

And he preceded that, a little before, with this:

> "It consarns me as all things that touches a fri'nd consarns a fri'nd."

And this is another of his remarks:

> "If I was Injin born, now, I might tell of this, or carry in the scalp and boast of the expl'ite afore the whole tribe; or if my inimy had only been a bear"– and so on.

We cannot imagine such a thing as a veteran Scotch Commander-in-Chief comporting himself in the field like a windy melodramatic actor, but Cooper could. On one occasion Alice and Cora were being chased by the French through a fog in the neighborhood of their father's fort:

> "*Point de quartier aux coquins!*" cried an eager pursuer, who seemed to direct the operations of the enemy.
> "Stand firm and be ready, my gallant 60ths!" suddenly exclaimed a voice above them: "wait to see the enemy; fire low, and sweep the glacis."
> "Father! father!" exclaimed a piercing cry from out the mist; "it is I! Alice! thy own Elsie! spare, O! save your daughters!"
> "Hold!" shouted the former speaker, in the awful tones of parental agony, the sound reaching even to the woods, and rolling back in solemn echo. " 'Tis she! God has restored me my children! Throw open the sally-port; to the field, 60ths, to the field; pull not a trigger, lest ye kill my lambs! Drive off these dogs of France with your steel!"

Cooper's word-sense was singularly dull. When a person has a poor ear for music he will flat and sharp right along without knowing it. He keeps near the tune, but it is *not* the tune. When a person has a poor ear for words, the result is a literary flatting and sharping; you perceive what he is intending to say, but you also perceive that he doesn't *say* it. This is Cooper. He is not a word-musician. His ear was satisfied with the *approximate* word. I will furnish some circumstantial evidence in support of this charge. My instances are gathered from half a dozen pages of the tale called *Deerslayer.* He uses "verbal," for "oral"; "precision," for "facility"; "phenomena," for "marvels"; "necessary," for "predetermined"; "unsophisticated," for "primitive"; "preparation," for "expectancy"; "rebuked," for "subdued"; "dependent on," for "resulting from"; "fact," for "condition"; "fact," for "conjecture"; "precaution," for "caution"; "explain," for "determine"; "mortified," for "disappointed"; "meretricious," for "factitious"; "materially," for "considerably"; "decreasing," for "deepening"; "increasing," for "disappearing"; "embedded," for "enclosed"; "treacherous," for "hostile"; "stood," for "stooped"; "softened," for "replaced"; "rejoined," for "remarked"; "situation," for "condition"; "different," for "differing"; "insensible," for "unsentient"; "brevity," for "celerity"; "distrusted," for "suspicious"; "mental imbecility," for "imbecility"; "eyes," for "sight"; "counteracting," for "opposing"; "funeral obsequies," for "obsequies."

There have been daring people in the world who claimed that Cooper could write English, but they are all dead now—all dead but Lounsbury. I don't remember that Lounsbury makes the claim in so many words, still he makes it, for he says that *Deerslayer* is a "pure work of art." Pure, in that connection, means faultless—faultless in all details—and language is a detail. If Mr. Lounsbury had only compared Cooper's English with the English which he writes himself—but it is plain that he didn't; and so it is likely that he imagines until this day that Cooper's is as clean and compact as his own. Now I feel sure, deep down in my heart, that

Cooper wrote about the poorest English that exists in our language, and that the English of *Deerslayer* is the very worst than even Cooper ever wrote.

I may be mistaken, but it does seem to me that *Deerslayer* is not a work of art in any sense; it does seem to me that it is destitute of every detail that goes to the making of a work of art; in truth, it seems to me that *Deerslayer* is just simply a literary *delirium tremens.*

A work of art? It has no invention; it has no order, system, sequence, or result; it has no lifelikeness, no thrill, no stir, no seeming of reality; its characters are confusedly drawn, and by their acts and words they prove that they are not the sort of people the author claims that they are; its humor is pathetic; its pathos is funny; its conversations are – oh! indescribable; its love-scenes odious; its English a crime against the language.

Counting these out, what is left is Art. I think we must all admit that.

How To Tell

a Story

THE HUMOROUS STORY AN AMERICAN DEVELOPMENT.– ITS DIFFERENCE
FROM COMIC AND WITTY STORIES.

First published in the *Youth's Companion* in October, 1895, this
story originated when Twain was asked how "The Celebrated
Jumping Frog of Calaveras County" came to be written. "How To
Tell a Story" explores the technique of the humorous narrative
with various examples, such as the ghost story, "The Golden
Arm," in which Twain effectively demonstrates the
importance of the pause.

I do not claim that I can tell a story as it ought to be told.
I only claim to know how a story ought to be told, for I have been
almost daily in the company of the most expert story-tellers for
many years.

There are several kinds of stories, but only one difficult kind –
the humorous. I will talk mainly about that one. The humorous
story is American, the comic story is English, the witty story is
French. The humorous story depends for its effect upon the *manner*
of the telling; the comic story and the witty story upon the *matter*.

The humorous story may be spun out to great length, and may
wander around as much as it pleases, and arrive nowhere in
particular; but the comic and witty stories must be brief and
end with a point. The humorous story bubbles gently along, the
others burst.

The humorous story is strictly a work of art – high and delicate art – and only an artist can tell it; but no art is necessary in
telling the comic and the witty story; anybody can so it. The art
of telling a humorous story – understand, I mean by word of mouth,
not print – was created in America, and has remained at home.

The humorous story is told gravely; the teller does his best
to conceal the fact that he even dimly suspects that there is anything funny about it; but the teller of the comic story tells you
beforehand that it is one of the funniest things he has ever heard,
then tells it with eager delight, and is the first person to laugh
when he gets through. And sometimes, if he has had good success, he is so glad and happy that he will repeat the "nub" of it
and glance around from face to face, collecting applause, and then
repeat it again. It is a pathetic thing to see.

Very often, of course, the rambling and disjointed humorous
story finishes with a nub, point, snapper, or whatever you like
to call it. Then the listener must be alert, for in many cases the
teller will divert attention from that nub by dropping it in a carefully casual and indifferent way, with the pretence that he does
not know it is a nub.

Artemus Ward used that trick a good deal; then when the
belated audience presently caught the joke he would look up with
innocent surprise, as if wondering what they had found to laugh
at. Dan Setchell used it before him, Nye and Riley and others use
it today.

But the teller of the comic story does not slur the nub; he
shouts it at you – every time. And when he prints it, in England,
France, Germany, and Italy, he italicizes it, puts some whooping
exclamation-points after it, and sometimes explains it in a
parenthesis. All of which is very depressing, and makes one want
to renounce joking and lead a better life.

Let me set down an instance of the comic method, using an
anecdote which has been popular all over the world for twelve
or fifteen hundred years. The teller tells it in this way:

THE WOUNDED SOLDIER

In the course of a certain battle a soldier whose leg had been
shot off appealed to another soldier who was hurrying by to carry

him to the rear, informing him at the same time of the loss which
he had sustained; whereupon the generous son of Mars, shoul-
dering the unfortunate, proceeded to carry out his desire. The
bullets and cannon-balls were flying in all directions, and presently
one of the latter took the wounded man's head off—without,
however, his deliverer being aware of it. In no long time he was
hailed by an officer, who said:

"Where are you going with that carcass?"

"To the rear, sir—he's lost his leg!"

"His leg, forsooth?" responded the astonished officer: "you
mean his head, you booby."

Whereupon the soldier dispossessed himself of his burden,
and stood looking down upon it in great perplexity. At length
he said:

"It is true, sir, just as you have said." Then after a pause he
added, *"But he* TOLD *me* IT WAS HIS LEG!!!!!"

Here the narrator bursts into explosion after explosion of thun-
derous horse-laughter, repeating that nub from time to time
through his gaspings and shriekings and suffocatings.

It takes only a minute and a half to tell that in its comic-story
form; and isn't worth the telling, after all. Put into the humorous-
story form it takes ten minutes, and is about the funniest thing
I have ever listened to—as James Whitcomb Riley tells it.

He tells it in the character of a dull-witted old farmer who
has just heard it for the first time, thinks it is unspeakably funny,
and is trying to repeat it to a neighbor. But he can't remember
it; so he gets all mixed up and wanders helplessly round and
round, putting in tedious details that don't belong in the tale and
only retard it; taking them out conscientiously and putting in
others that are just as useless; making minor mistakes now and
then and stopping to correct them and explain how he came to
make them; remembering things which he forgot to put in in their
proper place and going back to put them in there; stopping his
narrative a good while in order to try to recall the name of the

soldier that was hurt, and finally remembering that the soldier's name was not mentioned, and remarking placidly that the name is of no real importance, anyway – better, of course, if one knew it, but not essential, after all – and so on, and so on, and so on.

The teller is innocent and happy and pleased with himself, and has to stop every little while to hold himself in and keep from laughing outright; and does hold in, but his body quakes in a jelly-like way with interior chuckles; and at the end of the ten minutes the audience have laughed until they are exhausted, and the tears are running down their faces.

The simplicity and innocence and sincerity and unconsciousness of the old farmer are perfectly simulated, and the result is a performance which is thoroughly charming and delicious. This is art – and fine and beautiful, and only a master can compass it; but a machine could tell the other story.

To string incongruities and absurdities together in a wandering and sometimes purposeless way, and seem innocently unaware that they are absurdities, is the basis of the American art, if my position is correct. Another feature is the slurring of the point. A third is the dropping of a studied remark apparently without knowing it, as if one were thinking aloud. The fourth and last is the pause.

Artemus Ward dealt in numbers three and four a good deal. He would begin to tell with great animation something which he seemed to think was wonderful; then lose confidence, and after an apparently absent-minded pause add an incongruous remark in a soliloquizing way; and that was the remark intended to explode the mine – and it did.

For instance, he would say eagerly, excitedly, "I once knew a man in New Zealand who hadn't a tooth in his head"– here his animation would die out; a silent, reflective pause would follow, then he would say dreamily, and as if to himself, "and yet that man could beat a drum better than any man I ever saw."

The pause is an exceedingly important feature in any kind of story, and a frequently recurring feature, too. It is a dainty thing, and delicate, and also uncertain and treacherous; for it must be exactly the right length—no more and no less—or it fails of its purpose and makes trouble. If the pause is too short the impressive point is passed, and the audience have had time to divine that a surprise is intended—and then you can't surprise them, of course.

On the platform I used to tell a negro ghost story that had a pause in front of the snapper on the end, and that pause was the most important thing in the whole story. If I got it the right length precisely, I could spring the finishing ejaculation with effect enough to make some impressive girl deliver a startled little yelp and jump out of her seat—and that was what I was after. This story was called "The Golden Arm," and was told in this fashion. You can practice with it yourself—and mind you look out for the pause and get it right.

THE GOLDEN ARM

Once 'pon a time dey wuz a monsus mean man, en he live 'way out in de prairie all 'lone by hisself, 'cept'n he had a wife. En bimeby she died, en he tuck en toted her way out dah in de prairie en buried her. Well, she had a golden arm—all solid gold, fum de shoulder down. He wuz pow'ful mean—pow'ful; en dat night he couldn't sleep, caze he want dat golden arm so bad.

When it come midnight he couldn't stan' it no mo'; so he git up, he did, en tuck his lantern en shoved out thoo de storm en dug her up en got de golden arm; en he bent his head down 'gin de win', en plowed en plowed en plowed thoo de snow. Den all on a sudden he stop (make a considerable pause here, and look startled, and take a listening attitude) en say: "My *lan'* what's dat!"

En he listen—en listen—en de win' say (set your teeth together and imitate the wailing and wheezing singsong of the wind),

"Bzzz-z-zzz"–en den, way back yonder whah de grave is, he hear a *voice!*–he hear a voice all mix' up in de win'–can't hardly tell 'em 'part–"Bzzz-zzz–W-h-o–g-o-t–m-y–g-o-l-d-e-n *arm?*–zzz–zzz–W-h-o g-o-t m-y g-o-l-d-e-n *arm?*" (You must begin to shiver violently now.)

En he begin to shiver en shake, en say, "Oh, my! *Oh,* my lan'!" en de win' blow de lantern out, en de snow en sleet blow in his face en mos' choke him, en he start a-plowin' knee-deep towards home mos' dead, he so sk'yerd–en pooty soon he hear de voice agin, en (pause) it'us comin' *after* him! "Buzz–zzz–zzz–W-h-o–g-o-t–m-y–g-o-l-d-e-n–*arm?*"

When he git to de pasture he hear it agin–closter now, en a-*comin'!*–a-comin' back dah in de dark en de storm–(repeat the wind and the voice). When he git to de house he rush upstairs en jump in de bed en kiver up, head and years, en lay dah shiverin' en shakin'–en den way out dah he hear it *agin!*–en a *comin'!* En bimeby he hear (paused–awed, listening attitude)–pat–pat–pat–*hit's a-comin' upstairs!* Den he hear de latch, en he *know* it's in de room!

Den pooty soon he know it's a-*stannin' by de bed!* (Pause.) Den–he know its a-*bendin' down over him*–he cain't skasely git his breath! Den–den–he seem to feel someth'n *c-o-l-d,* right down 'most agin his head! (Pause.)

Den de voice say, *right at his year*–"W-h-o–g-o-t–m-y–g-o-l-d-e-n *arm?*" (You must wail it out very plaintively and accusingly; then you stare steadily and impressively into the face of the farthest-gone auditor–a girl, preferably–and let that awe-inspiring pause begin to build itself in the deep hush. When it has reached exactly the right length, jump suddenly at that girl and yell, "*You've* got it!"

If you've got the *pause* right, she'll fetch a dear little yelp and spring right out of her shoes. But you *must* get the pause right; and you will find it the most troublesome and aggravating and uncertain thing you ever undertook.)

THE MAN THAT CORRUPTED HADLEYBURG

Written at the end of a disastrous decade in which Twain was
forced to declare bankruptcy, faced a debt close to $100,000, and
mourned the death of his favorite daughter, "The Man That
Corrupted Hadleyburg" reflects Twain's increasing cynicism about
the hypocrisy of society. The story was first published in *Harper's
Magazine* in December of 1899 and appeared in *The Man That
Corrupted Hadleyburg and Other Stories and Essays* from
Harper & Brothers, New York and London, in 1900.

I

It was many years ago. Hadleyburg was the most honest and
upright town in all the region round about. It had kept that reputation unsmirched during three generations, and was prouder of
it than of any other of its possessions. It was so proud of it, and
so anxious to insure its perpetuation, that it began to teach the
principles of honest dealing to its babies in the cradle, and made
the like teachings the staple of their culture thenceforward through
all the years devoted to their education. Also, throughout the for-
mative years temptations were kept out of the way of the young
people, so that their honesty could have every chance to harden
and solidify, and become a part of their very bone. The neighboring towns were jealous of this honorable supremacy, and
affected to sneer at Hadleyburg's pride in it and call it vanity; but
all the same they were obliged to acknowledge that Hadleyburg
was in reality an incorruptible town; and if pressed they would
also acknowledge that the mere fact that a young man hailed from
Hadleyburg was all the recommendation he needed when he went
forth from his natal town to seek for responsible employment.

But at last, in the drift of time, Hadleyburg had the ill luck to offend a passing stranger—possibly without knowing it, certainly without caring, for Hadleyburg was sufficient unto itself, and cared not a rap for strangers or their opinions. Still, it would have been well to make an exception in this one's case, for he was a bitter man and revengeful. All through his wanderings during a whole year he kept his injury in mind, and gave all his leisure moments to trying to invent a compensating satisfaction for it. He contrived many plans, and all of them were good, but none of them was quite sweeping enough; the poorest of them would hurt a great many individuals, but what he wanted was a plan which would comprehend the entire town, and not let so much as one person escape unhurt. At last he had a fortunate idea, and when it fell into his brain it lit up his whole head with an evil joy. He began to form a plan at once, saying to himself, "That is the thing to do—I will corrupt the town."

Six months later he went to Hadleyburg, and arrived in a buggy at the house of the old cashier of the bank about ten at night. He got a sack out of the buggy, shouldered it, and staggered with it through the cottage yard, and knocked at the door. A woman's voice said "Come in," and he entered, and set his sack behind the stove in the parlor, saying politely to the old lady who sat reading the *Missionary Herald* by the lamp:

"Pray keep your seat, madam, I will not disturb you. There— now it is pretty well concealed; one would hardly know it was there. Can I see your husband a moment, madam?"

No, he was gone to Brixton, and might not return before morning.

"Very well, madam, it is no matter. I merely wanted to leave that sack in his care, to be delivered to the rightful owner when he shall be found. I am a stranger; he does not know me; I am merely passing through the town tonight to discharge a matter which has been long in my mind. My errand is not completed, and I go pleased and a little proud, and you will never see me again. There is a paper attached to the sack which will explain everything. Good-night, madam."

The old lady was afraid of the mysterious big stranger, and was glad to see him go. But her curiosity was roused, and she went straight to the sack and brought away the paper. It began as follows:

> "TO BE PUBLISHED: or, the right man sought out by private inquiry— either will answer. This sack contains gold coin weighing a hundred and sixty pounds four ounces —"

"Mercy on us, and the door not locked!"

Mrs. Richards flew to it all in a tremble and locked it, then pulled down the window-shades and stood frightened, worried, and wondering if there was anything else she could do toward making herself and the money more safe. She listened awhile for burglars, then surrendered to curiosity and went back to the lamp and finished reading the paper:

> "I am a foreigner, and am presently going back to my own country, to remain there permanently. I am grateful to America for what I have received at her hands during my long stay under her flag; and to one of her citizens—a citizen of Hadleyburg—I am especially grateful for a great kindness done me a year or two ago. Two great kindnesses, in fact. I will explain. I was a gambler. I say I WAS. I was a ruined gambler. I arrived in this village at night, hungry and without a penny. I asked for help—in the dark; I was ashamed to beg in the light. I begged of the right man. He gave me twenty dollars—that is to say, he gave me life, as I considered it. He also gave me fortune; for out of that money I have made myself rich at the gaming-table. And finally, a remark which he made to me has remained with me to this day, and has at last conquered me; and in conquering has saved the remnant of my morals; I shall gamble no more. Now I have no idea who that man was, but I want him found, and I want him to have this money, to give away, throw away, or keep, as he pleases. It is merely my way of testifying my gratitude to him. If I could stay, I would find him myself; but no matter, he will be found. This is an honest town, an incorruptible town, and I know I can trust it without fear. This man can be identified by the remark which he made to me: I feel persuaded that he will remember it.
>
> "And now my plan is this: If you prefer to conduct the inquiry privately, do so. Tell the contents of this present writing to any one who is

likely to be the right man. If he shall answer, 'I am the man; the remark
I made was so-and-so,' apply the test—to wit; open the sack, and in it
you will find a sealed envelope containing that remark. If the remark men-
tioned by the candidate tallies with it, give him the money, and ask no
further questions, for he is certainly the right man.

"But if you shall prefer a public inquiry, then publish this present writ-
ing in the local paper—with these instructions added, to wit: Thirty days
from now, let the candidate appear at the town-hall at eight in the even-
ing (Friday), and hand his remark, in a sealed envelope, to the Rev. Mr.
Burgess (if he will be kind enough to act); and let Mr. Burgess there and
then destroy the seals of the sack, open it, and see if the remark is correct;
if correct, let the money be delivered, with my sincere gratitude, to my
benefactor thus identified."

Mrs. Richards sat down, gently quivering with excitement, and was soon lost in things—after this pattern: "What a strange thing it is!... And what a fortune for that kind man who set his bread afloat upon the waters!... If it had only been my husband that did it!—for we are so poor, so old and poor!..." Then, with a sigh—"But it was not my Edward; no, it was not he that gave a stranger twenty dollars. It is a pity, too; I see it now..." Then, with a shudder—"But it is *gambler's* money! the wages of sin: we couldn't take it; we couldn't touch it. I don't like to be near it; it seems a defilement." She moved to a farther chair.... "I wish Edward would come, and take it to the bank; a burglar might come at any moment; it is dreadful to be here all alone with it."

At eleven Mr. Richards arrived, and while his wife was saying, "I am *so* glad you've come!" he was saying, "I'm so tired—tired clear out; it is dreadful to be poor, and have to make these dismal journeys at my time of life. Always at the grind, grind, grind, on a salary—another man's slave, and he sitting at home in his slippers, rich and comfortable."

"I am so sorry for you, Edward, you know that; but be comforted: we have our livelihood; we have our good name—"

"Yes, Mary, and that is everything. Don't mind my talk—it's just a moment's irritation and doesn't mean anything. Kiss me—there, it's all gone now, and I am not complaining any more. What have you been getting? What's in the sack?"

Then his wife told him the great secret. It dazed him for a moment; then he said:

"It weighs a hundred and sixty pounds? Why, Mary, it's for-ty thou-sand dollars—think of it—a whole fortune! Not ten men in this village are worth that much. Give me the paper."

He skimmed through it and said:

"Isn't it an adventure! Why, it's a romance; it's like the impossible things one reads about in books, and never sees in life." He was well stirred up now; cheerful, even gleeful. He tapped his old wife on the cheek, and said, humorously, "Why, we're rich, Mary, rich; all we've got to do is to bury the money and burn the papers. If the gambler ever comes to inquire, we'll merely look coldly upon him and say: 'What is this nonsense you are talking? We have never heard of you and your sack of gold before;' and then he would look foolish, and—"

"And in the meantime, while you are running on with your jokes, the money is still here, and it is fast getting along toward burglar-time."

"True. Very well, what shall we do—make the inquiry private? No, not that: it would spoil the romance. The public method is better. Think what a noise it will make! And it will make all the other towns jealous; for no stranger would trust such a thing to any town but Hadleyburg, and they know it. It's a great card for us. I must get to the printing-office now, or I shall be too late."

"But stop—stop—don't leave me here alone with it, Edward!"

But he was gone. For only a little while, however. Not far from his own house he met the editor-proprietor of the paper, and gave him the document, and said, "Here is a good thing for you, Cox—put it in."

"It may be too late, Mr. Richards, but I'll see."

At home again he and his wife sat down to talk the charming mystery over; they were in no condition for sleep. The first question was, Who could the citizen have been who gave the stranger the twenty dollars? It seemed a simple one; both answered it in the same breath—

"Barclay Goodson."

"Yes," said Richards, "he could have done it, and it would have been like him, but there's not another in the town."

"Everybody will grant that, Edward—grant it privately, anyway. For six months, now, the village has been its own proper self once more—honest, narrow, self-righteous, and stingy."

"It is what he always called it, to the day of his death—said it right out publicly, too."

"Yes, and he was hated for it."

"Oh, of course; but he didn't care. I reckon he was the best-hated man among us, except the Reverend Burgess."

"Well, Burgess deserves it—he will never get another congregation here. Mean as the town is, it knows how to estimate *him*. Edward, doesn't it seem odd that the stranger should appoint Burgess to deliver the money?"

"Well, yes—it does. That is—that is—"

"Why so much that-*is*-ing? Would *you* select him?"

"Mary, maybe the stranger knows him better than this village does."

"Much *that* would help Burgess!"

The husband seemed perplexed for an answer; the wife kept a steady eye upon him, and waited. Finally Richards said, with the hesitancy of one who is making a statement which is likely to encounter doubt.

"Mary, Burgess is not a bad man."

His wife was certainly surprised.

"Nonsense!" she exclaimed.

"He is not a bad man. I know. The whole of his unpopularity had its foundation in that one thing—the thing that made so much noise."

"That 'one thing,' indeed! As if that 'one thing' wasn't enough, all by itself."

"Plenty. Plenty. Only he wasn't guilty of it."

"How you talk! Not guilty of it! Everybody knows he *was* guilty."

"Mary, I give you my word – he was innocent."

"I can't believe it, and I don't. How do you know?"

"It is a confession. I am ashamed, but I will make it. I was the only man who knew he was innocent. I could have saved him, and – and – well, you know how the town was wrought up – I hadn't the pluck to do it. It would have turned everybody against me. I felt mean, ever so mean; but I didn't dare; I hadn't the manliness to face that."

Mary looked troubled, and for a while was silent. Then she said, stammeringly:

"I – I don't think it would have done for you to – to – One mustn't – er – public opinion – one has to be so careful – so –" It was a difficult road, and she got mired; but after a little she got started again. "It was a great pity, but – Why, we couldn't afford it, Edward – we couldn't indeed. Oh, I wouldn't have had you do it for anything!"

"It would have lost us the good-will of so many people, Mary; and then – and then –"

"What troubles me now is, what *he* thinks of us, Edward."

"He? *He* doesn't suspect that I could have saved him."

"Oh," exclaimed the wife, in a tone of relief, "I am glad of that. As long as he doesn't know that you could have saved him, he – he – well, that makes it a great deal better. Why, I might have known he didn't know, because he is always trying to be friendly with us, as little encouragement as we give him. More than once people have twitted me with it. There's the Wilsons, and the Wilcoxes, and the Harknesses, they take a mean pleasure in saying, 'Your *friend* Burgess,' because they know it pesters me. I wish he wouldn't persist in liking us so; I can't think why he keeps it up."

"I can explain it. It's another confession. When the thing was new and hot, and the town made a plan to ride him on a rail, my conscience hurt me so that I couldn't stand it, and I went

privately and gave him notice, and he got out of the town and
staid out till it was safe to come back."

"Edward! If the town had found it out–"

"*Don't!* It scares me yet, to think of it. I repented of it the minute
it was done; and I was even afraid to tell you, lest your face might
betray it to somebody. I didn't sleep any that night, for worrying.
But after a few days I saw that no one was going to suspect me,
and after that I got to feeling glad I did it. And I feel glad yet,
Mary–glad through and through."

"So do I, now, for it would have been a dreadful way to treat
him. Yes, I'm glad; for really you did owe him that, you know.
But Edward, suppose it should come out yet, some day!"

"It won't."

"Why?"

"Because everybody thinks it was Goodson."

"Of course they would!"

"Certainly. And of course *he* didn't care. They persuaded poor
old Sawlsberry to go and charge it on him, and he went bluster-
ing over there and did it. Goodson looked him over, like as if
he was hunting for a place on him that he could despise the most,
then he says, 'So you are the Committee of Inquiry, are you?' Sawlsberry said that was about what he was. 'Hm. Do they require
particulars, or do you reckon a kind of a *general* answer will do?'
'If they require particulars, I will come back, Mr. Goodson; I will
take the general answer first.' 'Very well, then, tell them to go to
hell–I reckon that's general enough. And I'll give you some advice,
Sawlsberry; when you come back for the particulars, fetch a basket
to carry the relics of yourself home in.'"

"Just like Goodson; it's got all the marks. He had only
one vanity; he thought he could give advice better than any
other person."

"It settled the business, and saved us, Mary. The subject
was dropped."

"Bless you, I'm not doubting *that.*"

Then they took up the gold-sack mystery again, with strong interest. Soon the conversation began to suffer breaks – interruptions caused by absorbed thinkings. The breaks grew more and more frequent. At last Richards lost himself wholly in thought. He sat long, gazing vacantly at the floor, and by and by he began to punctuate his thoughts with little nervous movements of his hands that seemed to indicate vexation. Meantime his wife too had relapsed into a thoughtful silence, and her movements were beginning to show a troubled discomfort. Finally Richards got up and strode aimlessly about the room, plowing his hands through his hair, much as a somnambulist might do who was having a bad dream. Then he seemed to arrive at a definite purpose; and without a word he put on his hat and passed quickly out of the house. His wife sat brooding, with a drawn face, and did not seem to be aware that she was alone. Now and then she murmured, "Lead us not into t– . . . but – but – we are so poor, so poor! . . . Lead us not into. . . . Ah, who would be hurt by it? – and no one would ever know. . . . Lead us . . . ." The voice died out in mumblings. After a little she glanced up and muttered in a half-frightened, half-glad way –

"He is gone! But, oh dear, he may be too late! too late. . . . Maybe not – maybe there is still time." She rose and stood thinking, nervously clasping and unclasping her hands. A slight shudder shook her frame, and she said, out of a dry throat. "God forgive me – it's awful to think such things – but . . . Lord, how we are made – how strangely we are made!"

She turned the light low, and slipped stealthily over and knelt down by the sack and felt of its ridgy sides with her hands, and fondled them lovingly; and there was a gloating light in her poor old eyes. She fell into fits of absence; and came half out of them at times to mutter. "If we had only waited! – oh, if we had only waited a little, and not been in such a hurry!"

Meantime Cox had gone home from his office and told his wife all about the strange thing that had happened, and they had talked it over eagerly, and guessed that the late Goodson was the only man in the town who could have helped a suffering stranger with so noble a sum as twenty dollars. Then there was a pause, and the two became thoughtful and silent. And by and by nervous and fidgety. At last the wife said, as if to herself,

"Nobody knows this secret but the Richardses...and us...nobody."

The husband came out of his thinkings with a slight start, and gazed wistfully at his wife, whose face was become very pale; then he hesitatingly rose, and glanced furtively at his hat, then at his wife – a sort of mute inquiry. Mrs. Cox swallowed once or twice, with her hand at her throat, then in place of speech she nodded her head. In a moment she was alone, and mumbling to herself.

And now Richards and Cox were hurrying through the deserted streets, from opposite directions. They met, panting, at the foot of the printing-office stairs; by the night-light there they read each other's face. Cox whispered,

"Nobody knows about this but us?"

The whispered answer was,

"Not a soul – on honor, not a soul!"

"If it isn't too late to –"

The men were starting upstairs; at this moment they were overtaken by a boy, and Cox asked,

"Is that you, Johnny?"

"Yes, sir."

"You needn't ship the early mail – nor *any* mail; wait till I tell you."

"It's already gone, sir."

"*Gone?*" It had the sound of an unspeakable disappointment in it.

"Yes, sir. Time-table for Brixton and all the towns beyond changed today, sir – had to get the papers in twenty minutes earlier than common. I had to rush; if I had been two minutes later –"

The men turned and walked slowly away, not waiting to hear the rest. Neither of them spoke during ten minutes; then Cox said, in a vexed tone.

"What possessed you to be in such a hurry, I can't make out."

The answer was humble enough:

"I see it now, but somehow I never thought, you know, until it was too late. But the next time—"

"Next time be hanged! It won't come in a thousand years."

Then the friends separated without a good-night, and dragged themselves home with the gait of mortally stricken men. At their homes their wives sprang up with an eager "Well?"—then saw the answer with their eyes and sank down sorrowing, without waiting for it to come in words. In both houses a discussion followed of a heated sort—a new thing; there had been discussions before, but not heated ones, not ungentle ones. The discussions tonight were a sort of seeming plagiarisms of each other. Mrs. Richards said,

"If you had only waited, Edward—if you had only stopped to think; but no, you must run straight to the printing-office and spread it all over the world."

"It *said* publish it."

"That is nothing; it also said do it privately, if you liked. There, now—is that true, or not?"

"Why, yes—yes, it is true; but when I thought what a stir it would make, and what a compliment it was to Hadleyburg that a stranger should trust it so—"

"Oh, certainly, I know all that; but if you had only stopped to think, you would have seen that you *couldn't* find the right man, because he is in his grave, and hasn't left chick nor child nor relation behind him; and as long as the money went to somebody that awfully needed it, and nobody would be hurt by it, and—and—"

She broke down, crying. Her husband tried to think of some comforting thing to say, and presently came out with this:

"But after all, Mary, it must be for the best—it *must* be; we know that. And we must remember that it was so ordered—"

"Ordered! Oh, everything's *ordered,* when a person has to find some way out when he has been stupid. Just the same, it was *ordered* that the money should come to us in this special way, and it was you that must take it on yourself to go meddling with the designs of Providence – and who gave you the right? It was wicked, that is what it was – just blasphemous presumption, and no more becoming to a meek and humble professor of –"

"But, Mary, you know how we have been trained all our lives long, like the whole village, till it is absolutely second nature to us to stop not a single moment to think when there's an honest thing to be done –"

"Oh, I know it, I know it – it's been one everlasting training and training and training in honesty – honesty shielded, from the very cradle, against every possible temptation, and so it's *artificial* honesty, and weak as water when temptation comes, as we have seen this night. God knows I never had shade nor shadow of a doubt of my petrified and indestructible honesty until now – and now, under the very first big and real temptation, I – Edward, it is my belief that this town's honesty is as rotten as mine is; as rotten as yours is. It is a mean town, a hard, stingy town, and hasn't a virtue in the world but this honesty it is so celebrated for and so conceited about; and so help me, I do believe that if ever the day comes that its honesty falls under great temptation, its grand reputation will go to ruin like a house of cards. There, now, I've made confession, and I feel better; I am a humbug, and I've been one all my life, without knowing it. Let no man call me honest again – I will not have it."

"I – well, Mary, I feel a good deal as you do; I certainly do. It seems strange, too, so strange. I never could have believed it – never."

A long silence followed; both were sunk in thought. At last the wife looked up and said,

"I know what you are thinking, Edward."

Richards had the embarrassed look of a person who is caught.

"I am ashamed to confess it, Mary, but—"

"It's no matter, Edward. I was thinking the same question myself."

"I hope so. State it."

"You were thinking, if a body could only guess out *what the remark was* that Goodson made to the stranger."

"It's perfectly true. I feel guilty and ashamed. And you?"

"I'm past it. Let us make a pallet here: we've got to stand watch till the bank vault opens in the morning and admits the sack. . . . Oh dear, oh dear—if we hadn't made the mistake!"

The pallet was made, and Mary said:

"The open sesame—what could it have been? I do wonder what that remark could have been? But come; we will get to bed now."

"And sleep?"

"No: think."

"Yes, think."

By this time the Coxes too had completed their spat and their reconciliation, and were turning in—to think, to think, and toss, and fret, and worry over what the remark could possibly have been which Goodson made to the stranded derelict; that golden remark; that remark worth forty thousand dollars, cash.

The reason that the village telegraph office was open later than usual that night was this: The foreman of Cox's paper was the local representative of the Associated Press. One might say its honorary representative, for it wasn't four times a year that he could furnish thirty words that would be accepted. But this time it was different. His dispatch stating what he had caught got an instant answer:

"Send the whole thing—all the details—twelve hundred words."

A colossal order! The foreman filled the bill; and he was the proudest man in the State. By breakfast-time the next morning the name of Hadleyburg the Incorruptible was on every lip in America, from Montreal to the Gulf, from the glaciers of Alaska

to the orange-groves of Florida; and millions and millions of people were discussing the stranger and his money-sack, and
wondering if the right man would be found, and hoping some
more news about the matter would come soon—right away.

II

Hadleyburg village woke up world-celebrated—astonished—
happy—vain. Vain beyond imagination. Its nineteen principal
citizens and their wives went about shaking hands with each other,
and beaming, and smiling, and congratulating, and saying *this* thing
adds a new word to the dictionary—*Hadleyburg,* synonym for
incorruptible—destined to live in dictionaries forever! And the
minor and unimportant citizens and their wives went around acting in much the same way. Everybody ran to the bank to see the
gold-sack; and before noon grieved and envious crowds began
to flock in from Brixton and all neighboring towns; and that afternoon and next day reporters began to arrive from everywhere to
verify the sack and its history and write the whole thing up anew,
and make dashing free-hand pictures of the sack, and of Richards's
house, and the bank, and the Presbyterian church, and the Baptist church, and the public square, and the town-hall where the
test would be applied and the money delivered; and damnable
portraits of the Richardses, and Pinkerton the banker, and Cox,
and the foreman, and Reverend Burgess, and the postmaster—
and even of Jack Halliday, who was the loafing, good-natured, no-
account, irreverent fisherman, hunter, boys' friend, typical "Sam
Lawson" of the town. The little mean, smirking, oily Pinkerton
showed the sack to all comers, and rubbed his sleek palms together
pleasantly, and enlarged upon the town's fine old reputation for
honesty and upon this wonderful endorsement of it, and hoped
and believed that the example would now spread far and wide
over the American world, and be epoch-making in the matter of
moral regeneration. And so on, and so on.

By the end of a week things had quieted down again; the wild intoxication of pride and joy had sobered to a soft, sweet, silent delight – a sort of deep, nameless, unutterable content. All faces bore a look of peaceful, holy happiness.

Then a change came. It was a gradual change: so gradual that its beginnings were hardly noticed; maybe were not noticed at all, except by Jack Halliday, who always noticed everything; and always made fun of it, too, no matter what it was. He began to throw out chaffing remarks about people not looking quite so happy as they did a day or so ago; and next he claimed that the new aspect was deepening to positive sadness; next, that it was taking on a sick look; and finally he said that everybody was become so moody, thoughtful, and absent-minded that he could rob the meanest man in town of a cent out of the bottom of his breeches pocket and not disturb his revery.

At this stage – or at about this stage – a saying like this was dropped at bedtime – with a sigh, usually – by the head of each of the nineteen principal households –"Ah, what *could* have been the remark that Goodson made?"

And straightway – with a shudder – came this, from the man's wife:

"Oh, *don't!* What horrible thing are mulling in your mind? Put it away from you, for God's sake!"

But that question was wrung from those men again the next night – and got the same retort. But weaker.

And the third night the men uttered the question yet again – with anguish, and absently. This time – and the following night – the wives fidgeted feebly, and tried to say something. But didn't.

And the night after that they found their tongues and responded – longingly,

"Oh, if we *could* only guess!"

Halliday's comments grew daily more and more sparklingly disagreeable and disparaging. He went diligently about, laughing at the town, individually and in mass. But his laugh was the only one left in the village: it fell upon a hollow and mournful vacancy

and emptiness. Not even a smile was findable anywhere. Halliday carried a cigar-box around on a tripod, playing that it was
a camera, and halted all passers and aimed the thing and said,
"Ready! – now look pleasant, please," but not even this capital joke
could surprise the dreary faces into any softening.

So three weeks passed – one week was left. It was Saturday
evening – after supper. Instead of the aforetime Saturday-evening
flutter and bustle and shopping and larking, the streets were empty
and desolate. Richards and his old wife sat apart in their little
parlor – miserable and thinking. This was become their evening
habit now; the lifelong habit which had preceded it, of reading,
knitting, and contented chat, or receiving or paying neighborly
calls, was dead and gone and forgotten, ages ago – two or three
weeks ago; nobody talked now, nobody read, nobody visited –
the whole village sat at home, sighing, worrying, silent. Trying
to guess out that remark.

The postman left a letter. Richards glanced listlessly at the
superscription and the postmark – unfamiliar, both – and tossed
the letter on the table and resumed his might-have-beens and his
hopeless dull miseries where he had left them off. Two or three
hours later his wife got wearily up and was going away to bed
without a good-night – custom now – but she stopped near the letter and eyed it awhile with a dead interest, then broke it open,
and began to skim it over. Richards, sitting there with his chair
tilted back against the wall and his chin between his knees,
heard something fall. It was his wife. He sprang to her side, but
she cried out:

"Leave me alone, I am too happy. Read the letter – read it!"

He did. He devoured it, his brain reeling. The letter was from
a distant State, and it said:

> "I am a stranger to you, but no matter; I have something to tell. I have
> just arrived home from Mexico, and learned about that episode. Of course
> you do not know who made that remark, but I know, and I am the only

person living who does know. It was GOODSON. I knew him well, many years ago. I passed through your village that very night, and was his guest till the midnight train came along. I overheard him make that remark to the stranger in the dark—it was in Hale Alley. He and I talked of it the rest of the way home, and while smoking in his house. He mentioned many of your villagers in the course of his talk—most of them in a very uncomplimentary way, but two or three favorably; among these latter yourself. I say 'favorably'—nothing stronger. I remember his saying he did not actually LIKE any person in the town—not one; but that you—I THINK he said you—am almost sure—had done him a very great service once, possibly without knowing the full value of it, and he wished he had a fortune, he would leave it to you when he died, and a curse apiece for the rest of the citizens. Now, then, if it was you that did him that service, you are his legitimate heir, and entitled to the sack of gold. I know that I can trust to your honor and honesty, for in a citizen of Hadleyburg these virtues are an unfailing inheritance, and so I am going to reveal to you the remark well satisfied that if you are not the right man, you will seek and find the right one and see that poor Goodson's debt of gratitude for the service referred to is paid. This is the remark: 'YOU ARE FAR FROM BEING A BAD MAN. GO, AND REFORM.'

"HOWARD L. STEPHENSON"

"Oh Edward, the money is ours, and I am so grateful, *oh,* so grateful—kiss me, dear, it's forever since we kissed—and we needed it so—the money—and now you are free of Pinkerton and his bank, and nobody's slave any more; it seems to me I could fly for joy."

It was a happy half-hour that the couple spent there on the settee caressing each other; it was the old days come again—days that had began with their courtship and lasted without a break till the stranger brought the deadly money. By and by the wife said:

"Oh, Edward, how lucky it was you did him that grand service, poor Goodson! I never liked him, but I love him now. And it was fine and beautiful of you never to mention it or brag about it." Then, with a touch of reproach, "But you ought to have told *me,* Edward, you ought to have told your wife, you know."

"Well, I—er—well, Mary, you see—"

"Now stop hemming and hawing, and tell me about it, Edward.

I always loved you, and now I'm proud of you. Everybody believes there was only one good generous soul in this village, and now it turns out that you—Edward, why don't you tell me?"

"Well—er—er—Why, Mary, I can't!"

"You *can't?* *Why* can't you?"

"You see, he—well, he—he made me promise I wouldn't."

The wife looked him over, and said, very slowly,

"Made—you—promise? Edward, what do you tell me that for?"

"Mary, do you think I would lie?"

She was troubled and silent for a moment, then she laid her hand within his and said:

"No...no. We have wandered far enough from our bearings—God spare us that! In all your life you have never uttered a lie. But now—now that the foundations of things seem to be crumbling from under us, we—we—" She lost her voice for a moment, then said brokenly, "Lead us not into temptation.... I think you made the promise, Edward. Let it rest so. Let us keep away from that ground. Now—that is all gone by; let us be happy again; it is no time for clouds."

Edward found it something of an effort to comply, for his mind kept wandering—trying to remember what the service was that he had done Goodson.

The couple lay awake the most of the night. Mary happy and busy, Edward busy but not so happy. Mary was planning what she would do with the money. Edward was trying to recall that service. At first his conscience was sore on account of the lie he had told Mary—if it was a lie. After much reflection—suppose it *was* a lie? What then? Was it such a great matter? Aren't we always *acting* lies? Then why not *tell* them? Look at Mary—look what she had done. While he was hurrying off on his honest errand, what was she doing? Lamenting because the papers hadn't been destroyed and the money kept! Is theft better than lying?

That point lost its sting—the lie dropped into the background and left comfort behind it. The next point came to the front: *Had* he rendered that service? Well, here was Goodson's own evidence as reported in Stephenson's letter; there could be no better evidence than that–it was even *proof* that he had rendered it. Of course. So that point was settled. . . . No, not quite. He recalled with a wince that this unknown Mr. Stephenson was just a trifle unsure as to whether the performer of it was Richards or some other–and, oh dear, he had put Richards on his honor! He must himself decide whither that money must go–and Mr. Stephenson was not doubting that if he was the wrong man he would go honorably and find the right one. Oh, it was odious to put a man in such a situation–ah, why couldn't Stephenson have left out that doubt! What did he want to intrude that for?

Further reflection. How did it happen that *Richards's* remained in Stephenson's mind as indicating the right man, and not some other man's name? That looked good. Yes, that looked very good. In fact, it went on looking better and better, straight along–until by and by it grew into positive *proof*. And then Richards put the matter at once out of his mind, for he had a private instinct that a proof once established is better left so.

He was feeling reasonably comfortable now, but there was still one other detail that kept pushing itself on his notice: of course he had done that service–that was settled; but what *was* that service? He must recall it–he would not go to sleep till he had recalled it; it would make his peace of mind perfect. And so he thought and thought. He thought of a dozen things–possible services–but none of them seemed adequate, none of them seemed large enough, none of them seemed worth the money–worth the fortune Goodson had wished he could leave in his will. And besides, he couldn't remember having done them, anyway. Now, then– now, then–what *kind* of a service would it be that would make a man so inordinately grateful? Ah–the saving of his soul! That must be it. Yes, he could remember, now, how he once set himself the task of converting Goodson, and labored at it as much as–he was going to say three months; but upon closer examination it shrunk to a month, then to a week, then to a day, then to nothing. Yes, he remembered now, and with unwelcome vividness, that Goodson had told him to go to thunder and mind his own business—*he* wasn't hankering to follow Hadleyburg to heaven!

So that solution was a failure—he hadn't saved Goodson's soul. Richards was discouraged. Then after a little came another idea: had he saved Goodson's property? No, that wouldn't do—he hadn't any. His life? That is it! Of course. Why, he might have thought of it before. This time he was on the right track, sure. His imagination-mill was hard at work in a minute, now.

Thereafter during a stretch of two exhausting hours he was busy saving Goodson's life. He saved it in all kinds of difficult and perilous ways. In every case he got it saved satisfactorily up to a certain point; then, just as he was beginning to get well persuaded that it had really happened, a troublesome detail would turn up which made the whole thing impossible. As in the matter of drowning, for instance. In that case he had swum out and tugged Goodson ashore in an unconscious state with a great crowd looking on and applauding, but when he had got it all thought out and was just beginning to remember all about it, a whole swarm of disqualifying details arrived on the ground: the town would have known of the circumstance. Mary would have known of it, it would glare like a limelight in his own memory instead of being an inconspicuous service which he had possibly rendered "without knowing its full value." And at this point he remembered that he couldn't swim, anyway.

Ah—*there* was a point which he had been overlooking from the start: it had to be a service which he had rendered "possibly without knowing the full value of it." Why, really, that ought to be an easy hunt—much easier than those others. And sure enough, by and by he found it. Goodson, years and years ago, came near marrying a very sweet and pretty girl, named Nancy Hewitt, but in some way or other the match had been broken off; the girl died. Goodson remained a bachelor, and by and by became a soured one and a frank despiser of the human species. Soon after the girl's death the village found out, or thought it had found out, that she carried a spoonful of negro blood in her veins. Richards worked at these details a good while, and in the end he thought he remembered things concerning them which must have gotten mislaid in his memory through long neglect. He seemed to dimly remember that it was *he* that found out about the negro blood; that it was he that told the village; that the village told Goodson where they got it; that he thus saved Goodson from marrying the tainted girl; that he had done him this great service "without knowing the full value of it," in fact without knowing that he *was* doing it; but that Goodson knew the value of it, and what a narrow escape he had had, and so went to his grave grateful to his benefactor and wishing he had a fortune to leave him. It was all clear and simple now, and the more he went over it the more luminous and certain it grew; and at last, when he nestled to sleep satisfied and happy, he remembered the whole thing just as if it had been yesterday. In fact, he dimly remembered Goodson's *telling* him his gratitude once. Meantime Mary had spent six thousand dollars on a new house for herself and a pair of slippers for her pastor, and then had fallen peacefully to rest.

That same Saturday evening the postman had delivered a letter to each of the other principal citizens – nineteen letters in all. No two of the envelopes were alike, and no two of the superscriptions were in the same hand, but the letters inside were just like each other in every detail but one. They were exact copies of the letter received by Richards – handwriting and all – and were all signed by Stephenson, but in place of Richards's name each receiver's own name appeared.

All night long eighteen principal citizens did what their caste-brother Richards was doing at the same time – they put in their energies trying to remember what notable service it was that they had unconsciously done Barclay Goodson. In no case was it a holiday job; still they succeeded.

And while they were at this work, which was difficult, their wives put in the night spending the money, which was easy. During that one night the nineteen wives spent an average of seven thousand dollars each out of the forty thousand in the sack – a hundred and thirty-three altogether.

Next day there was a surprise for Jack Halliday. He noticed that the faces of the nineteen chief citizens and their wives bore that expression of peaceful and holy happiness again. He could not understand it, neither was he able to invent any remarks about it that could damage it or disturb it. And so it was his turn to be dissatisfied with life. His private guesses at the reasons for the happiness failed in all instances, upon examination. When he met Mrs. Wilcox and noticed the placid ecstasy in her face, he said to himself, "Her cat has had kittens"–and went and asked the cook; it was not so; the cook had detected the happiness, but did not know the cause. When Halliday found the duplicate ecstasy in the face of "Shadbelly" Billson (village nickname), he was sure some neighbor of Billson's had broken his leg, but inquiry showed that this had not happened. The subdued ecstasy in Gregory Yates's face could mean but one thing–he was a mother-in-law short: it was another mistake. "And Pinkerton – Pinkerton – he has collected ten cents that he thought he was going to lose." And so on, and so on. In some cases the guesses had to remain in doubt, in the others they proved distinct errors. In the end Halliday said to himself, "Anyway it foots up that there's nineteen Hadleyburg families temporarily in heaven: I don't know how it happened; I only know Providence is off duty today."

An architect and builder from the next State had lately ventured to set up a small business in this unpromising village, and his sign had not been hanging out a week. Not a customer yet; he was a discouraged man, and sorry he had come. But his weather changed suddenly now. First one and then another chief citizen's wife said to him privately:

"Come to my house Monday week–but say nothing about it for the present. We think of building."

He got eleven invitations that day. That night he wrote his daughter and broke off her match with her student. He said she could marry a mile higher than that.

Pinkerton the banker and two or three other well-to-do men planned country-seats–but waited. That kind don't count their chickens until they are hatched.

The Wilsons devised a grand new thing–a fancy-dress ball. They made no actual promises, but told all their acquaintance-ship in confidence that they were thinking the matter over and thought they should give it–"and if we do, you will be invited, of course." People were surprised, and said, one to another, "Why, they are crazy, those poor Wilsons, they can't afford it." Several among the nineteen said privately to their husbands, "It is a good idea: we will keep still till their cheap thing is over, then *we* will give one that will make it sick."

The days drifted along, and the bill of future squanderings rose higher and higher, wilder and wilder, more and more foolish and reckless. It began to look as if every member of the nineteen would not only spend his whole forty thousand dollars before receiving-day, but be actually in debt by the time he got the money. In some cases light-headed people did not stop with planning to spend, they really spent–on credit. They bought land, mortgages, farms, speculative stocks, fine clothes, horses, and various other things, paid down the bonus, and made themselves liable for the rest–at ten days. Presently the sober second thought came, and Halli-day noticed that a ghastly anxiety was beginning to show up in a good many faces. Again he was puzzled, and didn't know what to make of it. "The Wilcox kittens aren't dead, for they weren't born; nobody's broken a leg; there's no shrinkage in mother-in-laws; *nothing* has happened–it is an unsolvable mystery."

There was another puzzled man, too–the Rev. Mr. Burgess. For days, wherever he went, people seemed to follow him or to be

watching out for him; and if he ever found himself in a retired
spot, a member of the nineteen would be sure to appear, thrust
an envelope privately into his hand, whisper "To be opened at
the town-hall Friday evening," then vanish away like a guilty thing.
He was expecting that there might be one claimant for the sack,–
doubtful, however. Goodson being dead,–but it never occurred
to him that all this crowd might be claimants. When the great
Friday came at last, he found that he had nineteen envelopes.

III

The town-hall had never looked finer. The platform at the end
of it was backed by a showy draping of flags; at intervals along
the walls were festoons of flags; the gallery fronts were clothed
in flags; the supporting columns were swathed in flags; all this
was to impress the stranger, for he would be there in considerable force, and in a large degree he would be connected with the
press. The house was full. The 412 fixed seats were occupied; also
the 68 extra chairs which had been packed into the aisles; the
steps of the platform were occupied; some distinguished strangers
were given seats on the platform; at the horseshoe of tables which
fenced the front and sides of the platform sat a strong force of
special correspondents who had come from everywhere. It was
the best-dressed house the town had ever produced. There were
some tolerably expensive toilets there, and in several cases the
ladies who wore them had the look of being unfamiliar with that
kind of clothes. At least the town thought they had that look, but
the notion could have arisen from the town's knowledge of the
fact that these ladies had never inhabited such clothes before.

The gold-sack stood on a little table at the front of the platform where all the house could see it. The bulk of the house gazed
at it with a burning interest, a mouth-watering interest, a wistful
and pathetic interest; a minority of nineteen couples gazed at it
tenderly, lovingly, proprietarily, and the male half of this minority
kept saying over to themselves the moving little impromptu

speeches of thankfulness for the audience's applause and congratulations which they were presently going to get up and deliver.
Every now and then one of these got a piece of paper out of his
vest pocket and privately glanced at it to refresh his memory.

Of course there was a buzz of conversation going on – there
always is; but at last when the Rev. Mr. Burgess rose and laid his
hand on the sack he could hear his microbes gnaw, the place was
so still. He related the curious history of the sack, then went on
to speak in warm terms of Hadleyburg's old and well-earned reputation for spotless honesty, and of the town's just pride in this
reputation. He said that this reputation was a treasure of priceless value; that under Providence its value had now become
inestimably enhanced, for the recent episode had spread this fame
far and wide, and thus had focused the eyes of the American world
upon this village, and made its name for all time, as he hoped
and believed, a synonym for commercial incorruptibility.
[*Applause.*] "And who is to be the guardian of this noble treasure –
the community as a whole? No! The responsibility is individual,
not communal. From this day forth each and every one of you
is in his own person its special guardian, and individually responsible that no harm shall come to it. Do you – does each of
you – accept this great trust? [*Tumultuous assent.*] Then all is well.
Transmit it to your children and to your children's children. Today
your purity is beyond reproach – see to it that it shall remain so.
Today there is not a person in your community who could be
beguiled to touch a penny not his own – see to it that you abide
in this grace. ["*We will! we will!*"] This is not the place to make
comparisons between ourselves and other communities – some
of them ungracious toward us; they have their ways, we have ours;
let us be content. [*Applause.*] I am done. Under my hand, my
friends, rests a stranger's eloquent recognition of what we are;
through him the world will always henceforth know what we are.
We do not know who he is, but in your name I utter your gratitude, and ask you to raise your voices in endorsement."

The house rose in a body and made the walls quake with the thunders of its thankfulness for the space of a long minute. Then it sat down, and Mr. Burgess took an envelope out of his pocket. The house held its breath while he slit the envelope open and took from it a slip of paper. He read its contents—slowly and impressively—the audience listening with tranced attention to this magic document, each of whose words stood for an ingot of gold:

" 'The remark which I made to the distressed stranger was this: "You are very far from being a bad man; go, and reform." ' " Then he continued:

"We shall know in a moment now whether the remark here quoted corresponds with the one concealed in the sack; and if that shall prove to be so—and it undoubtedly will—this sack of gold belongs to a fellow-citizen who will henceforth stand before the nation as the symbol of the special virtue which has made our town famous throughout the land—Mr. Billson!"

The house had gotten itself all ready to burst into the proper tornado of applause; but instead of doing it, it seemed stricken with a paralysis; there was a deep hush for a moment or two then a wave of whispered murmurs swept the place—of about this tenor: "*Billson!* oh, come, this is *too* thin! Twenty dollars to a stranger—or *anybody*—*Billson!* tell it to the marines!" And now at this point the house caught its breath all of a sudden in a new access of astonishment, for it discovered that whereas in one part of the hall Deacon Billson was standing up with his head meekly bowed, in another part of it Lawyer Wilson was doing the same. There was a wondering silence now for a while.

Everybody was puzzled, and nineteen couples were surprised and indignant.

Billson and Wilson turned and stared at each other. Billson asked, bitingly,

"Why do *you* rise, Mr. Wilson?"

"Because I have a right to. Perhaps you will be good enough to explain to the house why *you* rise?"

"With great pleasure. Because I wrote that paper."

"It is an impudent falsity! I wrote it myself."

It was Burgess's turn to be paralyzed. He stood looking vacantly at first one of the men and then the other, and did not seem to know what to do. The house was stupefied. Lawyer Wilson spoke up, now, and said,

"I ask the Chair to read the name signed to that paper."

That brought the Chair to itself, and it read out the name.

"'John Wharton *Billson*.'"

"There!" shouted Billson, "what have you got to say for yourself, now? And what kind of apology are you going to make to me and to this insulted house for the imposture which you have attempted to play here?"

"No apologies are due, sir; and as for the rest of it, I publicly charge you with pilfering my note from Mr. Burgess and substituting a copy of it signed with your own name. There is no other way by which you could have gotten hold of the test-remark; I alone, of living men, possessed the secret of its wording."

There was likely to be a scandalous state of things if this went on; everybody noticed with distress that the short-hand scribes were scribbling like mad; many people were crying "Chair, Chair! Order! order!" Burgess rapped with his gavel, and said:

"Let us not forget the proprieties due. There has evidently been a great mistake somewhere, but surely that is all. If Mr. Wilson gave me an envelope – and I remember now that he did – I still have it."

He took one out of his pocket, opened it, glanced at it, looked surprised and worried, and stood silent a few moments. Then he waved his hand in a wandering and mechanical way, and made an effort or two to say something, then gave it up, despondently. Several voices cried out:

"Read it! read it! What is it?"

So he began in a dazed and sleep-walker fashion:

"'*The remark which I made to the unhappy stranger was this:*

"*You are far from being a bad man.* [The house gazed at him, marveling.] *Go, and reform.*'' [*Murmurs:* "Amazing! what can this mean?"] This one," said the Chair, "is signed Thurlow G. Wilson."

"There!" cried Wilson, "I reckon that settles it! I knew perfectly well my note was purloined."

"Purloined!" retorted Billson, "I'll let you know that neither you nor any man of your kidney must venture to –"

The Chair. "Order, gentlemen, order! Take your seats, both of you, please."

They obeyed, shaking their heads and grumbling angrily. The house was profoundly puzzled; it did not know what to do with this curious emergency. Presently Thompson got up. Thompson was the hatter. He would have liked to be a Nineteener; but such was not for him: his stock of hats was not considerable enough for the position. He said:

"Mr. Chairman, if I may be permitted to make a suggestion, can both of these gentlemen be right? I put it to you, sir, can both have happened to say the very same words to the stranger? It seems to me –"

The tanner got up and interrupted him. The tanner was a disgruntled man; he believed himself entitled to be a Nineteener, but he couldn't get recognition. It made him a little unpleasant in his ways and speech. Said he:

"Sho, *that's* not the point! *That* could happen – twice in a hundred years – but not the other thing. *Neither* of them gave the twenty dollars!"

[*A ripple of applause.*]

Billson. "I did!"

Wilson. "I did!"

Then each accused the other of pilfering.

The Chair. "Order! Sit down, if you please – both of you. Neither of the notes has been out of my possession at any moment."

A Voice. "Good – that settles *that!*"

The Tanner. "Mr. Chairman, one thing is now plain: one of these men has been eavesdropping under the other one's bed, and filching family secrets. It if is not unparliamentary to suggest it, I will remark that both are equal to it. [*The Chair.* "Order! order!"] I withdraw the remark, sir, and will confine myself to suggesting that *if* one of them has overheard the other reveal the test-remark to his wife, we shall catch him now."

A Voice. "How?"

The Tanner. "Easily. The two have not quoted the remark in exactly the same words. You would have noticed that, if there hadn't been a considerable stretch of time and an exciting quarrel inserted between the two readings."

A Voice. "Name the difference."

The Tanner. "The word *very* is in Billson's note, and not in the other."

Many Voices. "That's so—he's right!"

The Tanner. "And so, if the Chair will examine the test-remark in the sack, we shall know which of these two frauds—[*The Chair.* "Order!"]—which of these two adventurers—[*The Chair.* "Order! order!"]—which of these two gentlemen—[*laughter and applause*]—is entitled to wear the belt as being the first dishonest blatherskite ever bred in this town—which he has dishonored, and which will be a sultry place for him from now out!" [*Vigorous applause.*]

Many Voices. "Open it!—open the sack!"

Mr. Burgess made a slit in the sack, slid his hand in and brought out an envelope. In it were a couple of folded notes. He said:

"One of these is marked, 'Not to be examined until all written communications which have been addressed to the Chair—if any—shall have been read.' The other is marked 'The Test.' Allow me. It is worded—to wit:

"'I do not require that the first half of the remark which was made to me by my benefactor shall be quoted with exactness, for it was not striking, and could be forgotten; but its closing fifteen words are quite striking, and I think easily rememberable; unless *these* shall be accurately reproduced, let the applicant be regarded as an impostor. My benefactor began by saying he seldom gave advice to any one, but that it always bore the hall-mark of high value when he did give it. Then he said this—and it has never faded from my memory: *"You are far from being a bad man—"'"*

Fifty Voices. "That settles it—the money's Wilson's! Wilson! Wilson! Speech! Speech!"

People jumped up and crowded around Wilson, wringing his hand and congratulating fervently—meantime the Chair was hammering with the gavel and shouting:

"Order, gentlemen! Order! Order! Let me finish reading, please." When quiet was restored, the reading was resumed—as follows:

"'*"Go, and reform—or, mark my words—some day, for your sins, you will die and go to hell or Hadleyburg*—TRY AND MAKE IT THE FORMER."'"

A ghastly silence followed. First an angry cloud began to settle darkly upon the faces of the citizenship; after a pause the cloud began to rise, and a tickled expression tried to take its place; tried so hard that it was only kept under with great and painful difficulty; the reporters, the Brixtonites, and other strangers bent their heads down and shielded their faces with their hands, and managed to hold in by main strength and heroic courtesy. At this most inopportune time burst upon the stillness the roar of a solitary voice—Jack Halliday's: *"That's* got the hall-mark on it!"

Then the house let go, strangers and all. Even Mr. Burgess's gravity broke down presently, then the audience considered itself officially absolved from all restraint, and it made the most of its privilege. It was a good long laugh, and a tempestuously wholehearted one, but it ceased at last—long enough for Mr. Burgess to try to resume, and for the people to get their eyes partially wiped; then it broke out again; and afterward yet again; then at last Burgess was able to get out these serious words:

"It is useless to try to disguise the fact—we find ourselves in the presence of a matter of grave import. It involves the honor of your town, it strikes at the town's good name. The difference of a single word between the test-remarks offered by Mr. Wilson and Mr. Billson was itself a serious thing, since it indicated that one or the other of these gentlemen had committed a theft—"

The two men were sitting limp, nerveless, crushed; but at these words both were electrified into movement, and started to get up—

"Sit down!" said the Chair, sharply, and they obeyed. "That, as I have said, was a serious thing. And it was—but for only one of them. But the matter has become graver; for the honor of *both* is now in formidable peril. Shall I go even further, and say in inextricable peril? *Both* left out the crucial fifteen words." He paused. During several moments he allowed the pervading stillness to gather and deepen its impressive effects, then added: "There would seem to be but one way whereby this could happen. I ask these gentlemen—Was there *collusion?—agreement?*"

A low murmur sifted through the house; its import was, "He's got them both."

Billson was not used to emergencies; he sat in a helpless collapse. But Wilson was a lawyer. He struggled to his feet, pale and worried, and said:

"I ask the indulgence of the house while I explain this most painful matter. I am sorry to say what I am about to say, since it must inflict irreparable injury upon Mr. Billson, whom I have always esteemed and respected until now, and in whose invulnerability to temptation I entirely believed—as did you all. But for the preservation of my own honor I must speak—and with frankness. I confess with shame—and I now beseech your pardon for it—that I said to the ruined stranger all of the words contained in the test-remark, including the disparaging fifteen. [*Sensation.*] When the late publication was made I recalled them, and I resolved to claim the sack of coin, for by every right I was entitled to it. Now I will ask you to consider this point, and weigh it well: that stranger's gratitude to me that night knew no bounds; he said himself that he could find no words for it that were adequate, and that if he should ever be able he would repay me a thousand

fold. Now, then, I ask you this: Could I expect – could I believe –
could I even remotely imagine – that, feeling as he did, he would
do so ungrateful a thing as to add those quite unnecessary fifteen
words to his test? – set a trap for me? – expose me as a slanderer
of my own town before my own people assembled in a public
hall? It was preposterous; it was impossible. His test would contain only the kindly opening clause of my remark. Of that I had
no shadow of doubt. You would have thought as I did. You would
not have expected a base betrayal from one whom you had
befriended and against whom you had committed no offense. And
so, with perfect confidence, perfect trust, I wrote on a piece of
paper the opening words – ending with 'Go, and reform,'– and
signed it. When I was about to put it in an envelope I was called
into my back office, and without thinking I left the paper lying
open on my desk." He stopped, turned his head slowly toward
Billson, waited a moment, then added: "I ask you to note this:
when I returned, a little later, Mr. Billson was retiring by my street
door." [*Sensation.*]

In a moment Billson was on his feet and shouting:

"It's a lie! It's an infamous lie!"

The Chair. "Be seated, sir! Mr. Wilson has the floor."

Billson's friends pulled him into his seat and quieted him, and
Wilson went on:

"Those are the simple facts. My note was now lying in a different place on the table from where I had left it. I noticed that,
but attached no importance to it, thinking a draught had blown
it there. That Mr. Billson would read a private paper was a thing
which could not occur to me; he was an honorable man, and
he would be above that. If you will allow me to say it, I think his
extra word '*very*' stands explained; it is attributable to a defect of
memory. I was the only man in the world who could furnish here
any detail of the test-remark – by *honorable* means. I have finished."

There is nothing in the world like a persuasive speech to fuddle
the mental apparatus and upset the convictions and debauch the

emotions of an audience not practiced in the tricks and delu-
sions of oratory. Wilson sat down victorious. The house submerged
him in tides of approving applause; friends swarmed to him and
shook him by the hand and congratulated him, and Billson was
shouted down and not allowed to say a word. The Chair hammered and hammered with its gavel, and kept shouting.

"But let us proceed, gentlemen. Let us proceed!"

At last there was a measurable degree of quiet, and the
hatter said:

"But what is there to proceed with, sir, but to deliver
the money?"

Voices. "That's it! That's it! come forward, Wilson!"

The Hatter. "I move three cheers for Mr. Wilson, Symbol of
the special virtue which—"

The cheers burst forth before he could finish; and in the midst
of them—and in the midst of the clamor of the gavel also—some
enthusiasts mounted Wilson on a big friend's shoulder and were
going to fetch him in triumph to the platform. The Chair's voice
now rose above the noise—

"Order! To your places! You forget that there is still a document to be read." When quiet had been restored he took up the
document, and was going to read it, but laid it down again, saying,
"I forgot; this is not to be read until all written communications
received by me have first been read." He took an envelope out
of his pocket, removed its enclosure, glanced at it—seemed
astonished—held it out and gazed at it—stared at it.

Twenty or thirty voices cried out:

"What is it? Read it! read it!"

And he did—slowly, and wondering:

" 'The remark which I made to the stranger—[*Voices.* "Hello!
how's this?"]—was this: "You are far from being a bad man. [*Voices.*
"Great Scott!"] Go, and reform.'" [*Voice.* "Oh, saw my leg off!"]
Signed by Mr. Pinkerton the banker."

The pandemonium of delight which turned itself loose now

was of a sort to make the judicious weep. Those whose withers were unwrung laughed till the tears ran down; the reporters, in throes of laughter, set down disordered pot-hooks which would never in the world be decipherable; and a sleeping dog jumped up, scared out of its wits, and barked itself crazy at the turmoil. All manner of cries were scattered through the din: "We're getting rich—*two* Symbols of Incorruptibility!—without counting Billson!" "*Three!*—count Shadbelly in—we can't have too many!" "All right—Billson's elected!" "Alas, poor Wilson—victim of *two* thieves!"

A Powerful Voice. "Silence! The Chair's fished up something more out of its pocket."

Voices. "Hurrah! Is it something fresh? Read it! read! read!"

The Chair [*reading.*] " 'The remark which I made,' etc.: "You are far from being a bad man. Go," etc. Signed, "Gregory Yates." "

Tornado of Voices. "Four Symbols!" " 'Rah for Yates!" "Fish again!"

The house was in a roaring humor now, and ready to get all the fun out of the occasion that might be in it. Several Nineteeners, looking pale and distressed, got up and began to work their way toward the aisles, but a score of shouts went up:

"The doors, the doors—close the doors; no Incorruptible shall leave this place! Sit down, everybody!"

The mandate was obeyed.

"Fish again! Read! read!"

The Chair fished again, and once more the familiar words began to fall from its lips—" 'You are far from being a bad man—' "

"Name! name! What's his name?"

" 'L. Ingoldsby Sargent.' "

"Five elected! Pile up the Symbols! Go on, go on!"

" 'You are far from being a bad—' "

"Name! name!"

" 'Nicholas Whitworth.' "

"Hooray! hooray! it's a symbolical day!"

Somebody wailed in, and began to sing this rhyme (leaving out "it's") to the lovely "Mikado" tune of "When a man's afraid,

a beautiful maid –"; the audience joined in, with joy; then, just
in time, somebody contributed another line –

"And don't you this forget –"

The house roared it out. A third line was at once furnished –

"Corruptibles far from Hadleyburg are –"

The house roared that one too. As the last note died, Jack Halliday's voice rose high and clear, freighted with a final line –

"But the Symbols are here, you bet!"

That was sung, with booming enthusiasm. Then the happy house
started in at the beginning and sang the four lines through twice,
with immense swing and dash, and finished up with a crashing
three-times-three and a tiger for "Hadleyburg the Incorruptible
and all Symbols of it which we shall find worthy to receive the
hall-mark tonight."

Then the shoutings at the Chair began again, all over the place:
"Go on! go on! Read! read some more! Read all you've got!"
"That's it – go on! We are winning eternal celebrity!"

A dozen men got up now and began to protest. They said that
this farce was the work of some abandoned joker, and was an
insult to the whole community. Without a doubt these signatures
were all forgeries –

"Sit down! sit down! Shut up! You are confessing. We'll find
your names in the lot."

"Mr. Chairman, how many of those envelopes have you got?"
The Chair counted.

"Together with those that have been already examined, there
are nineteen."

A storm of derisive applause broke out.

"Perhaps they all contain the secret. I move that you open them
all and read every signature that is attached to a note of that sort –
and read also the first eight words of the note."

"Second the motion!"

It was put and carried—uproariously. Then poor old Richards got up, and his wife rose and stood at his side. Her head was bent down, so that none might see that she was crying. Her husband gave her his arm, and so supporting her, he began to speak in a quavering voice:

"My friends, you have known us two—Mary and me—all our lives, and I think you have liked us and respected us—"

The Chair interrupted him:

"Allow me. It is quite true—that which you are saying, Mr. Richards—this town *does* know you two; it *does* like you; it *does* respect you; more—it honors you and *loves* you—"

Halliday's voice rang out:

"That's the hall-marked truth, too! If the Chair is right, let the house speak up and say it. Rise! Now, then—hip! hip! hip!—all together!"

The house rose in mass, faced toward the old couple eagerly, filled the air with a snowstorm of waving handkerchiefs, and delivered the cheers with all its affectionate heart.

The Chair then continued:

"What I was going to say is this: We know your good heart, Mr. Richards, but this is not a time for the exercise of charity toward offenders. [*Shouts of* "Right! right!"] I see your generous purpose in your face, but I cannot allow you to plead for these men—"

"But I was going to—"

"Please take your seat, Mr. Richards. We must examine the rest of these notes—simple fairness to the men who have already been exposed requires this. As soon as that has been done—I give you my word for this—you shall be heard."

Many Voices. "Right!—the Chair is right—no interruption can be permitted at this stage! Go on!—the names! the names!—according to the terms of the motion!"

The old couple sat reluctantly down, and the husband whispered to the wife, "It is pitifully hard to have to wait; the shame will be greater than ever when they find we were only going to plead for *ourselves*."

Straightway the jollity broke loose again with the reading of the names.

" 'You are far from being a bad man—' Signature, 'Robert J. Titmarsh.'

" 'You are far from being a bad man—' Signature, 'Eliphalet Weeks.'

" 'You are far from being a bad man—' Signature, 'Oscar B. Wilder.' "

At this point the house lit upon the idea of taking the eight words out of the Chairman's hands. He was not unthankful for that. Thenceforward he held up each note in its turn, and waited. The house droned out the eight words in a massed and measured and musical deep volume of sound (with a daringly close resemblance to a well-known church chant)—" 'You are f-a-r from being a b-a-a-a-d man.' " Then the Chair said, "Signature, 'Archibald Wilcox.' " And so on, and so on, name after name, and everybody had an increasingly and gloriously good time except the wretched Nineteen. Now and then, when a particularly shining name was called, the house made the Chair wait while it chanted the whole of the test-remark from the beginning to the closing words, "And go to hell or Hadleyburg—try and make it the for-or-m-e-r!" and in these special cases they added a grand and agonized and imposing "A-a-a-a-*men!*"

The list dwindled, dwindled, dwindled, poor old Richards keeping tally of the count, wincing when a name resembling his own was pronounced, and waiting in miserable suspense for the time to come when it would be his humiliating privilege to rise with Mary and finish his plea, which he was intending to word thus: ". . . for until now we have never done any wrong thing, but have gone our humble way unreproached. We are very poor, we are old, and have no chick nor child to help us; we were sorely tempted, and we fell. It was my purpose when I got up before to make confession and beg that my name might not be read out in this public place, for it seemed to us that we could not bear it; but I was prevented. It was just; it was our place to suffer with the rest. It has been hard for us. It is the first time we have ever heard our name fall from any one's lips—sullied. Be merciful—for the sake of the better days; make our shame as light to bear as in your charity you can." At this point in his revery Mary nudged him, perceiving that his mind was absent. The house was chanting, "You are f-a-r," etc.

"Be ready," Mary whispered. "Your name comes now; he has read eighteen."

The chant ended.

"Next! next! next!" came volleying from all over the house.

Burgess put his hand into his pocket. The old couple, trembling, began to rise. Burgess fumbled a moment, then said,

"I find I have read them all."

Faint with joy and surprise, the couple sank into their seats, and Mary whispered,

"Oh, bless God, we are saved!—he has lost ours—I wouldn't give this for a hundred of those sacks!"

The house burst out with its "Mikado" travesty, and sang it three times with ever-increasing enthusiasm, rising to its feet when it reached for the third time the closing line—

"But the Symbols are here, you bet!"

and finishing up with cheers and a tiger for "Hadleyburg purity and our eighteen immortal representatives of it."

Then Wingate, the saddler, got up and proposed cheers "for the cleanest man in town, the one solitary important citizen in it who didn't try to steal that money—Edward Richards."

They were given with great and moving heartiness; then somebody proposed that Richards be elected sole guardian and Symbol of the now Sacred Hadleyburg Tradition, with power and right to stand up and look the whole sarcastic world in the face.

Passed by acclamation; then they sang the "Mikado" again, and ended it with,

"And there's *one* Symbol left, you bet!"

There was a pause; then —

A Voice. "Now, then, who's to get the sack?"

The Tanner (with bitter sarcasm). "That's easy. The money has to be divided among the eighteen Incorruptibles. They gave the suffering stranger twenty dollars apiece — and that remark — each in his turn — it took twenty-two minutes for the procession to move past. Staked the stranger — total contribution, $360. All they want is just the loan back — and interest — forty thousand dollars altogether."

Many Voices [derisively.] "That's it! Divvy! divvy! Be kind to the poor — don't keep them waiting!"

The Chair. "Order! I now offer the stranger's remaining document. It says: 'If no claimant shall appear [*grand chorus of groans*], I desire that you open the sack and count out the money to the principal citizens of your town, they to take it in trust [*cries of* "Oh! Oh! Oh!"], and use it in such ways as to them shall seem best for the propagation and preservation of your community's noble reputation for incorruptible honesty [*more cries*] — a reputation to which their names and their efforts will add a new and far-reaching lustre.' [*Enthusiastic outburst of sarcastic applause.*] That seems to be all. No — here is a postscript:

" 'P.S. — CITIZENS OF HADLEYBURG: There *is* no test-remark — nobody made one [*Great sensation.*] There wasn't any pauper stranger, nor any twenty-dollar contribution, nor any accompanying benediction and compliment — these are all inventions. [*General buzz and hum of astonishment and delight.*] Allow me to tell my story — it will take but a word or two. I passed through your town at a certain time, and received a deep offense which I had not earned. Any other man would have been content to kill one or two of you and call it square, but to me that would have been a trivial revenge, and inadequate; for the dead do not *suffer*. Besides, I could not kill you all – and, anyway, made as I am, even that would not have satisfied me. I wanted to damage every man in the place, and every woman – and not in their bodies or in their estate, but in their vanity – the place where feeble and foolish people are most vulnerable. So I disguised myself and came back and studied you. You were easy game. You had an old and lofty reputation for honesty, and naturally you were proud of it – it was your treasure of treasures, the very apple of your eye. As soon as I found out that you carefully and vigilantly kept yourselves and your children *out of temptation,* I knew how to proceed. Why, you simple creatures, the weakest of all weak things is a virtue which has not been tested in the fire. I laid a plan, and gathered a list of names. My project was to corrupt Hadleyburg the Incorruptible. My idea was to make liars and thieves of nearly half a hundred smirchless men and women who had never in their lives uttered a lie or stolen a penny. I was afraid of Goodson. He was neither born nor reared in Hadleyburg. I was afraid that if I started to operate my scheme by getting my letter laid before you, you would say to yourselves, "Goodson is the only man among us who would give away twenty dollars to a poor devil"– and then you might not bite at my bait. But Heaven took Goodson; then I knew I was safe, and I set my trap and baited it. It may be that I shall not catch all the men to whom I mailed the pretended test secret, but I shall catch the most of them, if I knew Hadleyburg nature. [*Voices.* "Right – he got every last one of them."] I believe they will even steal ostensible *gamble*-money, rather than miss, poor, tempted, and mistrained fellows. I am hoping to eternally and everlastingly squelch your vanity and give Hadleyburg a new renown – one that will *stick* – and spread far. If I have succeeded, open the sack and summon the Committee on Propagation and Preservation of the Hadleyburg Reputation.' "

A Cyclone of Voices. "Open it! Open it! The Eighteen to the front! Committee on Propagation of the Tradition! Forward – the Incorruptibles!"

The Chair ripped the sack wide, and gathered up a handful of bright, broad, yellow coins, shook them together, then examined them—

"Friends, they are only gilded disks of lead!"

There was a crashing outbreak of delight over this news, and when the noise had subsided, the tanner called out:

"By right of apparent seniority in this business, Mr. Wilson is Chairman of the Committee on Propagation of the Tradition. I suggest that he step forward on behalf of his pals, and receive in trust the money."

A Hundred Voices. "Wilson! Wilson! Wilson! Speech! Speech!"

Wilson [*in a voice trembling with anger.*] "You will allow me to say, and without apologies for my language, *damn* the money!"

A Voice. "Oh, and him a Baptist!"

A Voice. "Seventeen Symbols left! Step up, gentlemen, and assume your trust!"

There was a pause—no response.

The Saddler. "Mr. Chairman, we've got *one* clean man left, anyway, out of the late aristocracy; and he needs money, and deserves it. I move that you appoint Jack Halliday to get up there and auction off that sack of gilt twenty-dollar pieces, and give the result to the right man—the man whom Hadleyburg delights to honor—Edward Richards."

This was received with great enthusiasm, the dog taking a hand again; the saddler started the bids at a dollar, the Brixton folk and Barnum's representative fought hard for it, the people cheered every jump that the bids made, the excitement climbed moment by moment higher and higher, the bidders got their mettle and grew steadily more and more daring, more and more determined, the jumps went from a dollar up to five, then to ten, then to twenty, then fifty, then to a hundred, then—

At the beginning of the auction Richards whispered in distress to his wife: "O Mary, can we allow it? It—it—you see, it is an honor-reward, a testimonial to purity of character, and—and—

can we allow it? Hadn't I better get up and–O Mary, what ought we to do?–what do you think we–"[*Halliday's voice. "Fifteen, I'm bid!–fifteen for the sack!–twenty!–ah, thanks!–thirty–thanks again! Thirty, thirty, thirty–do I hear forty?–forty it is! Keep the ball rolling, gentlemen, keep it rolling!–fifty!–thanks, noble Roman! going at fifty, fifty, fifty!–seventy!–ninety!–splendid!–a hundred!–pile it up, pile it up!–hundred and twenty–forty!–just in time!–hundred and fifty–TWO hundred!–superb! Do I hear two h–thanks! two hundred and fifty!–"*]

"It is another temptation, Edward–I'm all in a tremble–but, oh, we've escaped *one* temptation, and that ought to warn us to–["*Six did I hear?–thanks!–six fifty, six f–SEVEN hundred!*"] And yet, Edward, when you think–nobody susp–["*Eight hundred dollars!–hurrah!–make it nine!–Mr. Parsons, did I hear you say–thanks–nine!–this noble sack of virgin lead going at only nine hundred dollars, gilding and all–come! do I hear–a thousand!–gratefully yours!–did some one say eleven?–a sack which is going to be the most celebrated in the whole Uni–*"] O Edward" (beginning to sob), "we are *so* poor!–but–but–do as you think best–do as you think best."

Edward fell–that is, he sat still; sat with a conscience which was not satisfied, but which was overpowered by circumstances.

Meantime a stranger, who looked like an amateur detective gotten up as an impossible English earl, had been watching the evening's proceedings with manifest interest, and with a contented expression in his face; and he had been privately commenting to himself. He was now soliloquizing somewhat like this: "None of the Eighteen are bidding; that is not satisfactory; I must change that–the dramatic unities require it; they must buy the sack they tried to steal; they must pay a heavy price, too–some of them are rich. And another thing, when I make a mistake in Hadleyburg nature the man that puts that error upon me is entitled to a high honorarium, and some one must pay it. This poor old Richards has brought my judgment to shame; he is an honest man: – I don't understand it, but I acknowledge it. Yes, he saw my deuces *and* with a straight flush, and by rights the pot is his. And it shall be a jack-pot, too, if I can manage it. He disappointed me, but let that pass."

He was watching the bidding. At a thousand, the market broke; the prices tumbled swiftly. He waited – and still watched. One competitor dropped out; then another, and another. He put in a bid or two, now. When the bids had sunk to ten dollars, he added a five; some one raised him a three; he waited a moment, then flung in a fifty-dollar jump, and the sack was his – at $1,282. The house broke out in cheers – then stopped; for he was on his feet, and had lifted his hand. He began to speak.

"I desire to say a word, and ask a favor. I am a speculator in rarities, and I have dealings with persons interested in numismatics all over the world. I can make a profit on this purchase, just as it stands; but there is a way, if I can get your approval, whereby I can make every one of these leaden twenty-dollar pieces worth its face in gold, and perhaps more. Grant me that approval, and I will give part of my gains to your Mr. Richards, whose invulnerable probity you have so justly and so cordially recognized tonight; his share shall be ten thousand dollars, and I will hand him the money tomorrow. [*Great applause from the house*. But the "invulnerable probity" made the Richardses blush prettily; however, it went for modesty, and did no harm.] If you will pass my proposition by a good majority – I would like a two-thirds vote – I will regard that as the town's consent, and that is all I ask. Rarities are always helped by any device which will rouse curiosity and compel remark. Now if I may have your permission to stamp upon the faces of each of these ostensible coins the names of the eighteen gentlemen who –"

Nine-tenths of the audience were on their feet in a moment – dog and all – and the proposition was carried with a whirlwind of approving applause and laughter.

They sat down, and all the Symbols except "Dr." Clay

Harkness got up, violently protesting against the proposed outrage, and threatening to –

"I beg you not to threaten me," said the stranger, calmly. "I know my legal rights, and am not accustomed to being frightened at bluster." [*Applause.*] He sat down. "Dr." Harkness saw an opportunity here. He was one of the two very rich men of the place, and Pinkerton was the other. Harkness was proprietor of a mint; that is to say, a popular patent medicine. He was running for the Legislature on one ticket, and Pinkerton on the other. It was a close race and a hot one, and getting hotter every day. Both had strong appetites for money; each had bought a great tract of land, with a purpose; there was going to be a new railway, and each wanted to be in the Legislature and help locate the route to his own advantage; a single vote might make the decision, and with it two or three fortunes. The stake was large, and Harkness was a daring speculator. He was sitting close to the stranger. He leaned over while one or another of the other Symbols was entertaining the house with protests and appeals, and asked, in a whisper,

"What is your price for the sack?"

"Forty thousand dollars."

"I'll give you twenty."

"No."

"Twenty-five."

"No."

"Say thirty."

"The price is forty thousand dollars; not a penny less."

"All right, I'll give it. I will come to the hotel at ten in the morning. I don't want it known; will see you privately."

"Very good." Then the stranger got up and said to the house:

"I find it late. The speeches of these gentlemen are not without merit, not without interest, not without grace; yet if I may be excused I will take my leave. I thank you for the great favor which you have shown me in granting my petition. I ask the Chair to keep the sack for me until tomorrow, and to hand these three five-hundred-dollar notes to Mr. Richards." They were passed up to the Chair. "At nine I will call for the sack, and at eleven will deliver the rest of the ten thousand to Mr. Richards in person, at his home. Good night."

Then he slipped out, and left the audience making a vast noise, which was composed of a mixture of cheers, the "Mikado" song, dog-disapproval, and the chant, "You are f-a-r from being a b-a-a-d man – a-a-a-a-men!"

IV

At the home the Richardses had to endure congratulations and compliments until midnight. Then they were left to themselves. They looked a little sad, and they sat silent and thinking. Finally Mary sighed and said,

"Do you think we are to blame, Edward – *much* to blame?" and her eyes wandered to the accusing triplet of big bank notes lying on the table, where the congratulators had been gloating over them and reverently fingering them. Edward did not answer at once; then he brought out a sigh and said hesitatingly:

"We – we couldn't help it, Mary. It – well, it was ordered. *All* things are."

Mary glanced up and looked at him steadily, but he didn't return the look. Presently she said:

"I thought congratulations and praises always tasted good. But – it seems to me, now – Edward?"

"Well?"

"Are you going to stay in the bank?"

"N-no."

"Resign?"

"In the morning – by note."

"It does seem best."

Richards bowed his head in his hands and muttered:

"Before, I was not afraid to let oceans of people's money pour through my hands, but – Mary, I am so tired, so tired –"

"We will go to bed."

At nine in the morning the stranger called for the sack and took it to the hotel in a cab. At ten Harkness had a talk with him privately. The stranger asked for and got five checks on a metropolitan bank–drawn to "Bearer,"–four for $1,500 each, and one for $34,000. He put one of the former in his pocketbook, and the remainder, representing $38,500, he put in an envelope, and with these he added a note, which he wrote after Harkness was gone. At eleven he called at the Richards house and knocked. Mrs. Richards peeped through the shutters, then went and received the envelope, and the stranger disappeared without a word. She came back flushed and a little unsteady on her legs, and gasped out:

"I am sure I recognized him! Last night it seemed to me that maybe I had seen him somewhere before."

"He is the man that brought the sack here?"

"I am almost sure of it."

"Then he is the ostensible Stephenson, too, and sold every important citizen in this town with his bogus secret. Now if he has sent checks instead of money, we are sold, too, after we thought we had escaped. I was beginning to feel fairly comfortable once more, after my night's rest, but the look of that envelope makes me sick. It isn't fat enough; $8,500 in even the largest bank notes makes more bulk than that."

"Checks signed by Stephenson! I am resigned to take the $8,500 if it could come in bank notes–for it does seem that it was so ordered, Mary–but I have never had much courage, and I have not the pluck to try to market a check signed with that disastrous name. It would be a trap. That man tried to catch me; we escaped somehow or other; and now he is trying a new way. If it is checks–"

"Oh, Edward, it is *too* bad!" and she held up the checks and began to cry.

"Put them in the fire! quick! we mustn't be tempted. It is a

trick to make the world laugh at *us,* along with the rest, and—
Give them to *me,* since you can't do it!" He snatched them and
tried to hold his grip till he could get to the stove; but he was
human, he was a cashier, and he stopped a moment to make sure
of the signature. Then he came near to fainting.

"Fan me, Mary, fan em! They are the same as gold!"

"Oh, how lovely, Edward! Why?"

"Signed by Harkness. What can the mystery of that be, Mary?"

"Edward, do you think—"

"Look here—look at this! Fifteen—fifteen—fifteen—thirty-four.
Thirty-eight thousand five hundred! Mary, the sack isn't worth
twelve dollars, and Harkness—apparently—has paid about par
for it."

"And does it all come to us, do you think—instead of ten
thousand?"

"Why, it looks like it. And the checks are made to 'Bearer,' too."

"Is that good, Edward? What is it for?"

"A hint to collect them at some distant bank, I reckon. Perhaps
Harkness doesn't want the matter known. What is that—a note?"

"Yes, It was with the checks."

It was in the "Stephenson" handwriting, but there was no signature. It said:

> "I am a disappointed man. Your honesty is beyond the reach of temp-
> tation. I had a different idea about it, but I wronged you in that, and
> I beg pardon, and do it sincerely. I honor you—and that is sincere too.
> This town is not worthy to kiss the hem of your garment. Dear sir, I made
> a square bet with myself that there were nineteen debauchable men in
> your self-righteous community. I have lost. Take the whole pot, you are
> entitled to it."

Richards drew a deep sigh, and said:

"It seems written with fire—it burns so. Mary—I am miserable again."

"I, too. Ah, dear, I wish—"

"To think, Mary—he *believes* in me."

"Oh, don't, Edward—I can't bear it."

"If those beautiful words were deserved, Mary—and God knows I believed I deserved them once—I think I could give the forty thousand dollars for them. And I would put that paper away, as representing more than gold and jewels, and keep it always. But now—We could not live in the shadow of its accusing presence, Mary."

He put it in the fire.

A messenger arrived and delivered an envelope.

Richards took from it a note and read it; it was from Burgess.

> *"You saved me, in a difficult time. I saved you last night. It was at cost of a lie, but I made the sacrifice freely, and out of a grateful heart. None in this village knows so well as I know how brave and good and noble you are. At the bottom you cannot respect me, knowing as you do of that matter of which I am accused, and by the general voice condemned; but I beg that you will at least believe that I am a grateful man; it will help me to bear my burden.*
> [Signed]   "BURGESS."

"Saved, once more. And on such terms!" He put the note in the fire. "I—I wish I were dead, Mary, I wish I were out of it all."

"Oh, these are bitter, bitter days, Edward. The stabs, through their very generosity, are so deep—and they come so fast!"

Three days before the election each of two thousand voters suddenly found himself in possession of a prized memento— one of the renowned bogus double-eagles. Around one of its faces was stamped these words: "THE REMARK I MADE TO THE POOR STRANGER WAS—" Around the other face was stamped these: "GO, AND REFORM. [SIGNED] PINKERTON." Thus the entire remaining refuse of the renowned joke was emptied upon a single head, and with calamitous effect. It revived the recent vast laugh and concentrated it upon Pinkerton; and Harkness's election was a walkover.

Within twenty-four hours after the Richardses had received their checks their consciences were quieting down, discouraged;

the old couple were learning to reconcile themselves to the sin which they had now committed. But they were to learn, now, that a sin takes on new and real terrors when there seems a chance that it is going to be found out. This gives it a fresh and most substantial and important aspect. At church the morning sermon was of the usual pattern; it was the same old things said in the same old way; they had heard them a thousand times and found them innocuous, next to meaningless, and easy to sleep under; but now it was different: the sermon seemed to bristle with accusation; it seemed aimed straight and specially at people who were concealing deadly sins. After church they got away from the mob of congratulators as soon as they could, and hurried homeward, chilled to the bone at they did not know what—vague, shadowy, indefinite fears. And by chance they caught a glimpse of attention to their nod of recognition! He hadn't seen it; but they did not know that. What could his conduct mean? It might mean—it might mean—oh, a dozen dreadful things. Was it possible that he knew that Richards could have cleared him of guilt in that bygone time, and had been silently waiting for a chance to even up accounts? At home, in their distress they got to imagining that their servant might have been in the next room listening when Richards revealed the secret to his wife that he knew of Burgess's innocence; next, Richards began to imagine that he had heard the swish of a gown in there at that time; next, he was sure he *had* heard it. They would call Sarah in, on pretext, and watch her face; if she had been betraying them to Mr. Burgess, it would show in her manner. They asked her some questions—questions which were so random and incoherent and seemingly purposeless that the girl felt sure that the old people's minds had been affected by their sudden good fortune; the sharp and watchful gaze which they bent upon her frightened her, and that completed the business. She blushed, she became nervous and confused, and to the old people these were plain signs of guilt—guilt of some fearful sort or other—without doubt she was a spy and a traitor. When they were alone again they began to piece many unrelated things together and get horrible results out of the combination. When things had got about to the worst, Richards was delivered of a sudden gasp, and his wife asked,

"Oh, what is it?—what is it?"

"The note—Burgess's note! Its language was sarcastic, I see it now." He quoted: "'At bottom you cannot respect me, *knowing*, as you do, of *that matter* of which I am accused'—oh, it is perfectly plain, now, God help me! He knows that I know! You see the ingenuity of the phrasing. It was a trap—and like a fool, I walked into it. And Mary—?"

"Oh, it is dreadful—I know what you are going to say—he didn't return your transcript of the pretended test-remark."

"No—kept it to destroy us with. Mary, he has exposed us to some already. I know it—I know it well. I saw it in a dozen faces after church. Ah, he wouldn't answer our nod of recognition—*he* knew what he had been doing!"

In the night the doctor was called. The news went around in the morning that the old couple were rather seriously ill—prostrated by the exhausting excitement growing out of their great windfall, the congratulations, and the late hours, the doctor said. The town was sincerely distressed; for these old people were about all it had left to be proud of, now.

Two days later the news was worse. The old couple were delirious, and were doing strange things. By witness of the nurses, Richards had exhibited checks—for $8,500? No—for an amazing sum—$38,500! What could be the explanation of this gigantic piece of luck?

The following day the nurses had more news—and wonderful. They had concluded to hide the checks, lest harm come to them; but when they searched they were gone from under the patient's pillow—vanished away. The patient said:

"Let the pillow alone; what do you want?"

"We thought it best that the checks—"

"You will never see them again – they are destroyed. They came from Satan. I saw the hell-brand on them, and I knew they were sent to betray me to sin." Then he fell to gabbling strange and dreadful things which were not clearly understandable, and which the doctor admonished them to keep to themselves.

Richards was right; the checks were never seen again.

A nurse must have talked in her sleep, for within two days the forbidden gabblings were the property of the town; and they were of a surprising sort. They seemed to indicate that Richards had been a claimant for the sack himself, and that Burgess had concealed that fact and then maliciously betrayed it.

Burgess was taxed with this and stoutly denied it. And he said it was not fair to attach weight to the chatter of a sick old man who was out of his mind. Still, suspicion was in the air, and there was much talk.

After a day or two it was reported that Mrs. Richards's delirious deliveries were getting to be duplicates of her husband's. Suspicion flamed up into conviction, now, and the town's pride in the purity of its one undiscredited important citizen began to dim down and flicker toward extinction.

Six days passed, then came more news. The old couple were dying. Richards's mind cleared in his latest hour, and he sent for Burgess. Burgess said:

"Let the room be cleared. I think he wishes to say something in privacy."

"No!" said Richards: "I want witnesses. I want you all to hear my confession, so that I may die a man, and not a dog. I was clean – artificially – like the rest; and like the rest I fell when temptation came. I signed a lie, and claimed the miserable sack. Mr. Burgess remembered that I had done him a service, and in gratitude (and ignorance) he suppressed my claim and saved me. You know the thing that was charged against Burgess years ago. My testimony, and mine alone, could have cleared him, and I was a coward, and left him to suffer disgrace –"

"No – no – Mr. Richards, you –"

"My servant betrayed my secret to him –"

"No one has betrayed anything to me –"

–"and then he did a natural and justifiable thing, he repented of the saving kindness which he had done me, and he *exposed* me – as I deserved –"

"Never! – I make oath –"

"Out of my heart I forgive him."

Burgess's impassioned protestation fell upon deaf ears; the dying man passed away without knowing that once more he had done poor Burgess a wrong. The old wife died that night.

The last of the sacred Nineteen had fallen a prey to the fiendish sack; the town was stripped of the last rag of its ancient glory. Its mourning was not showy, but it was deep.

By act of the Legislature – upon prayer and petition – Hadleyburg was allowed to change its name to (never mind what – I will not give it away), and leave one word out of the motto that for many generations had graced the town's official seal.

It is an honest town once more, and the man will have to rise early that catches it napping again.

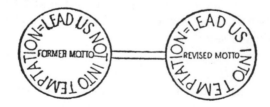

THE $30,000 BEQUEST

Published in *Harper's Magazine,* December 10, 1904, "The $30,000
Bequest" perhaps reflects Twain's own familiarity with the lure of
money. Twain wrote the story after his family had retired to
Florence, Italy in the hope of restoring his wife's health.
"The $30,000 Bequest" also was featured in the collection,
The $30,000 Bequest and Other Stories, published
by Harper & Brothers in 1906.

I

Lakeside was a pleasant little town of five or six thousand inhabitants, and a rather pretty one, too, as towns go in the Far West. It had church accommodations for 35,000, which is the way of the Far West and the South, where everybody is religious, and where each of the Protestant sects is represented and has a plant of its own. Rank was unknown in Lakeside—unconfessed, anyway; everybody knew everybody and his dog, and a sociable friendliness was prevailing atmosphere.

Saladin Foster was book-keeper in the principal store, and the only high-salaried man of his profession in Lakeside. He was thirty-five years old, now; he had served that store for fourteen years; he had begun in his marriage-week at four hundred dollars a year, and had climbed steadily up, a hundred dollars a year, for four years; from that time forth his wage had remained eight hundred—a handsome figure indeed, and everybody conceded that he was worth it.

His wife, Electra, was a capable helpmeet, although—like himself—a dreamer of dreams and a private dabbler in romance. The first thing she did, after her marriage—child as she was, aged only nineteen—was to buy an acre of ground on the edge of the town, and pay down the cash for it—twenty-five dollars, all her fortune. Saladin had less, by fifteen. She instituted a vegetable garden there,

got it farmed on shares by the nearest neighbor, and made it pay
her a hundred per cent a year. Out of Saladin's first year's wage
she put thirty dollars in the savings-bank, sixty out of his second,
a hundred out of his third, a hundred and fifty out of his fourth.
His wage went to eight hundred a year, then, and meantime two
children had arrived and increased the expenses, but she banked
two hundred a year from the salary, nevertheless, thenceforth.
When she had been married seven years she built and furnished
a pretty and comfortable two-thousand dollar house in the midst
of her garden-acre, paid half of the money down and moved her
family in. Seven years later she was out of debt and had several
hundred dollars out earning its living.

Earning it by the rise in landed estate; for she had long ago
bought another acre or two and sold the most of it at a profit
to pleasant people who were willing to build, and would be good
neighbors and furnish a general comradeship for herself and her
growing family. She had an independent income from safe investments of about a hundred dollars a year; her children were growing
in years and grace; and she was a pleased and happy woman.
Happy in her husband, happy in her children, and the husband
and the children were happy in her. It is at this point that this
history begins.

The youngest girl, Clytemnestra – called Clytie for short – was
eleven; her sister, Gwendolen – called Gwen for short – was
thirteen; nice girls, and comely. The names betray the latent
romance-tinge in the parental blood, the parents' names indicate
that the tinge was an inheritance. It was an affectionate family,
hence all four of its members had pet names. Saladin's was a curious and unsexing one – Sally; and so was Electra's – Aleck. All day
long Sally was a good and diligent book-keeper and salesman;
all day long Aleck was a good and faithful mother and house-
wife, and thoughtful and calculating business-woman; but in the
cosey living-room at night they put the plodding world away, and
lived in another and a fairer, reading romances to each other,

dreaming dreams, comrading with kings and princes and stately
lords and ladies in the flash and stir and splendor of noble palaces
and grim and ancient castles.

II

Now came great news! Stunning news—joyous news, in fact.
It came from a neighboring State, where the family's only surviv-
ing relative lived. It was Sally's relative—a sort of vague and
indefinite uncle or second or third cousin by the name of Tilbury
Foster, seventy and a bachelor, reputed well-off and correspond-
ingly sour and crusty. Sally had tried to make up to him once,
by letter, in a by-gone time, and had not made that mistake again.
Tilbury now wrote to Sally, saying he should shortly die, and
should leave him thirty thousand dollars, cash; not for love, but
because money had given him most of his troubles and exasper-
ations, and he wished to place it where there was good hope that
it would continue its malignant work. The bequest would be found
in his will, and would be paid over. *Provided,* that Sally should
be able to prove to the executors that he had *taken no notice of
the gift by spoken word or by letter, had made no inquiries concerning the moribund's progress towards the everlasting tropics, and had
not attended the funeral.*

As soon as Aleck had partially recovered from the tremendous
emotions created by the letter, she sent to the relative's habitat
and subscribed for the local paper.

Man and wife entered into a solemn compact, now, to never
mention the great news to any one while the relative lived, lest
some ignorant person carry the fact to the death-bed and distort
it and make it appear that they were disobediently thankful for
the bequest, and just the same as confessing it and publishing
it, right in the face of the prohibition.

For the rest of the day Sally made havoc and confusion
with his books, and Aleck could not keep her mind on her affairs,
nor even take up a flower-pot or book or a stick of wood

without forgetting what she had intended to do with it. For both were dreaming.

"Thir-ty thousand dollars!"

All day long the music of those inspiring words sang through those people's heads.

From his marriage-day forth, Aleck's grip had been upon the purse, and Sally had seldom known what it was to be privileged to squander a dime on non-necessities.

"Thir-ty thousand dollars!" the song went on and on. A vast sum, an unthinkable sum!

All day long Aleck was absorbed in planning how to invest it, Sally in planning how to spend it.

There was no romance-reading that night. The children took themselves away early, for the parents were silent, distraught, and strangely unentertaining. The good-night kisses might as well have been impressed upon vacancy, for all the response they got; the parents were not aware of the kisses, and the children had been gone an hour before their absence was noticed. Two pencils had been busy during that hour—note-making; in the way of plans. It was Sally who broke the stillness at last. He said with exultation—

"Ah, it'll be grand, Aleck! Out of the first thousand we'll have a horse and a buggy for summer, and a cutter and a skin lap-robe for winter."

Aleck responded with decision and composure—

"Out of the *capital?* Nothing of the kind. Not if it was a million!"

Sally was deeply disappointed; the glow went out of his face.

"Oh, Aleck!" he said, reproachfully. "We've always worked so hard and been so scrimped; and now that we are rich, it does seem—"

He did not finish, for he saw her eye soften; his supplication had touched her. She said, with gentle persuasiveness—

"We must not spend the capital, dear, it would not be wise. Out of the income from it—"

"That will answer, that will answer, Aleck! How dear and good you are! There will be a noble income, and if we can spend that—"

"Not *all* of it, dear, not all of it, but you can spend a part of it. That is, a reasonable part. But the whole of the capital—every penny of it—must be put to work, and kept at it. You see the reasonableness of that, don't you?"

"Why, ye-s. Yes, of course. But we'll have to wait so long. Six months before the first interest falls due."

"Yes—maybe longer."

"Longer, Aleck? Why? Don't they pay half-yearly?"

"*That* kind of an investment—yes; but I sha'n't invest in that way."

"What way then?"

"For big returns."

"Big. That's good. Go on, Aleck. What is it?"

"Coal. The new mines. Cannel. I mean to put in ten thousand. Ground floor. When we organize, we'll get three shares for one."

"By George, but it sounds good, Aleck! Then the shares will be worth—how much? And when?"

"About a year. They'll pay ten per cent. Half-yearly, and be worth thirty thousand. I know all about it; the advertisement is in the Cincinnati paper here."

"Land, thirty thousand for ten—in a year! Let's jam in the whole capital and pull out ninety! I'll write and subscribe right now—tomorrow it may be too late."

He was flying to the writing-desk, but Aleck stopped him and put him back in his chair. She said:

"Don't lose your head so. We mustn't subscribe till we've got the money; don't you know that?"

Sally's excitement went down a degree or two, but he was not wholly appeased.

"Why, Aleck, we'll *have* it, you know—and so soon, too. He's probably out of his troubles before this, it's a hundred to nothing he's selecting his brimstone-shovel this very minute. Now, I think—"

Aleck shuddered, and said:

"How *can* you, Sally! Don't talk in that way, it is perfectly scandalous."

"Oh well, make it a halo, if you like, *I* don't care for his outfit, I was only just talking. Can't you let a person talk?"

"But why should you *want* to talk in that dreadful way? How would you like to have people talk so about *you,* and you not cold yet?"

"Not likely to be, for *one* while, I reckon, if my last act was giving away money for the sake of doing somebody a harm with it. But never mind about Tilbury, Aleck, let's talk about something worldly. It does seem to me that that mine is the place for the whole thirty. What's the objection?"

"All the eggs in one basket – that's the objection."

"All right, if you say so. What about the other twenty? What do you mean to do with that?"

"There is no hurry; I am going to look around before I do anything with it."

"All right, if your mind's made up," sighed Sally. He was deep in thought awhile, then he said:

"There'll be twenty thousand profit coming from the ten a year from now. We can spend that, can't we, Aleck?"

"No, dear," she said, "it won't sell high till we've had the first semi-annual dividend. You can spend part of that."

"Shucks, only *that* – and a whole year to wait! Confound it, I –"

"Oh, do be patient! It might even be declared in three months – it's quite within the possibilities."

"Oh, jolly! oh, thanks!" and Sally jumped up and kissed his wife in gratitude. "It'll be three thousand – three whole thousand! how much do we spend, Aleck? Make it liberal – do, dear, that's a good fellow."

Aleck was pleased; so pleased that she yielded to the pressure and conceded a sum which her judgment told her was a foolish extravagance – a thousand dollars. Sally kissed her half a

dozen times and even in that way could not express all his joy
and thankfulness. This new access of gratitude and affection carried Aleck quite beyond the bounds of prudence, and before she
could restrain herself she had made her darling another grant – a
couple of thousand out of the fifty or sixty which she meant to
clear within a year out of the twenty which still remained of the
bequest. The happy tears sprang to Sally's eyes, and he said:

"Oh, I want to hug you!" And he did it. Then he got his notes
and sat down and began to check off, for first purchase, the luxuries which he should earliest wish to secure. "Horse – buggy –
cutter – lap-robe – patent-leathers – dog – plug hat – church-pew –
stem-winder – new teeth – say, Aleck!"

"Well?"

"Ciphering away, aren't you? That's right. Have you got the
twenty thousand invested yet?"

"No, there's no hurry about that; I must look around first,
and think."

"But you are ciphering; what's it about?"

"Why, I have to find work for the thirty thousand that comes
out of the coal, haven't I?"

"Scott, what a head! I never thought of that. How are you getting along? Where have you arrived?"

"Not very far – two years or three. I've turned it over twice; once
in oil and once in wheat."

"Why, Aleck, it's splendid! How does it aggregate?"

"I think – well, to be on the safe side, about a hundred and
eighty thousand clear, though it will probably be more."

"My! isn't it wonderful! By gracious! luck has come our way
at last, after all the hard sledding. Aleck!"

"Well?"

"I'm going to cash-in a whole three hundred on the missionaries – what real right have we to care for expenses!"

"You couldn't do a nobler thing, dear; and it's just like your
generous nature, you unselfish boy."

The praise made Sally poignantly happy, but he was fair and just enough to say it was rightfully due to Aleck rather than to himself, since but for her he should never have had the money.

Then they went up to bed, and in their delirium of bliss they forgot and left the candle burning in the parlor. They did not remember until they were undressed; then Sally was for letting it burn; he said they could afford it, if it was a thousand. But Aleck went down and put it out.

A good job, too; for on her way back she hit on a scheme that would turn the hundred and eighty thousand into half a million before it had had time to get cold.

III

The little newspaper which Aleck had subscribed for was a Thursday sheet; it would make the trip of five hundred miles from Tilbury's village and arrive on Saturday. Tilbury's letter had started on Friday, more than a day too late for the benefactor to die and get into that week's issue, but in plenty of time to make connection for the next output. Thus the Fosters had to wait almost a complete week to find out whether anything of a satisfactory nature had happened to him or not. It was a long, long week, and the strain was a heavy one. The pair could hardly have borne it if their minds had not had the relief of wholesome diversion. We have seen that they had that. The woman was piling up fortunes right along; the man was spending them – spending all his wife would give him a chance at, at any rate.

At last the Saturday came, and the *Weekly Sagamore* arrived. Mrs. Eversly Bennett was present. She was the Presbyterian parson's wife, and was working the Fosters for a charity. Talk now died a sudden death – on the Foster side. Mrs. Bennett presently discovered that her hosts were not hearing a word she was saying; so she got up, wondering and indignant, and went away. The moment she was out of the house, Aleck eagerly tore the wrapper from the paper, and her eyes and Sally's swept the columns

for the death notices. Disappointment! Tilbury was not anywhere mentioned. Aleck was a Christian from the cradle, and duty
and the force of habit required her to go through the motions.
She pulled herself together and said, with a pious two-per-cent
trade joyousness:

"Let us be humbly thankful that he has been spared; and–"

"Damn his treacherous hide, I wish–"

"Sally! For shame!"

"I don't care!" retorted the angry man. "It's the way *you* feel,
and if you weren't so immorally pious you'd be honest and say so."

Aleck said, with wounded dignity:

"I do not see how you can say such unkind and unjust things.
There is no such thing as immoral piety."

Sally felt a pang, but tried to conceal it under a shuffling
attempt to save his case by changing the form of it–as if changing the form while retaining the juice could deceive the expert
he was trying to placate. He said:

"I didn't mean so bad as that, Aleck; I didn't really mean
immoral piety, I only meant–meant–well, conventional piety, you
know; er–shop piety; the–the–way, *you* know what I mean,
Aleck–the–well, where you put up the plated article and play
it for solid, you know, without intending anything improper but
just out of trade habit, ancient policy, petrified custom, loyalty
to–to–hang it, I can't find the right words, but *you* know what
I mean, Aleck, and that there isn't any harm in it. I'll try again.
You see, it's this way. If a person–"

"You have said quite enough," said Aleck, coldly; "let the subject be dropped."

"*I'm* willing," fervently responded Sally, wiping the sweat from
his forehead and looking the thankfulness he had no words for.
Then, musingly, he apologized to himself. "I certainly held threes–I
know it–but I drew and didn't fill. That's where I'm so often weak
in the game. If I had stood pat–but I didn't. I never do. I don't
know enough."

Confessedly defeated, he was properly tame now and subdued. Aleck forgave him with her eyes.

The grand interest, the supreme interest, came instantly to the front again; nothing could keep it in the background many minutes on a stretch. The couple took up the puzzle of the absence of Tilbury's death notice. They discussed it every way, more or less hopefully, but they had to finish where they began, and concede that the only really sane explanation of the absence of the notice must be – and without doubt was – that Tilbury was not dead. There was something sad about it, something even a little unfair, maybe, but there it was, and had to be put up with. They were agreed as to that. To Sally it seemed a strangely inscrutable dispensation; more inscrutable than usual, he thought; one of the most unnecessarily inscrutable he could call to mind, in fact – and said so, with some feeling; but if he was hoping to draw Aleck he failed; she reserved her opinion, if she had one; she had not the habit of taking injudicious risks in any market, worldy or other.

The pair must wait for next week's paper – Tilbury had evidently postponed. That was their thought and their decision. So they put the subject away, and went about their affairs again with as good heart as they could.

Now, if they had but known it, they had been wronging Tilbury all the time. Tilbury had kept faith, kept it to the letter; he was dead, he had died to schedule. He was dead more than four days now and used to it; entirely dead, perfectly dead, as dead as any other new person in the cemetery; dead in abundant time to get into that week's *Sagamore,* too, and only shut out by an accident; an accident which could not happen to a metropolitan journal, but which happens easily to a poor little village rag like the *Sagamore.* On this occasion, just as the editorial page was being locked up, a gratis quart of strawberry water-ice arrived from Hostetter's Ladies' and Gents' Ice-Cream Parlors, and the stickful

of rather chilly regret over Tilbury's translation got crowded out
to make room for the editor's frantic gratitude.

On its way to the standing-galley Tilbury's notice got pied.
Otherwise it would have gone into some future edition, for *Weekly
Sagamores* do not waste "live" matter, and in their galleys "live"
matter is immortal, unless a pi accident intervenes. But a thing
that gets pied is dead, and for such there is no resurrection; its
chance of seeing print is gone, forever and ever. And so, let
Tilbury like it or not, let him rave in his grave to his fill, no
matter—no mention of his death would ever see the light in thee
Weekly Sagamore.

IV

Five weeks drifted tediously along. The *Sagamore* arrived regularly on the Saturdays, but never once contained a mention of
Tilbury Foster. Sally's patience broke down at this point, and he
said, resentfully:

"Damn his livers, he's immortal!"

Aleck gave him a very severe rebuke, and added, with
icy solemnity:

"How would you feel if you were suddenly cut off just after
such an awful remark had escaped out of you?"

Without sufficient reflection Sally responded:

"I'd feel I was lucky I hadn't got caught with it *in* me."

Pride had forced him to say something, and as he could not
think of any rational thing to say he flung that out. Then he stole
a base—as he called it—that is, slipped from the presence, to keep
from getting brayed in his wife's discussion-mortar.

Six months came and went. The *Sagamore* was still silent about
Tilbury. Meantime, Sally had several times thrown out a feeler—
that is, a hint that he would like to know. Aleck had ignored the
hints. Sally now resolved to brace up and risk a frontal attack.
So he squarely proposed to disguise himself and go to Tilbury's
village and surreptitiously find out as to the prospects. Aleck

put her foot on the dangerous project with energy and decision. She said:

"What can you be thinking of? You do keep my hands full! You have to be watched all the time, like a little child, to keep you from walking into the fire. You'll stay right where you are!"

"Why, Aleck, I could do it and not be found out – I'm certain of it."

"Sally Foster, don't you know you would have to inquire around?"

"Of course, but what of it? Nobody would suspect who I was."

"Oh, listen to the man! Some day you've got to prove to the executors that you never inquired. What then?"

He had forgotten that detail. He didn't reply; there wasn't anything to say. Aleck added:

"Now then, drop that notion out of your mind, and don't ever meddle with it again. Tilbury set that trap for you. Don't you know it's a trap? He is on the watch, and fully expecting you to blunder into it. Well, he is going to be disappointed – at least while I am on deck. Sally!"

"Well?"

"As long as you live, if it's a hundred years, don't you ever make an inquiry. Promise!"

"All right," with a sigh and reluctantly.

Then Aleck softened and said:

"Don't be impatient. We are prospering; we can wait; there is no hurry. Our small dead-certain income increases all the time; and as to futures, I have not made a mistake yet – they are piling up by the thousands and the tens of thousands. There is not another family in the State with such prospects as ours. Already we are beginning to roll in eventual wealth. You know that, don't you?"

"Yes, Aleck, it's certainly so."

"Then be grateful for what God is doing for us, and stop worrying. You do not believe we could have achieved these prodigious results without His special help and guidance, do you?"

Hesitatingly, "No-no, I suppose not." Then, with feeling and admiration, "And yet, when it comes to judiciousness in watering a stock or putting up a hand to skin Wall Street I don't give in that *you* need any outside amateur help, if I do I wish I–"

"Oh, *do* shut up! I know you do not mean any harm or any irreverence, poor boy, but you can't seem to open your mouth without letting out things to make a person shudder. You keep me in constant dread. For you and for all of us. Once I had no fear of the thunder, but now when I hear it I–"

Her voice broke, and she began to cry, and could not finish. The sight of this smote Sally to the heart and he took her in his arms and petted her and comforted her and promised better conduct, and upbraided himself and remorsefully pleaded for forgiveness. And he was in earnest, and sorry for what he had done and ready for any sacrifice that could make up for it.

And so, in privacy, he thought long and deeply over the matter, resolving to do what should seem best. It was easy to *promise* reform; indeed he had already promised it. But would that do any real good, any permanent good? No, it would be but temporary–he knew his weakness, and confessed it to himself with sorrow–he could not keep the promise. Something surer and better must be devised; and he devised it. At cost of precious money which he had long been saving up, shilling by shilling, he put a lightning-rod on the house.

At a subsequent time he relapsed.

What miracles habit can do! and how quickly and how easily habits are acquired–both trifling habits and habits which profoundly change us. If by accident we wake at two in the morning a couple of nights in succession, we have need to be uneasy, for another repetition can turn the accident into a habit; and a month's dallying with whiskey–but we all know these commonplace facts.

The castle-building habit, the day-dreaming habit–how it grows! what a luxury it becomes; how we fly to its enchantments at every idle moment, how we revel in them, steep our souls in them, intoxicate ourselves with their beguiling fantasies – oh yes, and how soon and how easily our dream-life and our material life become so intermingled and so fused together that we can't quite tell which is which, any more.

By-and-by Aleck subscribed for a Chicago daily and for the *Wall Street Pointer.* With an eye single to finance she studied these as diligently all the week as she studied her Bible Sundays. Sally was lost in admiration, to note with what swift and sure strides her genius and judgment developed and expanded in the forecasting and handling of the securities of both the material and spiritual markets. He was proud of her nerve and daring in exploiting worldly stocks, and just as proud of her conservative caution in working her spiritual deals. He noted that she never lost her head in either case; that with a splendid courage she often went short on worldly futures, but heedfully drew the line there – she was always long on the others. Her policy was quite sane and simple, as she explained it to him: what she put into earthly futures was for speculation, what she put into spiritual futures was for investment; she was willing to go into the one on a margin, and take chances, but in the case of the other, "margin her no margins" – she wanted to cash-in a hundred cents per dollar's-worth, and have the stock transferred on the books.

It took but a very few months to educate Aleck's imagination and Sally's. Each day's training added something to the spread and effectiveness of the two machines. As a consequence, Aleck made imaginary money much faster than at first she had dreamed of making it, and Sally's competency in spending the overflow of it kept pace with the strain put upon it, right along. In the beginning, Aleck had given the coal speculation a twelvemonth in which to materialize, and had been loath to grant that this term might possibly be shortened by nine months. But that was the feeble work, the nursery work, of a financial fancy that had had no teaching, no experience, no practice. These aids soon came, then that nine months vanished, and the imaginary ten-thousand-dollar investment came marching home with three hundred per cent profit on its back!

It was a great day for the pair of Fosters. They were speechless for joy. Also speechless for another reason: after much watching of the market, Aleck had lately, with fear and trembling, made her first flyer on a "margin," using the remaining twenty thousand of the bequest in this risk. In her mind's eye she had seen it climb, point by point—always with a chance that the market would break—until at last her anxieties were too great for further endurance—she being new to the margin-business and unhardened as yet—and she gave her imaginary broker an imaginary order by imaginary telegraph to sell. She said forty thousand dollars profit was enough. The sale was made on the very day that the coal—venture had returned with its rich freight. As I have said, the couple were speechless. They sat dazed and blissful that night, trying to realize the immense fact, the overwhelming fact, that they were actually worth a hundred thousand dollars in clean, imaginary cash. Yet so it was.

It was the last time that ever Aleck was afraid of a margin; at least afraid enough to let it break her sleep and pale her cheek to the extent that this first experience in that line had done.

Indeed it was a memorable night. Gradually the realization that they were rich sank securely home into the souls of the pair, then they began to place the money. If we could have looked out through the eyes of these dreamers, we should have seen their tidy little wooden house disappear, and a two-story brick with a cast-iron fence in front of it take its place; we should have seen a three-globed gas-chandelier grow down from the parlor ceiling; we should have seen the homely rag carpet turn to noble Brussels, a dollar and a half a yard; we should have seen the plebeian fireplace vanish away and a recherché, big base-burner with isinglass windows take position and spread awe around. And we should have seen other things, too; among them the buggy, the lap-robe, the stove-pipe hat, and so on.

From that time forth, although the daughters and the neighbors saw only the same old wooden house there, it was a two-story brick to Aleck and Sally; and not a night went by that Aleck did not worry about the imaginary gas-bills, and get for all comfort Sally's reckless retort, "What of it? We can afford it."

Before the couple went to bed, that first night that they were rich, they had decided that they must celebrate. They must give a party—that was the idea. But how to explain it—to the daughters and the neighbors? They could not expose the fact that they were rich. Sally was willing, even anxious, to do it; but Aleck kept her head and would not allow it. She said that although the money was as good as in, it would be as well to wait until it was actually in. On that policy she took her stand, and would not budge. The great secret must be kept, she said—kept from the daughters and everybody else.

The pair were puzzled. They must celebrate, they were determined to celebrate, but since the secret must be kept, what could they celebrate? No birthdays were due for three months. Tilbury wasn't available, evidently he was going to live forever; what the nation *could* they celebrate? That was Sally's way of putting it; and he was getting impatient, too, and harassed. But at last he hit it—just by sheer inspiration, as it seemed to him—and all their troubles were gone in a moment; they would celebrate the Discovery of America. A splendid idea!

Aleck was almost too proud of Sally for words—she said *she* never would have thought of it. But Sally, although he was bursting with delight in the compliment and with wonder at himself, tried not to let on, and said it wasn't really anything, anybody could have done it. Whereat Aleck, with a prideful toss of her happy head, said:

"Oh, certainly! Anybody could—oh, anybody! Hosannah Dilkins, for instance! Or maybe Adelbert Peanut—oh, *dear*—yes! Well, I'd like to see them try it, that's all. Dear-me-suz, if they could think of the discovery of a forty-acre island it's more than

I believe they could; and as for a whole continent, why, Sally Foster, you know perfectly well it would strain the livers and lights out of them and *then* they couldn't!"

The dear woman, she knew he had talent; and if affection made her over-estimate the size of it a little, surely it was a sweet and gentle crime, and forgivable for its source's sake.

v

The celebration went off well. The friends were all present, both the young and the old. Among the young were Flossie and Gracie Peanut and their brother Adelbert, who was a rising young journeyman tinner, also Hosannah Dilkins, Jr., journeyman plasterer, just out of his apprenticeship. For many months Adelbert and Hosannah had been showing interest in Gwendolen and Clytemnestra Foster, and the parents of the girls had noticed this with private satisfaction. But they suddenly realized now that feeling had passed. They recognized that the changed financial conditions had raised up a social bar between their daughters and the young mechanics. The daughters could now look higher – and must. Yes, must. They need marry nothing below the grade of lawyer or merchant; poppa and momma would take care of this; there must be no mésalliances.

However, these thinkings and projects of theirs were private, and did not show on the surface, and therefore threw no shadow upon the celebration. What showed upon the surface was a serene and lofty contentment and a dignity of carriage and gravity of deportment which compelled the admiration and likewise the wonder of the company. All noticed it, all commented upon it, but none was able to divine the secret of it. It was a marvel and a mystery. Three several persons remarked, without suspecting what clever shots they were making:

"It's as if they'd come into property."

That was just it, indeed.

Most mothers would have taken hold of the matrimonial matter

in the old regulation way; they would have given the girls a talking to, of a solemn sort and untactful – a lecture calculated to defeat
its own purpose, by producing tears and secret rebellion; and the
said mothers would have further damaged the business by request-
ing the young mechanics to discontinue their attentions. But this
mother was different. She was practical. She said nothing to any
of the young people concerned, nor to any one else except Sally.
He listened to her and understood; understood and admired.
He said:

"I get the idea. Instead of finding fault with the samples on view,
thus hurting feelings and obstructing trade without occasion, you
merely offer a higher class of goods for the money, and leave nature
to take her course. It's wisdom, Aleck, solid wisdom, and sound
as a nut. Who's your fish? Have you nominated him yet?"

No, she hadn't. They must look the market over – which they
did. To start with, they considered and discussed Bradish, rising
young lawyer, and Fulton, rising young dentist. Sally must invite
them to dinner. But not right away; there was no hurry, Aleck said.
Keep an eye on the pair, and wait; nothing would be lost by going
slowly in so important a matter.

It turned out that this was wisdom, too; for inside of three
weeks Aleck made a wonderful strike which swelled her imaginary hundred thousand to four hundred thousand of the same
quality. She and Sally were in the clouds that evening. For the
first time they introduced champagne at dinner. Not real champagne, but plenty real enough for the amount of imagination
expended on it. It was Sally that did it, and Aleck weakly submit-
ted. At bottom both were troubled and ashamed, for he was a
high-up Son of Temperance, and at funerals wore an apron which
no dog could look upon and retain his reason and his opinion;
and she was a W.C.T.U., with all that that implies of boiler-iron
virtue and unendurable holiness. But there it was; the pride of
riches was beginning its disintegrating work. They had lived to
prove, once more, a sad truth which had been proven many times

before in the world; that whereas principle is a great and noble
protection against showy and degrading vanities and vices, poverty
is worth six of it. More than four hundred thousand dollars to
the good! They took up the matrimonial matter again. Neither
the dentist nor the lawyer was mentioned; there was no occasion, they were out of the running. Disqualified. They discussed
the son of the pork-packer and the son of the village banker. But
finally, as in the previous case, they concluded to wait and think,
and go cautiously and sure.

Luck came their way again. Aleck, ever watchful, saw a great
and risky chance, and took a daring flyer. A time of trembling,
of doubt, of awful uneasiness followed, for non-success meant
absolute ruin and nothing short of it. Then came the result, and
Aleck, faint with joy, could hardly control her voice when she said:

"The suspense is over, Sally—and we are worth a cold million!"

Sally wept for gratitude, and said:

"Oh, Electra, jewel of women, darling of my heart, we are free
at last, we roll in wealth, we need never scrimp again. It's a case
for Veuve Cliquot!" and he got out a pint of spruce-beer and made
sacrifice, he saying, "Damn the expense," and she rebuking him
gently with reproachful but humid and happy eyes.

They shelved the pork-packer's son and the banker's son,
and sat down to consider the Governor's son and the son of
the Congressman.

VI

It were a weariness to follow in detail the leaps and bounds
the Foster fictitious finances took from this time forth. It was marvelous, it was dizzying, it was dazzling. Everything Aleck touched
turned to fairy gold, and heaped itself glittering towards the firma-
ment. Millions upon millions poured in, and still the mighty
stream flowed thundering along, still its vast volume increased.
Five millions—ten millions—twenty—thirty—was there never to
be an end?

Two years swept by in a splendid delirium, the intoxicated Fosters scarcely noticing the flight of time. They were now worth three hundred million dollars; they were in every board of directors of every prodigious combine in the country; and still, as time drifted along, the millions went on piling up, five at a time, ten at a time, as fast as they could tally them off, almost. The three hundred doubled itself – then doubled again – and yet again – and yet once more.

Twenty-four hundred millions!

The business was getting a little confused. It was necessary to take an account of stock, and straighten it out. The Fosters knew it, they felt it, they realized that it was imperative; but they also knew that to do it properly and perfectly the task must be carried to a finish without a break when once it was begun. A ten-hours' job; and where could *they* find ten leisure hours in a bunch? Sally was selling pins and sugar and calico all day and every day; Aleck was cooking and washing dishes and sweeping and making beds all day and every day, with none to help, for the daughters were being saved up for high society. The Fosters knew there was one way to get the ten hours, and only one. Both were ashamed to name it; each waited for the other to do it. Finally Sally said:

"Somebody's got to give in. It's up to me. Consider that I've named it – never mind pronouncing it out loud."

Aleck colored, but was grateful. Without further remark, they fell. Fell, and – broke the Sabbath. For that was their only free ten-hour stretch. It was but another step in the downward path. Others would follow. Vast wealth has temptations which fatally and surely undermine the moral structure of persons not habituated to its possession.

They pulled down the shades and broke the Sabbath. With hard and patient labor they overhauled their holdings and listed them. And a long-drawn procession of formidable names it was! Starting with the Railway Systems, Steamer Lines, Standard Oil,

Ocean Cables, Diluted Telegraph, and all the rest, and winding up with Klondike, De Beers, Tammany Graft, and Shady Privileges in the Post-office Department.

Twenty-four hundred millions, and all safely planted in Good Things, gilt-edged and interest-bearing. Income, $120,000,000 a year. Aleck fetched a long purr of soft delight, and said:

"Is it enough?"

"It is, Aleck."

"What shall we do?"

"Stand pat."

Retire from business?"

"That's it."

"I am agreed. The good work is finished; we will take a long rest and enjoy the money."

"Good! Aleck!"

"Yes, dear?"

"How much of the income can we spend?"

"The whole of it."

It seemed to her husband that a ton of chains fell from his limbs. He did not say a word; he was happy beyond the power of speech.

After that, they broke the Sabbaths right along, as fast as they turned up. It is the first wrong steps that count. Every Sunday they put in the whole day, after morning service, on inventions – inventions of ways to spend the money. They got to continuing this delicious dissipation until past midnight; and at every séance Aleck lavished millions upon great charities and religious enter- prises, and Sally lavished like sums upon matters to which (at first) he gave definite names. Only at first. Later the names gradu- ally lost sharpness of outline, and eventually faded into "sundries," thus becoming entirely – but safely – undescriptive. For Sally was crumbling. The placing of these millions added seriously and most uncomfortably to the family expenses – in tallow candles. For a while Aleck was worried. Then, after a little, she ceased to worry, for the occasion of it was gone. She was pained, she was grieved, she was ashamed; but she said nothing, and so became an accessory. Sally was taking candles; he was robbing the store. It is ever thus. Vast wealth, to the person unaccustomed to it, is a bane; it eats into the flesh and bone of his morals. When the Fosters were poor, they could have been trusted with untold candles. But now they–but let us not dwell upon it. From candles to apples is but a step: Sally got to taking apples; then soap; then maple-sugar; then canned-goods; then crockery. How easy it is to go from bad to worse, when once we have started upon a downward course!

Meantime, other effects had been milestoning the course of the Fosters' splendid financial march. The fictitious brick-dwelling had given place to an imaginary granite one with a checker-board mansard roof; in time this one disappeared and gave place to a still grander home–and so on and so on. Mansion after mansion, made of air, rose, higher, broader, finer, and each in its turn vanished away; until now, in these latter great days, our dreamers were in fancy housed, in a distant region, in a sumptuous vast palace which looked out from a leafy summit upon a noble prospect of vale and river and receding hills steeped in tinted mists–and all private, all the property of the dreamers; a palace swarming with liveried servants, and populous with guests of fame and power, hailing from all the world's capitals, foreign and domestic.

This palace was far, far away towards the rising sun, immeasurably remote, astronomically remote, in Newport, Rhode Island, Holy Land of High Society, ineffable Domain of the American Aristocracy. As a rule, they spent a part of every Sabbath–after morning service–in this sumptuous home, the rest of they spent in Europe, or in dawdling around in their private yacht. Six days of sordid and plodding Fact-life at home on the ragged edge of Lakeside and straitened means, the seventh in Fairyland–such had become their program and their habit.

In their sternly restricted Fact-life they remained as of old—
plodding, diligent, careful, practical, economical. They stuck loyally
to the little Presbyterian Church, and labored faithfully in its
interests and stood by its high and tough doctrines with all their
mental and spiritual energies. But in their Dream-life they obeyed
the invitations of their fancies, whatever they might be, and
howsoever the fancies might change. Aleck's fancies were not very
capricious, and not frequent, but Sally's scattered a good deal.
Aleck, in her dream-life, went over to the Episcopal camp, on
account of its large official titles; next she became High-church
on account of the candles and shows; and next she naturally
changed to Rome, where there were cardinals and more candles.
But these excursions were as nothing to Sally's. His Dream-life
was a glowing and continuous and persistent excitement, and he
kept every part of it fresh and sparkling by frequent changes, the
religious part along with the rest. He worked his religions hard,
and changed them with his shirt.

The liberal spendings of the Fosters upon their fancies began
early in their prosperities, and grew in prodigality step by step
with their advancing fortunes. In time they became truly enormous. Aleck built a university or two per sunday; also a hospital
or two; also a Rowton hotel or so; also a batch of churches; now
and then a cathedral; and once, with untimely and ill-chosen play-
fulness, Sally said, "It was a cold day when she didn't ship a cargo
of missionaries to persuade unreflecting Chinamen to trade off
twenty-four carat Confucianism for counterfeit Christianity."

This rude and unfeeling language hurt Aleck to the heart, and
she went from the presence crying. That spectacle went to his
own heart, and in his pain and shame he would have given worlds
to have those unkind words back. She had uttered no syllable
of reproach—and that cut him. Not one suggestion that he look
at his own record—and she could have made, oh, so many, and
such blistering ones! Her generous silence brought a swift revenge,
for it turned his thoughts upon himself, it summoned before him

a spectral procession, a moving vision of his life as he had been leading it these past few years of limitless prosperity, and as he sat there reviewing it his cheeks burned and his soul was steeped in humiliation. Look at her life – how fair it was, and tending upward; and look at his own – how frivolous, how charged with mean vanities, how selfish, how empty, how ignoble! And its trend – never upward, but downward, ever downward!

He instituted comparisons between her record and his own. He had found fault with her – so he mused – he! And what could he say for himself? When she built her first church what was he doing? Gathering other blasé multimillionaires into a Poker Club; defiling his own palace with it; losing hundreds of thousands to it at every sitting, and sillily vain of the admiring notoriety it made for him. When she was building her first university, what was he doing? Polluting himself with a gay and dissipated secret life in the company of other fast bloods, multimillionaires in money and paupers in character. When she was building her first foundling asylum, what was he doing? Alas! When she was projecting her noble Society for the Purifying of the Sex, what was he doing? Ah, what, indeed! When she and the W.C.T.U. and the Woman with the Hatchet, moving with resistless march, were sweeping the fatal bottle from the land, what was he doing? Getting drunk three times a day. When she, builder of a hundred cathedrals, was being gratefully welcomed and blest in papal Roe and decorated with the Golden Rose which she had so honorably earned, what was he doing? Breaking the bank at Monte Carlo

He stopped. He could go no farther; he could not bear the rest. He rose up, with great resolution upon his lips: this secret life should be revealed, and confessed; no longer would he live it clandestinely; he would go and tell her All.

And that is what he did. He told her All; and wept upon her bosom; wept, and moaned, and begged for her forgiveness. It was a profound shock, and she staggered under the blow, but he was her own, the core of her heart, the blessing of her eyes, her all in all, she could deny him nothing, and she forgave him. She felt that he could never again be quite to her what he had been before; she knew that he could only repent, and not reform; yet all morally defaced and decayed as he was, was he not her own, her very own, the idol of her deathless worship? She said she was his serf, his slave, and she opened her yearning heart and took him in.

VII

One Sunday afternoon some time after this they were sailing the summer seas in their dream-yacht, and reclining in lazy luxury under the awning of the after-deck. There was silence, for each was busy with his own thoughts. These seasons of silence has insensibly been growing more and more frequent of late; the old nearness and cordiality were waning. Sally's terrible revelation had done its work; Aleck had tried hard to drive the memory of it out of her mind, but it would not go, and the shame and bitterness of it were poisoning her gracious dream-life. She could see now (on Sundays) that her husband was becoming a bloated and repulsive Thing. She could not close her eyes to this, and in these days she no longer looked at him, Sundays, when she could help it.

But she—was she herself without blemish? Alas, she knew she was not. She was keeping a secret from him, she was acting dishonorably towards him, and many a pang it was costing her. *She was breaking the compact, and concealing it from him.* Under strong temptation she had gone into business again; she had risked their whole fortune in a purchase of all the railway systems and coal and steel companies in the country on a margin, and she was now trembling, every Sabbath hour, lest through some chance word of hers he find it out. In her misery and remorse for this treachery she could not keep her heart from going out to him in pity; she was filled with compunctions to see him lying there, drunk and content, and never suspecting. Never suspecting—trusting

her with a perfect and pathetic trust, and she holding over him
by a thread a possible calamity of so devastating a –

"*Say*–Aleck?"

The interrupting words brought her suddenly to herself. She
was grateful to have that persecuting subject from her thoughts,
and she answered, with much of the old-time tenderness in
her tone:

"Yes, dear."

"Do you know, Aleck, I think we are making a mistake – that
is, you are. I mean about the marriage business." He sat up, fat
and froggy and benevolent, like a bronze Buddha, and grew earnest.
"Consider – it's more than five years. You've continued the same
policy from the start: with every rise, always holding on for five
points higher. Always when I think we are going to have some
weddings, you see a bigger thing ahead, and I undergo another
disappointment. *I* think you are too hard to please. Some day we'll
get left. First, we turned down the dentist and the lawyer. That
was all right – it was sound. Next, we turned down the banker's
son and the pork-butcher's heir – right again, and sound. Next we
turned down the Congressman's son and the Governor's – right
as a trivet, I confess it. Next, the Senator's son and the son of the
Vice-President of the United States – perfectly right, there's no per-
manency about those little distinctions. Then you went for
aristocracy; and I thought we had struck oil at last – yes. We would
make a plunge at the Four Hundred, and pull in some ancient
lineage, venerable, holy, ineffable, mellow with antiquity of a
hundred and fifty years, disinfected of the ancestral odors of salt
cod and pelts all of a century ago, and unsmirched by a day's work
since; and then! why, then the marriages, of course. But no, along
comes a pair of real aristocrats from Europe, and straightway you
throw over the half-breeds. It was awfully discouraging, Aleck!
Since then, what a procession! You turned down the baronets for
a pair of barons; you turned down the barons for a pair of viscounts; the viscounts for a pair of earls; the earls for a pair of

marquises; the marquises for a brace of dukes. *Now,* Aleck, cash-in!–you've played the limit. You've got a job lot of four dukes under the hammer; of four nationalities; all sound in wind and limb and pedigree, all bankrupt and in debt up to the ears. They come high, but we can afford it. Come, Aleck, don't delay any longer, don't keep up the suspense: take the whole lay-out, and leave the girls to choose!"

Aleck had been smiling blandly and contentedly all through this arraignment of her marriage-policy; a pleasant light, as a triumph with perhaps a nice surprise peeping out through it, rose in her eyes, and she said, as calmly as she could.

"Sally, what would you say to–*royalty?*"

Prodigious! Poor man, it knocked him silly, and he fell over the garboard-strake and barked his shin on the cat-heads. He was dizzy for a moment, then he gathered himself up and limped over and sat down by his wife and beamed his old-time admiration and affection upon her in floods, out of his bleary eyes.

"By George!" he said, fervently, "Aleck, you *are* great–the greatest woman in the whole earth! I can't ever learn the whole size of you. I can't ever learn the immeasurable deeps of you. Here I've been considering myself qualified to criticise your game. *I!* Why, if I had stopped to think, I'd have known you had a lone hand up your sleeve. Now, dear heart, I'm all red-hot impatience– tell me about it!"

The flattered and happy woman put her lips to his ear and whispered a princely name. It made him catch his breath, it lit his face with exultation.

"Land!" he said, "it's a stunning catch! He's got a gambling-hall, and a graveyard, and a bishop, and a cathedral–all his very own. And all gilt-edged five-hundred-per-cent stock, every detail of it; the tidiest little property in Europe. And that graveyard–it's the selectest in the world: none but suicides admitted; *yes,* sir, and the free-list suspended, too, *all* the time. There isn't much land in the principality, but there's enough: eight hundred acres in the graveyard and forty-two outside. It's a *sovereignty*—that's the main thing; *land's* nothing. There's plenty land, Sahara's drugged with it."

Aleck glowed; she was profoundly happy. She said:

"Think of it, Sally—it is a family that has never married outside the Royal and Imperial Houses of Europe: our grandchildren will sit upon thrones!"

"True as you live, Aleck—and bear scepters, too; and handle them as naturally and nonchalantly as I handle a yardstick. It's a grand catch, Aleck. He's corralled, is he? Can't get away? You didn't take him on a margin?"

"No. Trust me for that. He's not a liability, he's an asset. So is the other one."

"Who is it, Aleck?"

"His Royal Highness Sigismund-Siegfried-Lauenfeld-Dinkel-spiel-Schwartzenberg Blutwurst, Hereditary Grand Duke of Katzenyammer."

"No! You can't mean it!"

"It's as true as I'm sitting here, I give you my word," she answered.

His cup was full, and he hugged her to his heart with rapture, saying:

"How wonderful it all seems, and how beautiful! It's one of the oldest and noblest of the three hundred and sixty-four ancient German principalities, and one of the few that was allowed to retain its royal estate when Bismarck got done trimming them. I know that farm, I've been there. It's got a ropewalk and a candle-factory and an army. Standing army. Infantry and cavalry. Three soldiers and a horse. Aleck, it's been a long wait, and full of heartbreak and hope deferred, but God knows I am happy now. Happy, and grateful to you, my own, who have done it all. When is it to be?"

"Next Sunday."

"Good. And we'll want to do these weddings up in the very regalest style that's going. It's properly due to the royal quality of the parties of the first part. Now as I understand it, there is only one kind of marriage that is sacred to royalty, exclusive to royalty: it's the morganatic."

"What do they call it that for, Sally?"

"I don't know; but anyway it's royal, and royal only."

"Then we will insist upon it. More—I will compel it. It is morganatic marriage or none."

"That settles it!" said Sally, rubbing his hands with delight. "And it will be the very first in America. Aleck, it will make Newport sick."

Then they fell silent, and drifted away upon their dream-wings to the far regions of the earth to invite all the crowned heads and their families and provide gratis transportation for them.

VIII

During three days the couple walked upon air, with their heads in the clouds. They were but vaguely conscious of their surroundings; they saw all things dimly, as through a veil; they were steeped in dreams, often they did not hear when they were spoken to; they often did not understand when they heard; they answered confusedly or at random; Sally sold molasses by weight, sugar by the yard, and furnished soap when asked for candles, and Aleck put the cat in the wash and fed milk to the soiled linen. Everybody was stunned and amazed, and went about muttering, "What *can* be the matter with the Fosters?"

Three days. Then came events! Things had taken a happy turn, and for forty-eight hours Aleck's imaginary corner had been booming. Up—up—still up! Cost-point was passed. Still up—and up—and up! Five points above cost—then ten—fifteen—twenty! Twenty points cold profit on the vast venture, now, and Aleck's imaginary brokers were shouting frantically by imaginary long-distance, "Sell! sell! for Heaven's sake *sell!*"

She broke the splendid news to Sally, and he, too, said, "Sell! sell—oh, don't make a blunder, now, you own the earth!—sell, sell!" But she set her iron will and lashed it amidships, and said she would hold on for five points more if she died for it.

It was a fatal resolve. The very next day came the historic crash, the record crash, the devastating crash, when the bottom fell out of Wall Street, and the whole body of gilt-edged stocks dropped ninety-five points in five hours, and the multimillionaire was seen begging his bread in the Bowery. Aleck sternly held her grip and "put up" as long as she could, but at last there came a call which she was powerless to meet, and her imaginary brokers sold her out. Then, and not till then, the man in her was vanquished, and the woman in resumed sway. She put her arms about her husband's neck and wept saying:

"I am to blame, do not forgive me, I cannot bear it. We are paupers! Paupers, and I am so miserable. The weddings will never come off; all that is past; we could not even buy the dentist, now."

A bitter reproach was on Sally's tongue: "I *begged* you to sell, but you–" He did not say it; he had not the heart to add a hurt to that broken and repentant spirit. A nobler thought came to him and he said:

"Bear up, my Aleck, all is not lost! You really never invested a penny of my uncle's bequest, but only its unmaterialized future; what we have lost was only the increment harvested from that future by your incomparable financial judgement and sagacity. Cheer up, banish these griefs; we still have the thirty thousand untouched; and with the experience which you have acquired, think what you will be able to do with it in a couple of years! The marriages are not off, they are only postponed."

These were blessed words. Aleck saw how true they were, and the influence was electric; her tears ceased to flow, and her great spirit rose to its full stature again. With flashing eye and grateful heart, and with hand uplifted in pledge and prophecy, she said:

"Now and here I proclaim–"

But she was interrupted by a visitor. It was the editor and proprietor of the *Sagamore*. He had happened into Lakeside to pay a duty-call upon an obscure grandmother of his who was nearing the end of her pilgrimage, and with the idea of combining business with grief he had looked up the Fosters, who had been so absorbed in other things for the past four years that they had neglected to pay up their subscription. Six dollars due. No visitor could have been more welcome. He would know all about Uncle Tilbury and what his chances might be getting to be, cemeterywards. They could, of course, ask no questions, for that would squelch the bequest, but they could nibble around on the edge of the subject and hope for results. The scheme did not work. The obtuse editor did not know he was being nibbled at; but at last, chance accomplished what art had failed in. In illustration of something under discussion which required the help of metaphor, the editor said:

"Land, it's as tough as Tilbury Foster!—as we say."

It was sudden, and it made the Fosters jump. The editor noticed it, and said, apologetically:

"No harm intended, I assure you. It's just a saying; just a joke, you know—nothing in it. Relation of yours?"

Sally crowded his burning eagerness down, and answered with all the indifference he could assume:

"I—well, not that I know of, but we've heard of him." The editor was thankful, and resumed his composure. Sally added: "Is he—is he—well?"

"Is he well? Why, bless you he's in Sheol these five years!"

The Fosters were trembling with grief, though it felt like joy. Sally said, non-commitally—and tentatively:

"Ah, well, such is life, and none can escape—not even the rich are spared."

The editor laughed.

"If you are including Tilbury," said he, "it don't apply. He hadn't a cent; the town had to bury him."

The Fosters sat petrified for two minutes; petrified and cold. Then, white-faced and weak-voiced, Sally asked:

"Is it true? Do you know it to be true?"

"Well, I should say! I was one of the executors. He hadn't

anything to leave but a wheelbarrow, and he left that to me. It hadn't any wheel, and wasn't any good. Still, it was something, and so, to square up, I scribbled off a sort of a little obituarial send-off for him, but it got crowded out."

The Fosters were not listening—their cup was full, it could contain no more. They sat with bowed heads, dead to all things but the ache at their hearts.

An hour later. Still they sat there, bowed, motionless, silent, the visitor long ago gone, they unaware.

Then they stirred, and lifted their heads wearily, and gazed at each other wistfully, dreamily, dazed; then presently began to twaddle to each other in a wandering and childish way. At intervals they lapsed into silences, leaving a sentence unfinished, seemingly either unaware of it or losing their way. Sometimes, when they woke out of these silences they had a dim and transient consciousness that something had happened to their minds; then with a dumb and yearning solicitude they would softly caress each other's hands in mutual compassion and support, as if they would say: "I am near you, I will not forsake you, we will bear it together; somewhere there is release and forgetfulness, somewhere there is a grave and peace; be patient, it will not be long."

They lived yet two years, in mental night, always brooding, steeped in vague regrets and melancholy dreams, never speaking; then release came to both on the same day.

Towards the end the darkness lifted from Sally's ruined mind for a moment, and he said:

"Vast wealth, acquired by sudden and unwholesome means, is a snare. It did us no good, transient were its feverish pleasures; yet for its sake we threw away our sweet and simple and happy life—let others take warning by us."

He lay silent awhile, with closed eyes; then as the chill of death crept upward towards his heart, and consciousness was fading from his brain, he muttered:

"Money had brought him misery, and he took his revenge upon us, who had done him no harm. He had his desire: with base and cunning calculation he left us but thirty thousand, knowing we would try to increase it, and ruin our life and break our hearts. Without added expense he could have left us far above desire of increase, far above the temptation to speculate, and a kinder soul would have done it; but in him was no generous spirit, no pity, no—"

EVE'S DIARY

TRANSLATED FROM THE ORIGINAL

When obliged to meet requests for submissions to *Harper's Magazine* in July 1905, Twain turned to "Eve's Diary." His intent, he explained, was for Eve to refer to "Extracts from Adam's Diary," published in 1893, as "her unwitting and un[con]scious text, since to use any other text would have been an imbecility." The "Diary" was made into a book in 1906, and later collected along with "Extracts from Adam's Diary" in *The Private Lives of Adam and Eve* in 1931.

Saturday

I am almost a whole day old, now. I arrived yesterday. That is as it seems to me. And it must be so, for if there was a day-before-yesterday I was not there when it happened, or I should remember it. It could be, of course, that it did happen, and that I was not noticing. Very well; I will be very watchful, now, and if any day-before-yesterdays happen I will make a note of it. It will be best to start right and not let the record get confused, for some instinct tells me that these details are going to be important to the historian some day. For I feel like an experiment, I feel exactly like an experiment; it would be impossible for a person to feel more like an experiment than I do, and so I am coming to feel convinced that that is what I *am* – an experiment; just an experiment, and nothing more.

Then if I am an experiment, am I the whole of it? No, I think not; I think the rest of it is part of it. I am the main part of it, but I think the rest of it has its share in the matter. Is my position assured, or do I have to watch it and take care of it? The latter, perhaps. Some instinct tells me that eternal vigilance is the price of supremacy. [That is a good phrase, I think, for one so young.]

Everything looks better today than it did yesterday. In the rush of finishing up yesterday, the mountains were left in a ragged

condition, and some of the plains were so cluttered with rubbish
and remnants that the aspects were quite distressing. Noble and
beautiful works of art should not be subjected to haste; and this
majestic new world is indeed a most noble and beautiful work.
And certainly marvelously near to being perfect, notwithstand-
ing the shortness of the time. There are too many stars in some
places and not enough in others, but that can be remedied
presently, no doubt. The moon got loose last night, and slid down
and fell out of the scheme – a very great loss; it breaks my heart
to think of it. There isn't another thing among the ornaments and
decorations that is comparable to it for beauty and finish. It should
have been fastened better. If we can only get it back again –

But of course there is no telling where it went to. And besides,
whoever gets it will hide it; I know it because I would do it myself.
I believe I can be honest in all other matters, but I already begin
to realize that the core and center of my nature is love of the beautiful, a passion for the beautiful, and that it would not be safe
to trust me with a moon that belonged to another person and
that person didn't know I had it. I could give up a moon that I
found in the daytime, because I should be afraid some one was
looking; but if I found it in the dark, I am sure I should find some
kind of an excuse for not saying anything about it. For I do love
moons, they are so pretty and so romantic. I wish we had five
or six; I would never go to bed; I should never get tired lying on
the moss-bank and looking up at them.

Stars are good, too. I wish I could get some to put in my hair.
But I suppose I never can. You would be surprised to find how
far off they are, for they do not look it. When they first showed,
last night, I tried to knock some down with a pole, but it didn't
reach, which astonished me; then I tried clods till I was all tired
out, but I never got one. It was because I am left-handed and cannot
throw good. Even when I aimed at the one I wasn't after I couldn't
hit the other one, though I did make some close shots, for I saw
the black blot of the clod sail right into the midst of the golden

clusters forty or fifty times, just barely missing them, and if I could have held out a little longer maybe I could have got one.

So I cried a little, which was natural, I suppose, for one of my age, and after I was rested I got a basket and started for a place on the extreme rim of the circle, where the stars were close to the ground and I could get them with my hands, which would be better, anyway, because I could gather them tenderly then, and not break them. But it was farther than I thought, and at last I had to give it up; I was so tired I couldn't drag my feet another step; and besides, they were sore and hurt me very much.

I couldn't get back home; it was too far, and turning cold; but I found some tigers, and nestled in among them and was most adorably comfortable, and their breath was sweet and pleasant, because they live on strawberries. I had never seen a tiger before, but I knew them in a minute by the stripes. If I could have one of those skins, it would make a lovely gown.

Today I am getting better ideas about distances. I was so eager to get hold of every pretty thing that I giddily grabbed for it, some-times when it was too far off, and sometimes when it was but six inches away but seemed a foot—alas, with thorns between! I learned a lesson; also I made an axiom, all out of my own head— my very first one; *The scratched Experiment shuns the thorn.* I think it is a very good one for one so young.

I followed the other Experiment around, yesterday afternoon, at a distance, to see what it might be for, if I could. But I was not able to make out. I think it is a man. I had never seen a man, but it looked like one, and I feel sure that that is what it is. I real-ize that I feel more curiosity about it than about any of the other reptiles. If it is a reptile, and I suppose it is; for it has frowsy hair and blue eyes, and looks like a reptile. It has no hips; it tapers like a carrot; when it stands, it spreads itself apart like a derrick; so I think it is a reptile, though it may be architecture.

I was afraid of it at first, and started to run every time it turned around, for I thought it was going to chase me; but by-and-by

I found it was only trying to get away, so after that I was not timid
any more, but tracked it along, several hours, about twenty yards
behind, which made it nervous and unhappy. At last it was a good
deal worried, and climbed a tree. I waited a good while, then gave
it up and went home.

Today the same thing over. I've got it up the tree again.

Sunday

It is up there yet. Resting, apparently. But that is a subterfuge:
Sunday isn't the day of rest; Saturday is appointed for that. It looks
to me like a creature that is more interested in resting than in
anything else. It would tire me to rest so much. It tires me just
to sit around and watch the tree. I do wonder what it is for; I
never see it do anything.

They returned the moon last night, and I was *so* happy! I think
it is very honest of them. It slid down and fell off again, but I
was not distressed; there is no need to worry when one has that
kind of neighbors; they will fetch it back. I wish I could do something to show my appreciation. I would like to send them some
stars, for we have more than we can use. I mean I, not we, for
I can see that the reptile cares nothing for such things.

It has low tastes, and is not kind. When I went there yesterday evening in the gloaming it had crept down and was trying
to catch the little speckled fishes that play in the pool, and I had
to clod it to make it go up the tree again and let them alone. I
wonder if *that* is what it is for? Hasn't it any heart? Hasn't it any
compassion for those little creatures? Can it be that it was designed
and manufactured for such ungentle work? It has the look of it.
One of the clods took it back of the ear, and it used language.
It gave me a thrill, for it was the first time I had ever heard
speech, except my own. I did not understand the words, but they
seemed expressive.

When I found it could talk, I felt a new interest in it, for I
love to talk; I talk all day, and in my sleep, too, and I am very

interesting, but if I had another to talk to I could be twice as interesting, and would never stop, if desired.

If this reptile is a man, it isn't an *it,* is it? That wouldn't be grammatical, would it? I think it would be *he.* I think so. In that case one would parse it thus: nominative, *he;* dative, *him;* possessive, *his'n.* Well I will consider it a man and call it he until it turns out to be something else. This will be handier than having so many uncertainties.

Next week Sunday

All the week I tagged around after him and tried to get acquainted. I had to do the talking, because he was shy, but I don't mind it. He seemed pleased to have me around, and I used the sociable "we" a good deal, because it seemed to flatter him to be included.

Wednesday

We are getting along very well indeed, now, and getting better and better acquainted. He does not try to avoid me any more, which is a good sign, and shows that he likes to have me with him. That pleases me, and I study to be useful to him in every way I can, so as to increase his regard. During the last day or two I have taken all the work of naming things off his hands, and this has been a great relief to him, for he has no gift in that line, and is evidently very grateful. He can't think of a rational name to save him, but I do not let him see that I am aware of his defect. Whenever a new creature comes along, I name it before he has time to expose himself by an awkward silence. In this way I have saved him many embarrassments. I have no defect like his. The minute I set eyes on an animal I know what it is. I don't have to reflect a moment; the right name comes out instantly, just as if it were an inspiration, as no doubt it is, for I am sure it wasn't in me half a minute before. I seem to know just by the shape of the creature and the way it acts what animal it is.

When the dodo came along he thought it was a wildcat – I saw it in his eye. But I saved him. And I was careful not to do it in a way that could hurt his pride. I just spoke up in a quite natural way of pleased surprise, and not as if I was dreaming of conveying information, and said, "Well, I do declare if there isn't the dodo!" I explained – without seeming to be explaining – how I knew it for a dodo, and although I thought maybe he was a little piqued that I knew the creature when he didn't, it was quite evident that he admired me. That was very agreeable, and I thought of it more than once with gratification before I slept. How little a thing can make us happy when we feel that we have earned it.

Thursday

My first sorrow. Yesterday he avoided me and seemed to wish I would not talk to him. I could not believe it, and thought there was some mistake, for I loved to be with him, and loved to hear him talk, and so how could it be that he could feel unkind towards me when I had not done anything? But at last it seemed true, so I went away and sat lonely in the place where I first saw him the morning that we were made and I did not know what he was and was indifferent about him; but now it was a mournful place, and every little thing spoke of him, and my heart was very sore. I did not know why very clearly, for it was a new feeling; I had not experienced it before, and it was all a mystery, and I could not make it out.

But when night came I could not bear the lonesomeness, and went to the new shelter which he has built, to ask him what I had done that was wrong and how I could mend it and get back his kindness again; but he put me out in the rain, and it was my first sorrow.

Sunday

It is pleasant again, now, and I am happy; but those were heavy days; I do not think of them when I can help it.

I tried to get him some of those apples, but I cannot learn to throw straight. I failed, but I think the good intention pleased him. They are forbidden, and he says I shall come to harm; but so I come to harm through pleasing him, why shall I care for that harm?

Monday

This morning I told him my name, hoping it would interest him. But he did not care for it. It is strange. If he should tell me his name, I would care. I think it would be pleasanter in my ears than any other sound.

He talks very little. Perhaps it is because he is not bright, and is sensitive about it and wishes to conceal it. It is such a pity that he should feel so, for brightness is nothing; it is in the heart that the values lie. I wish I could make him understand that a loving good heart is riches, and riches enough, and that without it intellect is poverty.

Although he talks so little he has quite a considerable vocabulary. This morning he used a surprisingly good word. He evidently recognized, himself, that it was a good one, for he worked it in twice afterwards, casually. It was not good casual art, still it showed that he possesses a certain quality of perception. Without a doubt that seed can be made to grow, if cultivated.

Where did he get that word? I do not think I have ever used it.

No, he took no interest in my name, I tried to hide my disappointment, but I suppose I did not succeed. I went away and sat on the moss-bank with my feet in the water. It is where I go when I hunger for companionship, some one to look at, some one to talk to. It is not enough—that lovely white body painted there in the pool—but it is something, and something is better than utter loneliness. It talks when I talk; it is sad when I am sad; it comforts me with its sympathy; it says, "Do not be downhearted, you poor friendless girl; I will be your friend." It *is* a good friend to me, and my only one; it is my sister.

That first time that she forsook me! ah, I shall never forget that—never, never. My heart was lead in my body! I said, "She was all I had, and now she is gone!" In my despair I said, "Break, my heart; I cannot bear my life any more!" and hid my face in my hands, and there was no solace for me. And when I took them away, after a little, there she was again, white and shining and beautiful, and I sprang into her arms!

That was perfect happiness; I had known happiness before, but it was not like this, which was ecstasy. I never doubted her afterwards. Sometimes she stayed away—maybe an hour, maybe almost the whole day, but I waited and did not doubt; I said, "She is busy, or she is gone on a journey, but she will come." And it was so: she always did. At night she would not come if it was dark, for she was a timid little thing; but if there was a moon she would come. I am not afraid of the dark, but she is younger than I am; she was born after I was. Many and many are the visits I have paid her; she is my comfort and my refuge when my life is hard—and it is mainly that.

Tuesday

All the morning I was at work improving the estate; and I pur- posely kept away from him in the hope that he would get lonely and come. But he did not.

At noon I stopped for the day and took my recreation by flitting all about with the bees and butterflies and revelling in the flowers, those beautiful creatures that catch the smile of God out of the sky and preserve it! I gathered them, and made them into wreaths and garlands and clothed myself in them while I ate my luncheon—apples, of course; then I sat in the shade and wished and waited. But he did not come.

But no matter. Nothing would have come of it, for he does not care for flowers. He calls them rubbish, and cannot tell one from another, and thinks it is superior to feel like that. He does not care for me, he does not care for flowers, he does not care

for the painted sky at eventide – is there anything he does care
for, except building shacks to coop himself up in from the good
clean rain, and thumping the melons, and sampling the grapes,
and fingering the fruit on the trees, to see how those properties
are coming along?

I laid a dry stick on the ground and tried to bore a hole in
it with another one, in order to carry out a scheme that I had,
and soon I got an awful fright. A thin, transparent, bluish film
rose out of the hole, and I dropped everything and ran! I thought
it was a spirit, and I *was* so frightened! But I looked back, and
it was not coming; so I leaned against a rock and rested and panted,
and let my limbs go on trembling until they got steady again; then
I crept warily back, alert, watching, and ready to fly if there was
occasion; and when I was come near, I parted the branches of
a rose-bush and peeped through – wishing the man was about,
I was looking so cunning and pretty – but the sprite was gone.
I went there, and there was a pinch of delicate pink dust in the
hold. I put my finger in, to feel it, and said *ouch!* and took it out
again. It was a cruel pain. I put my finger in my mouth; and by
standing first on one foot and then the other, and grunting, I
presently eased my misery; then I was full of interest, and began
to examine.

I was curious to know what the pink dust was. Suddenly the
name of it occurred to me, though I had never heard of it before.
It was *fire!* I was as certain of it as a person could be of anything
in the world. So without hesitation I named it that – fire.

I had created something that didn't exist before; I had added
a new thing to the world's uncountable properties; I realized
this, and was proud of my achievement, and was going to run
and find him and tell him about it, thinking to raise myself in
his esteem – but I reflected, and did not do it. No – he would not
care for it. He would ask what it was good for, and what could
I answer? For it was not *good* for something, but only beautiful,
merely beautiful –

So I sighed, and did not go. For it wasn't good for anything; it could not build a shack, it could not improve melons, it could not hurry a fruit crop; it was useless, it was a foolishness and a vanity; he would despise it and say cutting words. But to me it was not despicable; I said, "Oh, you fire, I love you, you dainty pink creature, for you are *beautiful*—and that is enough!" and was going to gather it to my breast. But refrained. Then I made another maxim out of my head, though it was so nearly like the first one that I was afraid it was only a plagiarism: *"The burnt Experiment shuns the fire."*

I wrought again; and when I had made a good deal of firedust I emptied it into a handful of dry brown grass, intending to carry it home and keep it always and play with it; but the wind struck it and it sprayed up and spat out at me fiercely, and I dropped it and ran. When I looked back the blue spirit was towering up and stretching and rolling away like a cloud, and instantly I thought of the name of it—*smoke!*—though, upon my word, I had never heard of smoke before.

Soon, brilliant yellow-and-red flares shot up through the smoke, and I named them in an instant—*flames!*—and I was right, too, though these were the very first flames that had ever been in the world. They climbed the trees, they flashed splendidly in and out of the vast and increasing volume of tumbling smoke, and I had to clap my hands and laugh and dance in my rapture, it was so new and strange and so wonderful and so beautiful!

He came running, and stopped and gazed, and said not a word for many minutes. Then he asked what it was. Ah, it was too bad that he should ask such a direct question. I had to answer it, of course, and I did. I said it was fire. If it annoyed him that I should know and he must ask, that was not my fault; I had no desire to annoy him. After a pause he asked:

"How did it come?"

Another direct question, and it also had to have a direct answer. "I made it."

The fire was travelling farther and farther off. He went to the edge of the burned place and stood looking down, and said:

"What are these?"

"Fire-coals."

He picked up one to examine it, but changed his mind and put it down again. Then he went away. *Nothing* interests him.

But I was interested. There were ashes, gray and soft and delicate and pretty—I knew what they were at once. And the embers; I knew the embers, too. I found my apples, and raked them out, and was glad; for I am very young and my appetite is active. But I was disappointed; they were all burst open and spoiled. Spoiled apparently; but it was not so; they were better than raw ones. Fire is beautiful; some day it will be useful, I think.

Friday

I saw him again, for a moment, last Monday at nightfall, but only for a moment. I was hoping he would praise me for trying to improve the estate, for I had meant well and had worked hard. But he was not pleased, and turned away and left me. He was also displeased on another account: I tried once more to persuade him to stop going over the Falls. That was because the fire had revealed to me a new passion—quite new, and distinctly different from love, grief, and those others which I had already discovered—*fear.* And it is horrible!—I wish I had never discovered it; it gives me dark moments, it spoils my happiness, it makes me shiver and tremble and shudder. But I could not persuade him, for he has not discovered fear yet, and so he could not understand me.

Extract from Adam's Diary

Perhaps I ought to remember that she is very young, a mere girl, and make allowances. She is all interest, eagerness, vivacity, the world is to her a charm, a wonder, a mystery, a joy; she can't speak for delight when she finds a new flower, she must pet it and caress it and smell it and talk to it, and pour out endearing names upon it. And she is color-mad: brown rocks, yellow sand, gray moss, green foliage, blue sky; the pearl of the dawn, the purple shadows on the mountains, the golden islands floating in crimson seas at sunset, the pallid moon sailing through the shredded cloud-rack, the star-jewels glittering in the wastes of space – none of them is of any practical value, so far as I can see, but because they have color and majesty, that is enough for her, and she loses her mind over them. If she could quiet down and keep still a couple of minutes at a time, it would be a reposeful spectacle. In that case I think I could enjoy looking at her; indeed I am sure I could, for I am coming to realize that she is a quite remarkably comely creature – lithe, slender, trim, rounded, shapely, nimble, graceful; and once when she was standing marble-white and sun-drenched on a boulder, with her young head tilted back and her hand shading her eyes, watching the flight of a bird in the sky, I recognized that she was beautiful.

Monday noon. – If there is anything on the planet that she is not interested in it is not in my list. There are animals that I am indifferent to, but it is not so with her. She has no discrimination, she takes to all of them, she thinks they are all treasures, every new one is welcome.

When the mighty brontosaurus came striding into camp, she regarded it as an acquisition, I considered it a calamity; that is a good sample of the lack of harmony that prevails in or views of things. She wanted to domesticate it, I wanted to make it a present of the homestead and move out. She believed it could be tamed by kind treatment and would be a good pet; I said a pet twenty-one feet high and eighty-four feet long would be no proper thing to have about the place, because, even with the best intentions and without meaning any harm, it could sit down on the house and mash it, for any one could see by the look of its eye that it was absent-minded.

Still, her heart was set upon having that monster, and she couldn't give it up. She thought we could start a dairy with it and wanted me to help her milk it; but I wouldn't; it was too risky. The sex wasn't right, and we hadn't any ladder anyway. Then she wanted to ride *it, and look at the scenery. Thirty or forty feet of its tail was lying on the ground, like a fallen tree, and she thought she could climb it, but she was mistaken; when she got to the steep place it was too slick and down she came, and would have hurt herself but for me.*

Was she satisfied now? No. Nothing ever satisfies her but demonstration; untested theories are not in her line, and she won't have them. It is the right spirit, I concede it; it attracts me; I feel the influence of it; if I were with her more I think I should take it up myself. Well, she had one theory remaining about this colossus: she thought that if we could tame him and make him friendly we could stand him in the river and use him for a bridge. It turned out that he was already plenty tame enough—at least as far as she was concerned—so she tried her theory, but it failed; every time she got him properly placed in the river and went ashore to cross over on him, he came out and followed her around like a pet mountain. Like the other animals. They all do that.

Tuesday—Wednesday—Thursday—and today: all without seeing him. It is a long time to be alone; still, it is better to be alone than unwelcome.

I *had* to have company—I was made for it, I think—so I made friends with the animals. They are just charming, and they have the kindest disposition and the politest ways; they never look sour, they never let you feel that you are intruding, they smile at you and wag their tail, if they've got one, and they are always ready for a romp or an excursion or anything you want to propose. I think they are perfect gentlemen. All these days we have had such good times, and it hasn't been lonesome for me, ever. Lonesome! No, I should say not. Why, there's always a swarm of them around—sometimes as much as four or five acres—you can't count them; and when you stand on a rock in the midst and look out over the furry expanse, it is so mottled and splashed and gay with color and frisking sheen and sun-flash, and so rippled with stripes, that you might think it was a lake, only you know it isn't; and there's storms of sociable birds, and hurricanes of whirring wings; and when the sun strikes all that feathery commotion, you have a blazing up of all the colors you can think of, enough to put your eyes out.

We have made long excursions, and I have seen a great deal of the world—almost all of it, I think; and so I am the first traveller, and the only one. When we are on the march, it is an imposing sight—there's nothing like it anywhere. For comfort I ride a tiger or a leopard, because it is soft and has a round back that fits me, and because they are such pretty animals; but for long distance or for scenery I ride the elephant. He hoists me up with his trunk, but I can get off myself; when we are ready to camp, he sits and I slide down the back way.

The birds and animals are all friendly to each other, and there are no disputes about anything. They all talk, and they all talk to me, but it must be a foreign language, for I cannot make out a word they say; yet they often understand me when I talk back, particularly the dog and the elephant. It makes me ashamed. It shows that they are brighter than I am, and are therefore my superiors. It annoys me, for I want to be the principal Experiment myself—and I intend to be, too.

I have learned a number of things, and am educated, now, but I wasn't at first. I was ignorant at first. At first it used to vex me because, with all my watching, I was never smart enough to be around when the water was running up-hill; but now I do not mind it. I have experimented and experimented until now I know it never does run up-hill, except in the dark. I know it does in the dark, because the pool never goes dry; which it would, of course, if the water didn't come back in the night. It is best to prove things by actual experiment; then you *know*; whereas if you depend on guessing and supposing and conjecturing, you will never get educated.

Friday

Some things you *can't* find out; but you will never know you can't by guessing and supposing: no, you have to be patient and go on experimenting until you find out that you can't find out. And it is delightful to have it that way, it makes the world so interesting. If there wasn't anything to find out, it would be dull. Even trying to find out and not finding out is just as interesting as trying to find out and finding out, and I don't know but more so. The secret of the water was a treasure until I *got* it; then the excitement all went away, and I recognized a sense of loss.

By experiment I know that wood swims, and dry leaves, and feathers, and plenty of other things; therefore by all that cumulative evidence you know that a rock will swim; but you have to put up with simply knowing it, for there isn't any way to prove it—up to now. But I shall find a way—then *that* excitement will go. Such things make me sad; because by-and-by when I have found out everything there won't be any more excitements, and I do love excitements so! The other night I couldn't sleep for thinking about it.

At first I couldn't make out what I was made for, but now I think it was to search out the secrets of this wonderful world and be happy and thank the Giver of it all for devising it. I think there are many things to learn yet—I hope so; and by economizing and not hurrying too fast I think they will last weeks and weeks. I hope so. When you cast up a feather it sails away on the air and goes out of sight; then you throw up a clod and it doesn't. It comes down, every time. I have tried it and tried it, and it is always so. I wonder why it is? If course it *doesn't* come down, but why should it *seem* to? I suppose it is an optical illusion. I mean, one of them is. I don't know which one. It may be the feather, it may be the clod; I can't prove which it is, I can only demonstrate that one or the other is a fake, and let a person take his choice.

By watching, I know that the stars are not going to last. I have seen some of the best ones melt and run down the sky. Since one

can melt, they can all melt; since they can all melt, they can all
melt the same night. That sorrow will come – I know it. I mean
to sit up every night and look at them as long as I can keep awake;
and I will impress those sparkling fields on my memory, so that
by-and-by when they are taken away I can by my fancy restore
those lovely myriads to the black sky and make them sparkle again,
and double them by the blur of my tears.

After the Fall

When I look back, the Garden is a dream to me. It was beautiful, surpassingly beautiful, enchantingly beautiful; and now it
is lost, and I shall not see it any more.

The Garden is lost, but I have found *him,* and am content. He
loves me as well as he can; I love him with all the strength of my
passionate nature, and this, I think, is proper to my youth and sex.
If I ask myself why I love him, I find I do not know, and do not
really much care to know; so I suppose that this kind of love is
not a product of reasoning and statistics, like one's love for other
reptiles and animals. I think that this must be so. I love certain birds
because of their song; but I do not love Adam on account of his
singing – no, it is not that; the more he sings the more I do not get
reconciled to it. Yet I ask him to sing, because I wish to learn to
like everything he is interested in. I am sure I can learn, because
at first I could not stand it, but now I can. It sours the milk, but
it doesn't matter; I can get used to that kind of milk.

It is not on account of his brightness that I love him – no, it
is not that. He is not to blame for his brightness, such as it is,
for he did not make it himself; he is as God made him, and that
is sufficient. There was a wise purpose in it; *that* I know. In time
it will develop, though I think it will not be sudden; and, besides,
there is no hurry; he is well enough just as he is.

It is not on account of his gracious and considerate ways and
his delicacy that I love him. No, he has lacks in these regards,
but he is well enough just so, and is improving.

It is not on account of his industry that I love him – no, it is not that. I think he has it in him, and I do not know why he conceals it from me. It is my only pain. Otherwise he is frank and open with me, now. I am sure he keeps nothing from me but this. It grieves me that he should have a secret from me, and sometimes it spoils my sleep, thinking of it, but I will put it out of my mind; it shall not trouble my happiness, which is otherwise full to overflowing.

It is not on account of his education that I love him – no, it is not that. He is self-educated, and does really know a multitude of things, but they are not so.

It is not on account of his chivalry that I love him – no, it is not that. He told on me, but I do not blame him; it is a peculiarity of sex, I think, and he did not make his sex. Of course I would not have told on him, I would have perished first; but that is a peculiarity of sex, too, and I do not take credit for it, for I did not make my sex.

Then why is it that I love him? *Merely because he is masculine,* I think.

At bottom he is good, and I love him for that, but I could love him without it. If he should beat me and abuse me, I should go on loving him. I know it. It is a matter of sex, I think.

He is strong and handsome, and I love him for that, and I admire him and am proud of him, but I could love him without those qualities. If he were plain, I should love him; if he were a wreck, I should love him; and I would work for him, and slave over him, and pray for him and watch by his bedside until I died.

Yes, I think I love him merely because he is *mine* and is *masculine.* There is no other reason, I suppose. And so I think it is as I first said: that this kind of love is not a product of reasonings and statistics. It just *comes* – none knows whence – and cannot explain itself. And doesn't need to.

It is what I think. But I am only a girl, and the first that has examined this matter, and it may turn out that in my ignorance and inexperience I have not got it right.

Forty Years Later

It is my prayer, it is my longing, that we may pass from this life together – a longing which shall never perish from the earth, but shall have place in the heart of every wife that loves, until the end of time; and it shall be called by my name.

But if one of us must go first, it is my prayer that it shall be I; for he is strong, I am weak, I am not so necessary to him as he is to me – life without him would not be life; how could I endure it? This prayer is also immortal, and will not cease from being offered up while my race continues. I am the first wife; and in the last wife I shall be repeated.

At Eve's Grave

ADAM: Wheresoever she was, *there* was Eden.

. . .

ESSAYS

from the Introduction to
The Complete Short Stories
of Mark Twain

BY

CHARLES NEIDER

During [Mark Twain's] lifetime his stories appeared in volumes which I can only call hodgepodge, containing as they did anecdotes, jokes, letters, essays – all sorts of serious and humorous nonfiction along with the fiction. Twain was a man who was easygoing about borderlines. Some of his short pieces fluctuate between fiction and fact. And he was a fellow who had very definite notions about the appeal of the grab bag. When he was a publisher himself he got William Dean Howells, his friend, to edit a collection of accounts of true adventure. Howells put the pieces together according to a scheme, and after Twain had looked at it he gently advised Howells to mix things up, give them variety, so that the reader might be surprised. A formal scheme was about as appealing to him as a tight collar. Perhaps it was his unconventionality, his insistence on formlessness, which had left his stories in the lurch.

In almost any other writer's work it is easy to say, "This is a short story, whereas that is not." Take the cases of Joyce, Mann, James, Hemingway, Kafka, Lawrence. There is no hesitation about it: a short story belongs to a particular genre and has a relation to the whole of fictional writing in the same way that a watercolor has to the whole of painting, or a song to the whole of composition. Even in Chekhov it is easy to say what is a short story and what isn't. I say "even" because his stories are so gentle in their shading, so clearly lacking in formalism (although not in form), that he of all the writers mentioned might cause some trouble in this respect. In Twain's case it is quite another matter. I have the sense that Twain wrote primarily to satisfy an audience rather than the requirements of a genre. Whatever came to mind that aided his cause was grist for his mill. This is why we find sketches in which it is not possible to distinguish between fiction and fact.

He rarely bothered about the niceties of fiction. Fiction has a tone all its own, which the literary artist reveres. For him it is in a special sense greater than reality. It shapes reality, controls it. It is hard to imagine a James or a Flaubert inserting raw material, untransmuted, unmodulated, into his fictions. For Mark Twain such problems were beside the point. He simply disregarded them, although he was quite aware of them, more aware than he was accustomed to admit. Twain had enough of the frontier spirit to dislike "form." Form was likely to be something eastern. Or if not eastern then something worse: European. Henry James went to Europe to seek form, to saturate himself in it, the form of old societies, old art, old manners and buildings. Twain went to Europe to poke fun at it and to make us laugh. The product of the frontier thought he could see where form was growing hollow and becoming a fraud.

Twain had the artistic temperament without much of the artistic conscience. His genius was essentially western, its strength the land, the people, their language, and their humor. What he lacked was a studied eastern conscience to refine the great ore he mined. Perhaps such a conscience would have inhibited and eventually ruined him. Probably he knew best what was necessary for him. What he had, he had in great measure: the naked power of the man with the gift of gab. He knew what a yarn was, and what to do with it. He did not think that a good yarn needs prettifying, and he told it straight, without trimmings. His high jinks are remarkable – his love of mugging, of monologue, dialect, caricature. He is a great proponent of the tall story, piling details on until the story comes crashing down. At his best he is uproari-ous, and he is often at his best in his stories, as you will see.

It has been said that his stories are an important part of our literary heritage. It would be difficult, if not impossible, to dis-pute this statement successfully, presuming one cared to try. They are also part of our folklore. Twain is our writer closest to folk-lore, our teller of fairy tales. The Jumping Frog story is a living American fairy tale, acted out annually in Calaveras County. Whatever may be its dim origins (it has been claimed to be close kin to an old Greek tale; but the latter probably descended from a Hindu one, and so on), it is now our story, mirroring some-thing in us. "The Man That Corrupted Hadleyburg" is part of our moral heritage. These tales, together with several others, among them "The $30,000 Bequest" and "The £1,000,000 Bank Note," have been anthologized many times. Others – tales of moral indigna-tion such as "A Horse's Tale," and tales meant to shock, for example, *Captain Stormfield's Visit to Heaven,* are no less powerful and impor-tant for being less popular.

Twain is a dangerous man to write about. Unless you approach him with a sense of humor you are lost. You cannot dissect a humorist upon a table. Your first stroke will kill him and make him a tragedian. You must come to Twain with a smile. That is his prerogative: that he can make you do so or fail. In Twain it is not the line-by-line detail which is great, nor the day-by-day life – it is the mass, the contour, and the fragrance of a personal-ity. Who would want, here in this place, to try to dissect that? I shall just pursue a few thoughts briefly, and if I seem to be criti-cal at times, let the reader remember I love the man this side of honesty.

Twain poured his writing out in a stream, showering upon it all his gifts. Sometimes it carried everything before it but at others it failed naively. He was not the kind of versatile writer who is equally good at everything he puts his hand to. It is difficult to believe he could have written fastidious travel essays like

Hawthorne's or the delicate, subtle criticism of James; yet at times he appeared to be attempting both. He carried a broadsword which he sometimes tried to use on butterflies. He wrote very rapidly and was as proud as a boy of his daily output. He didn't strive for the polished effect – or rather he strove for it too seldom. When his mood changed he pigeonholed a manuscript, sometimes for years. He wasn't a good judge of his work. Being essentially a man of humor, he was rarely humorless regarding himself in relation to his work, He was unlike Flaubert and Proust and James in this respect. To be humorless regarding oneself – or at least regarding one's work – came sometimes be a great advantage. To be well balanced doesn't guarantee better-grade work.

There is, in a good deal of Twain's writing – in the Hadleyburg story, for example – a kind of naïveté which one feels is literary, a sort of refusal to infuse prose with the sophistication of the mature man. This no doubt reflects in some measure an attitude Twain had to the act of writing and to the nature of his audience. Writing was not the whole man. It may have even been at times the lesser man. And the audience, one seems to perceive, like his family, was largely composed of women: naive women, sheltered from the painful realities of a man's world. The moral pressure in Twain's work is generally considerable but the purely literary, the aesthetic pressure is occasionally so low as to form only a trickle. This aesthetic pressure, impossible to define, is what is necessary to the creation of a work of art. In some cases it stems from moments of transcendent well-being, in others from the depths of frustration or despair. But whatever the causes, the pressure must be there, inside one, for the effect to be achieved. Too great a pressure may be as devastating to a work as too little. Writers like Twain are more likely to suffer from too little.

In Twain's case there is often something pleasant in even the lesser pages, precisely because of the low pressure: he is relaxed and his mood is infectious. Twain rarely tries to overreach himself, to strain after an effect of greatness. This lesson of being relaxed while writing, although a dangerous one for young writers, is an invaluable one for the mature ones. The right balance of pressure when one is about to sit down to work–one's health, one's relation to the material, one's linguistic resilience, the play of one's mind–is really what is called inspiration; the balance is everything: the container, which is one's own complex state, must exactly suit the thing contained, which is the raw material about to be transfigured into art. It is a pity that Twain did not often take the pains to find the just balance for himself. But if he didn't, he at least substituted another virtue. He says somewhere, wryly, that he had the habit of doing, and of reflecting afterward. One contrasts this habit with an opposite one, the habit of reflecting to the point of disease, often found in the later works of Melville and James, as well as in portions of the works of Thomas Mann and Marcel Proust.

Twain doesn't strive to be an artist–*artiste*, he probably would have called it with a grin. He would have felt more comfortable wearing the term "journalist." He grew up a journalist, like Dickens, and was one of those hearty nineteenth-century scribblers who strayed into literature almost without realizing it. He had the journalist's instinct, in the way Defoe had, and in the way Hawthorne and James did not. This is not necessarily a handicap in the creation of literature. Insofar as it stimulates a sense of audience, a sense of common scene, and the use of native speech and lore – insofar, that is, as it inspires one to attempt a colloquy in common terms but with uncommon genius, it is a definite and rare gift. Its limitations are likely to be great also, the limitations of the known, and especially what is known to the particular group. Twain's writing was almost always a means to an end. He had few impersonal objectives in mind in the way of form, experiment, texture, design. He had the common touch and knew it was a blessing. He was enriched by it and made world-famous.

He possessed in a limited degree the craft discipline of the writer who sees his prose, who carefully examines, it, watching for design and effect, while at the same time listening to its music. Flaubert and Joyce were writers who intensely saw, and it is by no accident that we find in their work a brilliance of visual images.

It is a large part of Twain's greatness that he heard so well. His dialogue is extraordinary. One sometimes wonders if he had a phonographic memory. His ability to imitate styles of speech, with a vast array of accurate detail, is remarkable. His biographer, Albert Bigelow Paine, has written: "At dinner, too, it was his habit, between the courses, to rise from the table and walk up and down the room, waving his napkin and talking – talking in a strain and with a charm that he could never quite equal with his pen. It is the opinion of most people who knew Mark Twain personally that his impromptu utterances, delivered with that ineffable quality of speech, manifested the culmination of his genius." Twain and the oral tradition: both are related to the frontier. Yet some of his chief faults stem directly from this side of his genius – an occasional looseness of texture, a kind of stage or vaudeville timing for effect, an overindulgence in burlesque, a sense as if he were lecturing from a platform. Early in his public career he achieved success as a lecturer and as a maker of speeches, and no doubt this success, this practice, this buttressed confidence in a talent he long must have known he possessed had a crucial influence upon his work.

There is a certain transparency in Twain's work, like that to be found in fairy tales, One senses the machinery behind the silken screen. But in this very transparency there is a kind of potency also found in the fairy tales, a foreknowledge of events, a delight in repetition, in the spelling out of the known, a sort of tribal incantation. There is also something abstract in certain of his fictions, some sort of geometric approach to the art of narrative which, to the modern reader, is not quite satisfying. I refer to pieces like *The American Claimant* and *The Tragedy of Pudd'nhead Wilson*. The latter is a very imperfect work whose imperfections are traceable to its conception, or rather misconception, a fact which

Twain himself has revealed at some length. But when he speaks out of his own mouth, with the drawl and idiom and dialect, as he does in so many of his stories, he is unique, inspired, zany, wonderful.

Twain, like many other nineteenth-century novelists, is sometimes guilty of padding. This is often due to the economics of book production of his day. The two-volume work, sold by subscription, sometimes serialized, was as much the thing in those days as it isn't now. If a man had only a book and a half in him, that was too bad. He had to get up the half somehow or throw in the towel.

It is almost needless to add that in the story the impulse or the need to pad was at a minimum, and that consequently there is more economy of effect in Twain's stories than in most of his book-size works. One might even say that Twain felt most at home in the story, that it was the form most congenial to him, lover as he was of the yarn. It was the form which most effectively brought out his particular "voice." Some of his full-size books are more like a series of yarns strung together than works with an indigenous structure.

His best books, with the exception of his travel books, are those with a western scene. And his travel books largely owe their humor, their geniality, and their wisdom to his western orientation. The sentimentality of the frontier, which ranged all the way from an exaggerated regard for females to the most deadly sort of sadism; the lack of form in social behavior, together with certain codes of behavior which smack of juvenile delinquents; the relative contempt for the written as against the spoken word, the racy language; the attitudes toward dudes and the East, the two being almost synonymous; the impatience with the ways and principles of law— all these characteristics of the American frontier are to be found in Twain's best work, and they are the motor of that work. They are also to be found, in more disguised form, in the work of his star descendant, Ernest Hemingway.

Twain has a wonderful wisdom. He is so essentially sane that it is exhilarating to be in his company. By his way of life he seemed to say, "I am of the tribe of writers but I am saner than they. I know how to savor life." You expect a man like that to live a long life. Twain did. . . .

Charles Neider, American novelist, critic, and Mark Twain scholar, is the editor of *The Autobiography of Mark Twain* and *The Outrageous Mark Twain.* He is also the author of the recent novella, *A Visit to Yazoo.* The film *One-Eyed Jacks* is based on his novel, *The Authentic Death of Hendry Jones.*

Creatures of Circumstance:
Mark Twain

BY

ALFRED KAZIN

Only an American would have seen in a single lifetime the growth of the whole tragedy of civilization from the primitive forest clearing.
—BERNARD SHAW to Hamlin Garland, 1904

I went right along, not fixing up any particular plan, but just trusting to Providence to put the right words in my mouth when the time came; for I'd noticed that Providence always did put the right words in my mouth, if I left it alone.
—MARK TWAIN, *Huckleberry Finn*

All I wanted was to go somewheres; all I wanted was a change.
—MARK TWAIN, *Huckleberry Finn*

He was a redhead five feet, eight inches tall, liked to make it five feet, eight and a half, and he talked constantly. He had a professional drawl and a resonant twang even in private that struck William James as perverse, his brother Henry as wistful. But from the "lecture" platform on which he performed for a lifetime he was the delight of audiences from Western mining camps in the 1860s to Freud's Vienna in the 1890s. He would shuffle out on the stage in slippers, hands in his pockets, stare impassively at the eagerly waiting faces until the first giggles told him that he had them thoroughly at his mercy. "His carefully studied effects," Howells wrote in *My Mark Twain*, "would reach the first rows in the orchestra first, and a ripple in laughter back to the standees against the wall, and then with a fine resurgence come again to the rear orchestra seats, and so rise from gallery to gallery till it fell back, a cataract of applause from the topmost row of seats."

He had only to make some pleasantly derisive sounds to leave them "howling" with delight. "Howling," along with "astonishment," were among Samuel Langhorne Clemens's favorite words. They stood for the raw, total, unlimited gush of pleasure he expected to arouse by just talking. He was the champion funnyman, the smartest voice out of the West. When he was in his late sixties and lived on lower Fifth Avenue, people went into raptures at the sight of Mark Twain talking to a friend and followed him up the avenue for miles. "Howling" also stood for his scale of feeling; his scorn was equally extreme. The loud clarity and positiveness of his feelings explain the brightness of his style. Anything he said, because of the confidence with which he said it, sounded right. And all this arose not just from his love of talk, from his perfected and professional skill in writing as if he were still talking, but from his enjoyment of himself, which he exuded like the smoke from his ever-present cigar. There was a tradition in the South and on the frontier of "selling" oneself by talk. His father, a transplant from Virginia to Missouri who failed to make anything out of the "Tennessee land" he had once bought, talked his family into the dream that the land would yet make them rich. Talk would become the son's favorite show of power.

Long before he "astonished" all those drifters, prospectors, gamblers, and other stray journalists in Nevada, young Sam Clemens in Hannibal must have sounded like his Tom Sawyer— amazing the home folks by his inventiveness and spiel. His style was formed on his lifelong relish of himself as a performer. And forever pushing the performer into action was this perennial boy's awareness of being a favorite, a star. He expected people to hang on his words, and he always meant to "astonish" them, to take them over. The glow of his style would obscure the raw dread he got into *Huckleberry Finn*, the violence of *A Connecticut Yankee in King Arthur's Court.*

He was the favorite, the winner, the Jim Dandy all-American boy (and man: in old age his entourage spoke of him as "King"). Like many another "real live nephew of my Uncle Sam," he was always on stage; his delivery was sardonic and his message the wisecrack. All in the "American" style. And what was that style, now, but "irreligion," skepticism in all things, dissolution in any direction of the eternal verities? No one before the Civil War, no one not from the West, would ever have mustered the poker face to get away with "the calm confidence of a Christian with four aces." In Mark Twain everything went to express suspicion and to conceal hostility by laughing at something or someone established. He was a southern Presbyterian scornful of sky-blue transcendental Yankee idealism, a poor boy from a family that still believed itself to be "quality," and he was kept hysterical by expecting wealth from the "Tennessee land." An overpowering egotist as well as an always vulnerable one, he had acquired in mining camps, saloons, and newspaper offices a bumptiousness, a special swagger. He was everlastingly the verbal winner, the fastest mouth in Virginia City, San Francisco, and Hawaii.

What formed Mark Twain's perennial "act" was the underplayed but unmistakable attack on belief and believers. No matter how friendly he remained to the end of his life with the Reverend Joe Twichell, no matter how often he assured "Livy" that he might yet be as content with churchgoing as others in their prosperous Hartford set, a preeminent object of his many dislikes was the church, churchgoers, prayer meetings, and the complacent banalities of established clerics. A profoundly middle-class soul himself for all his mischievousness, the very type of the boastful, loud, frantically unsure promoter, he used his "low" experiences to needle the "quality" without for a moment sacrificing the aggressiveness of the one and his respect for the other. His striking doubleness in so many American activities, his histrionic expressions of guilt at being a divided soul, were the predicament that he turned into his greatest feat. Mark Twain never ceased to be Mr. Clemens.

What rankled most (in a nature that luxuriated in irritations) was Christianity's assumption of unity, a creation overseen by Providence. The truth was not in any organized body or systematic belief, for there was no single truth. It was certainly not in the mind alone, as Emerson had preached. There was nothing but the mixed-up pieces of our raw human nature. This realism was crucial to Mark Twain's enduring popularity; after Cooper, he was the first significant American writer to whom people turned just for pleasure, without thought of improving themselves. Just as his one great book is an example of what the French call le roman fleuve, the novel which carries life along like a river and is as wayward as the great river that flows through Huckleberry Finn, so his genius was always in some sense for the circumstantial, never the abstract formula. After Mark Twain, many an early American classic would seen too ardent. His large, ever-larger audience, in Europe as well as in America, made him the most loved and best rewarded of American writers. His humor—always on the attack— was certainly not "ardent" about anything. He lacked the intellectual will to give life one dominating shape. His work required none of the training needed to meet Captain Ahab when the great man ranted, "Who's over me? Truth hath no confines!"

Mark Twain's famous "naturalness," his ability beyond anything else to give an episodic quality to life, spoke to a generation not altogether alarmed by the recognition that there was no necessary connection between man and the universe. His genius for improvisation was as important as his instinct for ridicule. Nothing he ever wrote—not even the determinism of What Is Man? and his other outcries in old age against the old American confidence and self-approval—was deliberated for a pilgrim race to make use of. His worst books were written as spontaneously as his best, and many of his projects resembled promoters' schemes in Western lands that came to nothing. He thought Joan of Arc his best book. *Huckleberry Finn* was dropped for six years on the principle that "as long as a book would write itself, I was a faithful and interested amanuensis and my industry did not flag, but the minute that the book tried to shift to *my* head the labor of contriving its situations and conducting its conversations, I put it away and dropped it out of my mind." When he picked it up again, he did not understand how much this novel-as-river had been moving in some deep channel of its own. Before he turned the last ten chapters over to Tom Sawyer, he established in the book's harshest scene, the murder of Boggs and the simplicity of the people in this "little one-horse town in a big bend," the hateful yet comic truth written entirely from inside Southern society.

Emerson dreamed that the earth revolving in space was an apple and that he ate it. By contrast with the Romantic will to absorb the world into oneself, Mark Twain made the world laugh as he exposed the rawness and deceitfulness of human nature. He softened the awful truth by enjoying his own performance so much. There was nothing to fear – not yet. Mark Twain darkened only as the century did. The performer kept a certain lordly air, like Colonel Sherburn in *Huckleberry Finn* deriding the mob come to lynch him, even as he paraded the new Western frontiersman. He flourished in all possible American worlds and was free to comment on anything in his own way. He was a dissolvent of the old ways while unmistakably keeping some privileged independence and, like a good Southerner, his ancestral place.

Alfred Kazin is the Distinguished Professor of English at the City University of New York. His works include *The Inmost Leaf, New York Jew, On Native Grounds: An Interpretation of Modern American Prose Literature,* and *A Walker in the City.*